# CARTER

Book 1 in the Harlow Brothers Series

## BRIE PAISLEY

Cover art by Tiffany Black from T.E. Black Designs

Edited by Karen Mandeville-Steer of Karen's Book Haven Editing Services

Formatted by Brenda Wright from Formatting Done Wright

Photograph and photography by Christopher Correia of CJC Photography

Cover model BT Urruela

Cover model Jessie Reis

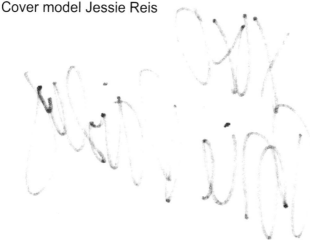

Carter

# DEDICATION

This book is for Cody, my one. Thank you, babe for inspiring me to write Carter. Because without you, I wouldn't have everything I needed to write this one.
I love you with all my heart, babe.

Brie Paisley

# PROLOGUE

## Shelby

It seems like a lifetime, since Carter Harlow entered my life.

We lived in the same small town where you couldn't go anywhere without seeing a familiar and friendly face. I was five years old, and he was six. I remember that day perfectly. We were at school, playing outside during recess. The school year was almost over, and it was a hot sunny day. The kids in my class played chase, or were in the sandbox making sandcastles. I was sitting on the swing, in my own little world. I didn't know how to swing yet without someone pushing me. My legs dangled, and I kicked the pebbled rocks with the tip of my shoes. I watched the other kids playing, seeing that they all had a playmate. It made me sad and envious that I didn't have that. All I wanted was someone to push me on the swing. I didn't have any friends back then, and maybe Carter knew what a lonely little girl I was.

Looking back, I didn't understand why my Mom didn't want anything to do with me, or why my Dad always smelled funny. But, Carter didn't make fun of my dirty clothes or say anything about how I hadn't bathed in a week. He walked right up to me, touched my hand holding tightly onto the chain of the swing, and looked right at me.

"I'm Carter. What's your name?"

I squinted my eyes at him, wondering if he was about to comment on why I was alone. Most kids made fun of me because I didn't have any friends. They would tease me relentlessly, but it seemed like Carter wasn't like the other kids at school. "Shelby."

He stared at me for a moment, then asked, "Can I push you?" I smiled brightly and nodded eagerly. All I wanted was a friend, someone to play with me. Carter took his hand off mine, and walked behind me. He grabbed a hold of the chains, and began to push me. I remembered laughing loudly, loving how high he pushed me. I also remembered holding on tightly to the chains and looking around the playground at the other kids. They didn't pay us any mind, and I told Carter to push me higher and higher. He did as I asked, laughing right along with me. I finally had someone to play with, and I felt happy. For the first time in my life, I felt just like all the other kids. I felt normal. I remembered how in just a short amount of time, I felt accepted.

When the bell rang for us to go back inside, Carter slowed me down and helped me off the swing. He held my hand as we walked back into the building, and I started to dread the moment when he would drop my hand and head back to class. I didn't want him to leave me. "Don't worry, Shelby. I'll see you after school." He said once we stopped at my classroom. I grinned and nodded at his promise. That one simple promise meant the world to me, and even if I didn't have any friends in my class, I knew I gained a new friend with Carter. When he met me right outside my classroom at the end of the day, I knew at the tender age of five, Carter would always keep his promises. Even though we'd just met we shared a bond, something special.

Thinking about it now, I was way too young to understand our connection. There was just something about that sweet, young boy. He quickly became my best friend, and there were hardly any moments when we weren't together.

Now that I'm older, I still don't understand the connection we had back then. Even when Carter and his family opened their arms and home to me when I needed them the most, I still didn't understand why he wanted to be around me. No one else in my family cared anything about me, and it was inevitable for me to fall head over heels in love with him. It didn't happen suddenly. It happened slowly over the years, time changed our relationship into something I couldn't live without. There are so many things I still look back on, and I try to figure out why Carter and I were so drawn together. Why, after everything we went through, he could just … let me go? I thought what Carter and I shared was special, one of a kind. But everything changed once he left for college.

When Carter Harlow broke my heart, I did what I knew best.

Brie Paisley

I ran.

# CHAPTER 1

## Shelby

Pulling the hood of my jacket over my head as I exit the bus station, I glance around me, nervous I'm being followed. I have no idea if Easton knows I've left or not, and I didn't stick around to find out. Shifting my heavy bag onto my other shoulder, I hope I didn't manage to lose anything. It was hell getting out of Charleston, South Carolina, and knowing my friends were the cause for my abrupt departure still puts a sick feeling in my gut. Betrayed by everyone I thought were the ones looking out for me. What a crock of shit. I've come to realize in the past few weeks the only person I can trust is myself.

I watch a man pass by, and I still as he nears me. My heart drums in my chest, and panic starts to take over. Letting my breath out when the man walks past me without a second glance, I run my hand down my face, wishing I wasn't so paranoid. I duck my head, as I make my way through the throng of people, trying to be as inconspicuous as possible. If I could be invisible, I would be. Briskly walking out of the arrival zone, I think about how much farther I have to go, before I'm back home in Columbus, Mississippi. I'm exhausted and running on fumes more than anything. I continue to ignore the busy people around me, as I slip inside the bathroom outside the bus station to find a somewhat clean, empty stall. I shut the door behind me, only letting myself glance over the surroundings. It smells awful in here, as if someone puked for days and didn't bother to clean it up. It's dirty. It's disgusting but for now, I'm safe.

I need to feel safe again.

I don't dare set my bag down on the nasty floor. Instead, I unroll some toilet paper and cover the lid of the commode with layers of it. I sit Indian style, putting my bag in my lap. Taking a deep breath, I will myself to relax. I don't know how I managed to get this far away from him, or how he hasn't found me yet. I'm sure my mother would be more than happy to tell him exactly where I'm headed, and the thought makes a lump form in my throat.

Easton Carrington. My lying, cheating, asshole of an ex-husband.

I shiver, just thinking about his name. Divorcing Easton, then leaving when I had, was the best decision I'd ever made. Although I'm afraid he'll come back for me, at least I'm free of him. Glancing down at my ring finger, I swallow hard seeing the faint tan line. I'd been married for seven years, and now, I'm … free. It's surreal, a bit terrifying, but I'm determined to move forward. I can't remember my time with Easton. Shaking my head, I clutch my half-moon and compass necklace, not wanting to think about him. Glancing down at it, I'm reminded of how much it means to me. Even after all these years, I've never lost it or taken it off. It's a simple thing: a small compass surrounded by a half moon with the words, 'no matter where' on it. Holding it tightly in my hand, I close my eyes realizing I'm starting over. Granted my situation isn't ideal, but at least I'm free of him. I push back the memories of how I got my keepsake, letting go of it. Opening my bag, I start rummaging through it until I find my bus ticket. I look at it, making sure all the information is correct. I'm in Atlanta, Georgia now, and in twelve hours I'll be back in my hometown. I sigh, not really acknowledging how I feel about going home for the first time in thirteen years. It's not something I've thought about in a very long time. I never thought I'd be going back to the place that holds so many good and bad memories. Or who I know I'll see once I get there.

Carter Harlow.

Years apart, and that one boy, well man now, is still able to make my heart race when I think of him and our past together. I know I promised myself I'd never return home but, I have nowhere else to go. Seeing Carter again outweighs the risk of being in Charleston, and I'll just have to deal with the repercussions later. I shake my head to keep the memories from overtaking me. I put my ticket safely back in my bag and pull out my wallet. I sigh, knowing my funds are low. The bus ticket wasn't very expensive, but then again, I didn't have much when I left South Carolina anyway. I only took enough so Easton wouldn't notice. I don't dwell on the fact that he made me resort to stealing, but then again, I only took what he owed me for all he's done. I wanted to take it all, just to show him how it feels to be outsmarted and deceived, but I couldn't do that no matter how much I wanted to. I'm a better person than I thought I was. Pulling out my money, I meticulously count each dollar and coin. Even digging to the bottom of my bag, making sure I don't miss anything. I huff out loud, seeing I only have one hundred and sixteen dollars and forty-seven cents left. It's going to be tight, but I have to make it on my low funds. I don't have a choice at this point. I refuse to go back to South Carolina and to that life. I've been in worse situations before, mainly as a child, but at least back then, I had friends to help me when I was in a bind. That makes me think of Annie and William Barrett. They practically raised me when my Mom wasn't around. They impacted my life and took care of me, showing me what a real family is like, and how people can really love one another. Now, it's just me. I'm alone again since the age of five, and I realize I don't like it. I won't give up though. I've come this far, and there's no going back.

Placing my wallet back inside my bag, I quickly zip it, not wanting to see the scrapbook of my times from back home. It's another keepsake, the one thing that I couldn't leave behind, besides my necklace. I lean back against the toilet, thinking I can do this. I tell myself this is just a bump in the road.

Carter

It's just an obstacle in the way. This dirty bathroom isn't the first disgusting place I've had to stay in for a few hours. It's not the first time I had to hide in a public place because I didn't have the money for a hotel room. I'm just happy this bathroom is warm, and I don't have to look over my shoulder every minute of every day since my hell began. That's what I compare my marriage to anyway. Don't get me wrong. In the beginning, it was perfect, or as perfect as it could be. I don't exactly know when things turned from great to shit. I don't know why I didn't see it coming, or I would've prepared better. I would've stood up to him and left sooner, rather than later. I wouldn't have lost everything to Easton in the divorce. I wouldn't have regretted marrying him. So many regrets and pain. It's more than any thirty-two year old woman should have to endure.

Hearing the bathroom door open, I cringe and my entire body tenses. The heavy door creaks loudly, and I see a woman's shoes from under my stall. The door beside my stall squeaks as it closes, and I barely breathe until she's finished emptying her bladder. It seems like forever until she's done, leaving as loudly as she came. I exhale slowly, telling myself I'm being paranoid again. There's no way Easton knows I'm here. "Come on, Shelby. Get your fucking head straight."

I shake my head, hating how my thoughts always go back to him. I have to learn not to think this way anymore. I'm alone again, and it's time I get used to it.

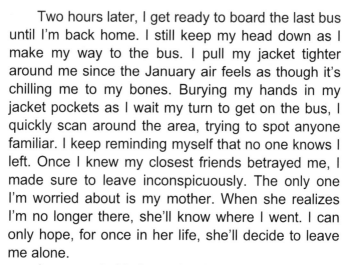

Two hours later, I get ready to board the last bus until I'm back home. I still keep my head down as I make my way to the bus. I pull my jacket tighter around me since the January air feels as though it's chilling me to my bones. Burying my hands in my jacket pockets as I wait my turn to get on the bus, I quickly scan around the area, trying to spot anyone familiar. I keep reminding myself that no one knows I left. Once I knew my closest friends betrayed me, I made sure to leave inconspicuously. The only one I'm worried about is my mother. When she realizes I'm no longer there, she'll know where I went. I can only hope, for once in her life, she'll decide to leave me alone.

A woman behind me clearing her throat startles me, letting me know to board the bus. I relax slightly and glance away from her, shifting my bag over my shoulder as I walk up the steps. Handing the bus driver my ticket, I refuse to make any eye contact with him, and look for a seat in the back. I want to be away from prying eyes. Away from everyone. I don't make eye contact with a single person already seated. I stare straight ahead, my eyes on the open seat two rows from the back. I sit down, immediately placing my bag beside me. I don't want anyone sitting next to me, but my hand rests on the bag just in case someone tries to take it. Once we're on the road, I'll count my items again. It's becoming more of an OCD habit to check on my things. Maybe it's because I know this bag is all I have now. The thought is depressing. I've never been attached to materialistic things, but change is never easy. It's hard and sometimes complicated, but I'm determined to push through the rough patches. I'm ready to start over with a new life, and forget my past.

Leaning my head against the window, I hear the bus driver announce he's getting ready to close the doors to start our long journey. I don't really hear much else. I'm thinking about how different my hometown is going to be. I wonder if my childhood home is still empty, or if Mom ended up selling it. I think about Annie and her husband, William. I wonder if they'll remember me after all these years. I block out thoughts of Carter Harlow and his family. Those memories are just too painful to think of right now.

Instead, I think of Annie and William.

Do they still live in their small house down the road from my childhood home? There were so many times when I was a child, I'd stay with them. They eventually became my family. Annie would fix me chicken and dumplings when I had a horrible day with Mom. William taught me how to change the oil in his truck. Both took care of me when Mom would be too busy for me, or when Dad was too drunk to care about anything. I even stayed overnight most weekends, and once Mom dropped me off for a full year so she could have her alone time. I don't know what I would've done if I didn't have them in my life. I also wonder about how they're doing. It's been thirteen years since I've seen either one of them. I never stayed in touch with them, and I feel the guilt rising in my chest. After all they've done for me, I should've at least called every once in a while. It feels like a slap in the face knowing how I've neglected them, when they've been nothing but kind to me. I wish I could call them now, but I don't have a cell phone anymore. I dropped it in a trash can somewhere in South Carolina before I got on my first bus. I knew keeping it that Easton would find a way to track me, and I couldn't have that.

I feel the bus jerk and the roar of the engine then soon after, the bus station is another memory. I wait until the driver takes us onto the highway before I finally take my hand off my bag. I still don't glance at any of the other passengers. I'm in my own world as I check on my belongings. I don't have much since I had to leave in such a hurry. I only had time to grab two pairs of jeans, a few T-shirts, and a pair of socks. I had a few pairs of panties, but I tossed them since I couldn't wash them after wearing them. I feel dirty, and probably smell. Pulling out the travel size deodorant, I quickly put some on. I also grab a disposable, travel size toothbrush. I brush my teeth, and put it back into the case once I'm done. Taking out the pack of baby wipes I picked up at a gas station, I wipe my hands and face. It's not ideal, but for now, it'll have to do. I set the discolored wipe aside, then I pull out my scrapbook. I lightly touch the front, staring at the picture on the front of the old me.

The person I was thirteen years ago. But I don't open it. I can't bear to look at the people from my past, and how much they impacted me. It was happier times back then. It was simple and not as fucked up as my life is now. I have to put my book away when my vision starts to blur.

I brush my fingers over my face, trying to make the tears stop from falling. I take a deep breath, placing my hand back on my bag. I lean back in the seat wishing I had my iPod. I know this ten-hour bus ride is going to seem a lot longer without something to pass the time. I pull my legs up to my chest, and lean my head on my knees as I wrap my arms around myself. I suddenly feel tired, and I know it's because of these past couple of weeks. I don't want to run anymore. I just want to get back to Annie and William. Back to happiness.

I just want to be home again.

I'm startled awake by a hand touching my shoulder. I jump, as a scream escapes my mouth. My heart begins race, and my hands start shaking. I look up, seeing the bus driver standing over me with a worried expression on his face. He holds his hands up, showing me he means no harm. Letting out a breath, I take off my hood and run my hands through my messy hair, while trying to give him a smile.

"I'm sorry, Miss. I didn't mean to startle you."

I shake my head as I say, "No, it's okay. Thank you for waking me. Have we arrived?"

I don't think I've convinced him I'm fine. He looks away with sad eyes, and I hear him say, "Yes, ma'am."

I try to smile, but end up turning away. I look out the window, noticing I'm back in Columbus, Mississippi. I can't believe I slept the entire way, but I'm grateful that I at least got one night of restful sleep. I can't recall the last time I slept more than a few hours at a time. I thank the bus driver for waking me, and he turns to leave as I grab my bag. I follow behind him, quickly getting off the bus. After finding a bathroom, and grateful to find an empty stall, I wash my face utilizing the free soap. My reflection catches my attention in the mirror as I use the scratchy paper towels to dry my face, but I don't recognize myself. My hair is oily and stringy looking. I can see my roots coming through the fake dye job, and I'm in need of a hot shower with lots of soap. For years, Easton loved it when I dyed my hair blonde. I'm not sure why. Maybe it was because he wanted to make me into someone else. Someone he could control and show off like some prized doll. Now, I just look pale, and my natural dark brunette roots make me feel trashy. Dull and lifeless eyes stare back at me, and I realize how lost and scared they seem. Once they were bright blue with a hint of green. So full of love back then, and I question if I'll ever get that light back. I have bags under my eyes from long sleepless nights. With a shaky hand, I graze the pink scar above my top lip. When I can't stand to look at the new scar any longer, I quickly move my hand to my cheek. I can see and feel my bones sticking out. I wonder if the people looking at me think I'm some poor sickly woman. That's exactly how I seem. Have I really lost that much weight? I glance down, realizing my jeans are hanging loosely on my hips, and my jacket's swallowing me. I briefly look back at myself, but then turn away from the mirror. I can't bear to look at myself anymore, disgusted with how much I've wasted away. I don't look like me, and I have no idea who I've turned into.

Swallowing down the lump in my throat, I exit the bathroom. I walk out of the bus station, ready to leave the past right where it needs to stay. Once outside, I take in my surroundings, leaning my head back and letting the morning sun warm my face. I close my eyes, loving the feel of it, and sigh deeply. It even smells the same. The air has a bit of humidity, but it's fresher. It smells like home, somewhere I remember and longed to be for a while since divorcing Easton. After a few moments, I raise my head and glance around me. I notice people coming out of the bus station, and I quickly pull my hood back over my head, tightly holding the strap of my bag. Even if these people are strangers, I still have the feeling of paranoia. I feel the urge to run, but force myself not to. It would draw more attention, so instead, I stare down Main Street, feeling a sense of déjà vu. I used to come down here multiple times when I was in high school. I remember these streets, and knowing I'm back home again makes my heart clench.

I turn left, starting my long walk to Annie and William's home. I could've gotten a taxi, but I didn't want to waste the money. I have this feeling I'm going to need every penny, so walking it is. I don't stop myself from looking at all the small businesses that are opening for the day. I soak up everything familiar, but different at the same time, as I pass by the Renasant Bank, the court house, a bistro, and a hardware shop. Across the street, there's a boutiques and a wedding dress shop. There's a new business across the street, and it seems more people are walking about than I remember. I make a right noticing the hair salon I used before is still in business. I desperately want to walk in to get my hair dyed back to my natural color, but my low funds stop me again. I will myself to pass by it, and notice how busy everyone seems going to work and starting their day.

I find myself envying them. Such mundane things people take for granted every single day. I used to be just like them. Getting up for work and stopping by Starbucks to get my morning coffee. I stop for a moment and stare at my dirty shoes. I shouldn't feel this way. I had a great job, and a great life with Easton, up until things slowly took a turn for the worse. I shouldn't feel so much regret for leaving my home town all those years ago, or letting my marriage turn into what it became. I can't help but think maybe if I'd paid more attention things wouldn't have happened the way it did. That maybe if I was stronger, and not so afraid, I could've done something to change it.

I don't know why I feel such deep regret for the way my life turned out. But the only thing I can do now is move forward, and try to put my past behind me.

I start walking again, hoping now that I'm home things will change this time around. I pass by Zachary's, a small restaurant on my left. My mouth starts to water thinking about their amazing food and my stomach growls. I can't stop for food since they're closed and because I'm broke. I think about stopping by McDonald's to grab something off their dollar menu, but that thought stops abruptly when I hear a siren go off. I jump, and my hand clutches my chest. I snap my head towards the sound, seeing a police car idling beside me. My heart instantly pounds in my chest and my stomach drops. My first thought is, what did I do wrong? Then my thoughts turn into panic. What if Easton knows where I am? Could he have connections here? Is the reach of his family's reputation really this far?

I stand as still as possible when the police officer steps out of his vehicle. I think about running, but I make myself stay where I am. If I'm in trouble, for whatever reason, running isn't an option. The officer makes his way towards me, and I realize he seems familiar. My eyebrows furrow, as I try and figure out how I know him. I watch him closely as he slowly takes off his sunglasses. When I see his face, I can't help but smile. "Caden? Is that really you?"

He grins widely, opening his arms. I immediately walk to him, letting him embrace me tightly. He rubs my back, and I take comfort in him. Caden slowly pulls me back, his grip lightly holding my shoulders. He looks me up and down, carefully taking in how I look. I can't help but turn away, ashamed of how awful I must seem. I still can't believe Caden Harlow is standing here, right in front of me. Then I realize if Caden's here, Carter will know I'm here soon. Caden is Carter's younger brother. I know all of Carter's brothers, since we grew up together, and use to hang around each other so much. Carter, Caden, Cason, Clark, and Caleb. Carter's the oldest out of the bunch, and he'll be thirty-three now. Caden and Cason are twins but from what I remember, are nothing alike. Cason has a scar on his right eyebrow, and it's always helped me make the difference between them. Caden was the jokester out of the group. He was always making everyone laugh, and playing pranks. Cason was the quiet one, but the one you could depend on whenever you needed anything. Then there's Clark, always wanting to save the day. The last I remember, he was thinking of joining the military. Caleb's the youngest and the nerdy, shy, one out of all the boys.

I glance back at Caden, shocked at how much he's changed since the last time I saw him. Once he was a skinny and lanky kid, but you'd never know that now by looking at him. He's put on muscle, and his arms are bigger than my entire body. His black officer's uniform hugs tightly against his upper body. I wonder if he flexed his muscles if it would rip? His dark brown hair is spiked in the front, short on the sides, and his deep blue eyes seem to make me feel warm and safe again. He's like the younger brother I never had. He starts to chuckle as I look him over. I smile and shake my head, knowing what he's about to say. "Checkin' me out, Shelby?"

His deep southern accent is such a familiar sound. The people I knew in South Carolina had an accent too, but theirs was more refined, almost as if they were too proper to speak with a twang. Hearing Caden's thick accent makes me instantly relax around him. He's safe, and for the first time in a long time, I feel at ease. "I can't believe how much you've changed," I reply, waving my hand up and down.

"Yeah, it's been a long time since you've been around. There's a lot you've missed." I feel a bit of guilt at his words, but I just nod my head. What's there to say? "Are you back in town for good or just passin' through?"

I sigh before I respond. "I'm not sure yet. I … I just needed to come home for a while." I hate I'm tripping over my words, but I'm not ready to talk about why I'm home again.

"That's good to hear. I couldn't believe my eyes when I saw you walking. I thought I'd seen a fucking ghost." I chuckle at his words, but it dies as he says, "I know Carter and Mama will be happy you're back," he stops when I start shaking my head.

"Please Caden, don't tell anyone I'm here yet. I … I'm not ready for anyone to know. Especially Carter. You understand, don't you?"

He looks away as if he's thinking about what I'm asking him. I know I'm putting him in an awkward position, but Carter cannot know yet. I can't let him see me like this, and I'm definitely not ready to face him. Caden nods and says, "Yeah, I understand. But, I won't lie to him. If he asks, I have to tell him. You of all people know why."

"I'd never ask you to lie to him. I remember our pact, even if it seems like forever ago since we made it." Caden nods, seeming to agree. And I do remember our little group pact we made years ago in our tree house. We made a promise never to lie to one another. Even at eleven years old, I saw what lies did to people. I watched my Mom and Dad fight on multiple occasions because my Dad claimed she was lying. I knew Mom lied to Dad before. Once I caught her kissing a man outside our home, and she told me to promise to never tell anyone. I didn't listen, immediately telling Carter, and Mom made sure I couldn't sit down for days after she found out I'd told.

"Good. Do you want a ride somewhere?" He asks as he points his thumb to his police car. I don't think twice about it before I nod my head and thank him as we both get in. I place my bag by my feet, and once I put on my seat belt, Caden slowly pulls out, heading north. We leave Main Street behind, and it's not until we pass by the Waffle House when he asks, "Where do you want me to take you?"

"Annie and William's, please." I glance at him and quickly add, "If they still live there. I haven't spoken to them in a long time." I turn away, absently staring out the window as I whisper, "A lot can change in thirteen years."

I don't know if Caden heard me since he didn't say anything about my last comment. He does begin to tell me Annie and William still live in their small house out on Jess Lyons Road. He doesn't ask me why I want to go there, he knows how much Annie and William mean to me. We all loved Annie and William. If we weren't at Caden's parents' home, we were at Annie and William's. We spent so much time there, that William built us a tree house in the backyard and put up a tree swing. Annie would make all kinds of food for us, and it always seemed like Thanksgiving Day when she did. These are the good memories. The ones I cherish and wish I could go back to relive again.

Caden's voice trails off as I think about the past. Our silence isn't uncomfortable. It's actually nice to be around someone I trust again. Someone I know who won't ask me twenty-one questions just to gain information about me to use later. I don't have to watch what I say, when I do talk. I don't have to worry about anything. It's such a relief to be with an old friend again. I want to break our silence, but then again, I want to relish in this peaceful feeling I'm having. It's a feeling I thought I'd never have again after everything that happened between Easton and I.

Then I wonder if Mom moving to Charleston had anything to do with how my life changed so much. I still have no idea why she chose to move down the street from us.

Things started to change quite drastically after Easton met my Mom. For years, I was able to come up with excuse after excuse to why Easton couldn't meet her. I didn't want him to see how selfish she was, or how she treated me. Easton didn't know about my past with Carter. I didn't tell him about how my father died, and how much I blamed my mother for it. He didn't know anything actually. I kept my precious memories to myself, only thinking of them as I fell asleep every night. I kept my secrets even closer, reminding myself every day of the pain I went through when Carter broke my heart into pieces. I didn't open up to anyone while I lived in South Carolina. I chose to keep everything locked away, thinking if I just stopped remembering the past it would eventually go away. It didn't, but I learned how to pretend to be perfectly put together.

"Are you sure you don't want to stop by and see Mama? I know she'll be ecstatic to see you." Caden's voice pulls me out of my head, putting a halt on the way my thoughts were going. I turn to face him, thinking of what to say. "It's fine if you don't want to. I just thought I'd ask again before I drop you off at the Barrett's."

I sigh, looking away. I do want to see Linda and Mitchell. I miss them just as much as I've missed Annie and William. But, I can't let anyone else see me this way. I feel as though I've hit rock bottom. I look and smell horrible. The last thing I want is for them to pity me, and question what happened. If anything, I don't want them to see how ashamed I am of myself. I could've changed how I came back, but I didn't. I was too weak. "Maybe some other time," I say quietly. I can't help but feel like a terrible person as his face falls. He nods, and I hope he understands why I don't want to see them yet, even if I haven't told him. Caden used to be very good at reading people, their emotions, and I don't think that skill ever left. He looks over at me for a moment, giving me a small smile. It reassures me he's not upset I turned down his request. "Tell me about everyone. How are they?" I add. I want to change the subject, and I do want to know how everyone has been.

Caden makes a right at the red light outside of town. Our ride is coming close to an end, and I realize I don't want it to. I want to talk to Caden for hours about what I've missed. "Who do you want me to start with? You've been gone a long time. A lot has changed."

I think about it for a few minutes before I decide. "Cason. Tell me about him." I knew it would be best to start with Caden's twin. Back when we were kids, they shared a bond none of us understood.

I watch his face light up as I mention Cason's name. He smiles, saying, "Cason is Cason." He chuckles loudly as if he's reliving a memory. "He owns a gym now. Mostly teaching the ladies how to defend themselves, and he seems to like being a personal trainer." He looks both ways at another stop sign before he turns right once more. I start to ask more about Cason, but Caden begins to give me more information. "Cason is probably the one that's changed the most. You remember how he used to be very quiet, never got into any trouble and was pretty smart in school." I nod, remembering before I left, Cason seemed the same as he always was. "Well, he's not like that anymore. None of us understood what happened. It happened shortly after you left, and we went through some shit with Carter. I don't really know what's going on with him, and that's saying a lot since I can always tell when something's off. He's always in a pissed off mood or picking fights for no reason. I've had to get him out of trouble more times than I'd care too."

I feel my chest tighten when he mentions Carter, but I ignore it. Caden doesn't speak for a few moments, and I don't interrupt him for a while. He seems lost in his thoughts, and I hate that Cason isn't the same as he once was. "What about Clark and Caleb?" I ask, hoping to take his mind off his troubling twin.

"Clark's deployed right now. He joined the Army as soon as he turned eighteen, and he calls home every chance his gets. He's always been the hero type out of all of us. Now, Caleb, he's doing pretty well. He's getting ready to graduate at MIT."

"Really? Wow, that's amazing. I always knew Clark would join the military. It's all he ever talked about, and Caleb's one of the smartest people I know. It doesn't surprise me he went to MIT."

"Yeah, I'm proud of both of them, but I can't help but worry about Clark getting deployed so much. This will be his fourth deployment, and he tries to play it off when he comes home that he's not affected by what he has to do or sees, but Carter and I notice it. He's not the same, and I can't say I blame him. I don't know if I could handle seeing the shit he does. "

I clench my jaw, turning my head away, hearing Caden mention Carter again. No matter how long it's been, just hearing his name makes my chest ache. It's like when you love someone so much, then suddenly they're not apart of your life anymore, any type of conversation about them makes you miss the good times. The times when you were happy. I don't respond to Caden, letting the silence take over the car again. Glancing out the window, I watch the houses pass by. It's strange how everything seems the same, but completely different. My stomach fills with butterflies as we pass over the railroad tracks, knowing any moment we'll be at Annie and William's home.

Caden expertly takes a sharp curve, and I see their house. It's exactly how I remember it. It's a small two-story house, with a country feel to it. The paint is now a pale yellow, instead of the bright color it was before I left. The yard is beautifully manicured, and I can't help but remember how I used to help Annie plant flowers in the spring. Caden pulls into their gravel driveway and parks. He doesn't turn off his police car, letting it idle. I think he knows I need to do this part on my own, and I really don't want Caden seeing me break down. I can already feel the tears burning in my eyes, and a lump forming in my throat.

I unbuckle my seat belt, then place my bag in my lap. Right before I open the door, I feel Caden's hand on my shoulder. "Here's my cell," he says as he hands me a piece of paper. "If you ever need anything, anything at all, call me. Even if it's just to talk or if you need a ride." I take the piece of paper, holding onto it like a lifeline. I nod, but I can't look at him. My eyes are full of unshed tears, and I don't dare blink. I don't want to cry.

Instead of saying anything, he pulls me into his arms, hugging me tightly. I squeeze him, hoping he understands how grateful I am for the ride, even if I can't tell him at the moment. I slowly pull away, quickly getting out of the car. Shutting the door, I glance up at the front porch. I've made a lot of memories on that front porch. The Harlow boys and I would eat popsicles on the swing in the summer. We would play Go Fish and I Spy once we got bored. I had my first kiss on that porch. Many nights of kissing, actually.

I swallow, and shake my head as I will the memories to stop. I rearrange my bag strap on my shoulder and place the piece of paper in my pocket, as I walk towards Annie and William's home. I hear Caden pulling out of the driveway, and I have to make myself not run to the house when Annie steps outside. Tears continue to fill my eyes as I get closer. Reaching the porch, I take the steps one at a time, careful not to trip. I get to the top, a place that I've been a thousand times, and grin when I see Annie smiling brightly back at me. It seems surreal seeing she hasn't changed that much in thirteen years. Her hair is all gray now, and a few more wrinkles cover her face, but everything else looks the same. Her honey brown eyes light up as I walk closer. I'm about a foot taller than she is, but that's never stopped her from taking me in her arms.

"Hi, Annie." I hear a gasp from her, and I wrap my arms around her small frame. I can't even describe how I feel at this very moment. I don't stop the tears from falling. I don't stop the cries that escape, but Annie never says a word. She rubs my back, letting me cry. I slowly pull away when my tears finally seem to dry up. I wipe my face with the back of my hands, and let out a laugh when Annie takes the dish towel off her shoulder. She wipes her face, then waves it back and forth afterwards.

I don't know how to explain my unexpected visit, but Annie doesn't give me the chance to even try. "Come on inside. I'll get you set up in your old room, and we can talk later." I nod, following her inside the house. I shut the screen door behind me, as a sense of calmness washes over me. Even as a little girl, Annie and William's home always seemed relaxing. It was as if I knew I belonged here instead of with my Mom. I always felt as if I were apart of The Barrett family, and there was never a time I didn't feel safe and loved. Their house still feels this way. I grin, noticing their home hasn't changed that much either. The hardwood floors are still the same dark color. Their couch still looks old, but comfortable. Pictures still cover the walls, and I walk over to inspect a few new ones on the entertainment center. I remember asking Annie once, why she didn't have any children of her own. She smiled at me, saying, "I have you and the boys. That's all I need." I was too young to really understand, but as I got older, I realized Annie and William had tried for years, and it just never happened for them. Maybe that's why fate brought me to them. Maybe some higher power saw how awful Mom was, and sent me here. I still remember the day I met them. I was seven, and I'd gotten lost in Wal-Mart while Mom was shopping. Annie found me, and helped me look for her. I remember Annie made me feel safe, and I was so comfortable around her. Once we realized Mom had left me, Annie took me back to her house and made me supper. Mom didn't come get me until the next day, but after that, I came over every day to see them.

I hear Annie calling for William, and I drop my bag, thankful to be brought out of my memory. I sit down on the comfy couch, as Annie walks into the kitchen. I can see her from where I'm sitting and watch her pull a plate out of the cabinet. I assume she's fixing a plate of food when she turns, making her way to the stove. My head snaps right as I hear heavy footsteps. I already know who it is, and when I see him, I jump off the couch and run to him. He immediately opens his arms, embracing me as he always did when I was younger. I close my eyes, taking in his familiar smell of motor oil and of the outdoors. "It's been way too long, Shelby."

I let him go and nod. "I know. It's good to be home."

"Come on, you two. I got breakfast waitin'," Annie interrupts. I smile and William places a hand on my back as we walk into the kitchen. I'm still shocked at how William and Annie haven't changed much over the years. William's jet black hair is still streaked with grey. His dark brown eyes still have warmth in them, and you can't help but smile when he does. I take a seat, and shake my head seeing how much taller William is compared to Annie's small frame. But they just fit together. They're the couple that you could never picture one without the other. When you're around them, you can't help but feel their love, just like now. I look away, as they share a sweet peck on the lips, and feel my face flush. Even after all this time, I still feel as though I'm intruding on their sweet moments.

Annie sets a plate full of food in front of me, and my mouth instantly starts to water. I lick my lips and devour the food. I scarf down the scrambled eggs, then move onto the crispy bacon. I have most of my food eaten before Annie places a glass of orange juice in front of me. I drink the entire glass before I notice the concerned looks from Annie and William. I glance a way, wiping my mouth. Neither one say anything about how I'm eating my food, and I'm glad for it. I don't want to explain anything. Maybe one day I'll talk to Annie about it, but right now, I don't want them feeling sorry for me.

Annie places a hand on top of mine, and I know she understands. I can see it in her eyes. She pats my hand as she asks, "When did you get back in town?"

I sigh in relief when she doesn't ask me anything I'm not ready to talk about yet. "An hour ago, actually. I was walking from the bus stop when Caden saw me and offered to give me a ride."

William nods, as Annie responds, "Oh, Caden, he's such a sweetheart. You know Caden and Cason still stop by from time to time. I know Clark and Caleb would if they were here. Carter used to come by more, but he hasn't lately."

"Really?" I nervously pick at my jacket, hoping that today isn't a day Carter randomly stops by.

"Of course they do. It's always nice to see the boys and spend time with them."

"Caden was here this past Sunday, helping me work on the old pick-up," William chimes in. I nod, making sure I eat my food slowly, and more lady like. Annie and William continue to talk about the Harlow boys, and my heart clenches every single time

## Carter

Carter's name is mentioned. Neither Annie nor William seem to notice how quiet I become, but I like hearing more about how things are going. We all finish eating, but none of us leave the table. Annie and William ask me how college was, if I liked South Carolina, and what my job was. I give them a brief summary of my time there, not wanting to go into detail about my life back then. I mainly talk about my job I had as an accountant. They both seem proud of me when I tell them I was the branch supervisor, and how I was going to get a promotion for the district manager if I hadn't left. They don't ask why I left, but I notice the look from them. They seem to communicate in a secret language that I'm not privy to. I don't tell them anything about Easton, or how we were married for seven years. I don't tell them anything about Mom moving to South Carolina, and ruining everything I had going for me. As the thought crosses my mind, I realize maybe Mom doing everything she did was my way of coming home. Maybe everything that happened, did for a reason, even if I don't know what the reason is yet.

Annie stands as she starts to clear the table, and I quickly get up to help her. "Let me take care of this, and William will carry your bag upstairs for you."

"Are you sure you don't need any help?"

"I think I can handle a few dishes. Go on, I'm sure you would like to lay down from all the travelin'."

"Thank you, Annie." I give her a hug and a kiss on the cheek, hoping she knows how much I appreciate her gentle nature. William follows me into the living room, stopping me before I can pick up my bag. I know better than to protest, and follow him upstairs. I suddenly feel tired, and I know it's because I'm exhausted from traveling, not to mention from having a home cooked meal. My room is still where it was the last time I was here years ago. Down the hall, first door on the right. William opens the door, and I can't believe how nothing has changed except the bed has upgraded to a full instead of a twin.

William doesn't say anything as I walk further into the room and touch my old porcelain dolls on the dresser. Annie let me pick out some of them for my birthday when I was fourteen. I turn around, seeing William standing by the door, watching me carefully. I wonder if he thinks I'm going to run away again or break down seeing my old room. It's strange to think they kept it all this time. "Everything is exactly how I left it last. Except the bed of course."

William nods, then says, "Annie and I always knew you'd come home when you were ready."

I look away, not wanting my emotions to get the best of me. I sit down on the bed and let out a deep sigh. "Are you sure it's alright if I stay here?" I glance up at him, quickly adding, "Just until I get back on my feet."

William sits on the bed beside me, and lets out a heavy breath before saying, "This house has and will always be your home too. It doesn't matter how long you've been gone. You know you can stay here as long as you'd like, for however long you need." He pats my leg, then gets up. William starts to walk out of my room, but then stops, and turns back to me. "I'm glad you're back where you belong. We sure have missed you."

"I've missed y'all too," I mutter, then he's gone, letting me have a moment to take in everything. It's a welcoming feeling. A sense of belonging somewhere in the world again, and I'm proud of myself for making the decision to come back here. I could never regret being back, with the two most gracious people I know.

Thoughts of how amazing Annie and William are, begin to make me sob. I wish I never left. I wish I would've stayed, letting their love keep me safe. I slowly lay down, letting all the bad memories of the past shed with my tears.

# CHAPTER 2

## Carter

The cold January air hits my face as I step out of my truck, but the sun shining makes my mood better. Shutting the door behind me, I hope today isn't filled with dread like it normally is. It began months ago when Dad told me he was getting ready to retire. I knew exactly what that meant before he told me, and I've been avoiding making the very big decision about taking over our family law firm ever since. I flip my keys around my finger as I begin to walk to our building on Main Street, working through my conflicted thoughts. Dad called me a few nights ago, asking if I'd given the offer anymore consideration. Of course I have. It's something that never leaves my mind, and I know I'm putting it off for no reason. I just don't know if I want the responsibility of running the firm. My father runs a tight ship, and maybe it's more a feeling than the thought of not being able to live up to his legacy. I'll never be as good as him and even though I've been doing this for years, I just can't shake the uneasy feeling I get when I think of the firm being solely mine. It's the doubt, and the fear of change that makes me question my decision so much.

My stomach grumbles, and I'm reminded I didn't get breakfast with my family this morning. It's been a tradition since I was a kid to have an early breakfast with my Mom, Dad, and, my annoying at times, brothers. Mom called me first thing this morning when I was twenty minutes late, but I didn't have the extra time today. It's my own fault for staying up so late talking with Bethany. And it's not the romantic, stay up all night fucking, or spilling your guts to someone kind of night. It was a night trying to talk her out of doing her usual nerdy thing, and wanting me to come over to get another tattoo. Bethany and I are more like brother and sister. She annoys the hell out of me like a sister would, and I give her hell at the guys she dates when she does date. She's smarter than any chick I know, and I've told her more than once she'd give Caleb a run for his money. I'd known her since Dad handled her parent's divorce about five years ago. Bethany is ten years younger than me, but when I saw her sitting in the lobby, waiting for her parents to be finished with all the divorce papers, something compelled me to talk to her. She was eighteen then, still a kid in my eyes, but our sibling like relationship bloomed from then on. She apprentices at a local tattoo shop, and I have to keep reminding her I'm not her damn guinea pig. I did let her do a piece on my back, just to show the owner of the tattoo shop, Theo, she's a brilliant artist.

My thoughts of talking to Bethany last night slip away from my mind, as Mrs. Baker calls out to me. I raise my hand in a friendly wave, knowing she'll be over around lunch to give us sandwiches from the Bistro she owns across the street. Mrs. Baker isn't the only one about to open their business for the day. I wave at a few more people as they pass by. I love the south. Everyone's just friendly, and it doesn't matter if I barely know some of the new business owners.

Flipping my keys around my finger once more, I glance around Main Street where my father's firm is located, before unlocking the door. It's a fairly new spot for us. We moved a few years ago, hoping the new location would pull in more clients. The move worked out in our favor for sure. Most days we're so busy that I've told Dad a few times he needs to hire another lawyer to pick up the slack. But I wouldn't trade those busy days for anything. Those days keep my mind away from thoughts of taking over the firm, and thoughts of the past that still to this day haunt me. Just as I'm about to unlock the door to start another day, I stop in my tracks. My eyes land on a slender woman wearing a gray oversized jacket, walking on the other side of the street. Seeing her makes me do a double take, and I squint trying to make out her face. She's looking down at her feet, which isn't working in my favor, but I can't help the overwhelming sense that I know her. Something about her seems familiar, but I can't put my finger on as to why that is. I continue to stare at her like some creepy stalker, and one name that still stops me in my tracks, takes over my mind.

Shelby Ross.

I sigh, knowing I've done this countless of times. I think I see her in strangers or think that I can smell her sweet perfume. I thought I would go mad at how many times I swore Shelby was walking down this very street, or how many times I had to look twice at someone that reminded me of her. Memories try to wash over me, but I push them out of my mind. I can't go down this road. Just being reminded of her memory is painful, and I reach up to rub my chest. Instead of looking away, like a man possessed, I watch the woman walk further down Main Street. I watch her as she takes in the town, almost as if she's been here before. I can't deny just seeing this mysterious woman makes me want to run across the street just to look at her face. It's like a force is willing me to go to her. I shake my head, only for a moment, thinking maybe I have finally lost my mind. The only other time I felt this strong pull to someone was with Shelby. But, this can't be her. The Shelby I knew would never come back to Columbus. I'd never get to see her again, or even hear her voice. After all this time that I've been away from her, it still hurts like hell knowing I'm the reason she'll never come back into my life. Every single day, since I stupidly pushed her away and let her go, I've regretted it. There's not one day that I don't wake up, and she's the first person I think of. She's also the last person that crosses my mind before a restless sleep overtakes me.

Over the years, I've figured out there's only one person that enters our lives and becomes permanently ingrained into our soul. It's that one person that will forever be with us, even if they're not physically here. Shelby was that person for me, and I'll never meet anyone like her again. She's etched into my heart, mind, and soul. I've tried to let her go, and accept she's never coming back. It's not like I've been sitting at home for thirteen years pining over the one that got away. I've dated a few women, but none ever lasted.

How could I ever try to really commit when my heart belongs to someone else?

The woman leaves my sight, and I finally pull my gaze away from the spot I last saw her. I drop my head sighing, feeling a deep sense of regret I haven't felt in months. It hits me like a ton of bricks, and I swallow hard trying to push back the emotions threatening to take over. I don't dare look over my shoulder. As I unlock the door to the firm, I tell myself I have to stop doing this. I can't always stay hung up on my one.

I have to let her go, but I don't know how. I realize that no matter how much time has passed, Shelby Ross will stay with me forever.

# Carter

At five o'clock on the dot, I lock the doors to Harlow: Attorneys At Law. Glancing out the front window, I make sure no one is about to stop in for a late consultation. When I don't see anyone, I shut the blinds, making my way to my small corner office. Dad has already left for the day, and I told Mary, our secretary, to head home about an hour ago. Wednesday's are always the slowest day of the week, and I for one, am grateful for the reprieve. Being a family and divorce lawyer makes me wonder if there's a thing such as a good marriage anymore. It seems every day we get more and more couples coming in and wanting a divorce. I shake my head thinking of the last client that came in today. He came in like a man on a mission, demanding we help him. Supposedly, his wife was cheating, and when I told him without documented proof, there was no way I could help him get everything he wanted in the divorce. Needless to say, the man left with another disappointment after our consultation. I turn and switch off the light in my office once I've put away all the files I'm working on, pushing that final client out of my mind. I have to remind myself multiple times a day that I can't let other people's horrible marriage affect me. I rub my hand on my neck, as I take a look around my office, making sure I haven't forgotten anything for the day.

My father's practice isn't big, but it suits us perfectly. We rent the building from a local real estate company that gives us a great price, and with the tan walls and new hardwood floors, I can't complain. I just don't know if I want it all. Caden, Cason, Clark, and Caleb all went for what they really wanted to do with their lives. Me, I had to be just like my Dad. Maybe some part of me wanted to impress him, since I'm the first born, and the expectations were high. I shake my head at this train of thought. Dad wouldn't care if I was a janitor at the high school. I know what he'd say, but being a lawyer is all I've ever known, and all I've ever wanted to be. I still have my doubts, and I often think maybe if I was happier with the way my life was going I wouldn't feel this way. Maybe it's just the responsibility that comes with taking over everything Dad built. I don't want to fuck up and disappoint him.

My phone starts to ring, and I chuckle when I see Bethany's name on the screen. "Didn't I just talk to you?" I answer, jokingly.

"Ha-ha, very funny, Carter. You off yet? We should get everyone together and play some Call of Duty later."

I unlock the door, awkwardly placing the phone on my shoulder. "Hell no. The last time we played you kicked our asses. I have no desire to be humiliated by a chick playing video games again."

"Don't be such a Debbie Downer. Come on, Carter. I'm bored, and Theo kicked me out of the shop today. Again."

I grab my phone, sighing loudly as I make my way to the parking lot behind our building. I listen to Bethany complain about not being able to tattoo anyone the entire way to my pick-up. Finally, she stops her ranting, and I try to get in a word. "Beth, look, I've told you countless times, you need to stand up to Theo. Tell him it's time he gives you a chair." When she doesn't say anything for a moment, I add, "Why can't we do something else besides something we all know you're better at? What about bowling?" I hope changing the subject about the tattoo shop will ease the conversation elsewhere. I can't even count how many times I've heard the same complaints about her being sent home for no reason.

"Well," I hear her talking to someone, and I wonder where she's at. "Sorry, Wal-Mart is insane right now." Ah, that explains everything. "We can try bowling, I guess." She sounds defeated. I open my mouth to respond, but she cuts me off. "I don't know why you're being such a bitch about playing video games with me."

"Because you hog all the zombies! Then the rest of us are up shit creek when it gets in the higher rounds." I glance around, hoping no one's listening to my conversation. I feel like a bitch since my voice got higher than normal. I can't help it with Bethany. She knows how to irritate me like my brothers.

"Psh, whatever. I'll call Cason, and you call Caden. Meet up in thirty?"

"I'll be there."

"Good. Be prepared to get your ass kicked at bowling too."

I shake my head, ending the call, not wanting to argue with her. She probably will kick all our asses tonight. I don't know how she does it, but pretty much anything Bethany does she excels at. I push the unlock button on my truck keys, and climb inside. I turn on my Bluetooth and once it connects, I call Caden. As it rings, I pull out of the parking lot and head north. It takes a bit longer to get out onto the crowded roads of downtown, since everyone has just closed shop for today.

I hang up when Caden doesn't answer. I wonder if he's still on his shift, and I realize I have no idea since I didn't see him this morning. That's another reason I love having breakfast with my family every morning. We talk about our plans for the day, and it makes seeing my brothers easier. We're all close, Caden and Cason more than the rest of us, since they share their weird twin bond, but overall we try to at least hang out every chance we get. Caden's shifts are always changing, and I know some days he doesn't enjoy it. I can understand why. Working a split shift one day, a half day the next, and then the night shift can really get old. I toss my phone in the passenger seat as I make my way through the afternoon traffic. I really don't pay attention to everyone around me as I drive at a snail's pace. My mind has been preoccupied all day with memories of Shelby and I when we were younger. A lot younger. I don't know why I was thinking of our childhood, instead of our teenage years. I know it has a lot to do with the woman I saw earlier today. Since seeing her, all I can think about is Shelby. I have to stop this. I'm starting to sound like a love sick puppy.

Thankfully, if anyone noticed today, they didn't say anything.

I try to call Caden once more as I finally break out of the heavy traffic, and turn left at the red light by Chili's. When he doesn't answer again, I leave him a voice mail, letting him know what the plans are for the evening. I pull in the parking lot behind one of my favorite restaurants, and find a parking spot in front of the newly added, GT Lanes. I haven't been here since it just opened a few months ago. I park and rub my chin as I turn on the radio. I turn it down low, thinking about getting some Mexican food after we finish bowling for the night. It's convenient having a Mexican restaurant and a frozen yogurt place right beside the bowling alley.

Unbuckling my seat belt, I prop my elbow on the side of the door, and stare out the window, as I wait for everyone to arrive. These are the moments I hate the most. The time alone, time to think about shit I don't really want to address even to myself. But try as I might, the damn memories pour into my mind, like an endless marathon of the most annoying TV show. I eventually just let the memory come, and close my eyes, remembering the past so vividly. At a time when nothing seemed to stop Shelby and I from just being ourselves. At a time, I was too naïve to believe that she wasn't my forever.

*I glanced down at Shelby, and I can't help but laugh at her. She's trying so hard to climb the rope that leads to our newly built treehouse William made for us. I've told her three times to use the ladder, but*

Brie Paisley

she's too stubborn to give up. I watch her fall on her butt again, and she frowns up at me then shakes her head. "Shel, why can't you just climb the ladder like I told you?" I said as I leaned on the rail, looking down at her.

"If you can do it, I know I can," she snapped, determined more than ever to do exactly what I did.

"Don't get mad when I laugh at you for falling again."

"Shut up, Carter. You watch. I'm going to do it, and then you're going to give me those Skittles you keep hidden from me!"

"Alright, if you can climb that rope without falling, I'll give you the entire bag of them."

"You promise?" Even at the age of ten, I could tell how much a promise meant to her. She asked me to promise the simplest of things, even when she knew I would do anything she asked.

"I promise, Shel. Now, get your skinny butt up here." She nodded, and I continued to watch her. She pushed her hair out of her face, then gripped the rope tightly. She stood still for a few moments, and I almost asked her if she was going to climb up. When she jumped and started to climb, I couldn't help but smile. I could already tell she was set on getting my bag of goodies.

I could hear her breath coming out faster as she got closer to the opening in the floor of the treehouse. I moved away from the rail when I didn't see her anymore, and hovered over the squared opening to watch her more. I started to cheer her on, *and bent down to help her off the rope as she reached the opening. I took her small hand and helped her up. I dropped her hand, and noticed she was beaming. "I told ya I could do it."*

*Laughing, I said, "I knew you would do it, Shel. Come on and I'll get you my Skittles." I took her hand again, and she followed me inside the treehouse. We came here a lot on the weekends, and when we didn't have school. Most days, we stayed up here and played Uno or Monopoly. Sometimes Caden, Cason, and Clark came up here too, but most days it was just Shelby and I. Mom said Caden, Cason, and Clark were too little to climb up to the treehouse, but I think she just said that because she didn't want them to get hurt.*

*Mr. William told us we could come over anytime we wanted to play in the treehouse. I liked coming here with Shelby, and I think she liked getting away from her Mom. I didn't like Mrs. Tabitha, but I didn't tell Shelby that. I also didn't tell Shelby she smelled funny, and her clothes were dirty. When I first met Shelby, she was sitting on the swings at school by herself. I knew how the other kids treated her. They were mean to her because she wasn't like them. But as I turned and looked at her bright blue eyes, still smiling from climbing the rope, I couldn't imagine not having her as my best friend. I dropped her hand, and we sat down on the floor as I grabbed my bag of Skittles. I didn't really like them, but I knew Shelby loved them. We sat across from each other, and I handed her the prize she won fair and square.*

"Thank you, Carter," she said as she took the bag out of my hands. I watched her as she started to shovel the sweet candies in her mouth, as if she hadn't eaten anything today. It made me sad knowing she was so skinny, and how she always seemed to be starving every time she ate. She stopped, and looked at me with sad eyes. I hated when she looked at me like that.

"What's wrong, Shel?"

She placed the bag beside her, and she looked away for a moment. I waited, hoping she would tell me for once what's really going on with her parents. I've overheard my Mom and Dad talking about them before, and none of it sounded good. "Carter, do you think you're Mommy and Daddy love each other?"

"What kind of question is that?" I really didn't know how to answer her.

"I mean, do your parents fight all the time? I've seen how your parents hug you and tell you they love you." I barely heard her say, "My Mommy tells me she hates me sometimes."

I moved beside her and took her hand again. She glanced at me, and I could see tears building in her eyes. "Don't cry, Shelby." I watched a tear slide down her cheek, and it made my stomach hurt seeing her so sad. I might not understand the meaning of love, but I did know that Shelby was my best friend. I didn't like her Mom was mean to her, and would say nasty things to her. "When your Mom says those things to you, just remember that I love you, Shelby. And I know my parents love you, too."

*She wiped her cheek and asked, "You promise?"*

*"I promise. I'll always love you, Shelby."*

I rub my eyes, making myself stop the memory from continuing. I still remember the feelings that ran through me seeing Shelby so hurt. I did keep my promise, too. Even if I never see her again, I hope she knows I never once stopped loving her. I run my hands down my face, trying to push away the unsettling emotions in the pit of my stomach. I have to rub my chest when my heart starts to ache, and turn off the radio as Springsteen by Eric Church comes on. I can't bear to listen to that song. It makes me think of the past, and of all the times I was with Shelby, a time when I thought we'd never be apart. But times change. People change, and promises of a ten-year old mean nothing now.

I turn off my truck, leaning my head against the seat. I close my eyes, trying to keep myself rooted where I am. As soon as I'm comfortable, I jump, hitting my arm on the door, when a loud tap comes to my left. I turn seeing Bethany standing beside my truck. She's laughing, even holding her sides, knowing she scared the shit out of me. Shaking my head, I grab my wallet then get out of the truck. I shut the door and lock it, as she continues to laugh. "Laugh it up while you can," I say and smile at her. It's a rare moment when she catches me off guard like that, and I give her props for getting me.

"I wish I recorded that." She stops to laugh more then says, "That was awesome. I can't believe I finally got you!"

"Remember it because that's the last time, Beth."

"You say that now, but I'll wait for another chance. What were you thinking about anyways? You looked so sad."

I start to walk towards the bowling alley, noticing Bethany beside me. "Nothing really. Just trying to get my head in the game for tonight." I look away, hoping she buys what I'm selling. I don't want to talk about Shelby. I don't want to be reminded how I need to let it go. Everyone close to me knows the story. They all know how I still zone out thinking about her, and every time they tell me I need to move on. They all loved Shelby, except Bethany, because she never knew her, but the rest of my family wished she would come back. I know my Mom still talks about her and tells me all the time how I should go find her. The thing is, I know where Shelby is. I know she's happy, living her life how she wants. Who am I to fuck up what she has? I'd rather stay here, being miserable, than mess with her happiness.

"Uh huh." Her eyes narrow, and I know she doesn't believe me. "Well, I hope you prepared enough because I'm bringing my A-game."

"Good. You're going to need all of it to win." I don't dwell on her not so subtle way of not believing me, but I'm glad she doesn't push for more. I'm actually grateful she didn't want to pick me apart about it. The thing about Bethany is she's the easiest person to spill all my deepest secrets to, but I always make her work for it. I don't like opening up those wounds, and I'd much rather leave them be.

"You keep on talking shit. Whatever makes you feel better about losing."

I laugh as we walk inside the bowling alley. I hold the door open for her and ask, "Why are you always so competitive?"

"I don't like to lose, Carter. You know this." She's right. From the moment we started becoming friends, I noticed how she had to be the best at everything she did. It didn't matter if it was just us hanging out, and doing our normal gaming night, she had to win. I didn't really understand why she thought she had to be the best, but I have a feeling it has something to do with her parents. I never really asked, knowing it's still a sore subject to bring up. Not to mention every time I tried to get her to open up, she would get defensive, and would say she didn't want to talk about it. I learned quickly not to bring it up again.

I don't comment on what she says, as we make our way to the front counter and reserve a lane for us. I stand behind Bethany as she gives the size of her bowling shoes to the cashier, and I take a look around. This is my first time here, and I can already tell this will be a new spot for us to hang out at. The vibe is laid back, yet it's exciting. It's just like any other bowling alley, except it's a huge building. They have twenty-four lanes and over half are already occupied. The lights are dim, but they have colorful flashing lights making the alley seem multi-colored, plus it's eye catching. They have Hotline Bling by Drake playing over the speakers, and it's hard not to bob my head to the beat.

Bethany grabs her shoes, and I step up to the counter to do the same. After we're set to get started, we head to our lane. We sit in the chairs by our lane, as we put on our bowling shoes, and I look up when I see someone moving in front of me. "Finally decide to show up, Cas?"

"Yeah, had to close up the gym, and since Beth is always last minute telling anyone plans, it was unavoidable."

"Like you had any plans made," Bethany says, and I laugh when Cason flips her the bird. Cason sits down and begins to lace his bowling shoes. I don't know about Bethany, but I've always known the difference between Caden and Cason. Even if they're identical twins, they couldn't be any more different than they are. I finish lacing my shoes, and I sit in the chair in front of the small keyboard to put in our names on the score-board.

I put in all our names, but before I finish, I turn to Cason to ask, "Heard anything from, Caden?"

Cason adjusts his hat, turning it backward before he responds. "Yeah, he said he'll be here in an hour." I nod, and click enter, putting our names on the overhead board. Afterward, we go to find our bowling balls. It takes us a bit of looking around for them, since more people are coming in to bowl for the night. It's been a long time since I've bowled, and

I can only hope I don't embarrass myself or let Bethany kick my ass.

Bethany picks up an eight-pound ball, and turns to me with a huge grin on her face. "Prepared to lose, old man?"

I take the dark blue twelve-pound ball off the rack, ignoring the old man comment. "Keep up the shit talk. When I kick your ass, you owe me a beer."

"I'll take that bet."

"What are we betting?" Cason asks as he chooses his bowling ball.

"Well, Carter seems to think he's going to kick my ass tonight. I bet he can't."

As we walk back to our lane, Cason says, "I'd like to see you lose, Carter. Beth's the man at everything. If I were you, I'd back out now while you can."

"Hell no. I'm taking the bet. Bethany, what do you say?"

She places her ball on the ball rack in front of our lane, as she says, "Let's make it interesting then. If you win, I'll buy you a twelve pack of whatever kind of beer you want."

"Alright, and if you win?"

She smiles, and I get a feeling I'm not going to like what she says. "If I win." She turns, looking around the alley, then answers with, "You have to ask that chick out." I glance in the direction she's pointing, noticing a short blonde laughing at something a woman says. I raise my eyebrows, wondering why in the world Bethany chose this girl.

The blonde is attractive, but I can't say I'm not apprehensive about this bet.

I think about it for a minute, before making up my mind, telling Bethany, "It's a bet then." We shake on it, and we start our game. I'm suddenly more determined to win against Bethany, and her trying to play matchmaker.

It's official.

Not only do I suck at bowling, but I also got my ass handed to me. Cason and Bethany's scores make me want to never play this game again. I can't count how many times I gutter-balled, or flat out just missed the bowling pins in general. How could that even happen? I've been asking myself that over and over. I'm glad Caden ended up not showing up because he surely would've given me hell for losing so badly. But a bet is a bet. I shake my head, rubbing my neck, as I make my way over to the blonde Bethany picked out. I glance over my shoulder before approaching the blonde and notice Bethany and Cason watching me, and it makes me regret taking that stupid bet. I should've listened to Cason when he told me not to take it, but no. I just had to do it, not knowing Bethany would beat me.

I stow my hurt pride, as I think of what to say to the blonde. As I get closer, I see she's watching me. She smiles, then blushes as she looks away. Maybe this whole bet thing will work in my favor. The blonde isn't the hottest chick I ever seen. She's just average, but she's easy on the eyes. Her blonde hair falls down to her shoulders, and she tucks some behind her ear. As I get closer, I notice she has light blue eyes, but I don't look into them long.

Shelby's eyes are a darker shade of blue with a hint of green in them.

I sigh, pushing that thought away. I cannot compare the blonde with Shelby. No one will be able to take her place, but it's time I really start to move on or at least try. I stop, letting a couple and their kids pass by. The blonde looks at me again, and I grin. I decide to make my move when she steps away from her group. "Hi, I'm Carter," I say as I hold out my hand for her.

She laughs, but she does shake my hand. "I'm Summer. It's nice to meet you." Alright, maybe my hand shaking was a smooth move. I let go of her hand, and she tucks another strand of hair behind her ear. I stare at her for a moment, hoping that maybe I'll feel something for Summer, but nothing's happening. I feel nothing for this girl, and I know this isn't a good thing. There's no zing, no heart racing. It's just another person standing in front of me. I turn away from her, and notice Bethany motioning me to talk to Summer more. I shake my head, turning back to Summer. She seems a bit lost and not knowing what to say. She looks to her friends, and I know if I don't do something now, this embarrassing bet will have been all for nothing. I won't back down, and even if I don't feel anything for Summer, maybe I can at least make another friend.

"So, uh, you like bowling?" I curse at myself, thinking I'm horrible at making small talk or even trying to flirt. I'm rusty. I haven't been on a date in almost a year, and I just know Summer is going to tell me she's not interested.

She giggles then says, "Yeah, my friends and I come here all the time. How about you? I don't think I've seen you here before."

I'm caught off guard for a moment at her response. I really thought she would tell me to fuck off, or make up a reason to go back to her friends. "I haven't bowled in a long time, and this is my first time here." I turn back to Bethany and Cason, noticing they've left. "Do you want to grab a drink and talk more? It's too loud in here to have a proper conversation."

Summer grins, nodding her head. She reminds me of those bobble head dolls, and I rub my chin to hold back a chuckle. "Yes, I'd love to. Let me tell my friends bye, and I'll meet you out front." I nod once, and head to the front counter.

After paying and getting my shoes back on, I make my way outside and wait for Summer. I glance around the parking lot, hoping to see Bethany and Cason. They would be a nice buffer until I can get to know Summer more. I pull out my phone when I don't see them, and notice I have a text from Bethany.

*Told you I'd kick your ass. Have fun with the blonde. She's cute so don't fuck up.*

I close out the text, deciding not to respond. Leave it to Bethany to rub in my horrible bowling skills. I slide my phone back in my pocket, placing my hands in my front pockets. I should've brought a jacket with me, noticing how cold it's gotten. I start pacing, waiting for Summer to come out. Thankfully, I don't have to wait long for her. She comes outside all smiles and staring right at me. "Would you like to sit, and grab some food at this Mexican place?" I ask, pointing at the restaurant.

"Yeah, sure. That would be great." We walk side by side next door to the Mexican restaurant, but neither of us says anything. I honestly don't know what to say, and I find I'm unsure how to go about this date if I could even call it that. I can only hope things aren't this awkward as we get inside the restaurant. I open the door for her, and just as I'm about to walk in behind her, I get another text. I lag behind Summer, pulling out my phone to see what the text says. I can't help but laugh when I see Bethany's newest demand.

*Tell me all the deets later.*

Yeah, that's highly unlikely. Bethany's going to be waiting a while for that one.

# CHAPTER 3

## Shelby

Annie and I sit out on the back porch, enjoying our morning coffee. It's become our new ritual. I find that I enjoy the coolness of the morning air, and how comfortable I feel just … being here. The past three months of being back home have been amazing for me. Every day I feel more and more like the old me, not the woman Easton tried to make me become. There's been a slow change in me with each passing day, but staying home all the time to heal, has been helpful. I also have Caden to help keep my spirits up when things aren't going as well, or if I'm having a horrible day. Annie and William have been patient, not pushing me to talk about the past. But I can tell from their sad stares some days it's hard for them to avoid it.

I feel Annie's gaze on me now, but I don't look her way yet. I stare at the old worn out treehouse wondering if it's safe to climb. The treehouse used to be my safe haven. I take a sip of my coffee, putting off Annie as long as I can. I know she's been working up to asking me about my time in South Carolina.

I've managed to change the subject every time she brings it up, or if I think she's going to ask me about it. I know it'll help if I open up to her, or at least get the horrible dreams I've been having under control. I just don't have the words to explain. If anything, I'm ashamed of myself for letting Easton's controlling ways happen for so long. I should've been smarter, and not so afraid to leave until things got so out of control.

"Shelby, when are you going to open up with what happened?" Annie asks softly. I sigh, knowing my time is up for hiding the truth. I turn in my chair, setting my coffee mug on the small outdoor table. I look into Annie's light brown eyes, and she gives me a sweet smile, encouraging me to talk to her. Before it was so easy to talk to Annie about everything. It came naturally, and I still feel that way, but I don't want her to see me differently.

I look away, staring at the old treehouse again, wishing I had the courage like I did when I was a child. It was so simple back then. I turn back to Annie when I feel her hand on mine. She squeezes my hand, and I take a deep breath. "I don't really know where to start," I say as a nervous laugh escapes me.

"Start wherever you want. You don't have to tell me anything, but just know I'm here when you're ready. I don't want to see the sadness in your eyes anymore, or hear you crying yourself to sleep."

I clench my jaw willing the tears that threaten to spill away. I didn't know she could tell how I'm struggling to leave my past behind me, or how I can't seem to stop the cries at night. It's always worse before sleep takes me. "I know I can tell you anything, Annie. I just …" I swallow hard and have to clear my throat before I tell her, "I just didn't know how much his words could affect me. I didn't know how difficult leaving, and putting that life behind me was going to be so hard. I thought …" I shake my head, trying not to let the memories take over. "I thought leaving and coming home would be the best option for me. And so far, it's been wonderful. But his words …" I wipe a tear as it slides down my cheek, and Annie moves her chair closer to mine. She takes my hand, placing it in her lap as I continue to talk. "The thing is when I first met Easton, he was perfect. I don't know what happened or where things went so horribly wrong, but I never knew someone could be so hateful for no reason. I didn't know how much his demeaning words would affect so much of who I am." Annie doesn't utter a single word as I talk about the past thirteen years. I don't tell her everything, but I know she understands why. I can only get a few words out before I finally break down. When it gets to the worst parts, Annie just holds me as I cry. It feels good to let it out and to talk about some of it. As my tears finally dry up, I feel lighter and more hopeful than I have in a long time. I know telling Annie won't magically cure me, but it's a start.

We stay out on the porch for hours it seems, talking about everything. Annie doesn't bring up anything I've told her. Instead, she fills me in on what's been going on lately since I've become a hermit. She tells me more about the nice family that moved into my childhood home, and about their children. I can't help but laugh when Annie says she's taken over the bingo night at the community center. I remember how she always made time to go every week, and it makes sense for her to run it now. I do notice how she doesn't speak much of the Harlow's. I want to think it's because of how Carter and I left things all those years ago, and I hope she knows how much I appreciate it. I hold no ill feelings towards Carter, those feelings have long passed, but I can't know if he's moved on yet. I don't want to know if he's doing well for himself, or if he's found someone to make him happy. He's my first love, and I know eventually I'm going to see him. It's unavoidable in our small town. I tell myself it won't bother me if I see him, but I honestly don't know if that'll hold true.

Much later, William finally comes outside, asking if we're hungry. Annie and I share a knowing glance, and we laugh as we make our way inside. I place the coffee mugs in the sink, and lean against the counter as I watch Annie and William banter playfully back and forth. I smile, enjoying listening to them bicker about nothing. I turn away when William sweetly kisses Annie, and walk to the fridge to start making sandwiches for us. I place everything I know we like on the counter when Annie lightly touches my back. "I've got this under control."

"I can help, it's no problem." She shakes her head and ushers me to sit down. I sigh and unwillingly take a seat at the table. Annie has always been this way, and I remember how she used to shoo me out of the kitchen when I stayed here when my mother left for a year. As I got older, she let me help some, and she taught me how to cook. I watch her as she moves swiftly around the kitchen, humming to herself. William's reading the paper, and I realize how peaceful and easy it is here with them. I don't have to pretend, or try to be perfect. I don't have to watch what I do or say. It's an amazing feeling, one that I'm glad I'm able to experience again.

My stomach drops and I snap my head towards the front door when I hear the doorbell chiming. I don't know why my hands start to sweat, or why suddenly I want to run and hide in my room. I sit like a statue as William folds his paper in half, then slowly walks to answer the door. I know for a fact Easton has no idea where I am. At least, that's what I'm telling myself. I slowly take a deep breath, trying to calm myself down. I've done this every single time since leaving South Carolina. I can only hope one day the fear of Easton finding me will dissipate.

I instantly relax when I hear William's laugh and a familiar voice. William moves to the side to let Caden in, and I smile at him when he sees me. "Annie, we have enough food for one more?" William asks.

"Of course. Come have a seat, Caden." Annie turns back to fixing lunch as Caden grabs a chair from the laundry room, then places it beside me.

"Couldn't stay away?" I playfully ask. Caden has been visiting randomly since I returned, and I want to think it's because he's checking in with Annie and William. I haven't gotten the courage to ask him about Carter, or if he knows I'm here. I have a feeling if he did know, he'd be over to talk to me.

"You know me, Shel. No one can resist Annie's food."

I laugh as William chimes in with, "How right you are. It's the reason for this." He points to his pot belly. "Right here." We laugh as William sits down with us. Soon after, Annie places a plate stacked high of sandwiches. After pouring us all a glass of sweet tea, she sits down, and we dig in.

"Thank you for the food, Mrs. Barrett," Caden says. I laugh, knowing Annie doesn't like it when anyone calls her that.

"Caden, you know not to call me that." She shakes her head and mumbles something about making her feel old.

I sit back as I listen to William and Caden talk about restoring an old truck William bought at an auction a few weeks ago. Some of it I understand, but I quickly get lost as they start talking about rebuilding the engine, and what all goes into that. "She'll be a beauty once we get all the parts, and put her back together," Caden says.

"She sure will. It's going to be a challenge, but I made a list of parts we can take to Carl's Auto later. It's over there on the table by the phone."

"I'll get it," I tell William. I get up and start rummaging through the pile of mail looking for the list. As I flip through the mail pile, my face falls seeing all of Annie and William's mail has past due notices on them. I glance back at them, and start to feel guilty. Here I am, bumming off them and they're behind on bills. I wonder how bad it is, and as I find the list, I decide it's time to get a job, and start helping them. It's the least I can do for all they've done for me.

I look up at the old treehouse, thinking about climbing up, and taking the chance that the old wood will hold. Caden stands behind me telling me that I shouldn't do it, but I want to. I've stared at it since I've been back, and I remember how safe it was being up there when I was younger. It felt as though it was the only place I could climb high enough to escape everything going wrong in my life. Although Annie and I talked this morning, I still feel the need to just sit in my old sanctuary.

"I really don't think this is a good idea, Shelby. No one's been up there in years."

"You chicken, Caden?" I ask, glancing back at him.

"No, I just don't want to die trying to climb up there."

"You were always the dramatic one." I turn back to the treehouse then say, "If Cason were here, he'd do it with me."

Caden laughs, then says, "I know he would. He's always been the risk taker out of all of us. I don't know, Shel. I think Annie and William will be highly upset if they find our broken bodies when they get back from the store."

"Stop being such a pansy." Caden laughs, but he doesn't respond. With my mind made up, I walk to the warped ladder. I hear Caden say a few choice words, but he reluctantly comes up behind me. I slowly start to climb the old ladder, hoping Caden isn't right. The last thing I need is a trip to the emergency room. I tense when I hear the wood making noises, but I don't stop. Slowly, I climb higher until I reach the floor opening. I glance down at Caden, and smile knowing I've almost made it. He shakes his head, and I take the last step up.

Once I see the porch of the treehouse, I look around, making sure everything at least seems sturdy enough to hold my weight. A rush of fear races through me, but I push it down. I'm this far, and I won't back down now. I place both hands on the wooden floor, pulling myself up. The floor creaks loudly, and I still for a few moments. I can feel the wind blowing on my face, and I take a deep breath, hoping to calm my racing heart down. Gently, I put more weight on the floor, and stop when I get on my hands and knees. "Shelby?"

My arms start to shake from climbing, holding myself up, and from being so tense, but I manage to call back down to Caden so he doesn't worry. "I'm fine. It's holding." *For now at least*, I think to myself. As I stand, my knees wobble, and I hold my arms out to steady myself. I take a light step forward, making my way to the rail so I can let Caden know I'm alright. Once I reach the railing, and Caden sees me, I grin widely. I can't believe I'm back in my childhood safe place, and taking everything in seems surreal. I can see the entire backyard now, along with the neighbors outside having a cookout. It's peaceful being able to look down at the world below me, and I've never felt so free. I close my eyes as the wind picks up again, and the sun finally makes an appearance. The sunlight warms my face, and I tilt my head back basking in its warmth.

I open my eyes and turn my head when I hear Caden walking up to me. He looks scared, and I burst out in laughter at his expression. "Stop laughing! I swear, Shel if I die from climbing up here, I'm coming back to haunt you as a ghost."

"Stop complaining, Caden. It's fine. Look," I move away from the rail and start jumping. Caden rushes to the rail, holding on for dear life. "It's holding just fine. This treehouse is sturdy, and William built it, so we both know he did it properly."

With wide eyes, Caden lets go of the rail with one hand and wipes the sweat off his forehead.

"Don't do that again. Jesus, do you want this thing to fall apart? And I trust William's carpenter skills, I just don't trust how old this wood is."

"Lighten up, Caden. Obviously, if it was going to fall apart, it would've done so by now. Come on, let's go inside." I have to beckon Caden a few times before he finally follows me inside. I have to duck as I walk through the door, but once inside, I'm able to stand tall. Glancing around the room, it's as though I never left. The horror posters I'd collected as a teen still hang on the walls. They're torn on the edges, but otherwise, still look in good condition. The bean bags we used to sit on are still in the corner, along with some old magazines. A small shelf to the right holds some of my favorite mix tapes, and I notice some action figures from one of the brothers. Caden doesn't speak as I take it all in, and I'm glad for it. I need a moment to reminisce, to miss all the things I wished I could have again. I make my way to the single window in the treehouse, and gaze outside. So many memories want to rush over me, but only one in particular stands out more than the others.

I reach in my shirt and grab my necklace. I hold onto it tightly as I close my eyes, and let the last memory of my father surface. To the time when I was twelve and had no idea what loss was until that day.

*Tears pour down my face, mixing with the rain. It made it hard to see, but I didn't stop running. I didn't care who saw me, and didn't hear anyone if they tried. The rain mixed with the thunder drowned out everything around me. I only had one thing on my mind, and I knew where I needed to go. The one place where I felt the safest. To the place where nothing could hurt me. My breath came out in pants, my lungs burned from exertion, but I didn't stop. I couldn't stop until I got there. Water splashed against my bare legs as I ran through puddles of water, and I almost slipped and fell when I rounded the corner to Annie and William's backyard. I was unsure if they were home, but if they were I knew they'd give me the space I needed.*

*Once I reached the ladder to the treehouse, I quickly climbed up, and had to stop once I reached the top to wipe my face. The rain fell down on me, and I stood still for a moment, letting it wash over me. I was soaking wet by the time I walked inside, but I didn't care. I was cold and wet, but nothing could take away the pain I felt. I sat down in the corner and pulled my legs to my chest. I leaned my head on my knees, and I had no idea how I still had tears streaming down my cheeks. My chest felt like it was being torn in two, and I started shaking feeling how cold my clothes were on my skin. I didn't know how long I sat all alone in the corner, crying hysterically before I heard him. I knew he'd come. He was there when the sheriff told me about my Dad's accident. The news shouldn't have shocked me as much as it did. I knew my dad was drunk. I knew he didn't have anything to live for, not even me. My mother made sure of that. But it's the pain of knowing he not only killed himself, but he also murdered a mother, father and one of their children. Their little girl was the only one that survived. I didn't know if she'd live through the pain and suffering of the news once she found out her family was dead. I let out a scream just thinking about it, of how selfish he was. Now, not only is my life utterly shattered, but so is that little girl's.*

*"Shelby?"*

*I lifted my head, hearing his voice, and when he sat beside me, I leaned into him. He pulled me tighter into his embrace as I cried out, and gripped his shirt in my hands. "Why, Carter? Why did he do this to me?" I screamed over and over. I knew he didn't have the answers. I knew my Dad had a problem, but I thought he was getting better. But once my mother left to go on her selfish trip, Dad started drinking again. I never thought he was this bad off. I never thought he could be stupid enough to drive while intoxicated. The only saving grace out of the whole situation was Mom had made sure Annie and William looked after me while she was gone. I pleaded with her to let me stay with Dad, but she refused to listen. With Dad being all alone, I was just waiting for something bad to happen. I just had a feeling he would go off the deep end.*

*My soaked shirt clung to me as Carter stroked my back. My cries finally stopped, but I didn't move out of Carter's arms, even if he was soaked from the rain. Somehow, his warmth was making me feel warm too. He was my other safe place. The one person I knew that would never leave me. "She did this to him."*

*"What do you mean, Shel?"*

*"My horrible mother. She did this! If she hadn't left for God knows what, he would still be here. That family would still be here. That little girl wouldn't be an orphan now." I raised my head, and turned away from Carter. The tears were back and a lump formed in my throat. It burned, and I felt it all the way down to my stomach.*

*"Shelby, I … I don't know what to say. I'm so sorry."*

*"Yeah, I am too. He was getting better. He'd stopped drinking again, and he actually was my Dad." I faced Carter as I asked, "Why did she leave him? I don't understand it, Carter. If she'd never left, if she wasn't so selfish, he'd still be here, and so would that family. I hate her. I hope she never comes back."*

*"I know you're angry, but you can't talk like that. Shelby, your dad was sick and it's not anyone's fault. I can't explain why your dad chose to drink and drive, but you and I both know he never meant to hurt anyone."*

*I stood and I pointed my finger in his face. I didn't want to direct my anger at him, but I couldn't help it. "Don't you say that! I hate her. I don't want her to come back, and it is her fault for what happened. If she never left he wouldn't have started drinking. If she hadn't left, then he wouldn't have gotten in the car. He wouldn't have …" My voice broke, but I don't stop. My anger was fueling me, and I had to say it out loud because then, I wouldn't feel like I could die. "I blame her for what happened to that family. It is her fault. Dad drank because my mother didn't love him. Don't tell me otherwise. You didn't live through it. You didn't see what I did. Don't you dare say it's only because he was sick!" My tears flowed down my face again, and I slowly lowered my arm when Carter stood. He didn't say anything, but I knew he understood. Carter had always understood me.*

*He took me in his arms again when I started shaking and held me as I let the pain and anger out. He didn't have to say anything because I knew he'd always be here for me. He was my best friend, and I knew he'd forgive me for yelling at him. As all the emotions poured out of me, I realized that if Carter were to ever leave me, I didn't think I could survive it.*

"Shelby?" Caden's voice pulls me out of one of the many bad memories I have. I unclench my hand around my necklace, placing it back inside my shirt. I sigh, and glance back at him with tears in my eyes.

"Want to go somewhere with me?" I ask with a shaky voice.

"Yeah, sure. Where do you want to go?"

I look back out the window as I say, "I want to go see my Dad."

The drive to the cemetery is quiet and shorter than I remembered. Caden drives as I sit in the passenger seat of his car, and the silence is welcome. I haven't been to my father's grave in a long time. I used to go before I left for South Carolina, but once I started a new life there, I couldn't make myself return.

I stare out the window, trying to keep the tears away. I don't want to have a breakdown in the car, or in front of Caden. It seems all I do lately is cry, or feel the darkness creeping in around my heart. I have a feeling Caden understands my pain. I turn to him with tears in my eyes as he squeezes my hand. He looks at me with his deep blue eyes, and I can tell he knows. The Harlow brothers and I were so close. They all shared my pain, and just having Caden here, means more to me than he knows. I couldn't do this on my own. He slowly lets my hand go, and I face the window again. I try to focus on the cars around us, and the buildings we pass as we make it further out of the city, but it's all a blur. I blink rapidly, failing at holding back the tears. I don't wipe them away as they fall, choosing to let out all the pain out. Caden stops and parks the car, turning to me to ask, "Do you want me to go with you?"

I shake my head, staring at my hands in my lap. "Thank you, but this is something I need to do alone." He doesn't respond, and after a moment, I open the car door. I know if I need him, he'll be right here for me. I take a deep breath as I exit the car, and make my way towards my father's grave. It's strange how nothing has seemed to have changed since the last time I was here. It's a typical cemetery, although a depressing place to visit, the grounds keeper has kept the place nice and clean. I slowly walk down the familiar path that leads to his grave, and as I get closer, my chest starts to tighten. I almost want to run, to get away from the never-ending sadness I start to feel. But, this is something I have to do. This is something I *need* to do. I remember coming here and sitting by my Dad's grave just to talk to him. Now it seems silly, but as a child and even as a teenager, it was comforting to have somewhere to go and talk about what was going on in my life, or just to get things off my chest.

Especially when Mom was her normal hateful self. This was the place I always would run to when I needed to escape. Even from Carter, sometimes.

Once I reach my destination, I sit on my legs in front of his headstone. I touch the words etched on the stone, wishing I had more time with him. I sigh deeply, feeling the sadness overwhelm me, and I don't stop the tears from falling. It hurts to remember all the times Dad was sober. All the times I could rely on him, and would be the father every little girl needed. But as I got older, I noticed his drinking more and more. I noticed how he wasn't my 'Dad' as much, choosing the bottle over spending time with me, or even helping me with my homework. I don't know if he knew I saw the pain from my Mom's actions. I knew my father loved her, and I'll never understand why she didn't love him the same. I have more bad memories than good, but I'll always cherish the good times, and the times he was actually with me. Not passed out on the couch, or slumped over the toilet. It does seem bitter sweet how much he was himself before Mom left for a year. He was the perfect Dad then. He seemed happy and so carefree.

"I'm sorry we didn't have more time together. I know now that you did what you thought was the only option left. I know you battled your addiction every single day, but I can't regret anything. Even some of the bad. I'm not angry anymore for you leaving me behind. I've forgiven you for what you did to that family. It's taken me a long time to accept that you couldn't help it, and I hope wherever you are, you're finally at peace." Somehow, I feel lighter and even though the pain is there, I know it'll be more bearable than before. Maybe it's knowing I can come here at anytime again that makes me feel this way. Maybe it's knowing even though Dad isn't here anymore, at least I have a place to come to talk to him when I feel so lost in this big world. I touch his stone one last time as I get up, and make my way back to Caden's car. With each step, my chest loosens and my tears dry up. I wipe my face with the palms of my hands, and I smooth my two toned hair back from my face.

I reach the car and see Caden leaning against the front waiting for me. He doesn't say anything as he sees me. He walks to the passenger side, opens the door for me, and soon we're heading back to

Carter

Annie and William's home. Caden rolls the windows down, and I lean my head back against the seat, letting the wind blow on my face. I close my eyes, holding my hand out the window, feeling free once again.

And I realize, coming home was the best thing for me.

# CHAPTER 4

## Carter

I walk into the Waffle House and my mouth instantly waters. I nod and wave to all the Sunday regulars, as I make my way to our booth in the back of the restaurant. I slide in, not even bothering to look at the menu. I always get the same thing, and the only time Caden, Cason, and I have to tell the waitress our orders is if someone new has just been hired, or if they order something different. I enjoy coming here every Sunday with my younger brothers after our daily workouts. It's become another tradition, just like us going to Mom and Dad's every morning during the weekdays. Plus it's nice to come to a place that has friendly service, and I can always count on seeing more than one person I know. Tables and booths fill the small area, and there seems to be more people here than last Sunday. The stools by the counter are all full, and the cooks behind the counter rush to fill orders. I'm surprised our booth is open, but I have a feeling our regular waitress had something to do with that. I see her wave at me, and I return the gesture.

# Carter

I look out the bay windows, seeing the heavy traffic. Rubbing my hand on my jaw, I realize I forgot to shave. I've had a lot on my mind, and Dad has been asking almost every day about my decision on taking over the firm. I know he's ready to retire, and a part of me wants to say yes, more out of obligation than anything. I don't know if it would be a good idea for me to say no because that would mean Dad would sell the firm. I sigh, hating how I can't seem to make up my mind, and I feel as though I've taken a step backward with it. I drop my hand from my chin and look to the door when I see Caden and Cason walk in. They spot me instantly, and I laugh when they race to the booth. Cason hates to sit on the inside, and I know Caden always tries to beat him to it, just to piss him off. I shake my head as they reach the booth. They are arguing and pushing each other. I can't be anywhere without them bickering like children.

"Will you two stop," I scold, trying to diffuse the situation before it escalates. It's happened more than once. One would think since they're twins they wouldn't fight so much, but they do. They might be identical, but they are two different people completely. Caden mumbles as he slides into the booth, and Cason has a satisfied smirk on his face. "Can you two please chill out for at least an hour?"

Caden rolls his eyes as Cason says, "It's not my fault Ms. Prissy over here," he elbows Caden on the arm. "Gets upset every time he doesn't get his way."

Brie Paisley

"Cason, I swear. If you don't shut the fuck up, I'm going to beat your ass at the gym tomorrow."

I shake my head, knowing I've heard this conversation a million times. "You wish you could beat my ass. Not my fault you can't handle my moves." Caden clenches his jaw, and I can't help but laugh at them both.

My laugh turns into a groan when my phone chimes. Caden smiles as Cason shakes his head. It's sad really that we all know who it is. "That poor girl just can't take a hint, can she?" Caden asks.

I pull out my phone as I say, "It's my fault more than anything. I should've made it clear when I lost that stupid bet that nothing was going to happen." I don't open the message, deciding to deal with Summer later. It's been six months since Bethany's stupid bet, and I tried to like Summer, I really did. I just couldn't connect with her, and now she's like a leech. She refuses to accept that I have zero feelings for her and that just blows my mind. I've never given her any reason to think there was going to be anything between us.

"You know, if she doesn't chill out with the million texts a day, you might have to get a restraining order," Caden says, and I'm actually considering it. At first, she wasn't bad, but lately it's becoming hard to ignore the constant texts, or the random visits at my office. Dad has also noticed, and he's warned me more than once I need to put a stop to it.

"I'll try to talk to her first before I do that. Surely this time she'll take a hint."

"I don't know about that. Haven't you already told her over and over you're not into her?" Cason chimes in.

"I think it's funny." I stare at Caden, wondering what the hell he means. This shit isn't funny. It's downright creepy and border-line psychotic behavior.

"Of course you'd think my creepy stalker is hilarious." Cason chuckles and I huff as I lean back in my seat.

"Who knows, maybe this Summer chick already has a secret fan club dedicated to you, Carter."

"Alright Caden, you've had your fun." Cason and Caden laugh loudly, and I can't stop the grin from forming. In a way, I guess it is funny. It seems I always attract the strange ones, but a stalker is a first for me. I've dated a few women here and there, but nothing has been serious. It's more for me to not feel alone, than me wanting to settle down.

We quiet down once our waitress, Kelly, comes to take our orders. I don't have to tell her mine since I always get the same thing, but she nods her head and writes down Caden and Cason's order. She's quick with bringing back our drinks, and I inwardly cringe when my phone goes off five times in a row. Caden smiles as Cason looks as though he wants to punch someone. This time I do open the messages, and I'm not surprised when I see they're all from Summer.

*Why won't you answer me?*

*Okay you're pissing me off.*
*Stop ignoring me.*
*Carter please we need to talk.*
*I guess you're busy.*

I take a deep breath before replying. I can feel the irritation rising, and it's becoming really hard not to be a dick to her when she does things like this.

*I'm having brunch with bros. We'll talk later.*

I don't even set my phone all the way down before she messages me right back. Caden bursts out laughing, making the other customers stare, and Cason cracks his knuckles looking bored or angry. I'm not sure which one it is since Cason is hard to read.

*Where are you?*

I know better than to tell her where I am and instead of saying anything back, I turn off my phone and lay it on the table. "She doesn't know when to quit, does she?" Cason asks.

"Apparently not. I'll talk with her later. I can't keep letting her blow up my phone and repeatedly show up at the office."

"And how do you plan on breaking her love connection?" Caden pipes in.

I roll my eyes, wishing I could smack that shit eating grin off his face. "I'll think of something."

"Sure you will."

"You can stop at any time with being a dick bag," I snap. He holds up his hands in surrender, and I try to reign in my temper with him. He just has a way of getting to me the most out of all my brothers.

Carter

Thankfully Kelly brings our food before Caden and I have words. She places our plates in front of us, and Cason and I politely thank her.

"Thanks, Sugar," Caden says to her, and Cason and I both shake our heads. Kelly beams and blushes as she walks away.

"Can you not fuck our new waitress? Jesus man, we just got used to her." Cason does have a point. Caden will fuck anything with legs and a vagina.

"It's not my fault you didn't tap that last one before I did."

"Really? I have standards, unlike you."

I take a deep breath, hating to be the oldest and the one that has to calm everyone down. "Okay, we get it. Caden is a man-whore, but can we not discuss this while I eat? I really would like not to vomit all over the place." Cason grins and Caden says something under his breath that I don't catch, but at least they cool it and begin eating.

Halfway through the meal, Caden has to go and ruin it. "So, what are you going to do about Dad retiring? You know it's time to man up, and just take over the firm already."

I glare at him, lower my silverware, and wipe my mouth. He continues to eat, as though what he just said wasn't that big of a deal. Cason avoids eye contact with me, staring down at his plate. "Look, I get you don't understand why I'm having second thoughts, but for once can you please stay the fuck out of it?"

"Why are you getting your panties in a wad? I'm just asking, hell everyone wants to know what you're going to do. And it's not like Dad's making you do anything. I just know if you don't take it, and Dad sells, you'll regret it eventually." Caden sighs then shovels a fork full of eggs into his mouth. He at least swallows before saying, "I know you don't think you want the responsibility of running the firm, but I also know you're the man for the job."

"Your confidence in me is shockingly surprising." And it is. I had no idea Caden felt this way about me taking over the firm, and in a way his words give me the boost I need to make the choice. I still don't have my mind made up completely, but knowing my brother has my back means more than I'll ever tell him. He'd never let me live that down.

"Well the way I see it, if I need a lawyer I know I can come to you, and how am I going to do that if some douche takes over?"

I laugh and Cason says, "Yeah you'll need a lawyer if you keep banging everything that has tits." And this of course leads to them bickering again, but I can't quit laughing at them to try and stop it. Even when the entire restaurant stares at us, I can't seem to stop.

My laughter finally dies down when I hear a loud crash. It's loud enough that Caden and Cason stop their bitching, and we turn towards the sound. I watch as an average size woman wearing the Waffle House uniform bends down, and from what I can guess, she dropped something. Her back is to me, but something is telling me to watch her. It's like that time months ago when I saw the slender woman walking down Main Street. There's just no way I could forget feeling that way. I won't lie, it's freaking me out a bit because there's no reason for me to be feeling this. But I can't deny something deep down is telling me I need to pay attention. The woman seems to be cleaning in a hurry, and I'm sure she's embarrassed more than anything. I suddenly want to see her face as she stands, and that's when I realize she's not so average after all. She has an hour-glass figure, and the black pants she's wearing make her ass look delectable. Her dark brown hair is pulled back into a low pony-tail, and I wonder what it would feel like wrapped around my hand as I fuck her from behind.

Whoa, what the fuck?

I shake my head, and that's when I notice Caden and Cason sharing one of those twin moments. They stare at one another, and I wonder if they can read each other's thoughts. It's strange to me when they do this. "What's up with you two?" Both look at me, but Caden looks away first. "Seriously, y'all are freaking me out with that twin bond shit. What gives?"

Caden still doesn't look at me, which is unusual for him but Cason says, "I'm going to the restroom, then we can head out." I frown, wondering why he wants to rush out of here. He gets up from the booth and before he turns to leave he says, "Plus you have a stalker to take care of, right?"

"Yeah, thanks for reminding me," I snap back. Cason smirks, heading towards the bathrooms. I watch him for a moment, then I turn my gaze to Caden. "You going to tell me what that was all about?"

He leans back, propping an arm on the top of the booth as he smiles at me. "Wouldn't you like to know?"

"Whatever man. I'm going to head out then. Cason's right. I have to take care of this Summer problem." I toss my napkin in my plate, and drink the last of my sweet tea. I slide out of the booth, leaving a hefty tip for Kelly. "I'll catch you later."

"Say hi to Summer for me," he says, and it takes all the strength I have not to smack him on the back of his head. I leave our table, and I can still hear him laughing all the way to the register to pay.

After paying, I quickly walk out, and stop once I get to my truck. "Are you fucking kidding me!" I glance back at the bay window we sat by, and I watch Caden with his signature shit eating grin, holding two thumbs up. Those fucking assholes. I flip him off and turn to look at the words written on the back of my truck window. 'Wash me, dick face' it says. I'm not sure how I missed them, or I should say, Caden, writing on my window. Shaking my head, I unlock my truck and think sometimes I hate having such annoying brothers.

Carter

I pull up at my house and after parking, I turn my phone back on. A few minutes pass before the texts start pouring in. All twenty-seven messages are from none other than Summer. I have to admit, she sure is persistent, also annoying as fuck. I don't even go through them all. I send her a quick message telling her to come over so we can talk about her stalker behavior, and I send her my address. I hit send before thinking it might not be such a good idea telling her where I live, but I'm confident I can get through to her about leaving me alone. She of course responds, but I don't message her back.

I grab my gym bag before locking everything up, and make my way inside. Stepping through the door, I sigh in relief as the cool air hits me. Being that it's June in Mississippi, it's hot as hell outside. I'm grateful for the cool air, and I drop my bag down by the door and my keys in the bowl on the table next to it. My home isn't very big, it's perfect for just me. As soon as you enter, you're in the living room, and you can see the modern kitchen as well. It's open and I like that I didn't have to do much to it when I bought it. Mom and Bethany helped me fill it with furniture and they also painted the walls with neutral colors. It makes it feel like home to me. There's three bedrooms and two bathrooms, but only one room and bathroom get used. Caden and Bethany have stayed a few times in the guest rooms, but it's the back porch that gets the most attention. Most Saturday nights everyone comes over and we grill out, sitting by the fire pit if it's not too warm out. It's perfect for entertaining and most days when I'm off work, I sit outside with a cold beer and just think about … life in general.

I shake my head and make way to the fridge when my phone pings again. I don't bother checking since I know it's Summer. I set my phone down on the counter as I open the door and pull out a bottle of water. I take a big gulp, slowly setting it down when I hear the doorbell go off. I rub the back of my neck as I walk to the door thinking Summer must have sped the whole way here. She got here a lot faster than I thought she would. I still don't know what I'm going to say to her without sounding like a heartless dick, but I also know I have to be stern so she gets the picture.

Needless to say, I'm not looking forward to this conversation.

I wait a moment before I open the door, getting my head in the game. Slowly opening it, I'm surprised to see Summer in the shortest shorts known to man. I blink when I notice she's wearing a low-cut shirt that leaves nothing to the imagination. I make a mental note to make sure not to let her use her body against me, but I am a man and I can't help but gaze at her long tanned legs longer than I meant to. "Hi Carter," she says in a sultry voice, and I snap my head up to her eyes.

She blushes and smiles at me. Dammit, she knows exactly what she's doing. I have to be careful around her. "Come on in." I open the door further for her as I let her inside. I shut the door as she walks around the living room, taking in my home. I cross my arms watching her as she stops to look at the pictures I have of my family and me. There's a few of Bethany and me, and she tenses up when she notices those. "Want anything to drink?"

She turns around and says, "No, thank you. You have a nice house."

"Thanks. It suits me." This is harder than I thought it would be. Summer isn't someone I can just freely talk to, and I'm at a loss of how to go about this. I still don't understand how one date with her six months ago led to her acting like a damn stalker. Sure we've talked and texted, but other than that, nothing ever came out of that one date. I walk over by the sectional that takes up most of the living room as I ask, "Do you want to sit down?" She nods and takes a seat beside me.

I start to tell her why I asked her over, but she beats me to it. "Look, Carter, I know why you asked me to come over."

"You do?" I say, shocked she even guessed it.

"Yeah, but," she sighs and looks away for a moment before glancing back. "I'm not that type of girl."

I frown, utterly confused to what she means. "I'm going to need you to explain what you mean by that."

She shakes her head. "I'm not just some girl you can ignore, and then call or text me when you need a booty call. It's all or nothing. And here lately, I just don't understand you. One minute everything is perfect, then like today you ignored me all day. Until now that is because you need something."

I back away a bit, frowning and hold up my hands. "What the hell are you talking about?" Is she seriously acting like we're a couple?

"Don't play dumb with me, Carter. You'll get what you want then you'll be done with me."

Okay, I've obviously missed something. I had no clue she thought this way and I'm still reeling over this. "Summer, I honestly have no idea how you can say I want anything from you." She opens her mouth to say something, but I shake my head at her. "No, don't speak, I need you to listen very carefully. I only asked you out because of a bet I lost. I know it sounds horrible, but I'm being honest right now. I took you on one date, just one. Yes, we've talked, and I thought we were friends, but that's all you are to me." I rub the back of my neck again, feeling the tension rising by the second. "I really don't know why you thought I was more than just a friend. I've never even made a move on you."

I watch her as she quickly gets off the couch, and she stands over me. "So, you're saying you feel nothing when you're with me?"

"Sorry, but no. I know that sounds harsh, but I need you to chill out with coming to my workplace and texting me all hours of the day." My head is staring to hurt. Apparently Summer isn't as smart as I thought either. I've told her more than once I didn't have feelings for her. I'm guessing she's in denial.

She shakes her head as if she's trying to shake away what I'm telling her. "I know what this is. You're playing hard to get. I've seen this before."

"Summer, I'm not playing any games with you. I'm telling you as nicely as I can, that I have zero feelings for you." When she looks at me with a puzzled look, I suck in a breath. I'm going to have to get through to her somehow. "Okay, Summer. I've tried to be nice, but I don't have any feelings for you at all. None, zilch, nada, and never going to happen." Jesus fucking Christ how many times am I going to have to tell her the same thing before she gets it. I can tell she's still not getting it. She stares at me with pleading eyes, almost begging me to tell her otherwise. I get up, realizing she just needs to leave. The best thing I can do is change my cell number and hope she eventually takes a hint. I open the front door and tell her, "I need you to leave."

"Are you seriously kicking me out?"

"Yes, I think it would be best if you leave and please don't text me anymore."

She huffs, but she does walk out the door. Before I shut her out, she snaps, "You will regret this. And when you're all alone, just remember you turned me down and shut me out." I stare at her as she turns on a heel and stomps away. Did that really just happen? I shut the door, still in shock at how that went. I knew she might not take my rejection well, but I think Summer needs to see a shrink or something.

I head back to the kitchen to grab my phone to call Bethany. If it wasn't for her stupid bet, I would've never met Summer. I dial Bethany's number, and it rings three times before she picks up. "What's up, buttercup?" Of course, she's cheerful and has not a care in the world. She didn't just experience the most mind-blowing conversation ever.

"Beth, we need to talk."

"Ooh, you sound lawyer-ish. Spill it, what happened?"

"Summer was just here."

It's quiet for a few moments, then I hear her sighing into the phone. "Okay, you want me to pull it out of you. Why was she there?"

"I asked her over so I could tell her to chill out with her stalker ways, as you already know."

"Alright, I'm sorry, okay? How was I supposed to know she'd be a creepy stalker? I didn't. But you agreed to that bet too. If I remember correctly, you seemed happy about meeting someone new."

"That's not the point, Beth. I wasn't looking, and I'm tired of you constantly pushing women on me. They've all ended either in me being a dick because I don't want anything serious, or they're just plain crazy." I rub my forehead with my knuckles then add, "I know you're trying to help but please, no more bets dealing with women, or playing matchmaker."

"Fine. No more bets, but it's time to move on, Carter. She's not coming back, and I hate seeing you alone all the time."

My heart clenches and my voice is softer as I say, "I know, Beth. I know."

"Carter," she starts, but I cut her off.

"It's fine. I'm not always alone. I have your annoying ass plus, Caden and Cason."

"You know that's not what I mean. But I get it. I know what it's like to want something you can't have."

"You do?" This is news to me, but then again, Bethany hardly talks about the men she's with.

"Yeah, I do, but we're not talking about me. Look, I'm headed to Theo's for a few hours, then I'll come over, and we can talk more. Make sure to have alcohol, I have a feeling we're going to need it."

I laugh, knowing she's right. "It's a done deal. See you later." I hang up and set my phone back down. I tap my fingers on the counter top, thinking about what Summer and Bethany said. They each have a point about me being alone. It makes me wonder if I'll ever meet someone I want to try and have something serious with. Yeah, it sucks being alone with no one to share my life with, but at the same time, a part of me doesn't want to be with someone. It sounds crazy and stupid, but I've tried to date. It never seems to work out.

It's as if I'm cheating on the memories of Shelby and I created together. I just can't seem to make myself forget anything about her. It's a blessing and a curse, one that I don't know if I'll ever be able to get rid of, or if I even want to.

# CHAPTER 5

## Shelby

I wake up shaking, drenched in sweat. I toss the soaked covers off my body, and get out of bed trying to clear the nightmare out of my mind. I glance at the alarm clock on the small bed side table, seeing that it says 5:30am. I run my hand through my newly dyed dark brown hair and walk quietly to the hallway bathroom. I know Annie and William will be up in a few hours for church, but I don't want them to know I'm still having nightmares. When I first got here, they plagued me every single night. It got so bad I would wake up screaming most nights. But lately, I've only been getting them a few times a week.

Opening the bathroom door, I'm grateful it doesn't creak, as I walk to the sink. I turn on the cold water then splash my face, trying to get my racing heart to calm down. "It's just a dream. It's not real," saying to myself in the mirror. Drying my face off, I repeat the mantra a few more times before it sinks in. I'm still not sure why I'm still having dreams that are so vivid I can't tell if they're real or not. And it's always the same one. It never changes, and I don't know why that is. I gaze at myself, wondering if I'll ever fully get over what I went through with Easton, and even though I've gained the much needed weight back, the light in my eyes has yet to return. Most days I'm okay but I still feel lost, and I have no idea how to fix that part of me. It's as if something is just … missing. I turn away from the mirror, trying to put a stop to my overactive thoughts, and make my way downstairs. I decide since I'm up, I'll start making breakfast, and hopefully it'll help wash away the nightmare. Of the hopeless feelings that try to take over, and of the past memories that blend in with my time with Easton.

I tiptoe, trying to avoid the spots on the stairs that make the most noise, and I'm glad for the street light outside. It makes it easier to walk to the kitchen in the dark. Once I get there, I turn on the light. I squint for a moment, letting my eyes adjust, and walk towards the sink. After washing and drying my hands, I start to get everything ready to make breakfast. I don't do this very often. Mostly because Annie refuses to let me help, but at least she's letting me watch her cook. I know Annie loves to cook for everyone, so I don't protest too much about it. It's the mornings like this when I'm able to do something nice for her and William. I quickly grab everything I need to start cooking and make a mental list of things I need to do today while I whisk up the eggs.

Sunday is the day I make sure, while Annie and William are gone to church, to clean the entire house. If either one of them are here, they make sure I can't get anything done. I've been doing a good job of getting the task finished while they're gone for a few hours. It's my way of giving back to them for letting me stay here, and helping me get back on my feet. I've also been secretly paying some of the bills with the new job I got about three months ago at the Waffle House in town. I was a little disappointed when I couldn't find an open job for my degree, but I'm happy I at least have some sort of income now. It makes me feel less guilty knowing I'm helping Annie and William, and I also have some extra money left over to put into my new savings account. While working at the Waffle House isn't my dream job, the manager's nice enough to let me have Sundays off, and she's been giving me all the shifts I can get. I repeat my mental list of things to do as I turn the bacon down on low heat.

I pour the eggs into the other pan, and when I turn around to get the toast ready, I jump and hold in a scream when I see Annie sitting at the table. "You scared me," I say with a huff.

"I smelled bacon, and I knew you were up. Thought I'd keep you company."

I nod and take in a deep breath, telling myself to calm down. I hate that I'm still so jittery at every little thing. "Want some coffee?"

"I can make it." While Annie busies herself with that task, I grab the bread off the top of the microwave and slather some pieces with butter. I pop them in the toaster oven as Annie asks, "Did you have another nightmare?"

I close my eyes, hating she knows. I try to hide it, but somehow she always seems to know. The breakfast was probably a dead giveaway, since I'm never up this early unless I have a nightmare. "Yes." I turn around, leaning against the counter, and I watch her as she pulls two coffee mugs from the cabinet above the coffee pot.

"Do you want to tell me about it?"

*Not really.* "It's always the same one." I hope she doesn't push me into talking about it. I have a hard enough time forgetting after I have one.

"It might help if you tell me. I don't want to push you or pry but," she sighs as she pours us coffee, then looks to me. "You're keeping everything bottled inside. I know you don't want to remember, and I can't imagine what it was like with that … man." Annie shakes her head, and she takes a deep breath. For a moment I thought she was going to cuss, or say something nasty. I've never heard a bad word come out her mouth. "I just want you to know you can tell me anything. I think you know by now I'm never going to judge you, and maybe if you talk about those nightmares, I can help you figure out why you keep having them."

I glance down at my feet, not wanting to meet her gaze. She's right, and I know she is. It's just hard for me to open up, it's always been that way. Growing up, I kept a lot of my feelings hidden, and maybe it is time I change that about myself. But it's hard to break old habits. I turn around to stir the eggs, and hear the ping of the toaster. I open the toaster door, turn it off, and leave the toast inside as I try to explain to her about my reoccurring nightmare. "It's always the same. I don't understand why, but it never changes. I'm always back in South Carolina, with Easton. At first he's happy, and I feel happy again. We're outside his home, and it's bright and sunny out." I swallow hard, concentrating on getting the eggs done. This is the part I hate talking about. "Things … things drastically change in the dream. I don't know why or what I did, but his face turns dark and his eyes grow cold. The sun suddenly disappears, and I flinch when the thunder starts. I feel so afraid of him. I feel hopeless, like I don't matter, as he starts with his hateful words." I take the eggs and bacon off the stove, turning off the heat as I do, but I can't turn around yet. I place the food on the counter and shut my eyes, willing the tears away. I don't want to cry over Easton and the shit he put me through. I want to be stronger than that, and I don't want to give him all the power anymore. "He calls me worthless. He tells me how I'll never get anywhere without him and with each word, I shrink back. Then suddenly without any warning, he's right in my face. He's yelling those damning words and then …" Slowly opening my eyes as I turn around, I push myself off the counter and grab the coffee Annie poured for me. Annie watches me the entire time, and when I sit down she grabs my hand. She squeezes it hard, encouraging me to go on. I look down at my coffee mug as I say, "That's when he backhands me and knocks me down. I fall on the cold hard ground as the thunder roars above us, then the rain starts pouring down. Easton stands over me, still yelling as I hold my hand to my stinging cheek. I ask him repeatedly to stop, but he doesn't. But that isn't the worst part."

I get the courage to look at Annie, and my heart clenches when I see tears in her eyes. It kills me knowing she's having to hear this, and there's not a thing she could've done to stop it. To stop any of the bullshit I had to face on a daily basis. "Carter is there." I watch her frown, confusion written all over her face. "I know. It's something I can't wrap my head around. He's there standing off to the side. Easton never sees him, but I do. He's twenty years old in my dream, and it's crazy that he looks exactly like he did when I last saw him. Annie …" My voice breaks for a moment, and I run a hand through my hair. I gaze at her, and I know she can see and feel my pain. "I call for him. Every single time. I yell and plead for him. Annie, I call for him until my throat is raw and hoarse. I reach for him, begging him to help me, to save me. Easton begins to beat me, he kicks me in my ribs over and over, but my eyes never leave Carter's. My tears mix with the rain, but the vilest part of it …" A tear slides down my face, and I quickly wipe it away. I clear my throat, trying to get a handle on my emotions. Once I feel in better control of myself, I finish telling her my dream. "Carter turns his back on me. I'm being beaten and I fear it'll never stop, but he just walks away. And every time he does, I scream the most agonizing scream I can.

Because it kills me. It's the part when I wake up, I feel as though I've lost my heart and a part of my soul. I don't understand it. I haven't seen Carter in thirteen years. Why would I have nightmares about him now? Why would he be in my nightmares with Easton?"

"It could be a number of reasons," she starts. I wipe the tear that rolls down my cheek as she continues. "But I think it's because of how you and Carter left things." I glance down at my cooling coffee, really taking in what she's saying. It's possible and since I told her the entire story of why I left a few weeks ago, she would be the best one to make sense of it all. An outsider opinion is always best when trying to figure everything out. "What you and Carter had, it was special. Love like that doesn't just go away, and knowing neither one of you had that closure. It's no wonder why you're dreaming about him. And thank you for talking to me about what's going on in that head of yours." I glance up seeing her smile, and I'm glad I told her. I do feel better about it, and I certainly have a different aspect on my reoccurring nightmare.

"Thank you for listening. I know it's not easy to listen to all the horrible things I went through, but I'm glad I have you to talk to again." We sit and talk about normal things for a while, and I think it's Annie's way of taking my mind off my nightmare and the feelings I'm experiencing. I have to admit, I have no clue how I went so long without Annie. She's the mother I've always wanted, and she does everything

Carter

in her power to help me and everyone around her. I hate knowing it's my own fault for not keeping in touch for all those years, and I know there's nothing I can do to get them back. I can only enjoy the time I have with her and William now.

Annie talks on and on about her new knitting club, and she gets up to refill her coffee mug. I love how she's so animated when she talks, and I can tell she's proud of her newfound hobby. She laughs as she tells me about some of her mishaps, and I can't control my laughter when she talks about another lady who is just as bad. "You should've seen her face, it was priceless. I swear I thought she'd made a sock." I place a hand under my chin as she says, "Poor woman. We all thought it was the smallest sock, but turns out, she was making a glove of some sort." She laughs some more, seeming to think more of the memory.

"Sounds like I need to stop by just to watch y'all," I say, trying to control my laughter.

"Oh, you'll definitely get a kick out of it." I watch as she turns to make her plate of almost forgotten food when she says, "I forgot to ask you. Did you ever finish that paperwork about your new social security card?"

"Yeah. I talked to a very nice woman a few days ago, and she was more than happy to help me get everything in order to change my name back." I'd made the decision a few weeks ago to change my last name back to my maiden name. I couldn't have my name being Carrington any longer, and I feel it's going to help me more in the long run to put the past behind me.

"That's great news. I think it's just what you needed." I nod, completely agreeing with her. Annie places a plate down in front of me and sits down.

"Where's yours?" I ask. It still amazes me how Annie always puts everyone first. It's humbling and comforting that I know someone isn't thinking about themselves like I'm used to.

"I'll eat once William decides to wake up. Go on, eat your breakfast."

I smile and say, "Yes, ma'am." We sit in a comfortable silence while I eat, but I know as soon as William comes into the kitchen. It's not the fact he made any noise, it's the look in Annie's eyes as she sees him. It makes my heart swell knowing how much she cares and loves him. I slowly push my plate away as William walks over to Annie and sweetly kisses her on the forehead.

"Good morning. Smells good down here," he says and begins to make his own plate. Annie gets up and does the same as I place my empty plate and coffee mug in the sink. I lean against the counter as they take a seat at the table, and listen to them talk about nothing in particular. I can't help but feel like an outsider looking in when they are so wrapped up in each other. It's not a bad feeling. It's more of a longing, an unfilled part of me that wishes I had that. I remember having that once. Thankfully, my phone starts ringing, pulling my thoughts away from those unwelcome emotions.

## Carter

I frown as I make my way to the living room where I left my phone charging the night before. Caden thought it would be a good idea for me to have one, and I'm still undecided if it was a good idea. I went a long time without one and now, I'm more annoyed when work calls, or when Caden texts me. Since it's still early in the morning, I already know it's work that's calling. And my suspicions are confirmed when I answer.

After a few moments on the phone, I hang up and turn to Annie and William. "That was Stephanie. She needs me to work a few hours today. Do y'all mind if I use the truck today?"

I know what William is going to say before he does. "Of course you can. I've told you to use it anytime you need to."

"Thank you. I should be back around two or three."

"Do you need anything from town? We're going to stop by the store before we come home," Annie asks. I tell her no and head upstairs to get ready for a busy shift. I already know if Stephanie's calling me in, it's going to be chaotic. Sunday mornings are usually the busiest, but I'm glad for the extra money. I'm also glad I know it's going to be busy. Those hours are the best thing for me since it quietens my thoughts, and helps me get a reprieve if only for a small about of time.

Busy isn't the word I'd use to describe how my shift is going. More along the lines of a damn mad-house. It's insanely busy, overcrowded, and I've been hiding in the back washing dishes for over two hours. Since being back home, I've managed to not run into anyone I knew. It's mostly because I've become a hermit, choosing to stay at Annie and William's versus taking the risk of meeting anyone I'd rather not see. But I know my hiding in the back is coming to an end as I see Stephanie looking around the restaurant. I know all the available waitresses are already filling orders left and right, and I feel bad that I'm taking the coward's way out. On the other hand, I'd much rather stay in the back with the comfort of washing dishes. "Shit," I say when Stephanie and I lock eyes. She all but runs to me, and I step away from my never ending pile of dishes and dry my hands off.

"Shelby, I need you out front." She must see the scared look on my face as she quickly adds, "Just serve coffee. We're drowning in customers." I nod, not wanting to go out of my comfort bubble. She swiftly goes back out to the thick crowd, and I tighten my ponytail then put my apron on. It's not that I have a problem taking orders, I would just rather not be around all these people. It makes me remember the times when Easton would make me go with him to all those boring charity events just to show off. It was his thing to let everyone know how successful he was, and how much of a Stepford wife I'd become.

I don't want to be reminded of that shit.

But no matter what I feel, I need this job, and I'll do whatever I need to so I can keep it. At least until something better comes along. I suck in a long and much needed breath, and make my way behind the counter. It's like a maze with so many workers, but I manage to get to the coffee makers unscathed. Once prepared, I put on a fake smile and start making rounds to the occupied tables and booths. I nod and politely speak only when necessary trying to hurry, and make everyone happy with getting their morning caffeine buzz.

Hours later, my feet and legs are killing me. No matter how many times I poured coffee or got something for the customer, it was never ending. Most days when I work, I'm in the back not really dealing with the needy customers, and I already wish I could go back in my hole. I did sneak away for a few moments for a bathroom break, but now it's time for me to get back to it. I look up at the clock, and sigh loudly when I notice it's barely after twelve. I quickly glance around the corner, seeing more people making their way inside. It's as if everyone decided they had to come eat here of all days. People are beginning to crowd at the front counter, getting a seat wherever they can. I can feel my heart beginning to race, and the urge to run. I don't do very well with crowds anymore, and I clench my jaw reminding myself I have to have my job. I can't very well run out the door and still expect to get paid. I push the uneasy feeling down as I walk behind the counter again to make more coffee. I bump into a few workers, and almost fall flat on my face trying to avoid being burned by the cook swinging around a hot plate. It's like an obstacle course just to get a mere five feet to my destination.

Finally, I get to the coffee pots. I stand in front of it as it brews, not paying attention to the throng of people around me. I stare directly in front of me, trying to drown out the noise. I start to zone out, when someone bumps into me. I turn and the waitress Kelly, quickly apologizes. I smile knowing it couldn't be avoided. There's just too many of us in one spot. Once the coffee is done, I grab two pots and carefully maneuver my way from behind the counter. I have to lift both pots above my head as someone ducks under me, and I swear to myself I'll never work another Sunday again. I shake my head and bring the hot coffee pots slowly down as I get into a safer zone. I turn my head to the direction of someone yelling for their much needed coffee fix, and that's when I see him.

Holy.

Fucking.

Shit.

My body freezes instantly, and my heart literally skips a beat. I feel my stomach fall, and I stop breathing. It happens so suddenly that I wouldn't have believed it if it not had happened to me. I never thought I would have this reaction to seeing the one person that held so much of me once upon a time. I stare, unable to make my body move and when I see him throw his head back in laughter, it sends chills down my entire body. I don't see the crowd anymore, they seem to slowly disappear as I watch Carter Harlow laugh with his brothers. Caden is half turned so I can see his face, and I know it's Cason with them. I don't even know how it's possible for Carter to look even more attractive now than he did the last time I saw him.

He's definitely not a boy anymore, he's all man.

His dark brown hair has a messy look going on, as if he just crawled out of bed and went about his day. He no longer has those boyish charms, but now he has an edge to him. I can't see his eyes, but I know they'll still have a hint of gold in them that I used to love to get lost in. I'm sure now, he has wrinkles around his eyes from years of laughing. I wonder if his lips are still as delectable as they once were on mine. On my body. He's definitely bulked up too. His shirt tightly hugs him in all the right places, and I know I need to stop staring. In the back of my mind, a little voice is telling me to get back to work and to stop gawking at him, but I can't seem to care about that stupid voice. I'm getting my fill, and I really could care less about anything else. Carter doesn't even know I'm here, and his presence is pulling me into a trance.

But suddenly the trance and the pull I'm feeling again, is gone. A customer walks right into me, making me drop the coffee pots. I snap out of my daze and quickly bend down. Now that my back is turned, my head clears. What the fuck am I doing? I silently thank the rude customer for knocking me out of my daze. One of the workers behind the counter hands me a towel, and I try to clean up the mess as quickly as possible. Stephanie comes to help me clean up the glass, and I make sure to keep my back to Carter. I can't let him see me. I know I'm being a coward, but now that I'm thinking clearly, I'm not ready to face him.

Once the mess is cleaned up, I make my way to the back. I don't care if I'm needed out front anymore. I'm confident everyone else can handle the madness. I dump the coffee soiled towels in the bucket under the sink and walk to the break room in the very back. It's not a very big area. It's just enough room to hold a table, a few chairs, and lockers on the side of the wall. At least there's a counter for a microwave, and a fridge off to the side of it. I pull out one of the metal chairs and sit down. I place my elbows on my thighs, leaning my head down on my hands. My feet are aching, and my heart will not stop thumping in my ears. I run both hands over my hair, trying to get a hold of myself. I knew this would eventually happen. I couldn't stop from seeing Carter again, no matter how much I stayed inside Annie and William's home. I just never expected to be affected so much just from seeing him again. It worries me and at the same time, it excites me. My emotions are all over the place, and I'm confused at how my body is reacting. Surely I still don't have feelings for him?

I don't want to believe I do, but deep down I know I still do. What Carter and I had, it was a one of a kind type of love. The kind that will leave you breathless if you ever get to witness it. The kind that will make you crave it knowing you can't have it. I've heard you never forget your first love, and now I can see why. I reach in my shirt and pull out my necklace. I look down at it, and grasp onto it tightly. I take a deep breath, trying to make my mind stop picturing Carter and how much he's changed. I can't deny the urge to get to know him as he is now, but I also know it's not a good idea.

Carter ripped my heart to pieces once, and I know I won't be able to survive it a second time. Some things are just better left alone, and I believe this is the way it has to be.

I place my necklace back in my shirt and snap my head up as I hear someone clearing their throat. My eyes lock with Cason's, and I can't help the grin crossing my face. I automatically can tell it's Cason from the scar on his right eyebrow that he got when we were kids. "You sure are a sight for sore eyes," he says, and I get up as he holds his arms. I walk in his embrace, but I don't hug him long. He's tense as hell and when I step back, I can see his jaw tensing. Well, that's strange.

"How did you know I was back here? Did Caden tell you I was back?" I fire off my questions quickly, wondering if Carter knows I'm here. I can't shake the nervous fluttering feeling in my stomach just thinking about it.

"He doesn't know." I frown at how he knows what I'm worried about, but I shrug it off. I'm sure if

Carter knew, he'd be the one back here instead of Cason. "I watched you leave, and I followed you back here. I doubt anyone will notice since they're so preoccupied with the crowd. And Caden didn't have to tell me, twin bond remember?" I don't even have to question the twin bond him and Caden share. Even as kids they shared it, and none of us understood it. Plus, Caden knew I worked here. He was the first person I told after I was hired.

"Yeah, I don't think anyone even noticed I left." I rub my forehead with the back of my hand and turn to sit back down. Cason follows me, and pulls out a chair beside me. It seems Carter and Caden aren't the only one that's changed a lot over the years. Cason still has the same features as Caden with the deep blue eyes and dark hair. Only Cason's is shorter than Caden's, and Cason has a hard and dangerous vibe about him. I can't put my finger on why, but I'm guessing it has something to do with what Caden told me about him when I first got back. Cason also has put on muscle and from what I can tell, he's got some ink done since I can see it barely showing from beneath his shirt sleeve. I can feel Cason's eyes on me, and it's starting to make me squirm in my seat. His gaze is a mixture of curiosity, and do I dare say, a bit of anger? "What?" I ask, wondering why he's staring at me so intently.

He rubs his chin, and turns his head toward the door, then back to me. He seems to consider what he wants to say, and I almost tell him to spit it out already when he says, "How long have you been back?"

Okay, not the question I was thinking he'd ask. "About six months."

I watch as his eyes take in my scar on my upper lip, and I look away. I silently beg him not to ask about it. "How long are you staying?"

I sigh in relief and turn back to him as I reply with, "I'm honestly not sure." When he clenches his jaw again, I add, "I just … I needed to come back and start over. Things are slowly getting better for me, and right now there's no reason for me to leave."

"I assume you're staying with Annie and William?"

"Yeah. They've been wonderful and welcomed me back with open arms."

He nods, knowing firsthand how amazing they are. "I've got to say, I didn't think you'd ever come back. And I can tell you've been through some shit. I won't ask, but I do want you to know Carter is going to fucking flip when he figures out your back, and you didn't go see him."

I cringe at his words, but everything he's saying is true. I'm such a coward, but who could blame me? "Look, I don't expect you to understand why I want to stay away from him. It's just not the right time."

"Yeah, I get it, I really do. There's a lot you've missed, not just with Carter. But, let me ask you this. If not now, when, Shelby? When is it going to be a good time for you? Carter is my brother, and I still think of you as my sister, but you weren't here, and you didn't have to see what I did. Or see the shit we all went through."

"I know I've missed a lot. I didn't want the world to suddenly stop when I left, but what choice did I have? And I don't know when I'll be ready. I just … I don't know how to face him, Cason." I'm trying not to get angry with him. I don't want to think he's trying to make me feel guilty of how things were left, but what does he know? I honestly don't know if he knows the whole story. I have no idea what Carter told him, or his family when I decided to leave. Not to mention, I feel as though he's not only pissed because I left Carter, but he seems angry I left him too. We once were all close. We used to share everything, and I just left them without saying goodbye. Okay, I do feel guilty about that.

"I don't want to push you into anything, but dammit, Shel. You need to see him. Even if it's just for closure for the both of you, but you need to at least talk to him. And I will not lie about seeing you either."

I figured as much since Caden said the same thing to me the day I got back. "I'll think about it, okay?" I hope he lets it go because this is all I can give him. The queasy feeling is back in the pit of my stomach, and I really don't want to talk about this anymore.

"Yeah, you think about it. And while you're at it, think about coming to see Mama. I know she'll be happy to see you again." He taps his knuckles on the table before standing. I watch him walk away, but before he leaves he turns back and says, "I may not know exactly what happened between you and Carter, but it's not fair to punish the rest of us for what happened. We used to be family, Shel. And family doesn't turn their back on each other."

I sit back in my chair shocked and even more confused than I was before. Is that what I'm doing? Am I punishing everyone that's cared about me because of Carter breaking my heart? I honestly don't think I am, but at the same time, it would be awkward and hard seeing them knowing Carter and I aren't together. I can't help, but feel the regret for running away all those years ago. And once again, I'm back to feeling lost and heavyhearted by the decisions I've made in my life.

# CHAPTER 6

## Carter

A couple of weeks has passed since seeing the mysterious woman at the Waffle House. It's strange all I can think of is her, of who she is, and if I'll see her again. A nagging thought has plagued me since that day, but damn if I know why. Shaking off the feeling, I pull up at Mom and Dad's house just like every other weekday. Parking my truck, I quickly make my way inside my childhood home. Just like any other time once inside I feel instantly at home and at times, I wonder why I ever left. I smile hearing Caden laughing and see everyone's crowded around the kitchen island in the middle. Mom busies herself with finishing up breakfast as Cason sits on the stool with a cup of coffee in front of him. Dad stands by Caden, and everyone looks up when I walk in.

"Well look what the cat drug in," Caden says and I roll my eyes at him. I'm tempted to flip him the bird, but Mom turns around. I walk over to hug her, then place a kiss her on her forehead. "It's about time you got here. Why are you always late?"

"What's with the third degree, Caden?"

He shrugs and says, "I don't know. I like busting your balls."

"Caden Michael Harlow, you know better than to talk like that in my house," Mom scolds him and Cason and I snicker.

"Sorry, Mama." It never ceases to amaze me. No matter how old we are, if Mom gets on to us, we still feel as though we're kids again. Mom goes back to finishing up our breakfast, and I make myself some coffee. Standing by Cason, I listen to Dad and Caden talk about his job and his upcoming work schedule. I sip on my coffee as he tells us about some of the people he's pulled over, and some of his stories are hilarious.

"I wish I'd videotaped it. It was fuc – freaking hilarious how the guy I pulled over reacted." I don't miss his almost slip up in front of Mom again. "Anyway, he just had a busted taillight. The way his eyes almost popped out of his head, I thought he was trying to hide drugs or something."

"How old was he," I ask.

"Seventeen. I think he might have pissed himself too."

"Caden, don't make me get my spoon out," Mom scolds him again. Cason, Dad, and I slowly back away. We all fear that damn wooden spoon. Mom has beat our asses more than once with it.

"What did I say now?"

"I don't like that language in my house."

"I can't say pissed? That's not a cuss word." I chuckle listening to Caden trying to get out of trouble. Some things never change.

"Caden, I'd shut up now if I were you," Dad warns. Caden throws up his hands in defeat, muttering to himself as he walks to the kitchen table.

"That boy will never learn," Dad says to no one in particular. He's partially right. Caden has grown up a lot over the years, but he still has that stubborn attitude he's always had.

Cason and I follow behind Dad when Mom tells us to go sit down at the table. We take our usual places as we wait for Mom to finish with whatever she's doing. None of us try to help her. After years of her telling us no, we know what to do now. "Has anyone heard from Clark lately?" I ask them. I haven't heard from him in a few weeks, and it worries me with him being on deployment again.

"I got an email from him about a week ago, but nothing since," Cason says.

"He called your mother and me last week. Should be getting another call soon," Dad responds and I nod.

"Well, I'm jealous. That dick hasn't spoken to me in a month." As soon as the words leave his mouth, Mom comes up behind him and whacks him with her whoopin' spoon. "Ow, Mama! What was that for?"

"Boy, I've told you about that mouth of yours."

Caden rubs his shoulder where she hit him as he says, "That hurt. I'm going to burn that stupid spoon one day." Cason and I do nothing but laugh.

Dad just shakes his head, knowing Caden is just going to keep digging that hole deeper and deeper.

"If you would just shut your mouth, you wouldn't get smacked," Cason says to Caden.

"You stay out of this, little brother." I lean my head back, and groan, knowing what's about to happen.

"Seriously? That again, huh. You were born three minutes before me."

"Here we go," Dad says. Mom and I say nothing as they bicker back and forth. Mom sets the food down on the table, and I tune out Cason and Caden's arguing. They do this so much it's just another normal day at the Harlow's for us. They were horrible as kids, but surprisingly they're still close. I have a feeling that's why they always argue. They're pretty much attached at the hip, and they even live together.

I load my plate down with Mom's fantastic cooking and finally, Caden and Cason shut up long enough to do the same. I start chowing down on Mom's cooking, and the table goes quiet while everyone else does the same. The silence doesn't last long, and I'm not surprised. It never does when you have Caden and Cason in the same room. "Are you going to train that chick at the gym, Cason?"

"Probably not. And no, I'm not banging her." Cason looks up to Mom and adds, "Sorry, Mama."

"You boys and your mouths are going to be the death of me. I know I raised you better than that." Mom shakes her head, and Dad places his hand on hers. They smile at each other and I look away, feeling as though I'm intruding on their moment.

"You should bang her. She's smokin' hot." And Caden ruins it.

"Dude, can you stop it already?" I tell him.

"Okay, Dad."

"You're such an a – pain." Caden smirks at my almost slip up in front of Mom. I think that's his plan.

Cason leans over and says, "I think we should take him outside, and teach him a lesson." I nod, actually considering it.

"Hey! Don't take his side. You're my twin, it's unnatural for you not to have my back."

"Where do you come up with this stuff, Caden?" It blows my mind at the shit that comes out of his mouth. His eyes narrow, then he gives Cason a knowing look. I glance at them both, wondering what that's about.

"Hey, Mama? Didn't you say you needed to drop off some sewing stuff to Mrs. Barrett?" Caden asks. Cason shakes his head, but has a cheeky grin.

"I did, but I can't go over there today." She and Dad both stare at me and I look around, thinking something's up.

"Carter, would you be a dear and take it by there for me?"

"Uh sure, Mama." Why is everyone staring at me?

"Yeah, I think that would be a great idea," Cason says and Caden grins, agreeing with him. Okay, now I really feel like I'm missing something here.

"Alright, what's going on?"

"Not a thing," Caden says a little too quickly for my liking.

"Whatever," I say as I look at my watch. "If I'm going, I need to head out now so I'm not late opening today."

I start to slide my chair back, but Dad speaks before I get up. "I'll open today. You take your time and visit with Annie and William. It's been a while since you've been over there."

I frown, having the feeling of uneasiness in the pit of my stomach. Dad hasn't opened the firm in, well shit, I can't remember it's been so long. "Why do I get the feeling y'all are setting me up for something?"

"Oh, honey. Just do as I asked." I concede, knowing I can't say no to my Mom.

I drive to Annie and William's house slower than I normally would. They don't live far from my parents, but it has been a long time since I've visited them. I always smile and talk to them when I see them in town, but as far as going to their home, it's been months. Possibly longer. I hate trying to avoid it, but shit it's a reminder of what I've lost. That was Shelby's home, no matter if she had a mother and a home of her own. So many of our memories were made at the Barrett's. But I can't say no to Mama, and even if I really don't want to do this, I will anyway since she asked me to.

Far from Home by Five Finger Death Punch plays softly on the radio as I pull up, and it suddenly takes me to the past. As I park, I stare at the front porch, remembering so vividly of the first time I kissed Shelby.

*I opened Shelby's door for her, and held out my hand. She smiled at me sweetly, as she placed hers in mine. I couldn't deny the tingling sensation that ran through me. It's amazing how much she made me feel and while with her, I felt so alive. I felt as though I was the luckiest sixteen year old ever. I realized, I never wanted this feeling to stop. My heart pounded in my chest as she slowly got out of my old Ford Ranger, and I lead her to the porch of Annie and William's home. She insisted I bring her back here after our time at the movies, and I didn't question it. I knew how much the Barrett's meant to her, and I'll gladly take her anywhere she wanted to go.*

*As we reached the top of the steps, I had to remind myself to breathe. My heart pounded in my chest thinking of what I wanted to do, and I could only hope Shelby felt the same way. Our relationship had grown more the older we got, and I knew she was afraid to ruin the close friendship between us. But I wanted her. I needed her, and I knew it a long time ago. Getting Shelby to realize this too, well that was an entirely different thing. I was putting everything on the line tonight. I knew I'd been pushing her more with each day to show her how amazing we were together, not just as friends. I'd been waiting for months it seemed, for this moment, and all the small touches, hand holding, and sweet words spoken over the years had paid off in my opinion. She didn't flinch or move away from my advances anymore. I could only hope making another bold move would make her finally realize I loved her.*

*I've always loved her.*

*I didn't know exactly when I knew it for sure, but I think it might have been the very first day I saw her on the swings on the playground. I knew she was special, and someone I wanted to be around. Slowly pulling her hand in mine, I bring it to my lips placing a kiss on her knuckles. I grinned when she blushed and looked away. I wanted her looking at me. I couldn't seem to get enough of looking into her deep blue eyes. They were stunning, even with just the porch light shining around her, I could see the sparkles of green in them. I could get lost in her eyes, and she didn't even know how much I wanted to. How much I could for the rest of my life if she'd only let me. I knew with me being sixteen and her fifteen, a lot of people would say we didn't know what love was, but they were wrong. I knew I loved her because without her, I felt as if a part of me was missing. Without her I didn't think of anything else, but being around her. Love is the only expression that can say to show how much I feel about her.*

*Pulling her closer to me, I used my other hand to brush her hair behind her ear. I watched her lips part as she stared into my eyes. I knew she felt exactly how I did. I could feel her racing heart on her wrist as I used my thumb to trace over her vein. Her chest rose with each breath, and I knew she was struggling to keep it hidden. Her pink tongue dipped out to wet her lips, and I knew she was ready. After months of thinking of nothing but her sweet succulent lips on mine, this moment seemed surreal. I ran my hand down her arm, loving the warm feel of her bare skin on mine. She closed her eyes, and I watched as chills rose up behind my touch. I stopped once I got to the top of her waist, and pulled her to my chest. Her hands rested on me as she steadied herself, but we never lost our gaze. She was just as entranced as I was.*

*"Carter," she said breathlessly.*

*I cupped her cheek in my hand, and leaned in closer to her lips. "Let me kiss you, Shel," I whispered. It was more of a plea than anything.*

*She closed her eyes, then said, "Yes." It was all I needed. I wasted no time in taking her mouth and brought her closer to me. Her lips tasted and felt exactly as I'd imagined. She tasted of mint from her gum, and her soft lips greedily took mine. Our sweet and gentle kiss was everything I thought it would be. It was perfect, it was memorizing, and I realized I wanted to kiss her for the rest of my life. I wanted to deepen the kiss, but instead I pulled away. I didn't want to rush her too soon, and I'd rather take my time, than her run away from me. She had a habit of running when she couldn't handle strong emotions, or when things got out of control.*

*She slowly opened her eyes, and she smiled up at me. I pecked her lips again, mostly because I couldn't resist. "I'll call you when I get home."*

*"Okay. Until then," she whispered back to me, and I watched her as she walked inside. When she shut the door, I turned to leave and walked away from the porch with the biggest smile on my face. Shelby had no idea how much that kiss meant to me, but I intended to show her starting tomorrow.*

I rub my eyes as the memory fades, and I have to adjust myself before stepping out of my truck. I shake my head, trying to get Shelby's fifteen year old lips out of my head. But the thing is, I can't. Now that I revisited the memory, her lips are all I can think and how many times she would kiss me. How every single time she'd take my breath away. The older we got, our kissing became more urgent and erotic. We couldn't seem to keep our hands to ourselves. "You've got to stop. Not going to look good with a boner when Annie answers the door," I tell my dick. He's not cooperating, and the last thing I need is to give poor old Annie a damn heart attack.

I end up tucking my stubborn cock up in my slacks, and reach over the seat to grab the bag of sewing stuff for Annie. I still have no idea why my whole family insisted I do this. It seems strange, but then again maybe this is their way of making me visit with the Barrett's. Before I shut the door, I take my blazer off, tossing it inside my truck. I'm not sure why I chose to wear it today knowing it's well over ninety degrees, but in my defense, I like to look the part at the firm. I set the bag of sewing supplies down, and quickly roll up my shirt sleeves. Shutting the truck door, I grab the bag and begin to walk towards the house. Walking up the steps, I wipe the sweat forming on my forehead. Today is humid, and my shirt begins to stick to my chest. Once I reach the door, I take a deep breath then knock. When it opens, I was expecting to see a smiling Annie.

I wasn't expecting to see her.

I wasn't expecting to feel as though someone hit me with a hammer in my chest.

I blink, thinking my brain is playing tricks on me. There's no way Shelby Ross is standing right in front of me. There's no way she's back. But as I rationalize it, it's real. She's real, she's here, and I can tell she's just as shocked as I am. Her eyes widen as she stumbles back for a moment. As though she was knocked back by a force like I was. I watch as her hand clutches her chest, and I drop the bag as I take her in. Her hair is longer than I've ever seen. It's touching her waist, and my hand twitches remembering how I used to run my fingers through it. Her blue eyes look me over, and I ache to pull her to me so I can see the hint of green in them. She looks the same but older, more mature, and she's filled out just like I knew she would. She's got the perfect hourglass figure and I have to shake my head, thinking how soft and luscious those curves would feel against me. My eyes graze down her beautiful face, and I frown when I notice a scar on her upper lip. I know she didn't have one the last time I saw her, and I instantly want to know what happened and how she got it. Now that I'm looking at her lips, they take me over the edge. I'm not sure if it's because I just remembered how they felt on mine or if it's just because of her, but I have to force myself to stay where I am.

She's not mine anymore. The thought is unwelcome, but it's the truth. I lost the right to claim her a long time ago.

Before I can ask her what she's doing here, I see Annie walk behind her. "Carter! What a wonderful surprise. Come on in." I clench my jaw, but I don't take my eyes off Shelby as I reach down and pick up the bag. I have a million questions for her, but they'll have to wait. I slowly walk inside as Shelby holds the door open for me. Passing by her, I notice how tense she seems. She carefully maneuvers around me, ever cautious not to touch me. It stings, but then again I don't think too much of it. I've thought about this moment numerous of times over the years, and not once did I think she'd ever come running into my arms. She hardly did that when we were together, and I shouldn't expect it now.

I finally pull my gaze from Shelby, and follow Annie into the living room. She sits on the old worn out couch, and pats the spot next to her. I walk around the coffee table, taking the seat by her. I set the bag on the table as I say, "Mama wanted me to drop this off." As the words leave my mouth I knew I'd been set up. Did they all know she was back? They must have, and I don't dwell on the unsettling feeling of being kept in the dark. I'll deal with my brothers later at the gym, but I'm not sure what to say to my parents.

"Thank you for dropping it off. And good timing too. I need this for the class tonight." Annie starts rummaging through the bag, and my eyes find Shelby's. She's still standing by the door, staring at her feet and I wonder what she's thinking. Her tense form lets me know she has her guard up. She crosses her arms, and her fingers turn white while holding onto herself so tightly. Wishing she would look at me, I wonder if she's glad to see me, or would she be happier if I just left? I can't tell, and it bothers me that I don't know what she wants anymore. I used to know everything about her and everything she wanted. But I fucked up. I know now that I did more damage than I thought. She seems guarded more than ever when she glances at me, clenches her jaw then looks away. The ache in my chest grows knowing I'm the reason she can't even bear to look at me. "Carter, you'll have to thank your mother for me. She really is a life saver."

"Yes ma'am she is, and I'll be sure to tell her when I see her later." I don't turn away from Shelby as I speak, and I will be talking to my Mom about this.

Reluctantly, I take my gaze off Shelby as Annie starts to stand and I frown, wondering what she's doing. "Okay, I'm going to take this over to the community center, and I'll be back in a few hours." She picks up the bag, hoisting over her shoulder as she winks at me.

"You're leaving? Right now?" Shelby asks. I can't help but grin knowing she doesn't want Annie to leave us alone.

"You'll be fine. It's time you two talked and caught up on things." Annie pats me on the shoulder as she walks by me, then over to Shelby. I watch Annie whisper something to Shelby, and her eyes dart to mine. She nods and Annie gives me one final glance before walking out the door.

It's an awkward silence now Annie's gone, and I honestly have no clue where to begin. I have so much to say, so much to ask, but now that it's just us I don't know where to start. I watch as she runs a hand through her dark brown hair, then she walks right by me into the kitchen. My eyes follow her movements, and I take in the rest of her. Before I was too caught up to notice her wearing shorts, and now that I can fully see her tanned bare legs, my dick starts to stir again. I chastise myself, willing my cock to behave. I hear the fridge open, and when I hear her voice, I get off the couch. "Do you want something to drink?"

I slowly make my way behind her, and it takes every bit of self-control not to touch her. I want to. I need to, but I don't. The urge is strong, so strong, I catch myself lifting my arm anyway. "No, I'm good." I watch her back straighten, and I realize I snuck up on her. She grabs a bottled water out of the fridge, closes it, and then moves to the counter by the stove. She turns around, and I notice she's holding onto the bottled water so tight it, makes a noise, and her hand turns white.

I start to move towards her out of instinct, but she holds up her hand as she says, "Don't, Carter. Just … just stay right there."

I clench my jaw and look away. Damn her and those walls, but I can't blame her. I sigh deeply as I pull out a chair at the table, and sit down. I rest my arms on my knees as I lean forward, glancing back at her. I still can't believe I'm looking at Shelby. My Shelby, even if she doesn't know it. She's always been mine, and my heart pounds in my chest as I silently reclaim her. "You look good, great actually," I confess.

"Thank you and you look … good, too."

I smirk, wondering if she meant to say that instead of something else. "How long have you been home?"

She starts to chew on her nail, and I have a feeling I'm not going to like her answer. "A little over six months."

I nod, trying not to show her how much that fucking hurts. But honestly, what did I expect? This is Shelby fucking Ross. The one who never stayed around when shit got rough, or when she couldn't handle when things got to be too much for her, and of course she wouldn't come rushing to see me. I have to look away, and bite the side of my cheek to reign in my overwhelming need to voice my problem with that. A thought comes to me from a few weeks ago when Caden, Cason, and I were at the Waffle House. I don't look at her when I ask, "That was you at the Waffle House, wasn't it?"

I close my eyes when she replies with, "Yes."

I knew something was up with Cason when he called me later that day. I could hear the anger in his voice, but I didn't ask him what was going on. Cason never likes to talk about feelings or anything like that, so I didn't think twice about it. But I should've known. Then I remember the time when I saw the slender woman walking down Main Street. The timing is right, and I know it was her. I feel stupid for not realizing it sooner. No woman has called to me like Shelby. No woman has made my heart, and soul ache to just see her again. Now that I have, it hurts more than anything knowing I hurt her so much she wouldn't even think of me. I know I fucked up all those years ago, and broke her heart, but fuck. Isn't years of knowing someone not enough? Is it not enough of how much we went through, and everything we shared? Shelby was my best friend since I was six years old. It's as if she forgot all those years we had. That's what kills me the most.

Do I mean nothing to her?

I open my eyes and abruptly stand. I glance at Shelby, and she's still chewing on that nail. I take her in one more time, then turn to leave. It's too painful to be around her knowing she's been right here for over six months. Knowing she's been right down the fucking road from me. She's here, but still not within my arms reach. My chest tightens and I have to swallow hard when a lump forms in my throat. I feel sick to my stomach, and I have to get the fuck out of here. I can't stand this … empty, lost feeling. I also have a nagging thought my brothers knew for a while, but I can't be angry with them. They saw firsthand how much I suffered after knowing Shelby ran to South Carolina. I don't know why they wanted me to see her now. If anything this just makes me want to go home, say fuck the world, and drink myself stupid for days.

I get to the front door and as I open it, I stop when I hear her call my name. "Carter, please don't be angry. I'm sorry. I … I just couldn't see you."

I don't look back, because if I do, I don't know if I'll be able to leave. I have to walk out the door. I have to get away and drink away this pain … something. "Yeah, I get it." I really don't get it, but I'm sure she'd rather I leave anyways. Since she saw me, it's as if she wished I never came over. I quickly walk out the door worried she might apologize again, but I just can't listen to it.

For the first time since I've known her, I walked away first.

# CHAPTER 7

## Shelby

I sit on my bed holding my phone in one hand, and my scrapbook is laying in front of me. Touching the front of the book, I close my eyes and take a deep breath. Since the run-in with Carter today, I've had a lot on my mind and mostly a lot of regrets. Seeing him today, and noticing how much hurt he had in his eyes, it almost broke me again. I never wanted to hurt him, but I wasn't ready to see him. I wasn't ready to face that sad look in his brown eyes, and I certainly wasn't ready to experience the overwhelming need to be in his arms again. I did try to be normal and carefree around him. I don't think I pulled it off, but I just couldn't act like nothing happened between us. I needed him to leave just so I wouldn't leap into those huge comforting arms. I need to take care of me first. I've come a long way from getting past the hurtful things Easton would say to me, but I still have a lot of healing to do. I'm still broken. I really don't know if I can put the pieces back together, and there's another part of me that's still angry at Carter for pushing me away all those years ago. If he hadn't, I wouldn't have left. I wouldn't have met Easton. I wouldn't have all these fucking regrets running rampant in my mind.

I snap my eyes open when my phone pings with a text message. Leaning against my headboard, I open the text and read it.

*I take it you're pissed at me.*

I roll my eyes at Caden's text. Of course, I'm mad at him. That ass knew Carter was coming over this morning. When he boldly asked how it went with Carter and me today, I instantly knew he had something to do with it. I wait a few moments, letting him sit and suffer before I send a text back.

*It was a low blow. A warning of some kind would've been nice.*

I set my phone down beside me, and grab my scrapbook. I place it in my lap, opening it to the first page. I smile seeing the picture of all of us sitting on Annie's porch for Halloween. Cason and Caden are dressed as cowboys, and they look adorable in their hats. I remember they both begged Linda, their mom, for days about buying them new cowboy boots. They of course got them. Clark is sitting in front of them wearing his Superman outfit. He was the hero out of us, and I swear he wore that costume for months after Halloween. But he didn't care. He wore that costume proudly, running around the neighborhood trying to do what heroes do. Caleb wasn't in this one since he was only a year old, but I remember Linda dressing him up in a pumpkin outfit. I can recall how we all thought he looked hilarious wearing it, and we got scolded more than once for making fun of him. My phone pings again, but I don't look away from the photo. For the first time, I'm seeing this photo as if I have brand new eyes. I never noticed it before, but as I lean in looking more closely, I see Carter staring at me. He was a pirate that year and I was sitting right by him. It didn't matter where we were, he and I were always together. Smiling, I remember how happy I was that year. I was Cinderella, and I never felt more like a princess. Annie and Linda made my costume by hand, and I helped pick out the crown. I was ten, so Carter was eleven. I frown as I start to flip through my book. In every picture I have of us, even if it's of everyone, Carter is always looking at me. He does it until we're older, maybe when I was fifteen.

I shut the book quickly and toss it in front of me. I don't know what to make of this revelation. I know it means something, but I push the thought away before it forms. I distract myself by picking up my phone and read Caden's message.

*I am sorry, Shel. But if we hadn't intervened, you would've never seen him.*

I sigh knowing he's right. If I could, I would've put it off longer than I had. I quickly fire back a response to him.

*I'm not mad. Next time promise me you'll give me some sort of warning.*

I chew on my nail again as I wait for him to reply back. When he doesn't immediately message me I set my phone down, and get up off the bed. Walking over to my dresser, I pull out some comfy pajamas. After grabbing everything I need and setting my necklace down on the bedside table, I go to the hallway bathroom and quickly take a shower. It's been a long, emotional draining day, and I can't wait to crawl in bed. I can only hope my nightmares won't return. After the shower, I poke my head in Annie and William's room to tell them goodnight. Annie smiles up at me from her book, and we giggle quietly when William snores loudly. I pull their door shut, and go back to my room. I shut off my light and turn on my lamp beside my bed. I push back the comforter and lie down, but before getting comfortable, I reach over and grab my necklace. I put it back on, and let out a huff when I hear my phone going off again. Leaning up to grab it, I quickly type in my password, and seeing the text makes my mouth goes dry.

*Here's your warning. I'm outside.*

I don't take the time to reply. I press his number, and it rings only once before he answers. "What the hell, Caden? Why are you outside?"

"I'm sorry, Shelby. You need to come with me, and we need to hurry."

Okay, now I'm starting to think the worst. "What's going on, Caden?" I throw the covers off me, and quickly pull off my pajama bottoms, putting on some shorts. I hear Caden talking to someone, but I can't make out their voice. "Caden? Please tell me what's wrong?"

"Are you coming outside?"

"I'll be down in a few." I hang up, knowing he's not going to tell me anything. I have no clue what's going on, and I shake out my hands to get them to stop the jitters. I slide on my sports bra and toss on a simple white T-shirt before letting Annie know what's going on. I slowly open the door to their room again, quickly relaying what I know. She doesn't ask too many questions, and I tell her I'll be back as soon as I can.

I have to force myself not to run down the stairs. I don't want to make a lot of noise since I know William is fast asleep. I snatch my purse off the floor by the couch, and forcefully open the door. I watch Caden for a second as he paces on the porch. He sees me, and I can tell he's worried. His eyebrows are drawn close together, and he looks pale. "Please tell me no one's hurt," I say as I walk out the door, closing it behind me.

"Ah, well. Here's the thing," he looks over his shoulder, and I follow his eyes. I see Cason leaning against what I assume is his truck, but I can tell by his body language, he's not happy. His arms and legs are crossed and the way he's looking at me, makes me take a step back. "Don't mind him. He's pissed, but we need your help."

I swallow, shocked for the first time since knowing Cason, I'm afraid of him. I shake off the feeling as I pull my gaze back to Caden and ask, "What do you need me to do?" I don't even ask what exactly he wants. I just sense they need me, and I'll help them however I can.

"Come on. I'll explain on the way." I nod, and follow Caden to Cason's truck. Cason says nothing to me, doesn't even look my way, as we climb in the truck.

Soon after, Cason skillfully and swiftly drives down the road. I sit in the back staring out the window, still wondering what the hell is going on. Caden and Cason don't say a word as we travel down the road, and I begin to see the familiar houses from my childhood. When we pass by Linda and Mitchell's home, I have a feeling I know where our destination will be. "Caden? I think it's about time you tell me what the fuck is going on."

He turns around, and I can barely make out his face in the dark truck. But from his voice, I can tell he's sincere when he says, "I'm sorry. I really am, but we had no choice. We didn't know what else to do." He straightens in his seat as he says, "It hasn't been this bad in a long time." I don't respond because I'm not sure if I was meant to hear that or not.

I try not to get frustrated at Caden for keeping me in the dark, but I have a good idea why he did. Whatever is going on, it has to do with Carter. It's the most logical reason why both brothers came to get me, and why they wanted to leave so suddenly. I know how the twins are. They're protective of family. No matter what. I use to be one they protected, but now I feel as though I did something wrong. I can't help but feel guilty, but I'm not sure what I should be feeling guilty about. I have a sense I'm about to find out.

Shortly after, Cason pulls up at a very modern home, and I can see another truck parked out front. There's also an old Volkswagen Beetle parked beside it. Cason parks, quickly gets out, then Caden does the same. I sit still in the back, unsure of what to do. My heart is pounding in my chest, and my stomach is doing flips. I snap my head to the door as it opens and Caden stares at me. "Come on, Shel. I really need you to get out of the truck and come inside." I want to ask why, or demand he tell me what the hell is happening but I don't. I just nod and slowly get out. I follow him towards the house, and Cason comes up behind me. I want to yell at them for boxing me in, but I have a feeling they did it on purpose.

This is their way of making sure I don't run away from whatever's happening. I can't say I blame them, but it does hurt knowing they think that's the first thing I'll do.

Caden opens the door and once inside, I hear him yelling. I don't even get a chance to look around the room. His booming voice stops me in my tracks, and Cason bumps into me. I feel his hands on my shoulders as he keeps me from falling, but I realize whose house I'm in. This is Carter's house. And whatever is going on at the back of the house isn't pretty.

"Fuck off, Beth! I told you I don't need your help. I don't need any of you. Just get the fuck out!" I swallow hard at his loud and hateful tone. I have to shake my head, willing myself to stay in the present and not let the past take over me. Easton would always tell me similar things, and I know Caden and Cason didn't bring me here for me to relive those hurtful years. But just being reminded of my past, my heart drums in my chest, and I start to back away from Carter's voice. Bumping into Cason once again, he holds me in place and I clench my jaw, knowing I can't run away like I wanted.

"Carter, if you don't stop with that I'll smack you sober. I'm not going anywhere until you put the bottle down, and tell me what happened." I wonder who this Beth is, and I also wonder what she's doing here. Caden takes a seat on the brown leather sofa, and I move into the kitchen. I set my purse down on the counter, but I don't dare go to the back where Beth and Carter are talking. I can feel the tension in the room, and I don't think me being here is going to help.

"I fucked up, that's what. I'm so stupid. You know, I thought just for a second, she'd be happy to see me."

"Let me guess. You saw, Shelby." I clench my jaw as I hear my name and at the sound of her hateful tone. Beth doesn't seem to like me even if she's never met me. I once again wonder what her relationship is with Carter.

"You can blame asshole one and two for that." I glance over at Caden. His head is down, and I can tell he feels responsible. Cason is still standing by the door guarding it, with his arms crossed, staring at his twin. "It's all my fault though. I drove her away. I pushed the right buttons knowing what she'd do, but I didn't think she would come back. I just can't, Beth. Please, just go." I can hear the agony in his voice, and it makes my chest hurt.

I don't hear either one of them talking for a moment, and jump when a door slams. I hear footsteps coming from down the hall, and I take a step back, nervous as to who I might see. Will it be Carter or this Beth chick that I know nothing about? My butt hits the kitchen island, and I hold my breath as I wait to see who's coming around the corner. Part of me hopes it's Carter just so I can see him again. It's stupid really. Earlier today I wanted nothing more for him to leave, to give me more time and space, but now I realize I'm just holding onto the anger and resentment I feel. I know it's not entirely Carter's fault for what I went through with Easton, but if he'd never pushed me away, or if he tried to come after me, maybe I wouldn't have gone through any of it.

The mental abuse. The loneliness I felt constantly or the public humiliation Easton put me through.

I push those unwanted thoughts away as the footsteps come closer. I think they belong to the woman Beth, as the steps are light and not heavy like a man's would be. I clutch the island's corner with my hand, feeling it go numb. My erratic heart is making me feel dizzy, but take a deep breath and will myself to focus. I have to stop being so weak and letting my emotions get the best of me. I frown when the mystery woman walks into my view. She's definitely not what I was expecting and not someone I thought Carter would hang around with. Let alone date. I ignore the twinge of jealousy that runs through me. She stops mid-way into the kitchen when she sees me, and for a moment, we both seem to be sizing each other up. She's a short woman, all curves, and I can't help but admire the colorful art work on her left arm. Her hair is blonde, hot pink, and black, and I find she can really pull off the punk rock look. She has a nose, lip, and an eyebrow piercing to complete her rebel personality. Her eyes narrow at me, and I know she's doing exactly what I am. I wonder what she sees in me, and dart my eyes away from her intense gaze.

"So, this is her?" She asks but I'm not sure who she's talking to. I clench my jaw, not liking the tone of her voice. It's as though she already hates me, but she doesn't even know me.

"Be nice, Beth. She's here to talk some sense into Carter," Caden says behind me.

Beth rolls her eyes and points a finger at me as she spits out, "You need to leave. You've done enough, and we definitely don't need you here now."

I suck in a breath, trying not to let her malicious words affect me. "First off," I start, but Beth shakes her head and cuts me off.

"Listen, I don't know who you think you are, but you need to leave. Now. Before I make you."

I flinch back at her harsh and violent words. Caden walks beside me, and I sigh when he starts to stick up for me. "I said be nice, Bethany. Lay off and take a breather." Caden turns to Cason as he says, "Cas, take her outside before she does something stupid."

"What the fuck, Caden? You can't just toss me out, and let her come back like nothing ever happened. This is bullshit, and we all know this is on her anyway." I can't find the words to stick up for myself. She's right and I know it.

"Cas, get her the fuck out of here before I lose my shit." I watch as Cason finally does what Caden asks, and a part of me wonders if Cason wanted me to feel the sting of Bethany's words. I can't help but feel a wave of sadness, and the guilt trying to consume me. I look down at my feet, blinking back the tears that try to fall. Bethany says something, but I don't hear her. I block her out as I shut my eyes, trying to forget why the hell I even agreed to come here. I should've known it would be a mistake to willingly come with Caden. I don't think he meant for Bethany and me to run into each other, but it happened and now it's just something else I need to repair. I can't stand the thought of her thinking such horrible things about me. She has no idea who I am or what I went through.

"Hey, you alright?" Caden asks as he puts a hand on my shoulder.

I clear my throat and nod as I reply, "Yeah. I'm fine."

"You know she didn't mean any of that. She's just pissed because Carter is acting the way he is. Just ignore her."

I glance up and say, "She's right though. None of this would've happened if I had handled seeing him earlier better, or never left to begin with." I lick my lips and shake my head as I add, "She may not like me, but I had a very good reason for leaving when I did and acted the way I did today. None of you understand."

Caden's hand on my shoulder tightens, and my heart aches in my chest when he says, "No matter what happened, we're all still here for you, Shel."

"You really mean that?"

"Yeah, I do. I know shit went down, and things didn't go the way we all hoped, but you're here now so that's all I care about." He takes his hand off my shoulder and says, "Let's go knock some sense into my dumbass brother."

I nod and follow him down the hallway. I notice the pictures hanging on the walls as we pass by them, and I feel a sense of longing when I see how happy everyone seems in them. I hate knowing I missed all this. I hate not knowing what happened to Carter after I left, and it makes everyone so worried about him now. It took me a long time to get over what happened the day Carter broke my heart. Actually, I never really got over it. It was more of pushing down the sorrow and pretending to be normal. That took two years, and it was a horrible two years.

# Carter

I almost run into Caden as he stops in front of a door and he turns to me before opening it. "I need to warn you. He's not going to be himself right now. He might say shit he doesn't mean, but he needs you." He sighs and swallows hard then says, "He's hurting, Shelby. Seeing you today, and then with the huge fight with Mom and Dad later, he didn't know what to do."

I glance at the door, as if it'll hold some sort of answers, but I know this is something I need to do. I have to let go of the past anger, and I need to remember that Carter was once my best friend. Somewhere along the way, I'd forgotten that. "I'll do my best, but I'm not sure if he'll even want me here." Saying it out loud makes my stomach take a dive. It's true, and my fears of seeing Carter angry still makes me want to run. Maybe this is my test to see how much I've overcome, but I still am unsure. Carter was my best friend a long time ago, but he's not the same person he once was. All I can do is try and if things get to be too much, I'll leave. Just knowing I have a way out makes my nerves ease by a small fraction.

"He does. He might not want to admit it, but he needs you. When you left the first time, it was really bad, but it's not my story to tell. I'll be outside if you need me, okay?"

I nod and watch him as he walks away. I push out a breath, trying to prepare myself for what I'm about to see. My hand shakes as I reach for the doorknob, but I will myself to be strong. I have to make sure Carter's okay, and hopefully I can talk some sense into him. I turn the knob and the door slowly opens. I cautiously step in the doorway taking everything in. Carter's room is everything I'd imagined it would be. Dark hardwood floors complete the light gray walls perfectly. There's a long dresser on one side, and a tall armoire sitting by the wall on the other side of the room. There's a few paintings to decorate the room, but the bed is what's holding my attention. It's a king size sleigh bed, and it's a little lighter than the floor. But it's not really the bed I'm taking in. Carter lies on his back with an arm over his face. He's not wearing a shirt, and I bite my lip seeing his perfectly shaped abs. I have to suck in a breath when he breathes deep, and his muscles contract. I run a hand through my hair, making myself look away. His comforter is tossed on the floor, and I also notice a Jack Daniels bottle on his bedside dresser. Seeing the bottle makes me think of my father and his drinking problem and it adds to my unease, but I force myself to slowly trudge into his room. My hands are still shaking, and my stomach drops when he reaches blindly for the half empty bottle of whiskey.

"Son of a bitch," he calls out, not realizing I'm here yet. I watch as he knocks the bottle off, spilling the brown liquid on the floor. He huffs out an aggravated breath and slaps both hands on his bed. His eyes are open, but they're staring up at the ceiling. It's now or never. I quietly shut the door and move further into his room. When I get closer to his bed, his eyes move to me. "Oh fuck. I must be really shit faced. Now I'm hallucinating."

I sigh before saying, "I'm not in your head, Carter."

He frowns, really taking me in and considering my words. "Why are you here then? You made it perfectly clear you didn't want to see me earlier today."

Sighing, I sit at the edge of his bed. I think carefully about what to say, but as I look into his deep brown eyes, I realize he needs the truth. "It's not because I didn't want to see you, Carter." He moves up in the bed and I confess, "I didn't know if you wanted to see me, and honestly I was more afraid than anything. And I'm here because your brothers, and some chick named Bethany are worried about you." I point to the now empty liquor bottle conveying what I mean. "Obviously, they have a reason to be concerned."

"They need to stay out of my business and leave me alone. I didn't ask for their help or yours for that matter."

I shift a leg onto the bed, and I don't miss Carter's gaze as he watches me do so. "I know you didn't ask for my help, but I'm here now. So you can stop with the asshole attitude because I'm not going anywhere."

He chuckles as he snaps back with, "You say that now. But you forget. I know you and sooner or later, you'll run away again like you always do. It's only a matter of time."

His words hit a nerve, but I close my eyes remembering what Caden said to me. I know he's drunk. I know he's upset and hurting. So instead of proving him right, I stay where I am. I kick off my flip flops, and place my other leg up on the bed sitting cross-legged. "A lot has changed in thirteen years, and I'm not going anywhere, Carter." I watch as he crosses his arms, and try not to drool as his biceps bulge. I clear my throat, and I don't miss his smirk as I ask, "What happened today? I know I wasn't the only one to drive you to drink."

"Why should I tell you? Not only have you forgotten what friendship means, you literally gave me the cold shoulder. So please excuse me if I don't want to bare my soul to you."

"Okay, you want to be difficult, fine. But for once, can you please put yourself in my shoes? You have no idea how much your words hurt me back then and yes, I know it's been a long time, but just remembering how you told me I meant nothing to you anymore still fucking hurts." I can't help but get angry at him. He doesn't have a fucking clue what those words did to me. They shattered me. They broke me into a million tiny little pieces. He was my world, my everything, and in one second, he destroyed everything we had and everything we shared. We stare at each other for a moment before he finally looks away. I don't want to place the blame solely on him, but he needs to wake up and see I'm here now. That I'm here for him.

"I am sorry, Shel." He rubs his face with is hands, and he groans out loudly. I pick at my nails, hoping he doesn't see what that sexy groan does to me. I start to feel … antsy. "Shelby?" I glance back up at him, and seeing the hurt and regret in his eyes makes my chest hurt for him. "I never wanted to hurt you. I know I fucked up, and I really can't blame you for not wanting to see me, but you have to realize it almost killed me seeing you today. It hit me all of a sudden that I didn't have my best friend anymore, and it made me realize how much I've missed having you in my life." He clenches his jaw as he adds, "I never knew how lost I really was until today. Seeing you again, it was as if someone tossed a bucket of ice cold water on me. It made me see how many mistakes I've made, and how I can never take any of it back." I watch him with wide eyes as he moves closer to me, and swallow hard as he takes my hand. My heart is beating rapidly, and my face flushes.

I glance down at his hand on mine, and I still can't believe how much his touch affects me. If anything, my body is reacting much stronger than it had before, and I realize how much I've missed this. His warm touch on my skin. The way my body seems to call out to him for more. I've missed him comforting me even when he's the one who needs it. I glance up at him, and he's gazing at our hands together. Maybe he does miss it too, not just our friendship. "Carter?"

He glances at me, gazes into my eyes, and says softly, "If I could take it back I would. If I could go back in time, I would've never let you leave. I would've changed so much, but I can't. All I can do is tell you how sorry I am. I've never regretted anything as much as not having you in my life." I blink quickly, trying to keep my tears from falling. I know he means every word he's saying. I can tell he's sincere, and it pains me knowing I wasn't there for him. "I don't expect things to go back to normal between us." He looks away but quickly looks back. He squeezes my hand as he says, "I'm hoping we can start over, and get to know one another as we are now. I miss my best friend, Shel. I miss us."

Taking in his words, I really think it over. A part of me wants to say yes. I would love nothing more than to have my other half back, but there's also another part of me that's afraid. I don't know if I can be anything but friends. I don't know if I have anything else to give him. "I don't know, Carter. I want us to be friends again, but I don't know if I can give anything else."

He nods, but I can tell my words hurt him. He masks it quickly and says, "Honestly, I'll take what I can get. I'm not asking you to do anything other than what you can. As long as you're here, I'm okay with that." He reluctantly takes his hand off mine, and I almost protest, but it's better this way. Friendship I can do. He moves to get off the bed, and I watch him with curious eyes. "I'm just going to throw on a shirt." When he fully stands, he sways and blinks his eyes.

"Maybe I should get one for you?"

"No. I've got it. That first step was a doozy though." I laugh loudly and he smiles, shaking his head. He rubs the back of his neck and makes his way to his closet. I stare after him, and notice he has a tattoo on his back. I try to take it all in before he disappears into his walk-in closet. From what I could tell, it's a heart with a sword through the top. I bite on my nail as I wonder what the barbed wire wrapped around it means. I also noticed how the heart was bleeding. I can't help but wonder what it symbolizes. I move my hand from my mouth, when Carter reemerges with a gray shirt on. He looks at me, and I see him sigh. Did he think I was going to leave? "Do you want anything to drink?"

"I'm fine." I move to the headboard and nod to the spot beside me. He quickly makes his way beside me, getting comfortable. I turn and ask, "You want to tell me about what happened with your parents?"

"I think I need another drink before I start with that."

"I think you've had enough for one night." I snicker when he gives me a 'what the fuck' look.

"I've missed hearing your laugh. I'm glad you came back, and you came over tonight. Even if I was being an ass to everyone."

My smile fades at the direction of his words. "I am too and you were a complete dick, but I forgive you." I scoot down, turning to my side as I pull his pillow under my head.

He grins as he watches me. "Getting comfortable?"

"I can't help it. Your bed is comfy, and it's just like old times." It does remind me of the times I would come over to his house, and we would lay in bed just like this, talking for hours. I hadn't realized how much I've missed being with him. Even if we're just friends again, I'm enjoying his company and it's not as painful knowing he's sorry for the things he's said or done. I might not be able to completely forgive him, but I know we'll get there. "Are you sobering up? Cause if you're feeling sick I'll go grab you a trash can."

"No I'm good, surprisingly." He gets comfortable and moves to his side to look at me and talk. I push the butterflies in my stomach away as he stares into my eyes. "Tell me about South Carolina."

"What do you want to know?" I don't miss how he knows that's where I went but then again, he knew I'd been accepted to the University of South Carolina, too.

"What was it like there?"

I have to tread carefully talking about this with him. I don't want him to know about my past with Easton. "It was different. Don't get me wrong, it was beautiful there and I loved all my professors, but it wasn't home."

"I know the feeling. I felt the same way being in Massachusetts." I don't ask about his time at Harvard Law. That time is still raw since that's where he was when he pushed me away. Instead, we steer clear of things that might upset us. I tell him about my degree and how much I enjoyed my job. He tells me about the firm and how he's worried about taking over once his Dad retires. Carter does most of the talking, and I soak up everything he tells me like a sponge. He talks about Bethany a lot, and I try not to let it bother me. I'm not sure why the thought of him with her brings out my jealousy, but I push it down trying to not think of it. He does say over and over how they're just friends, and I like knowing he's trying to reassure me. It seems we talk forever, and I find I'm enjoying it. A lot actually. I've missed just talking to him and being near him. I've also missed his gentle and caring nature. I realize the more he talks, the more I forget about my demons and the past I have. It's still there, but with him, he makes it bearable.

We both look to the door when we hear a loud knock. Caden sticks his head in, and when he sees us on the bed, he slings the door open, runs to the bed shouting, "SLUMBER PARTY!" I try to move out of his way, but he lands on one of my legs, and I can't help but laugh as I hold onto it.

"Caden! What the hell?" I'm still laughing as Carter scolds him like a child.

"What? I wanted to join the fun."

"Yeah, but you landed on Shelby." Carter pushes Caden, and when he almost falls off the bed, I have to hold my side from laughing so hard.

Tears fill my eyes at the look on Caden's face as he stands on the bed and declares, "Oh you're going down for that!" He jumps again, landing right on top of Carter. I decide to move before any more damage is done to my body, and stand by the bed as they wrestle like kids. They continue for a while fighting, and I know someone is about to get angry. Caden has Carter in a head lock and his face is turning red, but Carter isn't giving up.

They punch and slap each other, and I chuckle when Carter yells out when Caden bites him on the arm. Apparently Caden doesn't play fair. Cason walks into the room, and he rolls his eyes seeing them roughing each other up. Cason looks to me, nods, then starts to pull them off each other. He grabs Caden, yanking him off the bed. I cover my mouth with my hand, trying to hold in my laughing when Caden almost falls. He catches himself on Cason and by the look on his face, he's not happy about it.

"Dammit, Cas. You almost made me bust my ass."

"Serves you right! You bit me!" Carter yells.

Cason sighs as Caden yells back, "You shouldn't have started something you couldn't finish then." I slowly get back to my spot on the bed as Carter and Caden argue. I don't miss Cason raising his eyebrow at me, but I choose to ignore it. He can think whatever he wants.

"Alright, Caden. We all get it. You won. Say he won Carter, so he'll shut the fuck up."

Carter narrows his eyes at Cason, then inspects the huge bite mark on his arm. "You won, but just wait. Tomorrow your ass is mine."

"Don't make promises you can't keep, old ass."

"Caden, why can't you just take the win and call it a night?" I can tell Cason is getting frustrated with his twin. It's hilarious seeing them all together again, acting just like they used to, but it's bittersweet knowing Clark and Caleb aren't here to join the show.

"Truce?" Carter asks Caden.

"Truce. By the way, you need to call Bethany soon. She was livid, and then she burnt rubber in your driveway leaving." I look down hearing her name again. I can only guess what she thinks of me, and I know it's not filled with compliments. Her words replay in my mind again, and I start to feel the guilt creeping in. Funny how people's words have the power to drag us down when we felt so happy before.

I move to leave thinking it's time for me to go home, but Carter reaches over and grabs my hand. "Where are you going? It's movie time, and I'll deal with Bethany later. She's just butt-hurt."

"You want to watch a movie this late?" I ask.

"I'm down for a movie. What are we watching? I'll make the popcorn," Caden states, and I can't take my eyes off Carter's pleading eyes.

"Alright, but I get to pick the movie," I say and Caden squeals like a girl, then rushes out of the room. I glance at Cason and ask, "Is he alright?"

"I have no idea. I think Mama dropped him on his head more than the rest of us."

I grin, and when Cason leaves the room, I realize Carter has yet to take his hand off mine. He rubs his thumb back and forth on the back of my hand, and all those emotions I felt years ago with him come flying back. It scares me at how intense they are, and how they're stronger than ever. I swallow, and quickly take my hand out of his. I see a flash of hurt in his eyes, but I can't dwell on it. "I'm going to help Caden." I don't wait for his reply. I leave his hypnotizing gaze. I make my way to the kitchen to help Caden, trying so very hard to keep my heart from leaping out of my chest. Damn Carter, and his gentle touch.

# CHAPTER 8

## Carter

I massage the back of my neck, feeling the sudden tension building. Probably not the best move to touch Shelby like I had so soon, but dammit I couldn't help myself. There's just this force pulling me to her. I can't deny seeing her here, knowing she's going to try and give our friendship another shot thrills me unlike anything I've known before. Granted, I would love if it was more than just a friendship, but I know she's not ready for that. I didn't miss the fear in her eyes as I told her I missed her, but I'm determined more than ever to get her back where she needs to be. I feel as though I'm having to start all over with her again, but I'll do whatever's necessary to have her in my arms once more.

I get off the bed, thankful I'm somewhat more sober than before. Shelby helped me a lot with the sobering up and if she hadn't come over, I'd probably still be drinking. Which reminds me, I need to clean up my mess. I quickly race to the bathroom and grab a towel. I place the half empty bottle on the bedside dresser, and bend down to clean up the mess on the floor. It doesn't take long to soak up the alcohol, and once I toss the towel in the hamper, I make my way to find where Shelby went. My heart races thinking she might have left. Walking into the kitchen, I see her and Caden talking as the popcorn pops in the microwave. I sigh in relief seeing her, and when she glances at me then blushes, I can't help but grin back. My stomach takes a dive when she smiles at me, and I make myself walk into the living room. I can't slip up and touch her again. She's very skittish, and I'm afraid she'll bolt at any moment.

One way or another, I'll make her see I'm not letting her go anywhere now that she's back.

I take a seat by Cason on the couch as I wait on Caden and Shelby to finish with the popcorn. Cason lays the remote on the armrest and turns to me. I had a feeling he would have something to say, and I hope he doesn't say something I don't want to hear. "So, you and Shel good now?"

"I guess you could say that." I glance back into the kitchen, making sure Shelby can't hear me as I say, "It's complicated. She's down for us being friends again, but I want more than that." I'll always want more with her.

"I figured as much. Just take it slow. We all see how much of a flight risk she is right now. And you know something happened to her, right?"

I nod, knowing what he's talking about. "Yeah. She's definitely keeping something hidden." I pause, thinking of how she wouldn't really open up about her time in South Carolina. All that time there, but she had nothing to say? I don't buy it. Not to mention the new scar on her lip, and how her blue eyes have lost some of the fire I once loved to gaze at. "But one way or another, I'll get her to talk to me about it. And you're right. I have to be patient." I look right at Cason as I confess, "I can't lose her again."

He clenches his jaw and says, "I know. I'm not the best person to help, but I'll do whatever I can to make sure she doesn't leave." I don't question what he means, but I know he'll do what he says. I nod, but I don't respond.

Caden and Shelby finally make their way into the living room. Caden takes a seat with a bowl of popcorn on the recliner, and Shelby hesitates before sitting down by me with another bowl. She hands me the bowl, and Cason shoves his whole hand into the bowl making some spill over. "Seriously, man?"

He cups his hand, and tosses the popcorn in his mouth as he says, "What?" It comes out more as 'wuf' and I just shake my head.

I turn to Shelby seeing she's smiling again. I stare at her longer than I should, but I've missed seeing her smile. "What movie do you want to watch?"

"I'm not sure. Where's your movies?" I point to my movie collection, and she goes to pick one. I honestly had no intentions of watching a movie tonight, but when I noticed she froze and was getting ready to leave, it was the first thing I could think of to make her stay. Which reminds me I need to thank Caden for being on board with a last minute movie night. I watch her intently knowing she can't see me, as she looks over the section of horror movies. I know she's a horror movie buff, and over the years I've added a lot to my collection. I don't really care for them, but just knowing she loves them made me want to have them. Even when we were apart, I still bought them when a new one would release.

"Don't you dare pick Child's Play," Caden proclaims, and I turn and throw popcorn at him. Shelby turns around with a wicked grin, and I already know which one she chose. "I'm serious, Shel. That damn doll scares the shit out of me."

I watch as she rolls her eyes and says, "Stop being such a chicken."

"Yeah Caden, stop being such a chicken," Cason chimes in with a monotone voice.

"Call me a chicken one more time!" I laugh at how serious Caden is about being called a chicken. You would think someone called him a dick, or an asshole.

Shelby turns around and puts the movie in the DVD player, and makes her way back to me. I hand her the popcorn bowl, and we lock gazes as our hands brush over each others. She blushes and quickly looks away, but it's just a boost for me. She's still affected by me, and that's all I need to know to carry out my plan.

Slow and easy. I repeat the words a few times to be sure I remember them.

I watch her as she pulls her legs up beside her, and I find I like seeing her getting comfortable on my couch. I know I should be interested in the movie that's starting to play, but I can't take my eyes off her. I stare as she slowly eats her popcorn and, something so simple shouldn't be so fucking erotic.

It is because it's Shelby doing it.

I shake my head, and pull my gaze from her when I hear Caden groan out loudly and say, "Oh come on! I asked you not to pick this movie! Now I won't be able to sleep worth a shit." I chuckle as does everyone else knowing Caden's so full of it.

The movie plays on, and I try to stay focused on it. I really do, but I can't knowing she's right beside me. And the fact she's hogging all the popcorn. I lean over and lightly tap on her shoulder. As she looks at me, I gesture for her to move closer. I grin when she complies willingly, and even though she sits closer, she's careful not to touch me. I casually place my arm behind her, but I don't touch her. I know she's probably thinking about it since I noticed her chest rising and falling quickly, but I need her to get used to being around me again. Her eyes never once waver from the movie, and I have a feeling she's trying to ignore the fact I'm so close to her. I might be pushing it too fast, but fuck me if I can help it. I use my other hand to take some popcorn, and she tenses each time I do so. So much for slow and easy.

Thankfully, Caden keeps his comments to himself as the movie plays, but I can't help but laugh as he hides his face behind a pillow. I tap Shelby on her shoulder again, getting her to look at him and she snickers. When Chucky comes into play, he screams. We all burst out in laughter since he spilled popcorn everywhere while screaming at the top of his lungs, and almost jumping out of his chair. "You better clean that shit up once you find your balls," I tell him, and he just shakes his head.

"I told y'all I didn't want to watch this damn movie. I should make you clean it up."

"Caden, hush your mouth. I'm trying to watch the movie," Shelby says, and when Caden looks at me, all I can do is shrug my shoulders. We did say she could pick the movie and now, Caden just has to deal with it.

About halfway through, I notice Shelby's eyes begin to droop. She blinks several times, and I can tell she's fighting her sleep. I look at the clock on the wall behind us, seeing it's getting really late. When she starts to lean her head back, I grab the popcorn bowl out of her lap, hand it to Cason, then I gently guide her to my lap. I know she's tired since she doesn't even put up a fight, but I can't help feeling a rush of satisfaction. I move her long hair from her neck, and she snuggles her face on my legs. I close my eyes, and will my cock to behave. I really don't think she'll like my cock poking her in the cheek. I barely breathe having her this close, and I hope she can't hear my drumming heart. I know this moment can't last, but I'm taking it all in, committing it to memory. This is all I've ever wanted, and I have to tell myself that this doesn't mean she's mine. At least not yet.

# Carter

I see Cason get up out of the corner of my eye, and he walks over to Caden. I'm grateful when they both nod to me, and head towards the door. At least now I don't have to worry about Caden screaming again. I don't want this moment to end, and now that my brothers have left, I sigh in relief. I tune out the horror movie's creepy music, and gaze at Shelby. She looks so peaceful, and when I start to run my fingers through her hair, she sighs deeply.

I let the movie play once more before I decide to put her in my bed. I want time to stop, to make this last a lifetime, but I know I need to move her. She'll be more comfortable in bed. Carefully, I lift her head and slowly move off the couch. I know she's dead to the world when she doesn't even make a sound as I do so. I slide my hands under her, gently picking her up. I hold her close to my chest and my stomach dips as she nuzzles her head on my chest, and wraps her arms around my neck. I breathe in her sweet scent of her shampoo, and slowly make my way to my room. The whole way there, I feel the warmth of her skin on my hands. I want nothing more than to keep her exactly where she is and where she belongs. Having her back in my life again, I feel complete. I always knew there was a piece of me missing, but I didn't realize it was her until now. She's my other half, the part of me I can't live without, and I will fight like hell to keep her. As I push open my door with my foot, I swear to myself that I won't fuck up this time. I won't push her away like before, even if I thought those reasons were for the best. I don't care what I have to do this time. I won't stop until she's given herself to me completely.

I know she's going to fight me, but then again, she wouldn't be Shelby if she didn't.

I don't dare turn on the light, afraid she'll wake up and want me to take her home. I'm glad I left the blinds open, and the moon gives me enough light to walk to my bed. I bend, carefully setting her down. I pick the sheets and comforter off the floor, and place it over her body. I wonder for a second if I need to take off her jean shorts, but I quickly scratch that idea. The last thing I need is for her to think I tried to see her when she's vulnerable. After pulling the covers up to her shoulders, I push the hair out of her face. She sighs deeply again, and I linger longer on her cheek. I want nothing more than to kiss her and lay right by her, but I know I can't. I clench my jaw hating I'm going to have to either sleep on the couch or in one of the guest rooms. It's going to be fucking tempting as hell not to slip in and hold her all night. But I need her to trust me and if she wakes up with me in the bed, that definitely won't work in my favor. I rub her cheek with my thumb once, twice, and a third time before pulling away. Right as I'm moving my hand, she whispers my name, and I swallow hard hearing her say it. I wonder what she's dreaming about. Is she dreaming of me? Maybe it's her soul calling out to mine. I can feel that invisible force willing my body to touch her. To hold her and never let go. It would be so easy to listen to the force, to get in the bed, and do exactly what I want but I don't.

I lean down and kiss her softly on her forehead, then as hard as it is, I leave her to sleep.

I rub the back of my neck as I walk out of my room, and turn to shut the door. Making my way to the living room, I turn off lights as I go and shut off the movie and the TV. I pick up the popcorn bowls and set them down on the counter then I sit down on the couch, wondering if I should sleep here or across the hall from Shelby. I opt for the couch, that way I won't be as tempted to be in the same room as her. Distance is probably the best option tonight. I huff as I grab a pillow, and pull a blanket off the back of the couch.

As I finally get into a comfortable position, I blindly stare up at the ceiling. Sleep doesn't seem to be coming so instead, I think of Shelby. I probably shouldn't, but damn if I can help it. I think of her on my bed sleeping soundly, and imagine I'm there with her. I can feel myself pressed against her body and feel my arms wrapped around her. I think of her warmth, and how soft she felt in my arms as I carried her to bed. I long to actually do this with her. I long to have her all to myself again. Closing my eyes, I try not to let the regret of what I did to her surface. If I let it, it will take me under, smother me, and then if I come out of it, I'll be right where I was earlier. I don't want to go back to the dark place I was when I realized I royally fucked up with her thirteen years ago. It's something I'll probably never forgive myself for, and all I can do now is make it up to her. Show her how I've changed, and how much I wish I could take it back.

As I finally start to let sleep take me, the last thing that crosses my mind is how different our lives could've been if I hadn't pushed her away.

# CHAPTER 9

## Shelby

I slowly open my eyes thinking I must still be dreaming. I'm surrounded by the smell of Carter on his pillows. I don't think I've had such a peaceful night's sleep in years. I blink a few times and rub the sleep out of my eyes. Looking around the unfamiliar room, I realize I'm not dreaming. I'm still at Carter's house and in his bed. I must have fallen asleep during the movie, but I have no recollection of how I ended up here. Sitting up against the headboard, I push my hair out of my face. I'm still in shock that I'm here, in Carter's house. It's surreal, something I never thought would happen, but now that it has, I can't help but be skeptical. I have to remember to keep my guard up around him because I just can't let him totally back in my heart again.

Fear of being hurt again stops me from being too hopeful.

Smelling coffee, I slowly get out of bed wishing I had a toothbrush and some different clothes. But I'll have to make do with what I have. I smooth out the wrinkles on my shirt and use my fingers to brush through my hair. Slowly walking to the bedroom door, I take a deep and calming breath before opening it. Making my way down the hall towards the smell of coffee, I try to calm my nerves. My stomach feels like it's in knots, and I know it's because I'm about to see Carter again. Spotting him in the kitchen, my breath catches in my throat. My heart drums rapidly in my chest, and my face warms. He's leaning against the kitchen island, coffee cup to his lips. He hasn't noticed me yet as he reads the morning paper, and I take my fill before he does. His hair is disheveled, and he's either forgone shaving or forgotten. I find I like the scruffy look on him more than his clean face. Even his clothes seem wrinkled as if he got dressed in a hurry. He slowly looks up and when he sees me and smiles that heart stopping smile. Not kidding either. My heart literally feels as if it stopped beating knowing I'm the one that made him smile like that.

"Good morning."

I tuck some hair behind my ear, hoping my blush isn't showing like it feels. I like the sound of his morning voice. It's husky, deep, and I can't even lie and say it's not sexy. "Morning."

"How'd you sleep?"

I walk over to the stools, and sit down as I answer with, "Better than I have in a long time actually. I'm guessing you put me to bed?"

"That's good to hear, and yeah that was me. I figured you'd be more comfortable in a bed rather than the couch. Trust me, I feel like I was hit by a car last night."

"Did you sleep on the couch?"

He looks away, taking another sip of his coffee before he answers. "Yeah." I can't help but feel there's more he wants to say, but instead he adds, "Do you want some coffee?"

"Sure, that would be great." I watch him as he nods and turns to make my coffee. I lean my elbows on the counter, and bite my lip as I sneak a peek at his ass in his tight slacks. I wonder what he looks like naked. I know he's changed a lot since the last time I saw him, and I can't help but be curious. Time definitely has been good to him. He's much more attractive now than when he was twenty. Don't get me wrong, he's always been handsome and I've always thought so, but now he's a *man*. Maybe it's because I haven't seen him in so long. Maybe because it's been a very long time since I've felt a tender touch. Not to mention, how long it's been since I've had sex. All I do know is that I'm going to have to be extra careful around him. It's hard enough as it is not to fall back into our old patterns and knowing how I'm reacting to him, it's a disaster waiting to happen. I dart my eyes away from him as he turns back around, and places my coffee mug in front of me. I take a glance at him and grin seeing him staring back at me. He chuckles another sexy sound, and I can't get over how just one look; one sound from him, makes me feel as if I'm a teenager again. He continues to stare at me and finally I ask, "What are you staring at?"

He shrugs as he says, "You." I swallow hard, and I look down at my coffee. I quickly snap my eyes back to his as he touches my hand. "I still can't believe you're here. I feel like this is a dream."

"It's not," I whisper.

"Good. Because if it is, then I don't want to wake up."

I can't help but look away from his intense gaze, and take a sip from my mug. We sit in silence for a bit, neither one of us knowing what to say. Thankfully, Carter picks his paper back up and begins to read again. Our silence it comfortable even if I'm feeling nervous from just being near him. But I push the antsy feeling away, willing myself to act like a normal person. It's not an easy thing to do. Just imagine being around the one person who understands you more than anyone else ever could. Then add in the fact you're attracted to this person, have a history with them, know them inside and out. That plus a force willing you to jump in their arms. Yes, it's hard to stay where I am. A part of me already wants to forget about everything. All the hurt and shit I went through just to have him touch me. But the other part of me is afraid.

It's the fear that keeps me rooted where I am.

I drink the last of my coffee and watch as he folds his paper in half, then places it aside. He notices I'm finished with my coffee and takes my mug with his, placing them in the sink. I see him look at the clock, and I know my time with him is almost over. I can't deny the uneasy feeling that runs through me thinking about not seeing him. "What time do you work today?" I hope my question sounds as causal as I hope.

"I need to leave soon if I don't want Dad to chew me out again."

I frown, then remember Caden telling me he had a fight with his parents yesterday. I also recall how Carter didn't want to talk about it with me last night. "Want to talk about it?"

He rubs the back of his neck, and I realize that seems to be a tick of his now. He didn't do that when we were younger. "We just have a difference of opinions about the firm."

"And?" I can tell he's leaving something out by the way his eyes dart around me, instead of looking at me. Seems he hasn't lost all his younger traits.

He sighs then says, "And I might have gotten angry at them, and my brothers for keeping your homecoming from me."

"Okay. I can see why you would be upset about that, but that's more my fault than anything." His eyes snap to me and I add, "I asked Caden and Cason not to tell you. I assume one of them or both told your mom and dad. It wasn't my intention to cause you to fight with them."

"I know. I don't blame you, or them really. I ..." His jaw clenches as he says, "I was just angry and needed someone to blame. When I went over there, and Dad started questioning me about what my decision was about taking over the firm and I just snapped. Seeing you again, and knowing at the time you didn't want me to know it really hurt." I shrink back at his words, and I can't help but replay Bethany's words in my head. "I'm sorry, I don't want to make you feel bad about it. Trust me, I'm going to apologize to Dad at work and to Mom later this afternoon. I didn't handle anything like I should've yesterday. I'm more embarrassed than anything."

"Why would you be embarrassed?"

"Because my father's right. I'm avoiding taking over the firm and instead of confronting the reasons, I came home and got drunk. I should've taken responsibility instead of acting like well, the old me."

I'm not sure what to make of his last comment. I can only assume he's referring to the time after I left. "Why don't you want to take over the firm? I can't see anyone else doing it, but you. And do you really want someone else to take over?"

He seems to think about my questions before he answers with, "Honestly, I'm afraid." I open my mouth to ask why, but he adds, "What if I fuck it up? Or what if I can't live up to my father's reputation? I know it's a huge decision to make, and I've been going over it since Dad brought it up. It makes sense for me to step up, but at the same time I don't want to let him down."

I reach across the counter acting purely on instinct, and grab his hand. I watch him gaze at my hand on his and when he looks back at me, I know he feels what I do. Even if I can't give him anything else right now. I can be here for him like I used to be. I can help him more than anyone else because I understand him. "You won't fuck up, Carter. I know you have doubts and are worried, but I also know your Dad would've never asked you to take over the firm unless he knew you were ready." I squeeze his hand as I add, "You have to have more faith in yourself."

He places his other hand over mine and says, "Thank you. I needed to hear that, and it means a lot coming from you."

He looks down and shakes his head. He smiles, and I can't help but wonder what he's thinking. "What?"

"It's just … you coming back, being here right now, and telling me what I need to hear, it's like fate stepping in."

I give him a puzzled look as I ask, "What do you mean?"

He's still looking at our hands intertwined together as he explains. "It feels like this is how things were supposed to go. As if fate knew I needed you, and brought you back to me."

"Carter," I start, but he cuts me off.

"Don't shut me out, Shel." His eyes dart to mine, and the intensity of his gaze makes me suck in a breath. "You asked me, and I'm being honest with you. I promise it's not a ruse to get you back. I know you're not ready for that, but I was talking more along the lines of you coming back to me as my best friend. No one ever understood me like you did or knew what I needed to hear to make my choices easier. You do that." He lets my hands go, and I watch him closely as he walks around the island, slowly making his way to me. My damn heart won't stop racing, and I have to remind myself to breathe as he reaches me. I still as his hand cups my cheek, and savor the feel of his hand on me. His touch is gentle and warm, and I close my eyes taking in the sensations that run through me. My body seems to come alive at his sweet gesture. It's as if my soul is overjoyed to have him back in my life, simply touching me. I let out a deep sigh, and glance at him when I hear him speak softly. "I've missed you so damn much. You have no idea how happy it makes me that you're here." He traces his thumb on my cheek as he says, "I finally feel complete again."

I don't know what to say, so I just stare up at him. He smiles back at me, and slowly takes his hand off my face. I want to cry out at the loss of his warmth, but I know he needed to move away from me. I watch him as he walks back around the kitchen island, and swallow hard as he refuses to take his eyes off me. His gaze is intense, and I can't stop the warm sensations that form in my stomach. I go to grab my necklace, but stop midway. Carter frowns then asks, "What is it?"

I debate on whether, or not to tell him I still have his gift. Then again, maybe if he sees I've kept it all this time, he'll know I never forgot what we had. I reach into my shirt and pull out my keepsake. I hold it in my hand for a moment, and stare at it before letting it drop. Carter sucks in a breath when he sees it. I watch him closely as a variety of emotions cross his face. Shock, disbelief, and when he looks in my eyes again, he looks at me adoringly. As if he's seeing me again for the very first time, with such love in his eyes. "I know we didn't end things on a good note, but I couldn't bear to part with it. Every time I needed strength or a reminder of what I left behind, I would look at it, and just knowing I had a piece of you made things easier." I'm surprised by my admission, but at the same time, it feels good to open up to someone again. It's been so long since I felt like I could trust someone with how I really feel.

"I can't believe you kept it after all this time." He grins, shakes his head, and his eyes light up. "Do you remember what I said when I gave it to you?"

Of course I remember. It's committed to my memory, and it's one that I used to think of often. "I do. Instead of me giving you a graduation present, you gave me this." I glance down at my necklace, thinking back to that day. It was a happy day, and I was so proud of Carter for graduating, and getting accepted into Harvard Law. I wasn't expecting a gift from him, but I remember being excited when he showed me what he bought. I blink, coming back to the present as I say, "As you put the necklace on me, you said it was to remind me how much you loved me. That no matter how far apart we were, it wouldn't matter because our love for each other was strong." I glance away from him, as I repeat his sweet words from a lifetime ago. "I remember you saying, that my necklace was your way of giving me your heart and that we'd always be able to find one another."

I look back at Carter, noticing he's rubbing his chest. I want to ask him if he's alright. But I don't. I know that day meant so much to the both of us. I could see and feel how much he cared about me back then. Which made when he broke my heart that much more painful. He clears his throat before saying, "I'm glad you kept it, and it's brought you good memories when you needed them."

I suddenly feel shy, and a bit out of place. The emotions running through me scare the shit out of me, and the room feels as though it's closing in. Reliving the past then the emotions running through me now … it's too intense. I look away from him and place my necklace back in my shirt. I get off the stool and say, "I think I should head back to Annie and William's. I'm sure they're worried where I am." I don't look at Carter. I don't want to see the hurt in his eyes because he'll know what I'm doing. I hate that I can't seem to stay around him, but the wave of all the past emotions and the present ones colliding is overwhelming. I have to get away from it.

"Yeah, okay. I can drive you there since it's on my way." I nod and head back to his room to grab my shoes. I remind myself to breathe and stop over thinking everything. It's stupid of me to act this way, but going for so long without feeling any of this … it's frightening.

# Carter

I quickly slip on my flip flops, and walk back into the kitchen to grab my purse. Carter's sitting on the couch in the living room, and when he sees me, he makes his way to the door. We don't speak as I follow him to his truck, and I can't help but feel remorseful for shutting him out and running away. I just can't help it. I'd rather push him away, than have him hurt me again. Once we get to his truck, he opens my door like the perfect gentlemen, and I climb inside. It takes me a few tries before I'm able to get in since it's so high up, but Carter patiently waits until I'm situated then shuts my door. He climbs in and once I'm buckled in, he starts the truck and pulls out of the driveway.

The drive to Annie and William's is quiet, but thankfully short. When Carter pulls in at their house, I want to jump out and run to the safety of my room. I quickly undo my seat belt, but before I open the door Carter grabs my hand. I still and slowly look at him. "I'm sorry I overwhelmed you earlier. But I want you to know I meant every word. I still want us to start over and give our friendship another shot, but I need you to promise me something."

I relax in my seat and ask, "What do you want me to promise you?"

He lets out a rush of air then says, "That you won't run every time you feel the need to. If you want to get away or feel like you need space tell me, and I'll back off. I want you to promise that you won't shut me out, and you'll talk to me about why you feel the urge to get away."

I turn away and look out the window as I consider his request. Running a hand through my hair, I wonder if by making this promise will I be able to keep it? I sigh, turning back to him and say, "Carter, I can't promise you that." He looks away from me and rubs his chin. Before he can say anything, I add, "It's not that I won't promise you what you want. It's just going to take me some time to get used to opening up to you again, and getting used to feeling … the way I do when I'm around you." I glance down at my hand in his, and I can't believe I just told him that. "I went through a lot while I was in South Carolina, and all I can give you is, I'll try." I look back at him and see understanding in his eyes. "I will try to let you back in, but I just need you to be patient with me."

He squeezes my hand and responds with, "I can do that." I nod and reach for the door handle again. I open the door, and before I hop out he asks, "Can I see your phone?" I frown and shrug as I pull out my phone for him. He takes it from me, and I watch him as he punches in something. He hands it back, and I see he added his number into my contacts. I shake my head, and he says, "I'll call you later."

I smile as I get out of the truck, and when I turn to shut the door I whisper, "Okay. Until then." I shut the door, and I know he heard me by the grin on his face. When I get to the porch, he honks his horn and waves to me. I watch him as he leaves and I realize I'm still smiling as I walk inside.

## Carter

I can't help the wide grin that forms when I notice Carter messaged me. I feel like a teenager again, and it's all because of him. Two months of constant texting, late night phone calls, and hanging out … just feels right. I've kept to my word of trying not to run, and I've been getting better at not shutting him out. Plus it's always been easy to be around and talk to Carter. He just makes it simple, and he doesn't push me into talking. It seems as if we've never been apart, and I can't help the excitement that runs through me every time he calls, texts, or when I see him. I open the message, reading what he says, and let out a giggle. I don't giggle, at least I haven't in a long time, but Carter brings out the giddy part in me.

"Someone's in a good mood today," Annie says as she sits on the couch by me. She and William have picked up on my old self, and I can tell they like the improvement.

"Carter's being his usual self." I send him a quick response then lay my phone down. "Do you and William have any plans for tonight?" It's Saturday, and normally Saturday's are our game night or bingo night at the community center.

Annie glances at me and she asks, "Why? Does Carter want you to come over?"

"He said he's having a get together at his house later tonight. Since it's cooling off at night, he wants to sit around the fire pit. I told him I'd think about it because I knew Saturday's are our nights."

Annie smiles brightly as she says, "I think we can spare you for one night. Go have fun, I know you want to."

I grin knowing I'm busted. "Maybe a little, but y'all come first."

Annie starts shaking her head as she declares, "It's fine if you go. William and I can go to bingo and maybe go to the Steak House for dinner. See, you've given us a perfect reason to go out to eat."

"Are you sure?"

"Yes, Shelby. It's time William and I do something together besides watch TV all afternoon. Plus it'll be good for you to spend more time with Carter." She reaches over, patting my hand. "I've seen the changes he brings out of you, and I know he makes you happy. Now go on and get ready. We don't want to keep him waiting now would we?"

I laugh and reach over to hug her. "Thank you, Annie." I pull away and get up from the couch. Before walking away I turn back and tell her, "He does make me happy." I quickly glance away, and make my way upstairs. Admitting out loud how Carter makes me feel like the old me again is a huge revelation. I've known for a while, but I kept it to myself. I was afraid if I said it out loud or if I talked to anyone about it, it wouldn't be real anymore. I can't let my fears stop me from being happy. I've let it control me for a long time, but each day with Carter has shown me how to slowly let go of that fear. I can only hope one day I'll totally be free of it, and be able to finally live the life I deserve.

I'm a bundle of nerves as I park in Carter's driveway. I turn off William's truck, and lean back in my seat. I can hear the music coming from inside the house, and I know everyone's here since their vehicles are parked in front of the house. I'm not sure who was invited, and I didn't even think to ask. When Carter asked me to come, all I could think about was spending more time with him. I suck in a deep breath, and grab my Cupcake Vineyards wine and my purse. I hop out of my truck and slowly make my way to Carter's home.

Making my way to the door, I knock a few times. When Carter doesn't answer, I open the it and walk inside. Music assaults my ears from the living room, and I set my purse down by the couch before making my way to the back porch. As I get closer, I can see that's where everyone is. I can hear a lot of laughing and notice Caden is doubled over when I stop and stand by the back door. He's standing by the porch rail, and I sweep my gaze around seeing who all is here. Cason's sitting down by the outdoor table shaking his head at what I'm assuming is Caden. There's honestly no telling what's so funny, with the Harlow's you can never tell. A skinny blonde is sitting across from Cason, and I wonder if she came with one of the twins. I clench my jaw as the thought of her coming for Carter, but I shake the unwelcome thought off. I frown when I don't see Carter, and go to look for him. I don't get an inch away from my spot by the door when I feel a hand on my arm. I tense for a second before relaxing when I realize it's Carter who's touching me. "Going somewhere?" He asks with his deep husky voice, and there's no stopping my stomach from fluttering.

I slowly turn leaning my back on the door frame, and look up at him as I reply. "I was about to come looking for you." His eyebrows raise, as if he's surprised by my response. "You didn't answer the door, so I just let myself in," I add.

"Sorry about that. Caden insisted on playing this loud ass music, and I didn't hear the doorbell." I don't really hear the music anymore. I know it's playing, but all I can focus on is how close Carter is standing to me. I clutch the bottle of wine in my hand tighter as I take in his masculine scent, and swallow hard when he runs his fingers through his hair. It still looks damp from his shower, and he's kept the scruff tonight. I wonder how that scruff would feel against my legs or on my entire body. He gazes into my eyes, and my face flushes. He grins and fuck me, I'm glad he can't read my mind. It's shocking how intense being around him is, and how just looking at him is starting to turn me on. I watch him as he looks down. I see his mouth moving, but I'm staring at his lips instead of hearing what he's saying. "… for you?" He asks.

"What?" I shake my head, clearing my thoughts of Carter and I doing things that I know I'm not ready for.

He laughs and says, "Can I put your wine in the fridge for you?"

I glance down at the wine in my hand, and let out a nervous laugh and respond with, "Oh, right. Yeah, that would be great. Thanks." I awkwardly hand him the bottle, and when his fingers brush against mine, I suck in a breath.

"Hey, Shel. Get your ass out here and stop ignoring me!" And the trance is broken by Caden. I roll my eyes and give Carter a smile before pushing myself off the frame and walk outside. I make my way over to Caden, and glare at him before slugging him in the arm. "Ouch! What was that for?"

He rubs the spot on his arm, and I chuckle as I say, "You know why." And he does know why. He's a pest and his usual self. Even as a kid he was the same way. I see some things never change.

"I really don't, but I'll let it slide this one time. Just remember, I'm a cop, and I can arrest you for that."

"Oh really? I'd like to see you try. Plus you deserved it."

"Look now, I'm an officer of the law. It's my job to put cop beaters in jail." I try to hold back my laughter. I really do, but I can't. Caden is so serious, and I even hear Cason start laughing. "I don't see what's so funny. This is no laughing matter."

"Caden you're so full of shit," Cason says in between laughing, then adjusts his hat. Caden shakes his head and walks inside. Once I get control over myself, I take a seat by Cason. I glance over at the blonde, and she's in her own little world. She's staring off into the yard, and I give Cason a knowing look. He shrugs his shoulders, and I know then she's with Caden.

How Deep Is Your Love by Calvin Harris and Disciples starts playing, and I chuckle as Cason's face turns into a grimace. I hear Caden call out, "This is my jam," then proceeds to walk outside while singing, beer in hand, very loudly and off key. Cason groans, I laugh, and the blonde starts to bob her head, which in turn, makes me laugh louder. Caden starts to dance around the porch, and I wonder how many beers he's had already. I see movement out of the corner of my eye, and turn seeing Carter standing by the back door staring right at me. My laughter slowly dies as I notice the look in his eyes. It's a mixture of lust, desire, and dare I say love? I'm not entirely sure, but his gaze is making my heart beat faster than before. His eyes never leave mine as he comes closer to me, and I notice he's holding a glass of wine in one hand and a beer in the other.

He takes the seat by me as he places my wine in front of me then he leans over to whisper, "Are your ears bleeding like mine?"

I wasn't expecting that, but I recover quickly with, "I think it's almost over." As soon as the words leave my lips, Gotta Be Somebody by Nickelback comes on. Carter's head drops and Cason groans again as Caden starts trying to sing. And I say try because Caden's voice sounds like nails on a chalkboard. "Oh, God someone please make him stop," I say to no one in particular.

"Carter, do you have any duct tape? I think that'll shut him up," Cason asks.

"Actually, I think I do. Caden, this is your warning. Either stop that screeching sound you call singing, or Cason and I are going to tape your mouth shut." I snort before taking a drink of my wine. I know they're serious. Carter and Cason did tape Caden's mouth shut once when we were teenagers.

"I think you sound amazing, Caden." Blonde pipes in. I almost spit out my wine at the look on Cason's face and Carter just shakes his head.

"Don't worry, Sugar. They're just jealous because I was gifted with such a beautiful voice."

"Again, you're full of shit, Caden," Cason points at him.

"Why is everyone ganging up on me tonight?" Caden clutches his chest, feigning to be hurt and he stumbles to his seat by Blondie.

I take another sip of my wine as I say, "You were always such a drama queen."

"I second that," Carter says. I lean up to set my glass on the table and when I sit back in my chair, Carter places an arm on the back of my seat. I try to act like the small gesture goes unnoticed, but it totally doesn't. I'm very aware of his arm, so much so I can feel my entire body start to heat up. Carter carries on a conversation with his brothers, but I can't focus on what they're talking about. He's been doing this a lot when we're around each other, and I know what he's doing. He thinks he's slick, but I remember all too well he's done the same thing once before. He's trying to get me used to his touch, and his presence. Thing is, I'll never get used to him. He's just that one person that my body reacts differently with. Even if it's just a small thing like now. I can't seem to think straight around him when he does this. It should worry me that I'm still attuned to his every movement, but then again I knew when I saw him again that it would be this way. I had no idea I still cared so much for him even after not seeing him in thirteen years.

But love like ours doesn't just go away.

I try once more to pay attention to what's going around me, but Carter has placed his hand on my shoulder. I can feel the light rubbing of his fingers on my bare skin, and I lean into his touch more. It's been a very long time since I've had someone touch me like this. Gently and without a hidden agenda. I grab my glass of wine off the table and take a big gulp. I don't want to be reminded of Easton's callous intentions when he touched me. I shiver thinking about the shameful things he would do when I would cave for him. Just for a simple touch, caress, or to feel like he loved me.

"Are you cold?" Carter mistakes my shiver, but I don't correct him. Being that it's August, nights aren't cold enough for a jacket yet. I shake my head, and he says, "We'll start the fire in a minute. I can get a jacket for you."

I turn to him and say, "Always the gentlemen." He grins, and I add, "I'm okay, but thank you."

He pushes my hair off my shoulder as he says softly, "Okay, but you tell me if you need it." I grin and look away before he can see my blush. Carter's always been so caring, and I realize how much I've missed that about him.

"Can you two get a room already?"

"Dammit, Caden. Can you not stay out of anyone's business?" I shake my head as Carter cusses under his breath.

"It's kind of hard not to notice when you two are practically all over each other," Caden says sarcastically. I watch as the blonde, whose name I still don't know, beams when Caden puts his arm around her and pulls her closer.

"Would you leave them alone already? No one is saying anything about you trying to bust a nut later," Cason adds.

I hold in my laugh as Caden shrugs, and he states, "Sometimes you feel like a nut, and other times you feel like fucking vodka!" Cason, Carter, and I burst into laughter as Caden leans down and grabs a vodka bottle. The blonde frowns, looking around at us, no doubt wondering what was so funny.

"I don't get it. What's so funny?" I totally called that, and it makes me laugh even harder. Poor girl. She really is clueless.

Caden looks at her with a disbelieving look and says, "Never mind. Here." He hands her the vodka bottle. "Take a swig, Sugar." I wonder if Caden even knows the blonde's name. I've yet to hear him call her anything other than Sugar. I cringe as she takes a huge gulp of it and I can tell she instantly regrets that. She starts coughing and fanning her face. Caden rolls his eyes and says, "I told you a swig. Not chug the bottle!"

"Oh my God! It burns," she says in between coughing, and I can't help but feel a little sorry for her. Carter snickers beside me and Cason has a bored expression on his face.

Caden takes the bottle away from her and before he takes a drink he yells, "NO RAGRETS!"

I double over, holding my sides, hysterically laughing as Cason says, "I know you didn't just quote We Are the Millers."

Caden clears his throat and nods, saying, "I did. That movie is the best."

"What's We Are the Millers?" Blondie asks.

"I'll let you handle that, Caden." Cason gets out of his chair and walks inside. I tune out Caden trying to explain to the blonde what she doesn't understand, and turn to face Carter.

He still has an arm around me, but he's looking down at his phone. I watch him type out a message, but I can't see who he's talking to. Plus it wouldn't be right of me to spy on him. I take another drink of my wine as I lean back in my seat watching him. He's really interested in his phone, and I can't help wanting to know who has him so distracted. I eventually pull my gaze away from him, and start listening to Caden and the blonde. I quickly lose interest, plus I'm not really paying attention. I'm getting lost in my thoughts again, and feel the familiar urge to run. It's so frustrating when the feeling slowly starts. It begins as an uneasy feeling, then it builds into an absolute need. Imagine being around people, but feel totally out of place. It's a sense of not belonging anywhere, and I shake my head trying to make the urge go away. I have no reason to feel like this. I know I'm welcome here, and that I'm a part of the Harlow family again. Granted it's not as it was before, but it's a start. I down the last of the wine hoping it'll help turn my stupid flight response off even more.

I turn to Carter when he places his hand over mine and he asks, "Everything alright?" I give him a small smile, and it's funny how he knows I've slipped back into old habits. His touch grounds me and the urge slowly dissipates. "Need a refill?" He asks as he points to my glass.

"Yeah, that would be great."

He gets up out of his chair and says, "I'll be right back." I watch him walk into the house, and frown when he pulls out his phone again. I reluctantly turn my head away, wishing I wasn't jealous of a damn cell phone. It does sting a bit, knowing he asked me over to spend time together, and he's on his phone talking to God knows who.

I begin to wonder where he went to after a few moments pass. Come to think of it, Cason has been gone for a while too. Right before I get up to go find Carter, he reappears with Cason behind him. I smile when I see Carter holding another beer in one hand and my glass in the other. Cason is holding a bag full of wood, but my smile fades when I see Bethany walking behind Cason. I haven't seen her since the night Cason and Caden brought me over to talk to Carter. Seeing her here and remembering how she spoke to me, well it's not a pleasant feeling. I know she doesn't care for me, and it still shows. Carter places my wine in front of me, and I turn away from her angry gaze. I don't know what I've done for her to dislike me so much, but on the other hand, I'm starting not to give a shit about her or what she thinks of me. I've spent most of my adult life caring about what everyone thought of me, and being exactly who Easton wanted and expected me to be.

I won't do that again.

If Bethany doesn't want to get to know me and learn the truth, then fuck her. I'm done trying to please everyone else, and for once I'm doing what I want. I pick up my glass and watch as Carter pulls her off to the other side of the porch out of the corner of my eye. I try not to let my jealousy take hold, and I wish I could hear what they're talking about. It does seem like a heated conversation. I take another hefty drink of my wine when I noticed Carter looking at me, and I turn my attention to watch Cason start the fire in the fire pit.

Once he gets the fire situated, I stare into the flames before I sense someone sit beside me. "What's got your panties in a wad?" Caden asks, and I snicker at his choice of words.

"Why would you think that?"

"Oh, I don't know. Maybe because since someone showed up unannounced, you've been holding onto that glass like a lifeline."

I shrug, not really wanting to talk about it. I finish off my wine before saying, "I'm going to need a lot more wine before I tell you all my darkest secrets."

He takes my glass from me and says, "More wine coming up then." I chuckle as he leaves and he returns moments later with my refill.

One bottle of wine and five shots of vodka later, I feel pretty damn good. I know I'm drunk. I probably should've stopped after I finished off the bottle of wine, but I just couldn't seem to stop. It doesn't help every time I look over at Carter sitting across from me, Bethany is touching him or laughing at something he's said. Jealousy is a cruel bitch. Every time Carter would try to talk to me or even look my way, Bethany would ask him something. Pretty much anything to take his attention away from me, she did. I don't want to feel second best, but I do. Which is another reason I've let myself have so much to drink. Not to mention Caden hasn't helped me any tonight. He's been right by my side the whole night since Bethany has shown up, and it's as if he's been reading my mind. It could be the fact he's seen me clench my fists when I watch her touch Carter, and every time Caden would notice, he would pull out the vodka and tell me to drink.

The blonde is still here too, and she's been hanging all over Caden. Once she gets up for a bathroom break and I lean over to Caden and ask, "Do you even know her name?"

Cason pipes in and adds, "Yeah Caden, what's her name?"

Caden takes a drink of his beer before answering with, "The fuck if I remember."

I laugh, knowing I was right. "Wait, you brought a chick here, and you have no idea what her name is?" I ask him, and Cason rolls his eyes.

"What's wrong with that? She's been messaging me on Facebook, and she wanted to hang out."

I raise my eyebrows at his admission and Cason asks, "You met her on Facebook?"

"Yeah. So what? Something wrong with that?"

"It's like I don't even know you. Facebook is not a place to meet chicks. What if she's a serial killer? Or worse. What if she's like Summer?"

It doesn't go unnoticed how another girl could be worse than a serial killer, and I definitely don't miss Carter's head falling back. "Who's Summer?" I ask the twins.

Cason looks over to Carter, who by the way is letting Bethany lean on him, and says, "Sorry man."

I frown, as Caden hands the vodka bottle and tells me, "Here, drink up." I do as I'm told and feel the harsh burn of the clear liquid as I swallow. I hand him back the bottle as he explains who Summer is.

"Carter you remember, Summer?" Carter nods and groans and I turn away when he glances at me. I don't know if I can listen to his dating life. "Okay, Summer was this chick Carter met once. They went on one date and afterward, she started stalking him." Cason chuckles as Bethany rolls her eyes. "Anyways, Summer had it in her head that her and Carter were going to get married, and have three kids."

"I don't think it went that far, Caden." Carter states. I can only sit back and listen. My head starts to feel fuzzy hearing all this.

"I think it would've if you hadn't changed your number and told her to fuck off."

"I wasn't that harsh. But I did change my number," Carter tells everyone. They continue to talk about this Summer chick, and I can't help but feel sorry for her. Apparently she was obsessed with Carter, but I can't say I blame her. They crack jokes about how she would randomly show up at the firm, and I don't miss Bethany getting irritated as they keep going on and on about it.

When I start to get queasy I state, "I have to pee." I can't listen to them talk about some girl Carter was with. I awkwardly stand and sway. Caden starts to get up, but I give him a thumbs up letting him know I'm fine. Stumbling into the house, I hold onto the wall, making my way to the much needed bathroom. I suddenly regret drinking so much. My mouth feels dry, and I can barely focus on anything. I'm seeing double, and the booming music isn't helping. Thankfully, I don't puke while in the bathroom like I thought I would, but I do pee for a good five minutes though.

Once I wash my hands, a task harder than it should be while intoxicated, I walk out of the bathroom. I hear everyone laughing outside, but I'm not ready to go back out yet. Instead I head to the kitchen, and grab a bottled water out of the fridge. I walk to the side of the fridge, leaning against the wall as I take a few sips. I move my hair out of my face wishing I hadn't drunk so much. I can't even drive home now, and I'm going to have to stay here. I'm pretty sure all of us are drunk, and no one will be able to drive tonight. I lightly bang my head on the wall frustrated at myself. I can't listen to Caden talk about Summer anymore, and I can't stand to see Bethany hanging on Carter either. I'm stuck here and I don't like it.

I hear someone call my name, but I don't know which brother it is. The music drowns out the sound of their voice, and I don't move from my hiding spot to see who it is. A few heartbeats later, I see Carter beside me. "There you are. Why are you hiding?"

"Figured you wouldn't notice with you being preoccupied with Bethany." Shit. I didn't mean for that to come out, but it did.

He walks in front of me and he has a huge grin on his face. "Are you jealous?"

I frown and shake my head as I say, "What? No, I'm not jealous." Okay, yeah I am jealous, but he doesn't need to know that.

He raises an eyebrow, and I know he doesn't believe me. My heart drums in my chest when he lightly slowly traces his fingertips up my arm. "You don't have any reason to be jealous."

"Why's that?" I whisper.

His eyes stare into mine as he declares, "Because I only see you." I blink a few times, and I have to remind myself to breathe when he moves closer to me. His hand caresses my face, and his presence is beginning to overwhelm me. His gaze wavers for a moment when I lick my lips, and he whispers, "You're the only one I want." Just A Kiss by Lady Antebellum starts playing as his other hand grabs a hold of my waist. The song is everything I'm thinking. I don't know if I should stop him, or even if I want to. I don't want to mess things up, and I don't want to rush things with him either. But I do know I want him. I want to feel his gentle touch and his warmth. Everything about him is calling out to me. His eyes look into mine, seeming to plead with me, or to see if I'm really alright with him being where he is. He leans his head on my forehead, and I close my eyes when he mutters, "Let me kiss you."

It might just be the alcohol talking, but I breathe out, "Yes." He wastes no time taking my lips, and his kiss is everything I remembered and more. His lips are soft and greedily take mine, as if he's been dying to kiss me.

It's the closest I'll ever come to feeling euphoria.

I drop my water bottle, and my arms wrap around his neck pulling him closer. I run my fingers through his hair, and moan when he dips his tongue inside my mouth. I feel his fingers digging into my waist, but I don't care. I'm surrounded by Carter being consumed by his gentle, but demanding kiss. He slows his seductive mouth, and I know he doesn't want to rush our kiss. Instead he starts to take his time, tasting me, and sucking on my bottom lip. I take everything he gives, wanting, and needing more from him. My body craves him, and for the first time in a very long time, I feel my stomach clench with a familiar ache. I arch my hips towards him and savor the sensations running throughout my entire body. I want him more than I've thought possible. But he stops for a moment so I can catch my breath, and his hand on my waist moves to my face. He tilts my head the way he wants me, and sweetly pecks my lips. I don't want him to stop kissing me, or making me feel in absolute bliss. He slowly pulls away dropping his hands, and I swallow down the protest. I feel a sense of déjà vu, and that's when I remember our first kiss. Granted it wasn't as intense as it just was, but everything else was the same.

He backs a few steps away, as if he's trying to gain control over himself and his emotions. I'm grateful for the wall behind me, or I would've fallen on the floor by now. My head is swimming. It's a mixture of alcohol and the taste of Carter. "Oh fuck. Were y'all just making out?" We both snap our heads to Caden's voice, and I'm glad Carter pulled away when he did. Caden smiles, and Carter rubs the back of his neck. Caden holds his hand up and says,

"Hell yeah, bro. It's about fucking time." Carter grins, shakes his head, and gives Caden his high five.

Carter turns to me and says, "Ignore him. He's pretty wasted."

"What? Who's wasted? Not me, bro. I'm cool as a cucumber." I laugh knowing Carter's right. Caden is hammered.

"Alright, I'm cutting you off and putting your ass to bed."

"Ah man, don't be a buzzkill."

Carter takes Caden by the arms and says to me, "You can have my room. I'll tuck you in after I put this one to bed." I can only nod. My nerves suddenly coming to the surface.

I laugh as Caden slurs, "Night, Shelby." But it ends up sounding more like, knife Swelby.

I watch Carter lead Caden out of the kitchen, and I push myself off the wall. I pick up my water, and head towards Carter's room. I open the door, set my water down on the bedside table, and kick off my shoes before I sit on the bed. I wish I'd brought my pajamas but then again, I didn't know I wouldn't be sober enough to drive home. As I wait for Carter, I smile thinking about our kiss. I don't know if it means anything, or if we're going to start dating. All I do know is, I want to kiss him again. And again. Maybe in the morning we can talk about what our kiss meant, and where to go from there. I also try to push thoughts of where Carter's sleeping tonight out of my mind. The drunk me would love nothing more for him to climb in the bed and hold me. And if anything were to happen, let's say my lady parts are okay with that. But the sober me, the one that's slowly coming around, is telling me it's too soon. It's too fast. I've known Carter almost all my life, but we both have changed over the years. I need to get to know him as he is now and not the memory of how he was. I snap out of my inner dilemma when I notice someone has turned off the music and soon after, I hear a light tap on the door.

Carter walks in the room and I don't try to stop the grin from forming. "Hi."

He stays by the door, seeming unsure of what to do. "Hey. Comfortable?"

"I should've came prepared. Sleeping in jean shorts and a tank isn't going to be very comfortable."

"I can let you use one of my shirts if you want."

"Thank you. That would be much better." He nods and I watch him as he walks over to his armoire. He opens it and pulls out a plain white T-shirt.

He makes his way back and hands me the shirt, as he says, "I'll let you change."

I frown but nod. He quickly leaves the room, and I undress as soon as he shuts the door. I pull his oversized shirt over my head, and I'm glad I'm alone so he can't see me smell his shirt. It smells of him, his unique scent, and I neatly fold my clothes, setting them on his dresser by his bed. I crawl into bed, and I get under the covers as I wait for him to come back. My eyes start to get heavy as I wait, and I blink the sleep away. I feel my stomach flutter when he finally comes back in the room, and he smiles at me as he walks over to the bed.

Once he reaches me, he brushes my hair back and asks, "Do you need anything?" Well isn't that a loaded question. I need … him. I need his touch, and his hot mouth on my lips again. I need all of him. He must sense where my thoughts go because he says, "I'm sleeping in the guest room tonight."

I pout, yes childish but I'm still drunk, as I ask, "Why?"

He takes a deep breath and caresses my cheek and says, "Because you're drunk and when I make you mine again, I want you sober so you can remember everything I plan on doing."

I feel my face flush and swallow hard. "When?"

"Yes, Shelby. When. Not maybe, or second guessing these feelings between us."

I pull away from his hand as I roll on my back. He takes a seat by me and I say, "You sound sure of yourself. What if I wake up and don't remember any of this?"

"Don't worry about that. I'll help you remember if you forget, but I have a feeling you're going to think about our kiss for days." I lick my lips knowing he's right. There's no way I could ever forget that kiss. When I don't respond, he leans down and I hold my breath as he kisses my forehead. "Goodnight, Shelby."

He gets off the bed and I say, "Night, Carter." He shuts off the light and shuts the door. My last thought before I fall into a deep sleep is Carter's lips taking mine.

I wake with a huge smile on my face. I stretch, remembering everything that happened last night, and blush thinking about me wanting Carter to do more than kiss me. I am glad he was a gentleman and didn't take advantage of me. I have no idea what time it is, but I'm suddenly energized, and I need to see him. I need to confirm what I remember just to be sure my fucked up brain isn't playing tricks on me. I toss the covers off me and hop out of bed. I quickly make my way over to the dresser and grab my shorts. I almost trip trying to get them on, but thankfully crisis adverted.

Again, I chastise myself for not being prepared for another sleep over. I desperately want a toothbrush and a hairbrush. I make do again with my fingers, and smooth out my hair with the palms of my hands. I walk over to the bathroom in Carter's room, and almost jump with joy when I see his toothbrush and toothpaste by the sink. I don't think he'll mind if I use his toothbrush. I mean, he kissed me last night, and this is basically the same thing. I think about our kiss again, and smile widely as I quickly brush my teeth. When I'm finished, I clean up after myself and put everything back where it was. I look myself over before going to find him, and smile once more when I see the light shining back in my eyes.

# Carter

It's all because of Carter. It's funny how one simple, but passionate kiss can change things.

I have to stop myself from running out of the bathroom, but I manage to slow down. Before I open the door to find him, I take a deep breath stilling the nerves in my stomach. I haven't been this thrilled in a long time, and I relish in the rush that takes over me. But when I open the door, I'm not prepared to see him standing across the hall. My eyes graze over him, and seeing his naked chest makes my breath catch in my throat. I recover quickly, and blush when he notices me. He must have slept in the guest room across from his room, but my face falls when I see the look on his face. It's a mixture of regret and sadness.

I'm confused by his look and I instantly think something's wrong. He hasn't moved out of the doorway fully, and before I can ask what's wrong, I hear her voice. "Carter, come back to bed."

My stomach falls, and I swallow hard trying to get the lump that's forming in my throat to go away before I ask, "Please tell me that's not Bethany in there."

His jaw clenches and his head drops as the door opens so I can see her. She's sitting up in the bed wearing Carter's shirt, and it's all the confirmation I need. I don't even say anything before turning around, going back to his room, and quickly grab the rest of my things. "Shelby, it's not what it looks like." I still as I hear his voice noticing he's right behind me. I take a deep breath, trying to keep it together, and push past him. I hear him following me, but I just can't deal with him. I get to the living room, and slip on my shoes before bending down to grab my purse. I can't even bear to look him as he says, "Please, Shelby. Let me explain. I swear it's not what you think."

I put a hand on the door handle, but before I open it I turn and say, "Fuck you, Carter. Don't follow me either." I quickly turn away, not caring to see if my words hurt him. I race out the door and get to William's truck. I drop my clothes trying to dig for my keys in my purse. Unlocking the door, I toss my purse in the seat and bend down to pick the clothes back up.

Pulling out of the driveway, I see Carter standing on the porch with his arms crossed. I know I'm running, the very thing I was trying so hard not to do, but I cannot deal with this. Carter's house fades behind me and before I reach Annie and William's, I pull off to the side of the road. I cut the engine and place my head on the steering wheel. I close my eyes, hating that I fell for his lies. I should've known something was going on between him and Bethany. It all makes sense now why she didn't like me, and why she has been so hateful towards me. She has feelings for him. I should've seen it the first time I met her, but I missed it. I don't want to believe that Carter is that type of guy, but the facts are damning. And this isn't the first time he's done this. I should've seen there was something between them when he never once tried to get away from her advances last night, and then he kisses me only to sleep with her.

I lean back in my seat and let the tears finally fall. I feel as though my heart has literally been ripped out of my chest, and someone is punching me in the stomach. I think it hurts so much just because I was ready to be with him. I was ready to be happy, and move on. To make a better life for myself. I can't believe I trusted him. I let out a scream willing myself to be strong, but in my heart I know Carter Harlow has destroyed me.

Again.

It takes me back to a time I really don't want to relive. To a place that I thought my world was ending. But the stupid memory of Carter telling me he didn't want me, he didn't need me, surfaces anyways.

*It had been weeks since I had more than a ten-minute conversation with Carter. His calls didn't come as often as they used to. I missed talking to him, hearing his voice, and feeling our connection. I didn't want to think the worst, so I'd decided to surprise him. I pushed my fear of flying down and hopped on the first flight I could afford. It had also been a long time since he'd been able to come home, and I knew Harvard hadn't been easy for him. I also knew being away from his family had taken a toll on him, but I couldn't help but feel he was pulling away from me. I knew something was drastically changing when he didn't come home to visit my father's grave on the anniversary of his death with me. He'd never once forgotten, and I told myself he didn't do it on purpose. I knew he had a lot going on and I tried not to smother him, but I needed him too much to give up.*

*That's why I stood outside his fraternity house getting the courage to walk in and surprise him. He had no idea I was there and when he texted me yesterday, he said he would be spending the weekend studying for mid-term exams.*

*I pushed down the uneasy feeling in the pit of my stomach, and walked up the steps to the fraternity. As I got closer to the door, I could hear the loud music playing. I frowned, wondering if Carter was even there. There was no way he could concentrate if there was a party going on. I knocked loudly a few times before a guy answered the door. The guy looked me over, but he didn't say anything when he let me in. My eyes darted around the crowded living room seeing a mixture of alcohol, drugs, and of course half-naked sorority girls. I instantly felt out of place, knowing I didn't belong here. My stomach clenched, but I swallowed hard. I took a deep breath, making the flight rush dissipate only by a fraction. I pushed through the drunk college students trying to find Carter. I had no idea where he could be, or what room was his. I'd never been here before, let alone in a different state or city. This was all new to me, but I was determined to talk to him. I needed his reassurance everything was fine between us. I needed him to smile at me, and make my worries seem as though I was over thinking things. To remind me that this was nothing more than a bump in the road. That this was just a time in our lives that we had to deal with, and we'd come out stronger when it was over.*

*Just like he told me two years ago.*

*But I didn't have to look very hard for him. I stood still as I watched him in the kitchen taking shots out of a girl's cleavage. Afterward he pulled her by the waist, placing her under his arm, and for a moment I thought he was going to kiss her. My mouth dropped shocked he would do this, and I was confused as to why he lied to me. I felt my stomach start to ache, and rubbed my chest feeling my heart breaking one small piece at a time. I clenched my jaw as she smiled sweetly up at him. I wanted to scream. I wanted to yank her by her blonde hair and make sure she never looked at Carter that way again. I'd never been an angry person, but seeing Carter touching another woman, made my blood boil. The rage built, and I was afraid I wouldn't be able to stop my jealous outburst. But I didn't have to do anything. I didn't get a chance. A guy from the party bumped into me, and the commotion made Carter lock gazes with me. His smile instantly faded, and he quickly took his arm off the girl. I sighed when he started to walk toward me, but I couldn't stand to listen to more of his lies. I had to get out of there. I should've listened to my gut. I should've listened to the warning bells going off in my head, but I didn't. As I turned around ready to get the hell out of the house, Carter grabbed my wrist. At this point, I didn't* care what he had to say. I couldn't stand the thought of him being with someone else, and jerked my hand out of his. I heard him calling after me, but I didn't stop. I felt my heart breaking more, and tears threatened to spill.

Once I got outside, I closed my eyes fighting the tears from falling, and breathing was a bit easier. I blinked a few times, wondering how in the hell I was going to get back home. Then I heard him calling after me again. I dropped my head knowing I couldn't run away from this, and I told myself no matter how much it would hurt, I'd listen to what he had to say. "Shelby, what are you doing here?"

I pushed my hair out of my face as I said, "I wanted to surprise you, but I can see you're busy. Not studying like you told me." I shook my head, not wanting to believe he would be stupid enough to throw everything we had away. "Are you fucking her? And I need to know why you lied to me."

He stepped closer to me, and I held up my hands to stop him. "I'm sorry. I was going to study, but the guys wanted to relax and have a good time. I couldn't say no, I needed to let go for once."

I squinted my eyes at him not believing his bullshit excuse, and how he avoided my other question. "So, that gave you a reason to lie to me, forget about coming with me to see my Dad's grave, and to hang all over some other girl? I need to know, Carter. Did you sleep with her?"

"What? No, I've never cheated on you, and I'll never do that. It was just harmless fun, that's all. And

*I … I'm sorry. I know I lied, and I know I forgot to go with you."* He looked away and I frowned. He seemed to be deciding what to say, and I had a feeling I wasn't going to like it. *"Shel, I fucked up. I've been fucking up a lot, and I think … I think it would be best if we stopped seeing each other."*

*"Carter, what are you saying?"* No, he couldn't be saying this. After all we'd been through, he couldn't just leave me.

*"Look I'm distracted and constantly studying. I just don't need anything else keeping me from school."*

*"But you promised me."* I said with a shaky voice *"You told me we would make it work, and I know we can."* I won't believe it. He's pushing me away and I won't let him. We could get past this and eventually, I'd forgive him for lying and for flirting with another girl.

*"I know what I said."* I stepped back at his tone. *"This is the best thing for me right now, and I need you to understand that."*

I swallowed hard and shook out my hands. *"I don't understand, Carter. What are you saying? That you don't want me anymore? That you don't need me? Are you really throwing everything we have away for nothing?"*

I stopped breathing as he stayed silent for a few moments. My heartbeat was the only thing I could hear as I waited for him to either rip the rest of my heart out, or if we could forget about this stupid fight and move on. *"Yes."* I sucked in a breath and I bit my

*cheek to hold in my cry. "I'm sorry, Shelby. I can't do
this anymore."*

*"Carter, please don't do this!"*

*He wouldn't even look at me as he said, "It's
already done." I watched him turn and leave, in
complete and utter disbelief. He didn't look back as
he walked inside the house, leaving me alone
outside.*

*I waited for a few moments hoping he'd come
back. That he'd changed his mind, and didn't mean
any of what he said. But he didn't. Hot tears fell
down my cheeks, and I backed away from the
house. I held my chest with both hands, walking
alone in a city I didn't know, feeling the worse kind of
pain anyone could imagine.*

*I was alone, abandoned, heartbroken, and I
never thought Carter would be the one to make me
feel this way.*

A horn honks as it passes by, snapping me out
of the past. I watch the car as it fades into the
distance, and I'm grateful the person came when
they did. If not, I would've been stuck in that horrible
memory. I let a few more tears fall before I wipe my
eyes and face. I start the truck again, gaining a bit
more control over myself, and I pull back on the
road.

The short drive to Annie and William's is painful,
depressing, and I fear I'm falling down the same hole
as I did years ago. But the thing is, I don't know how
to stop it. I have no idea how I'm going to patch my
broken heart together again.

Carter

# CHAPTER 10

## Carter

I watch Shelby leave, and I know she's going to need a lot of convincing after this. Rubbing the back of my neck, I'm unsure of how in the hell I'm going to fix this. I make my way back inside when I can't see William's truck anymore, and slam the door shut behind me. I'm pissed the fuck off Bethany would do something like this. Stomping through the house heading to the guest room she's staying in, I forcefully open the door. "You have five fucking seconds to explain what the hell that was." I can't feel bad for yelling at her. This is such bullshit.

I never fucked Bethany.

I never fucking touched her.

I didn't even know she was in the same bed as me until I woke up this morning. This whole fucked up situation is just bullshit. I'm being blamed for something I didn't do, and a part of me is pissed at Shelby since she didn't even give me the chance to explain. And now she probably won't. She'll assume the worse not caring about the truth.

Just like she had thirteen years ago. I might have pushed her away letting her slip through my fingers, but I had good reasons for doing what I did. And there's so much more to the story than she knows.

"Why are you yelling at me? I didn't do anything."

"Bethany, don't test me right now. Shelby saw you were in here, and now she thinks we fucked."

She rolls her eyes and crosses her arms. "That's her problem, not mine. It's not my fault she runs away like a child every time something doesn't go her way."

"Is that really what you think of her?"

"Of course. Why else would she do it?"

I take a deep breath, finding it's getting harder by the second not to lose my temper. "First off, you have no idea what Shelby has been through, and it's none of your fucking business to know or to judge her." I point my finger at her saying, "Second, you forget I fucking know you, and you never do anything like this without an agenda. Thirdly, you and I have never slept in the same bed let alone the same room, so care to explain this to me?"

She looks away and huffs out a breath. I clench my jaw and let my hand drop waiting for her to tell me what the fuck she was thinking. "Carter, I'm going to tell you something, but..." She looks at me and says, "I don't think you're going to say the same thing back."

"What are you talking about?" I'm losing my patience with her. She better have a really good fucking excuse for doing what she did.

"Carter, I … I'm in love with you, okay? There I said it and now you know." What the fuck? Shocked doesn't even begin to explain how I feel about her admission. "I can see you're confused and shocked, so I'll explain a bit for you. I knew I had feelings for you about a year after we met. I knew you still loved … her, but I was willing to wait until you got over her. I thought it would only be a matter of time before you finally gave up on her after you told me some of what happened between you two, but I really didn't think she'd come back." I'm reeling from hearing her words and finding out she had feelings for me all this time. I stare at her utterly dumbfounded, and I have no idea what to say. "Carter, please say something."

"I don't know what to even think right now. What would you like me to say? Why would you push me to other women, but yet you say you love me? Not to mention I've seen you with other guys. This makes no fucking sense."

"I dated only to move on but when it never happened, I just used them. And I thought if you started dating again you'd forget about her."

I can only shake my head as I interrupt her before she can say anything else. "And then what? I'd come running to you? Why would you even think that?"

"Because, Carter. I thought you'd finally see me as more than a friend."

"I'll never see you that way, Bethany. It's always been her, and that'll never change." She balks at my words as if they slapped her in the face, but it's the truth. Even after thirteen years of not being with Shelby and her coming back, still hasn't made my feelings change. If anything, I want her more now than I ever did.

"You can't mean that. You just need more time, and you'll see there's something between us."

"What else do I have to do to show you that it's not going to happen? At least not romantically. You're my friend, or was fuck I don't know what to think of you anymore." I shake my head and walk out of the room. I need a minute to process this, and knowing one of my friends has probably ruined everything I had going with Shelby … is devastating. I don't know how this happened, or how I didn't see Bethany's feelings for me. But what shocks me the most is the cruelty I've noticed in her since Shelby has returned. It's as if she's a completely different person. I never knew she could be this way, and I wonder if she's showing her true colors. Sure she's played pranks on people and talked shit, but she's never done something that would hurt anyone else. What if this is how she really is, and I just got the version she wanted me to see? I stare at nothing as I walk into the living room and sit down on the couch. I lean my head back and run my hands down my face. I have no clue how to handle this, or how to get past this with Bethany. Can we even go back to being friends after her confession? Do I really want to be around someone like her? I don't know the answers. I don't know what to do, or how to get Shelby to listen to me.

Bethany royally fucked me over.

"Carter, there's something else I need to tell you."

I drop my hands to my sides when I hear her voice. I sigh deeply before asking, "What else could you possibly have to say?"

I feel the couch dip, but I don't turn to her when she starts talking. "There's a reason I didn't think Shelby would ever come back. When you told me she left you, I did some research. I found something, and I know she hasn't told you."

"Out with it already," I huff out.

"She was married, Carter."

I snap my head to her, but I don't believe it. "Why would you lie about something like that? Look I get you want me for yourself and it's not going to happen, but to lie to me. That's a low blow, Bethany."

"I'm not lying to you. I get you're pissed at me, but I swear I'm telling the truth." None of this is making sense. My head starts to pound taking everything in. I look away as she gets up and says, "I get you don't want to believe that she did move on and had another life without you, but it's the truth. Google it and see for yourself." She disappears for a moment, and she looks at me before she walks out the front door saying, "She doesn't deserve a second chance with you." I don't bother to get up, or to try and go after her when she slams the door shut. I don't have it in me.

Not only have I lost Shelby, but I've also lost a friend.

I arrive at Cason's Fitness Studio, and I'm glad my brothers aren't here yet. I need some time alone to work off my anger and frustrations. I definitely don't need Caden's smart ass comments because he'll only piss me off more than I already am. Cason's gym is similar to every gym. Basic equipment for lifting weights, and treadmills line the walls to the left. There's a huge ring in the middle of his gym for fighters of a variety of styles to come and develop their techniques. Behind the ring, blue padding mats are laid out for his self-defense lessons. There's also an office, locker rooms, and a private workout room in the back. Awards of the fighter's that's trained here line the walls, and inspirational quotes make it easy to keep the motivation going. It's a nice setup, and I'm glad Cason bought this place when he did. It's on the outside of town, but not so far away that it's a hassle to come to every day. Caden and Cason will be here soon, and I remind myself to ask where they were this morning when the shit hit the fan. And what happened to Caden's date? After Bethany left, I went looking for them but Caden wasn't in the room I put him in, and Cason's truck wasn't in the driveway.

Blondie was nowhere to be found, and I'm assuming either Cason ended up leaving late last night since he didn't have as much to drink, or they left this morning before anyone else woke up.

Either way, it would've been nice to have my brothers there to lean on, and to help me figure out what the fuck I'm going to do about Shelby. Not to mention help me process what Bethany told me. Now that I've had time to think about things, I'm too angry for talking. Which is why I'm at Cason's gym ready to go a few rounds with the punching bag. I drop my bag by the mats, and sit on the bench to quickly wrap my hands in tape. Once I'm satisfied, I get up to stretch my arms and neck. Walking in front of the heavy bag, all I have to think about is the shattered look on Shelby's face to get me going. I start hitting the bag with my right hand, then add my left, making sure to hit as hard as I can. My blood starts pumping along with my heart when I pick up my pace and punch the bag faster and faster. Sweat starts to coat my whole body, but I don't stop. I keep Shelby's heartbroken look focused in my mind fuels my anger more.

It makes the rage inside of me boil knowing I'm the reason she looked that way. I couldn't control Bethany's actions, but I should've known she was up to something last night. I move slowly around the bag keeping up with my punches, and replay how Bethany acted. She was flirting with me and touching me every chance she could. She wouldn't leave my side, and for the life of me I couldn't figure out why she was acting so different. I'm reminded of her texting me and asking to come over to talk, then before I could tell her no she showed up. I think of our argument and how spiteful she was when she realized Shelby was there hanging out. I knew Bethany didn't like that Shelby and I were becoming closer with each passing day. On multiple occasions Bethany would talk shit about Shelby and even though I told her to chill the fuck out, I never knew this was coming. If I had known beforehand of Bethany's feelings her intentions, I would've made sure to keep my distance and to keep her away from Shelby.

There's only one woman I've ever loved and still want more than anything. The sooner Bethany realizes that the better off I'll be.

The thing that drives my forceful jabs the most is the fact that Shelby was married. Not only did she leave everyone that cared for her behind she had moved on, or at least seemed to have moved on. I don't know how long she was married or when they divorced, but knowing it wasn't me she was with it fucking rips me apart. It's as if my soul is crying out in agony. I have no one to blame but myself. Even knowing that I'm still hurt she didn't tell me herself. I have no idea why she chose to keep that part of her life from me, and I have a feeling it has something to do with the scar on her lip. I want her to open up to me but God help me, if she tells me her ex hurt her, I'll probably end up in jail.

Brie Paisley

I stop for a moment to wipe the sweat off my forehead when I hear the door to the gym shut. I don't look to see who came in because I know it's my brothers. The only day the gym's closed is on Sunday's, and we're the only ones able to come and workout. I turn back to the punching bag still feeling the frustration of this morning.

I hear one of the twins come up behind me, and I don't stop what I'm doing when I realize it's Cason talking. "How long have you been here?"

I jab right twice then left once before saying, "I don't know. An hour or so."

"Oh shit. What happened?" Caden asks.

I choose not to answer yet, but Cason does. "What makes you think something's wrong?"

"Because he's here early and he's killing the punching bag."

"Carter, did something happen?" Cason asks, and I stop my assault on the bag knowing it's time to confide in my brothers.

Walking over to the bench, I rip off the tap on my hands. Using my shirt to wipe the sweat off my face, I take a deep breath before I begin. "Shelby thinks I fucked Bethany."

"Whoa, I need to sit down for this." Caden says as he takes a seat by me, and Cason stands in front of us with his arms crossed. "Alright, start from the beginning, but talk slowly because I have a bitch of a hangover."

I ball the white tape up and hold it in my hands. I need something to keep me grounded, and I stare at the ball of tape as I explain. "When I woke up this morning Bethany was in the bed with me. At first I thought I did something really fucking stupid, but I knew I hadn't because one I'm not that guy. Two, I wasn't that drunk. Thirdly, I kissed Shelby and would never do anything to fuck up another chance with her." I look up at Cason and he nods, knowing I'm right. Caden stays silent and I take it as my cue to continue. "I didn't want to wake Bethany because I knew Shelby was across the hall, and dammit I knew how it would look if anyone saw me walking out of the room with her still in the bed. I didn't know what else to do but to sneak out so I did or tried at least. As soon as I opened the door, Shelby was standing right in front of me." I drop my head staring at the ball of tape again. "Shelby saw Bethany in the room, and assumed I'd slept with her. She didn't even give me a chance to explain, and ran off before I could do anything."

"Damn. This is fucked, man."

I turn to Caden and say, "Oh you think? And what gave it away?" I clench my jaw and say, "I'm sorry. I'm just frustrated with that, and what Bethany told me soon after Shelby ran for the hills."

Caden slaps my shoulder as he says, "I get it. You're fucked and you're pissed."

"Caden, can you not make shit worse? Sometimes I really don't know how you're my twin."

"Hey! That really hurts my feelings."

Cason rolls his eyes as I but in. "Can you two not fight? Major issues going on, and I need help."

"You're right, tell us what happened with Bethany," Cason says and Caden nods in agreement.

"Y'all are not going to believe this, but she told me she's in love with me."

Cason frowns, and Caden all but yells, "What the fuck!"

"Wait, she really said that?" Cason asks.

"Yeah. She shocked the hell out of me too, but the more I thought about it the more it makes sense. She was all over me last night, and it was to make Shelby jealous." Cason starts to pace and Caden I think is stunned into silence. "There's one more thing too."

"You've got to be kidding me. What more could happen to you in such a short amount of time?"

"You read my mind, Caden." I rub the back of my neck as I say, "Shelby was married."

Cason stops pacing and stares at me with wide eyes. Caden lets out a deep breath before saying, "How are you not drunk right now? I mean I'm glad you're here instead of drowning in a bottle, but fuck. This is a lot to let sink in."

"Believe me, I've thought about it. You have no idea how much today fucking sucks."

"What do you need us to do?" Cason asks.

"Tell me what I need to do because right now, I'm fucking clueless."

Cason nods as Caden tells me, "I think the best thing you can do is give her some space. She's going to need some time to let off some steam, and I don't think it's going to do any good to try and talk to her while it's fresh on her mind."

"You probably shouldn't call or text her either," Cason adds. I nod, not really liking that I won't be able to try and explain, but they both have a point. Shelby isn't the type to let go of her anger easily. Her running away for thirteen years reminds me of that. "Caden and I will still talk to her, and hopefully between the two of us, we can get through to her and she'll actually listen when the time is right."

"Yeah, we'll double team her." I frown, and Cason shakes his head. "Wait that didn't come out right."

"No shit. I know what you meant, but you need to think before you speak." Caden shrugs his shoulders, but he knows I'm right.

"Don't worry, Carter. We'll help you get her back." I nod at Cason's words knowing he's telling me the truth. My brothers will do anything to help me and for that I'm grateful. Caden might say a lot of inappropriate things and Cason doesn't say much, but I know no matter what, they'll have my back.

I know I can always count on any of my brothers. Because we're family and family doesn't turn their back on a brother in need.

"Thank you both for this. I know I won't be able to fix this on my own." It's the truth. It's one thing that Shelby let me get close to her after everything I said to her years ago, but it's another for her to think I was with someone else. Damn, this feels like déjà vu. "Anyway, now that we have a game plan anyone want to tell me what happened to Blondie last night?"

"Who? What blonde?"

Cason and I stare blankly at Caden, wondering if he really is that hungover. "Seriously? You don't remember the skinny blonde that was hanging all over you last night?"

Cason shakes his head as Caden seems to think about my question. "The damn girl you met on Facebook," Cason explains.

"Oh right! Wow I must have drank way more than I thought. I really don't know. The last thing I remember is you," he says to me. "Putting me to bed. The rest is a fucking blur."

"Fucking hell. This better not come back to bite us in the ass." I don't say anything as Cason scolds his twin. Sometimes it's best to let them banter back and forth. Cason's the only one Caden really listens to when it counts. I sit back on the bench as they continue to argue, and I can't help but smile watching them.

Even with all their faults, there's no one I'd rather have in my corner than these two dipshits. They make life interesting, and just knowing they care enough to do whatever they can to help me, it makes me damn proud to call them brothers.

Two. Fucking. Weeks.

I can't stand it any longer. Two weeks of utter silence from Shelby is killing me, and I feel as if I'm going insane. I've tried to stick with the plan and be patient. I've tried to listen to Cason and Caden's advice but dammit, I can't stand it any longer. It's not enough just getting brief details of when my brothers see or talk to her. I need more. I need to see her, talk to her, or just text her. I'd settle for watching her at her workplace, or seeing her in passing. Anything at this point would do. Maybe it's the reassurance that things are going the way we hope is what I need. Mostly I just need to talk to her and try to explain shit didn't go down like she thought. I feel the guilt eating away at me, knowing she thinks I fucked someone else after kissing her. I'd never do that, have never done that, and I most certainly won't give up on my chance to make things right.

Which is why I'm sitting at my usual booth at the Waffle House with Caden and Cason. I need to see her, and I can't stand the distance any longer. "Are you sure this is such a good idea, Carter?" Caden asks. I rub the back of my neck hoping this wasn't a mistake. "I mean she hasn't even noticed we're here yet and the last time I talked to her, she wasn't keen on the idea of talking let alone seeing you."

He has a valid point, but I'm willing to risk it. "I have to see her. I can't wait any longer."

Caden shrugs as Cason says, "I have to agree with dipshit on this one. I don't think she's ready yet, Carter."

I clench my jaw not liking how both my brothers are against me seeing her. I look at both of them, seeing a worried expression written all over their faces. They have every right to be concerned, but dammit if I care. "One day, y'all will understand why I'm doing what I am. She slipped away from me once, and there's not a chance I'm going to let it happen again." They don't comment, and I'm glad for it. I need their support even if this turns out to be a shit move.

As if I can feel her presence, I look up and see her at a table not far from ours taking an order. I gaze at her willing her to glance my way. She quickly finishes taking the older couples order, and when she starts to move away from their table, she looks directly at me. She frowns then drops her head. I can tell she's not happy to see me, and as she walks towards our booth, I see her hand clenching at her side. She doesn't even look at me as she takes Caden and Cason's order. I start to tell her what I'd like, but she doesn't give me the chance. "I know what you want."

I sigh and drop my head as she storms off. I shake my head when Caden says, "I told you so."

"Could you not be an asshole right now?" I look up and tell Caden.

"I'm sorry, man. We told you she wasn't ready."

"I know, Caden." Cason backhands him on the shoulder, and they glare at each other. I search for Shelby as they start with their twin bond. I rest my hands under my chin as I watch her behind the counter filling drink orders, and bringing customers their food. She seems fine on the outside, but I know she's anything but that. She smiles and talks to her customers, but I can tell it's fake. Her entire body seems tense, and I watch her clench her jaw more than once. I have to admit, she's got the pretending part down, and I wonder how she managed to hone that skill so well. Before I fucked up years ago, Shelby wore her emotions on her sleeve. They were visible to anyone paying attention, but I always knew when something was bothering her, or if something was wrong. Like now. I can just sense it. It's as if my soul is connected to hers, and whenever she needs me, even if she doesn't see it, I just … know. I might not know how to fix this between us, but I'm going to do whatever it takes to make it right again. I can't go another day knowing she thinks I fucked Bethany. I haven't even talked to Bethany since she admitted her feelings. She's tried a few times, but I don't know what to say to her just yet. I don't know if we can even be friends again after all she's done. All her texts and calls go unanswered from me. At least until I can figure out what to do.

A few moments pass before Shelby comes back to our booth with our drinks. It guts me she won't even look at me. When she turns to walk away from me again, I get up from the booth and grab her wrist. She turns as she jerks her arm away from me, but it's the fear in her voice that makes me regret touching her. "Don't fucking touch me!" She stumbles backward as she clutches her arms to her chest with tears in her eyes.

"Shel, I'm sorry." She slowly backs away and the frightened look in her eyes is what makes me stay where I am. She turns away from me, and darts to the back of the restaurant. I run my hands down my face wondering if I should go after her, or give her some time alone. I stand for a few minutes before sitting back in the booth, and notice every single person in the Waffle House staring at me. I look around, and realize it's too quiet. I clench my jaw knowing I fucked up, and now everyone will probably think the worst. I close my eyes for a second trying to get a hold of myself. I can feel the immense regret and guilt trying to take over, but fight like hell to make it stop.

"Well that certainly didn't go as planned," Caden says.

I open my eyes, and glare at him. Cason just rolls his eyes, knowing now isn't the time to speak. I don't even bother to say anything back to Caden. He's right, and I should've listened to them. But I didn't, and now I have to live with that image of Shelby's face burned in my mind forever. I start to feel sick to my stomach the more I think about it, and decide I need to get the fuck out of here. I give my brothers one final glance before I get up and walk out of the restaurant. I don't bother looking back, and quickly get into my truck slamming the door shut behind me.

Before starting the engine and driving off, I bang my hands on the steering wheel as I scream out loud. I hold onto the wheel as tight as I can willing this immense sense of dread to go away. I don't care if anyone can see me. Half the town saw how Shelby ran away from me as if I hurt her. I don't understand why she reacted the way she had, and knowing I'm responsible guts me. I clench my jaw willing the pain in my heart to dissipate.

I have to get this regret and guilt out.

I have to get Shelby's terrified look out of my mind.

But damn if I know how or where to start.

# CHAPTER 11

## Shelby

I need air.

I need to escape.

I can feel the walls of the restaurant closing in on me, and I heave in a breath as I run out the back door. The humid air hits me, but I welcome it. I suck in a much needed breath, feeling my lungs burn, and pull at the collar of my shirt trying to clear my airway. My heart races rapidly in my chest, and it feels almost as if it's ready to burst. I lean my head back as the tears begin to roll down my cheeks, and bite my bottom lip trying to hold in the agonizing scream wanting to come out. I clutch my hands to my chest trying to keep myself together. It wasn't seeing Carter sitting with his brothers at their usual booth, or the fact Carter tried to talk to me that sent me into an emotional frenzy. It was the flashback of the past. It was the familiar pressure of Carter's hand on my wrist that did it for me.

All I could see was Easton grabbing me roughly. Easton's angry face and teeth clenching as he yelled at me. I couldn't get those images out of my head, and knowing I thought it was Easton grabbing me instead of Carter, it's something I never thought would happen. I know Carter would never hurt me. He'd never put me through half of what Easton did, but I can't control when the flashbacks come. I haven't had one since seeing Carter again until today. I honestly don't know why I went back to the dark place in my mind. Maybe it's because Carter caught me off guard. I wasn't expecting Carter to touch me, let alone grab me to get my attention.

I slowly open my eyes, and raise my head as I lean against the brick wall. I chastise myself for letting things between Carter and I go this far. I knew it was only a matter of time before he sought me out and with Caden and Cason constantly telling me to talk to him, I figured he'd eventually show up. I was hoping Carter would come to Annie and William's not where I work. My outburst is surely going to cause drama with my boss, but fuck if I could help it. I slowly slide down the wall ignoring the pain of the bricks on my back. I pull my knees to my chest, and lay my head down on my knees. I feel my chest start to ache, and I already know the reason why.

I miss Carter. I miss talking to him. I miss the way he makes me feel, and the way I always seem to have a smile on my face when I'm near him. I half expected him to follow me, but I know he won't. Not after he saw the way I reacted. It kills me knowing he thinks he caused me to flip out and run away, but that's not even the half of it. I just wasn't ready to face the truth of the morning I saw Bethany in his bed. Caden and Cason have made me question that morning more than once, but there's something that keeps holding me back. I don't want to be ripped into pieces again. I don't want to feel heartbroken, shattered, and most of all I don't want to feel the regret I have constantly consuming me. There's a hole inside of me and with each day I'm not with Carter, it grows and soon I don't think I'll ever be able to fill it. What scares me about the entire situation is, how am I going to move on if what I saw was the truth? How will I make it a second time around knowing this is the same exact feeling I had thirteen years ago? I don't want to do this again. I don't want to feel these fucked up emotions but a part of me, the one that still needs Carter, is telling me if I don't at least listen to what he has to say I'll never forgive myself. It's just hard to figure out which part of me wants what more. I could run away again, knowing if I don't get deeper involved with Carter I might not suffer as much if shit doesn't go well, or I could push these unwanted thoughts away and hear him out.

Run or stay?

I wish someone would just tell me what to do. It would make my life so much easier, but I know that won't happen. I can only decide what to do, even if it'll hurt more in the long run.

# Carter

I sit on the tree swing in Annie and William's backyard thinking over my options. It's been two days since the incident at work, and I'm still confused as to what I need to do. The sun is getting ready to set and I stare down at the ground, and kick a few rocks with the toe of my shoe as I weigh my options. Talk to Carter or not talk to him? Maybe I should pick a flower by the wooden fence, and try my luck with the petals. At least then I would know and stop going back and forth with my decision. I've talked to Annie about it, and although she helped bring more into perspective, she refused to tell me what I needed to do. She kept saying, "You already know, Shelby," but dammit if I know what she means by that. Annie's good at being cryptic with her words. I know I'm being childish by not making a choice, but when my heart's on the line, I need to take my time.

It didn't end so well for me last time.

I've decided I won't move away no matter the outcome. I'm comfortable being home, and I can't bear to be away from Annie or William again. They've helped me so much since I got back, and I can't even think about not seeing them every day. I just wish knowing what to do about Carter was as easy. I sigh deeply, and turn as I see something moving out of the corner of my eye. I watch Carter walking down the back porch steps and with each step closer, my heart beats faster. My stomach flutters at seeing him, and I notice how tired he looks. He hasn't shaved in several days, and his eyes look exhausted. I'm glad I'm not the only one losing sleep over this between us.

He stops a few inches in front of me and he grins when he sees me. We gaze at each other for a moment before he asks, "Can I push you?" I smile and look away remembering he asked me the same thing when we first met. He lightly touches my hand and when I glance up at him, I can tell he's not sure if he made the right move. His eyes hold so much pain and sorrow in them, and it makes me suck in a breath at the intensity. I slowly nod my head letting him know it's okay to touch me and to start pushing me. I make myself relax as his hand leaves mine, and he walks behind me. I feel his hands gently touching my lower back, and he slowly pushes me forward. I hold on tight to the rope of the swing and lean back as Carter continues to push me higher and higher. With each touch of his hands on my back, I feel myself letting go and the chains that bind my fragile heart release. I find myself grinning widely, and let out a loud laugh as he pushes me one final time. I feel as if I'm that broken five year old again, and nothing can hurt me.

It's not because I seemed to be flying. It's because Carter is here. It's because I know if I were to fall, Carter would be there to catch me.

He's always been there for me, and the one that never seemed to have left my heart. Annie's words replay in my mind as Carter slows me down, and I know what she meant now. I let my fear of being hurt overshadow what I really needed to do, and now that

Carter's here, I can have the much needed conversation with him. It doesn't seem strange to me how things have finally clicked into place since Carter showed up. It was always this way between us. No matter how much I fought within myself about us, or anything else, just being near him made my choices easier.

I come to a stop and Carter walks in front of me. I open my mouth to say something, but I have no idea where to start. I have so much to ask him and so much to tell him. At my continuous pause, he takes it as his cue to begin. "Can I explain first? Then you can tell me whatever you want, and if you still don't want to see me afterward I'll understand." My stomach clenches at his words wondering how bad it'll be. I also notice he seems unsure of how I'll react, and he stares at me until I nod my head. He takes a deep breath and says, "I know how bad it looked when you saw Bethany in the same bed I was in and trust me if the roles were reversed, I would've thought the exact same thing." I hold in a breath as he continues, afraid of what he'll say. "But I swear I never touched her. I promise you. I never slept with her, and I don't have any type of feelings for her what so ever." He pauses for a minute, and I let out the breath I was holding. I know he's telling me the truth. Caden and Cason have repeatedly told me that things didn't happen the way I thought, and I know neither one of them would tell me that if it weren't true. Plus I can see it in his eyes as they plead for me to believe him, and he has no reason to lie to me now. "I didn't even know she got in the bed with me let alone how she felt about me," he shakes his head and starts to rub the back of his neck.

"How she felt?" I ask even though I already knew Bethany had feelings for him.

He gazes at me as he says, "She told me she loved me." He says it as though it came as a shock, and I realize he didn't have a clue of how she felt. "If I'd known, I would've … hell, I don't know. I would've stayed away from her, or done something to prevent what she made you believe. I feel as if I should've known how she felt, but I either looked over it or just wasn't paying attention." I watch him as he squats down in front of me and holds onto the outside of my thighs. I swallow as his touch sends warmth throughout my entire body, and I definitely don't miss the comforting caress of his fingers. "Maybe I just didn't see it because there's only one woman I've ever loved, and still want." Licking my lips at his confession, I know I'm the one he's talking about. It's hard not to believe him, especially as his eyes fill with desire and longing. He reaches up to cup my cheek with one of his hands, and I let myself lean into his gentle touch.

All the reasons to stay away seem to fade to the back of my mind and for the life of me, I can't seem to remember why I wanted to stay away from him. Carter's always had that effect on me. I close my eyes as he rubs his thumb over my face and listen as he says, "I'm so sorry you thought I'd slept with her. I hope you know I would never do something like that, and I would never do anything to risk losing you again."

Slowly opening my eyes, hating I assumed the worst. I should've listened to him. I should've stayed to let him explain. "I'm sorry I took off before you could tell me this." I glance down saying, "All this could've been avoided if I hadn't run from you."

He raises my head with a finger under my chin and he whispers, "You have nothing to be sorry about. All we can do now is move forward. That is if you want to. I need you, Shel."

I grin at his sweet words as I reach up to hold his hand on my face. I look deep into his eyes and honestly tell him, "I need you too, Carter." He beams at me and I know he's happy I finally admitted my feelings out loud for him. It's a relief actually to let him know that I do need him. It's always been him. I hope he knows just how much, and that I'm putting my trust in him not to hurt me. I know I still have a long way to go before my past doesn't have a hold on me, but I also know it's time to let Carter be here for me. He'll help me get through the rough patches, and remind me of the good times.

I watch him curiously as he slowly drops his hand from my face and stands. He holds out a hand for me and asks, "Want to go somewhere with me?"

I place mine in his without question and answer with a simple, "Yes."

He helps me off the swing and pulls me to his chest. His hands hold me tightly, as close as I can be to him, as if he's afraid I'll take off at any second. I suck in a long breath taking in his manly smell, and he leans his head against mine as he asks, "You ready to go now?"

I let out a laugh and say, "Yes, Carter. Take me anywhere because from now on, wherever you go, I'll follow you."

He pulls back and gazes at me, and declares, "Good, because I'm never letting you go again."

I blush and look away as Carter parks his truck at the lock and dam. I'm reminded of all the times we used to come here when we were teenagers to make out. I hear him open his door, and moments later, I look up to him opening my side. I hop out with his help, and watch him as he reaches to the back seat. He pulls out a thick blanket and two pillows. He places them under his arm, and I laugh as I ask, "Did you come prepared for this?"

He shrugs as he says, "I'm always prepared. Plus I figured either I'd be here with you tonight, or I'd be here alone. Either way, I wanted to come and watch the stars."

I walk up to him and take a pillow out from under his arm and say, "Are you trying to seduce me?"

"Why? Is it working?" I playfully slap his arm and start to walk to the bed of his truck. Before I get too far, he takes my hand and pulls me back. I land against him, and my laugh slowly dies away as I look up at him. He gazes at me and I can't stop wanting him to lean down and take my lips. Instead of kissing me he says, "I've missed hearing you laugh."

"Still the charmer, I see."

He chuckles and says, "Only for you." I shyly look away and he slowly lets me go. I walk to the tailgate and let it down. I glance up to see him still standing there, watching me intently. I grin, as I climb up and wait for him to follow me.

"Are you going to stand there all night?" I finally ask when he's yet to move. He shakes his head and quickly makes his way over to me. I help him get the pillows and the blanket situated so it's comfortable for us, and I sit back against a pillow as he goes back to the front of his truck. I lean my head back as I hear Lovesong by Adele softly playing over the radio.

"Come dance with me," I hear Carter ask, and I don't waste a second before getting up and hopping off the truck. I wipe my hands off on my shorts hoping he won't feel how clammy they've become. Carter lightly grabs onto my waist, and I place my hand on his shoulder as my other sets in his hand. We stare deeply into each other's eyes as he leads me around with the music's beat. This song is perfect for us, and I can't help but feel he played this song on purpose. I don't mind though, and I don't comment on it either. I don't want to ruin our moment. It's everything I've been craving from him and I never want it to stop.

I let out a laugh when he catches me off guard making me do a turn. He dips me back, and holds me there for a moment as he stares into my eyes. I love seeing the smile on his face, and reach up to caress his scruff. His smile slowly disappears and his eyes fill with desire and lust. He guides me upright once the song is over, and I shiver when his hand travels down my arm. My eyes never leave his as he starts to lean into me. I ache for him to grab me and kiss me again, but he doesn't do that. I hope I hide my disappointment when he takes my hand, and leads me back over to the truck. He helps me climb up, and I take my spot as he sits beside me. I look towards the water, and listen to the waves crashing into the bank. I'm glad Carter parked us facing the water, and I rub my hands up and down my arms as I feel the cool breeze. I turn to Carter when I feel his arm wrap around me. He pulls me to his side, and I place my head on his shoulder sighing as his warmth surrounds me. Neither one of us say anything deciding not to break the silence. I don't mind it. I actually enjoy just sitting next to him, and letting him hold me. No words are needed and it doesn't seem possible, but I can feel how pleased he is with me just being here with him.

We eventually move to lay on our backs, and I curl up on my side against him with my head in the crook of his shoulder. He slowly runs his hand up and down my arm making sure I'm warm, and I look up to see his eyes are closed. The moon shines down on us brightly, and I'm glad so I can admire him. His other arm is under his head, and I grin seeing how relaxed he seems. His chest slowly rises

Carter

and falls, and I sigh deeply at hearing his heart beating strongly in his chest. It's a soothing sound one that makes the sensations of being complete fill me more than ever before. I realize the hole I felt days ago is starting to fill and I owe it all to him.

He slowly opens his eyes and when he looks down at me and smiles, my stomach dips. He raises up pushing my hair behind my ear. His touch is so kind and loving. He does it slowly and I take it all in, loving every second of it. "You know I never apologized for grabbing you the other day."

I want to look away, afraid he might see the truth of my past in my eyes, but I don't. His gaze holds mine and I can't seem to look away from him. "It's okay. I know you didn't mean to upset me."

"I know. But, I am sorry." He leans over me as he says softly, "I never want to see that look in your eyes again."

I let his words sink in before saying, "There are some things about my past I'm not ready to talk about yet," I swallow hard feeling my heart start to race just thinking about talking to Carter about my past. I know I can tell him anything. I know he won't judge me or feel sorry for me, but I'm not there yet. A part of me never wants him to know about my past, but that small voice in the back of mind is telling me eventually he's going to push me to tell him. "I can't promise you I'll ever be ready and it's not something I want to remember."

I hold onto his arm as he raises it to my top lip, and I hold my breath as he lightly touches the scar on it. I can guess he has an idea of what happened to me, but he doesn't say anything to push me to talk. At least not tonight. "You know I'll always be here for you, whenever you're ready."

"I know. You've always been here for me. Even when I was too stupid to see it."

I watch him as he smiles and shakes his head then he says, "Not stupid, Shel." He caresses my face with the palm of his hand as he leans down. He's inches from my lips and I slowly let out a breath. "Sometimes we have to lose something precious to us, before we realize how important is really was when we had it."

There's so much hidden behind those words, but I don't want to ask what he means. I can only focus on his lips and the word precious. "Am I something precious, Carter?"

"Yes. You're everything to me."

"You promise?"

"I promise with all that I am," he says and then he captures my mouth with his. His kiss is slow, precise, and it's filled with so much passion. It's tender, as if he's kissing me in the most delicate way he can manage. His hand continues to caress my face, and I let my hand roam up his back, to his neck, and finally they stop when I reach his hair. We both moan when our tongues touch, and I feel my entire body warming. It's not because I'm hot. It's because of his mouth, his touch, his very being, and the way he makes me feel whole again. Desire starts to take over and I wantonly move my hips closer to him. I need to feel him all over my body. His kiss starts to deepen as if he can feel my need for him rising. I pull him closer to my chest as his hand leaves my face and slowly makes its way to my leg. He gently pulls my leg over his, and he places his knee in between mine. He glides his hand up my leg, starting at my calf, to my knee, then to my thigh. He sucks on my bottom lip as he grabs onto my thigh tightly making me moan out loud for him.

I can feel his racing heart and it matches my own. I snap my eyes open as he pulls away. "Carter?" I ask breathlessly hoping he's not about to stop.

"If I'm going too fast just tell me to stop." I nod and I can't help but fall a bit more in love with him. He's always concerned for me. Always putting me first. It's still something I'm not used to and I know one day, I'll finally see that this is something Carter will always do for me.

He takes my mouth again, only this time, his kiss is more demanding and controlling. I grab onto him tighter enjoying it more with each dip of his tongue inside my mouth. Returning the kiss, I savor his taste and the way he feels against me. I arch my hips again as he cups my ass in his hand, and moan in his mouth when I feel his hard cock against my leg.

"Carter, please," I beg against his lips. I need him to ease this ache that's building. I'm afraid I'll burst if he doesn't do something soon.

He nips at my lips and leaves wet kisses on my cheek making his way down to my neck as he says,

"I have you, Shel." His hand on my ass slowly makes its way under my T-shirt, and my stomach quivers as he touches me. His palm is hot against my skin, but it feels so right. Carter kisses my neck as his hand continues to touch me, and when he takes a hold of my breast through my bra, he groans in my ear. The sound shouldn't sound so sexy, but I feel my pussy clench when he does it again. "Fuck, Shelby. I'd forgotten how good you feel."

"Don't stop," I cry out when he grabs my other breast. I arch my back letting him know how much I'm enjoying him caressing me.

"Should've taken you home so I can have my fill of you more thoroughly." He declares then nips at my earlobe. If he decides to stop, I think I might cry in frustration. Thankfully he doesn't, and his hand travels down. He stops his delectable kissing and looks at me. I suck in a breath, as his hand slips under my shorts, then under the band of my panties. Our breaths start to sound heavy panting, as I wait for him to touch me where I need him most. I feel him slowly touch my pussy, and I bite my lip as he runs a finger over my sensitive clit. My hips start to move searching for his fingers and I moan as he says, "Fuck," when he easily glides a finger inside of me. I close my eyes and lean my head back as he unhurriedly moves in and out of me. I dig my nails in his arm that's holding him up and my other on his shoulder. "Look at me, Shelby." I snap my eyes to his at his command, and he says in a husky voice, "I want to watch you come undone for me."

He adds another finger inside of me, and I gasp before calling out, "Oh, fuck, Carter." But I make damn sure not to look away. The moment is too intense for me to break our trance. He starts to speed up his movements, but they're still controlled. He curls his fingertips and wiggles them back and forth, hitting my G-spot. I almost close my eyes feeling the pleasure ripple through me. My hips move with his fingers, and my grip on him doesn't let up.

I can sense my orgasm coming on fast and Carter must feel it too. He leans down hovering over my lips and demands, "Let go for me, Shelby. Let me feel you come." Not even two seconds later, I feel my walls clenching around his fingers, and Carter captures my cries of pleasure with his mouth. I ride the waves of absolute bliss. Never wanting it to end. My entire body feels warm mixed with a numbing sensation followed right after.

It's ecstasy.

It's consuming.

I fear I'll never be able to get enough of the way Carter makes me feel.

I finally come down from my high and Carter slowly takes his hand out of my shorts. He lays his hand on top of my stomach, and he gazes at me with satisfaction gleaming in his eyes. He raises up to sweetly kiss my lips, and my grip on him finally releases. I let my leg that's over him fall beside my other one, and realize he's still hard. I start to lean up and reach down to please him but he stops me. "Lay with me."

I frown wondering why he doesn't want me to satisfy him. "You don't want me to return the favor?"

He chuckles, a sound I'm finding I like very much, and he pulls me back down by him. "I would love nothing more than for you to touch me and get me off, but I wanted to do something for you. I wanted to watch as you let go." He touches my lips as he says, "And seeing how beautiful you are while you came on my hand is enough for me."

"Carter, stop that," I say, and turn away. My face flushes and I'm thankful it's night and he can't see how red my face is. I don't know why I'm embarrassed.

"Don't be embarrassed. It was fucking hot as hell. And I definitely cannot wait to see you come undone again."

"You're so bad!"

We both laugh and he brushes my hair out of my face as he says, "I'm only what you need me to be, Shelby." I place my hand on his face taking him in and loving every second of it.

It's in this moment that I can't figure out why in the hell I've been running away from this man for so long. All this time I've spent away from him just seems cruel, and I tell myself there won't be any more running from him. He's everything I've ever needed, and it's time I start letting myself be with him and enjoy everything he has to offer me.

# CHAPTER 12

## Carter

Every day that I spend with Shelby, I can see the change in her. She's always smiling or laughing, and I've noticed she doesn't get lost in her thoughts as much. I'd like to think I've had a lot to do with that. We spend every chance we have together mostly at my house, watching movies or going out to eat. It's been three months since I got her back after the misunderstanding with Bethany, and I can only hope things between us continue to get better. I'm learning more about her than I've ever known, and I love how she's able to act the way she used to.

I'm finding I enjoy our routine, and I'm trying not to push her into anything she's not ready for. While I love kissing her sweet and seductive lips, I'm beginning to develop a serious case of the blue balls. I want to claim her, make her mine fully, but I want her to know it's not about the sex for me. I've craved this normalcy with her for so long, and now I'm living it almost every single day. I don't want to do anything to ruin it. But it is getting harder not to take her when I touch her, when I caress her soft skin, and especially when she begs me to fuck her. She makes it hard for me not to give into her desires and her need for me, but I want her to open up. I want her to tell me everything about her past, because I know it still haunts her. I've noticed over the past few months, every time I bring it up or ask a question about her time in South Carolina, she either avoids the question, or makes me forget with her luscious mouth. I'm a patient man, but fuck me I need her to open up fully to me. I need her to need me as much as I need her, but I can't be the man she wants if I can't help her get over the past.

Looking down at her sleeping next to me on the couch, I brush her hair out of her face. I pull her sleeping form closer to me, holding on tightly to her, because I have a feeling something is going to happen, and it'll rip us apart or she'll do what she does best. I hate I have that nagging feeling in the pit of my stomach about her up and taking off again, but I can't help it. Which is another reason why I need her to talk to me. She snuggles her face deeper in the crook of my arm, and I feel my heart clench with a familiar ache. She looks so peaceful and angelic like, as she sleeps and I know I have to have this with her every day for the rest of our lives. I want her to be mine totally and completely, not halfway like it is now. I just have no idea how to get her to talk to me without pushing her, and risking her running away from me. I cannot bear her leaving again. I cannot take knowing she'd rather run off instead of facing the problem that I can help her with. I know she's slowly getting better, but she should know more than anyone, that the past never stays where it belongs. Sooner or later it's going to smack us both in the face and I hope she knows no matter what she went through or what happened, I'll always be here for her.

That'll never change. No matter how much she tries to run from me or keep her past hidden, I'm not letting her go this time. I've never regretted something so much until I let her go thirteen years ago. Every single day without her, I knew I fucked up and made the wrong choice. Even if I thought I was doing the right thing for her. It was stupid of me to think I could live my life without her. I place a kiss on her forehead, wishing I could go back and change pushing her away. It seems like a waste I've been missing her for so long, knowing it didn't change anything. Sure she went to college, got a degree, and got married, but I never once stopped loving her. I've never stopped caring about her, or just thinking of her. I sigh, grateful she's here with me now, and maybe this is fate's way of giving me another chance with her. I'm glad for the second chance and it's one I'd never dreamed of having again.

When she starts to whimper in her sleep, I lightly run my fingers up and down her arm. She's done this multiple times and I've let it slide, not wanting to push her into telling me what her dreams are about. I want to know, need to know what makes her cry out sometimes in her sleep. Most of the time, she clutches my shirt as if she's holding on for dear life. I don't know how much more I can stand to watch and not confront her. Her pain in her cries chip away at my heart and my soul each time she calls out for me. Her breath comes out in pants, and I know this one is going to be bad. Her head starts to thrash back and forth and I gently shake her trying to wake her.

"No! Please, stop!" I clench my jaw hearing her plea.

"Shelby, wake up." I shake her a few times, but she's in her nightmare too deep. I don't know what to do, or how to help her. I pull my arm from under her head and lean over her, hoping the movement will wake her. It doesn't and I take a deep breath as I get off the couch. I know I have to get her out of the nightmare. She's starting to cry louder and she rolls to her side, as if she's trying to get away from something, or someone. I take a hold of her shoulders and shake her gently as I try to wake her.

She thrashes her arms out at me, fighting me off as she screams out, "Stop! Easton, please don't hurt me!"

I don't know what to do and hate that I feel so helpless. "Shelby, wake up!" Relief flows through me when her eyes open, but my stomach drops as I see the fear in her eyes. I slowly let go of her, and she covers her face with her hands as she begins to cry. I pick her up and sit down holding her tightly to me as she cries hysterically. I rub her back and tell her everything is fine now, but it seems no matter what I say, her sobs refuse to stop. I don't know who Easton is, but I have a feeling he's the reason for her nightmares. I want nothing more than to find this asshole, and beat the shit out of him for making Shelby go through this. I pull her back and wipe her tears away. She refuses to look at me and I softly ask, "Do you want to talk about it?"

She shakes her head and says, "It's nothing. I'm sorry you had to see that."

"This isn't the first time this has happened, Shel." I place a finger under her chin and make her look at me. "I think you need to talk about what's making you have these nightmares. It'll help you move on from them and you know I'm here for you no matter what."

More unshed tears fill her eyes, and I will her to open up to me. She sucks in a breath and leans forward as she says against my lips, "Make me forget, Carter." She takes my mouth urgently, and I want nothing more than to give her what she wants. I kiss her back, holding onto her thigh and caress her face. I can feel her tears as they fall on my face and I know I can't help her this way.

I slowly pull her back and plead, "Talk to me, Shel. I can't help you if you don't tell me what's really going on."

She recoils then quickly gets off me. Fucking hell. I know she thinks I'm rejecting her, but that's far from the truth. "I'll just go then. I can see you don't want me, and I'm sorry you have to deal with this shit."

I get off the couch and stand in front of her as I say, "No, you're not going anywhere until you explain why you keep having these nightmares, or why you keep shutting me out." I won't let her run away from this. Away from me.

"I can't, Carter." She shakes her head and says in a broken voice. "Please, don't make me."

I sigh, knowing this is probably going to hurt both of us, but she needs to get whatever's haunting her out. Taking her hand, I rub my thumb on the back of her hand as I say, "I need you to tell me. It's not because I want to push or hurt you, but because you need this. You can tell me, Shelby. Please let me carry some of that burden for you."

"You say that now, but trust me, you don't want to know."

"What do I have to do to make you see I'm here for you? That I want to help you and be the one you need? I can't do any of that when you continue to shut me out and run at every chance you get." I'm trying not to lose my temper, but fuck enough is enough.

She jerks her hand out of mine and steps back as she crosses her arms. "Fine. You want to know it all? Then I'll tell you, but I can promise you this, you're not going to like it."

I rub the back of my neck as I say, "I might not like it, but I'm willing to listen if it'll help you stop screaming out for me in your sleep." I close my eyes and let out a long breath. I open my eyes, then glance at her. Even if I'm about to fuck it all up, she has to know that I know she was married. I have a feeling this is what this entire situation is about. "Is it because of your ex-husband?"

Her eyes widen, and I know that's the last thing she thought I'd say. "How did you know I was married?"

"Bethany," is all I say and I know that's not what she wanted to hear.

"Really?" She lets out a laugh but there's nothing funny about this conversation. "I'm guessing she checked out my background then. Of course she'd tell you that. Of course she'd do everything she could to get you for herself." I start to stop her and tell her that's not why, but she doesn't give me the chance. "Let me guess, she probably painted my failed marriage in a perfect little picture didn't she?" Actually she didn't say anything about it, but I don't stop her from continuing. "There wasn't a single perfect thing about my ex-husband. There were no rainbows and sunshine and all that bullshit people say about being married. It was horrible. It was nothing more than a man trying to make me into someone I'm not, and constantly telling me I wasn't worth shit." I clench my hands to my side as her words continue to flow and she's right. I don't like this, or the way this conversation is going. "You want to know how my perfect life was? It was me always walking on eggshells. Being terrified of doing something wrong, and no matter how small it was, I always paid a price. At first, it was small things he'd say to me. But over the years, he didn't try to manipulate me. No, after my mother moved to South

Brie Paisley

Carolina, he wasn't so discrete about how he felt about me, or how much he thought I was nothing more than trash."

She turns away as if she's ashamed of what she's telling me. I want to comfort her tell her that bastard doesn't mean shit, but I'm rooted in place. I know she has more to say and more to tell me, but damnit as much as it hurts to see her this way, I have to let her finish. "The worst part about it, I wanted to be everything he wanted. I did every little thing he asked and more, but it was never good enough. My hair wasn't the way he wanted, I didn't dress sophisticated enough for his liking, or my favorite, I didn't please him the way he liked. It was always something, always his damning words cutting me deep to my soul. I'd much rather he had beat me than remind me how worthless I was. How I'd never amount to anything without him, and how he made me who I was." I stumble to the couch feeling as if I don't sit, I might fall to my knees. I thought it might be bad, but fuck I didn't realize how awful it was for her. I let my head fall as she continues on. "He made me want him. I hated how he'd go for weeks, and once for months without touching me or talking to me. He knew exactly what to do to make me do whatever he wanted, and I fell for it every time." My heart begins to ache hearing the agony in her voice. "I didn't think I was worth anything after a while. I thought no man would want me knowing how damaged and broken I was. After hearing the same hurtful words over and over, it's hard not to start believing them. My mother definitely didn't help. If I'd go to her and tell her what was going on, she'd tell me I needed to be better. I needed to stop being selfish, and be the perfect little wife I was expected to be. The thing is, Easton came at the perfect time and I don't know how he knew I was so vulnerable. Maybe he sensed it. I don't know, but at first he made me feel better. He made me forget."

I snap my head up hearing that and ask, "It's because of me, isn't it?" She slowly turns and I can see it in her sad eyes. It's my fault she went through all this. If I'd never pushed her away or let her go, she would've never had to endure any of it.

"You didn't want me anymore, Carter."

No, no, no. This wasn't how it was supposed to go. I stand up and pace in front of the couch. A wave of uncontrollable guilt comes over me and I yell, "Fuck!" I did this. I knew I fucked up, but knowing I'm the reason she was hurt so much over the years because of me … I can't take it. No wonder why she didn't want to see me when she first got back. No wonder she ran and shut me out so much. She didn't want me to know it's all on me for letting her go, and having to live through so much pain. But I tell myself I did it for the right reasons even if those reasons don't mean shit. Who am I kidding? I was selfish. I was young and I thought I didn't need her.

Was I ever fucking wrong.

I turn and look at her seeing tears falling down her face. I feel sick. I feel as if someone ripped my beating heart out of my chest, and all the breath in my lungs evaporate. "I'm so fucking sorry," I choke out and reach for her. She walks into my arms and she lets out another cry on my chest. I clench my jaw as I feel my own tears burning and a lump forms in my throat. I thought I regretted what I did before, but now the regret is almost too much to bear. I hold her tightly unwilling to let her go, and I can only hope she can forgive me.

She pulls back as she wipes her tears away. I push her hair out of her face and she takes a deep breath before asking, "Why, Carter? I have to know why you let me go."

I swallow, knowing no matter what I say, no matter my reasons, it'll never make up for what she went through. I hold her cheeks with both hands as I tell her, "I thought I was doing what was best for you. I knew you were putting your life on hold for me, and sitting around waiting for me to finish college. It killed me knowing you wanted to get away and live your life on your own, and I was doing nothing but holding you back." I slowly drop my hands as her tears start up again. "I was stupid, Shel. When you showed up at my fraternity house that night, and knowing you saw me hanging over that chick, I knew I'd fucked up. I never did anything with her. She was my buddy's chick, but it doesn't excuse anything. I shouldn't have lied to you, or been thinking about myself. The thing is, as I ran after you, something told me it was time to let you go. A voice in the back of my mind kept saying, 'stop hurting her and let her go'. I shouldn't have listened. Honestly, I don't know why I thought it was best for us to be apart, and I swear to you I've never stopped wishing I could take it back." My voice cracks and I step back, knowing there's nothing I can do to make her realize how much I want to go back and change everything. "Tell me you hate me, Shelby. Tell me how angry you are at me because if it had not been for me being so selfish, you would've never met that dick. You would've never went through hell and …" My voice breaks again and I can't find the words I want to say to make it right.

"I don't blame you anymore, Carter." I frown at her words, wondering why she's not yelling or running. "I did resent you at first for all the reasons you just said. But I can't hold you totally responsible for that. Yes, you might have been the catalyst, but in the end I choose to stay as long as I did."

"You wouldn't think that if you knew I came after you."

"What?"

I suck in a breath and rush out, "I came after you twice."

"I don't understand, Carter."

"The first time was two days after our fight. I rushed home and went straight to your house only to find you had already left. Your mother …" I rub the back of my neck, trying to get through this part. Shelby's mother is an evil bitch. "She answered the door and let's just say, she didn't paint a very pretty picture of me."

She steps closer to me and asks, "What did she tell you? Please, tell me, Carter."

Clearing my throat I say, "She told me how I'd never be good enough for you, and that you deserved to have a chance to start a life without me. She said you were glad I broke things off, and how happy you were for finally getting out of Columbus. Away from me. I shouldn't have believed her, but it didn't take me long to realize how I fucked up, and she hit every insecurity I had."

I can tell my words shock her. She shakes her head and starts to clench her jaw. "My fucking mother. I should've known. She's the reason for a lot of things, and I can't believe she would lie to you. She saw firsthand how broken I was when I came home after seeing you, and I should've known she was up to something when she literally pushed me out the door to run off to South Carolina." She huffs out a breath and adds, "She made running seem easy. Like it was my only option, so I did."

"I don't blame you for running. I knew what would probably happen when I decided to let you go, but I never thought any of this would happen. How are you not angry with me?" I truly want to know. I don't see how she can forgive me so easily.

"I was for a long time. But I can't be angry at you. Even if I don't agree with your reasons."

Walking to her, I pull her to me. Her hands land on my chest, and I run my hand through her hair as she looks up at me and I tell her, "I came for you a second time, too."

"Carter, please don't. Let's leave the past where it belongs."

I want to do as she asks, I really do, but she needs to know. "I have to, Shel. We're letting all past demons out, and if I don't it'll be like I'm keeping things from you."

She sighs, then says, "Alright."

I pull away from her and take her hand leading her to the couch. She straddles me willingly, as her hands rest on my shoulders and I hold onto her waist as I begin. "It was two years after not having you in my life, when one day I just couldn't take it anymore. I knew where you were only from keeping up with you on Facebook, and I caught a plane that same day to come see you. At the time, I hadn't thought it through. I just knew I needed you." I pause for a second, not wanting to remember how I felt as though I would die if I didn't see her. No words can explain how much I missed her, and I had this urge to be close to where she was. Her hand cups my face and I stare deep into her eyes hoping she sees how much I wish I could fix everything. "When I got to the campus, I looked for you for hours it seemed. Then when I'd almost given up, I saw you sitting by a tree. You weren't alone though. I watched as you laughed and seemed so happy. But when I started to walk towards you, I saw the guy you were with kiss you on the cheek, and I knew I had to leave. I knew my chance was over and I couldn't bear to take that happiness away from you." I remember that day all too clearly. I hated seeing her with someone else. I hated I lost my chance to make things right, and how my chest started to ache.

"Oh, Carter." I frown as she takes a deep breath. "That was Easton you saw me with." She looks away for a moment, then back to me. "I wasn't with him then. I know what day you're talking about. He tried for a whole year to get me to date him, but I couldn't let you go. Even when I finally gave him a chance and dated him for years, I never could let you go. I think he knew it too. Maybe that's why he was so cruel and hateful to me. I don't want to make excuses for what he did to me, but you were always the one, Carter." My stomach drops as the words leave her lips. All this time I thought I'd missed my chance, when I could've gotten her back. "Finish telling me what you want. I'm ready to move on from this."

Nodding, I suck in a much needed breath and tell her, "After seeing you with another man, things got really bad. I started to drink more and I came close to failing out of law school. I pushed my family away, ignoring them and not caring to see them when they came to check on me. I didn't deserve any of it. I didn't want their help or their kindness. I wanted to make myself suffer for losing you, and knowing it was all my fault. I was lost and I didn't know how to move forward."

Shelby surprises me when she leans forward and places a tender kiss on my lips. She takes her hand off my face and says, "I know exactly how you felt because I went through the same. Maybe not so much of losing myself in a bottle, but knowing loss is something I'm all too familiar with. But now that time for us is over. We're together now and I don't know about you, but I'm sick of living in the past. I'm tired of thinking about it, and remembering every single bad thing that's ever happened." I close my eyes as she runs her fingers through my hair. It seems crazy she's comforting me when I should be the one doing it to her. I open my eyes, gazing at her, and I can't help but fall more in love with her. "Why is it we can remember all the shitty things we've been through, and relive them so vividly?"

I move my hands up on each of her legs as I say, "I think it's because those moments define us. They mold and shape us to what and who we are today. It's because we want to remember so we can learn and not make the same mistakes again."

She grins and asks, "When did you get so wise?"

I smirk and say, "It comes with age, baby." She laughs and it's a sound that eases the guilt. It's still there, but knowing she doesn't hate me for all I've done and she can laugh with me, it helps tremendously. I stop my hands as they caress her face and lean up inches away from her tempting lips. "I am so sorry I fucked up, Shel. Please tell me I can make up for what I did. Tell me I can show you for the rest of my life how much you mean to me, and how much I need you by my side."

I watch as she licks her lips and she says softly, "I wouldn't have it any other way, Carter. I need you too much to run away from you again."

I sigh in relief and she has no idea how much those words mean to me. I move closer, hovering so closely to her lips as I demand, "Tell me you love me. Tell me how much you need me." I have to hear her say it. I know she loves me. I know she needs me more than anything, but hearing it and confirming it is exactly what will make me know she's mine.

She gazes into my eyes, and my heart drums heavily in my chest as I wait to hear the words I desperately yearn for. She takes a breath and I worry for a second she's not going to say what I want. "I love you, Carter." I smile and I rub my thumb over her face as she places her hands on mine. "I need you more than the air I breathe. I need you more than anything, and I can't see myself not ever needing you. I crave you, Carter."

I let my hand fall from her face and place it on her back, pulling her chest to mine. Her arms wrap around my neck as I say, "I love you, Shel. I've always loved you and nothing will ever change that." I close the small distance between us, taking her lips. I hear her sigh and tilt her head so I can deepen our kiss. I take my time with her. Savoring her taste, her smell, and the way she makes me feel. My heart, my soul, my entire being feels complete knowing she wants to be with me and to fight for what we have.

My hands travel down her body, and place them under her legs picking her up. My mouth doesn't leave hers as I start walking down the hall to my room. I hold her making sure to keep my grip tight, as I push the door open with my foot. I blindly feel for the light switch as I walk in the room and flip it on heading to the bed. Laying her down gently, to hover over her, she smiles at me as she holds onto my arms. I feel like the luckiest man alive.

As I caress her cheek, my heart beats rapidly in my chest knowing I'm about to finally make her mine.

Forever.

# CHAPTER 13

## Shelby

Carter stares down at me and I can see the lust and desire burning within his honey brown eyes. I reach up and take a hold of his neck pulling him down to me. I'm sick of waiting for him to take me. I know he's been waiting and being patient, before we took our relationship to the next level, but I've been more than ready. I knew from the moment he made me feel bliss in the back of his truck there was no going back.

Not now, not ever.

His mouth takes mine again and his kiss is so tender, full of passion, and I moan as his tongue caresses mine. I let my hands roam through this hair loving the feel of it against my fingers. Carter's hand runs up my leg, under my shirt, and he stops when he touches my bra. I arch my hips encouraging him to keep going, and to make me cry out with the pleasure only he can make me feel. He pulls his mouth off mine. I suck in a much needed breath, and turn my head to the side as he places hot kisses on my neck. His other hand grabs mine and he squeezes it, moving it above my head. It doesn't seem possible, but I can feel our connection. I can feel his love pouring into me, and he's barely touched me. My entire body zings with a delicious tingling sensation, and I slowly wrap my legs around his. There's no part of us not touching, or not being connected, and I want more.

I crave it.

I need it.

Just like I told him before, I have to have him like the air we breathe. After not feeling this kind of passionate love for so long, it's almost unbearable. He gently caresses my breast with his hand over my bra and I arch my back, trying to find more of his touch. He's turning me into a wanton woman, but thoughts of stopping his hands, or his body from not being this close, isn't even an option. I'd forgotten Carter's kind and loving nature. I'd forgotten how it felt to be loved by someone who truly cares and wants to spend every waking moment together. It's a powerful feeling. One that makes my heart flutter and makes my stomach dip.

When he bites my collar bone, I cry out but not in pain. No, Carter would never hurt me the way Easton had. My cries turn into a deep moan, and when his hips meet my aching pussy, I want to beg him to fuck me. I don't want him to take his time savoring me. I want him now. I need him now, and I don't think he knows just how much I do. "Carter, please." I moan with an unrecognizable voice. It doesn't sound like me. But I don't really think much about it. I'm already too far gone to care.

He nips at my earlobe, and with a husky voice he whispers, "I'm not rushing this, Shel. I have to savor you." He nips my lobe again. "To touch you in every way I can." I suck in a breath as his hands roam all over me attentively. "I have to have my fill of you and trust me." He raises up and we lock gazes as he says, "It's not going to be over any time soon." Fuck me. I don't know how to respond and he takes it as his cue to continue devouring me. He carefully moves down, and patiently pulls my shirt up. He leaves it covering my breasts, and my stomach jumps as I feel his breath tickling my skin. It's as if my body is hypersensitive, and every little caress is going to send me over the edge.

He plants sweet and tender kisses starting on my ribs, and I place my hands back in his thick hair as he moves around over my stomach. Hands are added to his kiss, and I lick my lips as I take in his warmth. All I can hear is the blood rushing to my brain. The familiar thump, thump of my heart and the ache, the need, shoots through me causing me to jerk him up to my mouth. Gone is his sweet and tender kiss. Carter takes my mouth like he's starving for me. Like he can't get enough and never wants it to end. His tongue dips in clashing with mine. Our teeth hit and when he pulls away quickly, he suddenly takes off my shirt. He tosses it off the bed and I don't look away from him to see where it lands.

Fuck the shirt. Fuck the clothes constricting us from touching skin to skin.

I feel my face flush as he gazes down at me seeing how much he appreciates my body, makes all my insecurities vanish. He slowly takes his forefinger, touching my necklace, moving down my chest over my racing heart, and slowly traces down between my breasts. My stomach is next, and his eyes follow his steady movement. Hungry and lustful eyes meet mine once he stops, and I swallow down a moan. I reach up to rid him of his shirt, but instead he takes both of my hands in his. He gently pulls me up and places me in his lap and my legs straddle his. I wrap my arms around his neck as he lets go of my hands, and my back arches instinctively when he runs both hands up it. Our eyes never waver as he brushes my hair out of my face, and I know I'm affecting him just as he is me. I hear his panting and see his chest rising and falling. I feel his hard cock against me, and I rock forward to make his cock touch my clit through our constricting clothes. The pressure is amazing and he groans as he closes his eyes. No words are needed because I know he wants me. I see it as he opens them and gazes at me adoringly. I've missed this look. I've missed the way my stomach flutters seeing him stare at me with such love and compassion. I move my hands down his chest taking my fill, and stop once I reach his waist. I wait to see what he does next, realizing the anticipation is really turning me on.

He cups my cheek, rubbing his thumb back and forth, before slowly sliding his hand down my neck. His touch is light, gentle, and he pushes my hair off my shoulder as he says softly, "You're so beautiful, Shelby." I close my eyes taking in his tender caress as he unhurriedly takes my bra strap and pulls it down. I feel the brush of his lips on my shoulder, and as he leaves small pecks following down where my strap hangs. His fingertips delicately run down my arm, leaving goosebumps behind. "I could spend all day showing you how much I love you." I can't stop the moan that escapes my lips hearing his words. Carter knows just what to say to make me fall even more in love with him. Just knowing he feels the same way as I do, thrills me unlike anything I've ever known before. I've never stopped loving Carter. Even if we were apart for so long, my feelings never changed. People say you never forget your first love, and I wholeheartedly believe that. I never thought he'd still care for me after learning some of the things I went through, but I should've known better. Carter's the most genuine person I've ever met, and he'd never turn his back on me. Especially when I need him the most. When he told me he loved me back, I felt my whole body let go of all the pain and suffering I'd experienced.

His love is all I've ever needed.

I open my eyes and keep them on him as he uses his other hand to tilt my head to the side, doing the same sweet and loving caress on my right arm. I cherish his touch, his caress. I shiver with pleasure when his hands roam to my back again, and he unsnaps my bra clasp. It slowly falls down as I pull my hands off his waist and he reaches to my front, grabbing the lacy bra tossing it on the floor. Before he can touch me again, I grab the bottom of his shirt quickly taking it off him. He grins at my sneaky and bold move, but I need his warmth touching me in every way I can get it. My breath catches in my throat as I stare at him, and even though I've seen him more than once with his shirt off. Being this close and feeling the sexual tension surrounding us, it seems as if I'm dreaming. I reach out my hand placing it over his fast pacing heart, just to be sure he's here. Looking up at him, he takes a hold of my hand and brings it to his lips. He presses light kisses all over my fingertips and pulls me to him. I place my hand on his shoulder as he takes my mouth again, and Carter's hands glide all over my upper body. When he cups my breast with both hands, he groans and I let out a squeal as he quickly flips me on my back. I don't have time to even get adjusted to the new position as he claims my mouth again, still kneading my breasts.

He hovers over me and one arm is placed beside my head holding himself up. Wrapping my legs around his waist, his other hand caresses my left breast firmly as I run mine up his back. His tongue dips into my mouth, and I twirl mine against his, loving how he tastes. When his hand moves to my other breast, I arch my hips, seeking the much needed attention to my aching clit. He presses his hips to mine, causing me to moan into his mouth, and I use my hands to pull him closer. Carter gives me a final peck on my lips, then moves down to my chin, slowly to down my neck, leaving me burning hotter than before with his kiss. He nips at my collar bone then kisses the sting of his bite away, before moving to my breasts.

He sucks and pulls at my sensitive nipple with his hot mouth. I can't stop from pushing my breasts to him wanting more. He chuckles then says, "You still love this?" He takes my other breast with his mouth, while his other hand kneads my other at the same time. He pinches my wet nipple with his forefinger and thumb before declaring, "I remember everything you love, Shel." I moan in agreement, thinking how could either one of us forget something that feels so fucking good. His hips press into me again as he takes one final nip at my breast. Then he starts to kiss down my ribs making it to my stomach, but once he reaches my pants he stops to look at me. I raise my head, wondering what he's up to as he traces his fingertips ever so lightly above my jeans. "Do you know what I want to do, Shel?"

I have an idea, but I breathlessly answer with, "No."

He grins, then plants a kiss under my belly button. He sits on his knees eyes focused on mine, as he unbuttons my jeans. I bite my lip wishing he'd hurry, but I don't speak. I can't form the words even if I wanted to. Carter has me in a seductive trance. One that I find I don't want to ever break. I glance down as he unzips my blue jeans, and I lift my hips when he starts to pull them down. Soon my jeans find the floor with the rest of my clothes, and all that's left is my panties. My head falls back down on the pillow when both of his hands glide up my legs. He reaches to the top of my panties, slowly pulling them down as I raise my hips for him. Glancing down at him, my nipples harden as he moves back in between my legs, and firmly grips my thighs. "Do you know now, Shelby?" He asks with a groan. He's inches away from my aching and wanting pussy. I arch my hips willing him to do exactly what I want him to.

"Carter, please," I cry out begging and pleading for him to devour me.

"Please what?"

I swallow, knowing he wants me to ask for it. My face flushes as does my whole body and I tell him, "You know what I want."

My eyes roll in the back of my head as his tongue licks me from top to bottom, and I'm left panting, craving more when he asks, "This what you want?"

He licks me again, and again, before I scream out, "Yes, please, Carter! More."

I feel the vibrations of his groan. A sound I'm loving more and more when he stops again. "I remember you loving this very much."

I raise up to my elbows and demand, "Carter, please stop teasing me and either fuck me, or use your tongue again." He chuckles, but he finally gives in and starts licking and sucking on my pussy. I fall back as I let out a cry of pleasure, arching my hips with his slow and deliberate strokes. His tongue dips in and out of me, and I don't try to stop the loud moans that escape me. He sucks hard on my clit as his hands on my thighs tighten their hold keeping me in place. I feel nothing but him. Nothing but sweet and blissful sensations raging havoc on my body. My stomach clenches as he nips at my sensitive clit and I push my hips closer to his mouth seeking more of his skillful tongue.

I instantly feel the familiar build of euphoria coming. I don't fight it. When Carter stops, I let out a frustrated groan wondering if he's just going to tease me all night. I open my eyes watching him as he hovers over me still wearing his jeans, as he says against my lips, "As much as I love your taste when you come, I want to be inside you. I have to feel you come undone on me. With me." I suck in a breath, finding I'm loving this side of him. When we had sex as teenagers it was sweet and innocent, since we were each other's firsts. But it was also awkward until after a few times. He never was controlling in the bedroom or assertive. It's a change. One that I'm thrilled to see happen.

I lean up desperate to rid him of his clothes as quickly as possible. My hands fumble with his belt, and I hear him snicker as I cuss. He takes my hands off his belt, and I stare into his eyes as he undresses. He has a satisfied grin, and I'm sure it's because I've turned into a sex fiend for him. I gaze down at his skillful hands as he unbuttons his jeans, and wet my lips wanting to taste him. My eyes slowly look him over, appreciative of his strong physique. He's not overly muscular, just enough to turn me on more as I take him in. My gaze is broken when he leaves the bed to discard his pants, and he stops for a second before taking off his boxer briefs. I glance up at him seeing him watching me, then he swiftly pulls his boxers down. I swallow deeply as my eyes travel down his body, and they stop at his rigid cock. I smirk when it jumps at my attention and look back up. I beckon him to take me with a crook of my finger, and he happily obliges.

He crawls over me, arms on either side of me, and I hold on to them needing to feel him more. He leans his head closer as I raise mine to kiss him deeply, passionately, and with so much love flowing through me into him. I can taste myself on him and the thought of him licking and pleasing me, makes my pussy clench with want and longing. I open my legs wider to accommodate him as he pushes his hips into me. I can feel his hard cock against me, his warmth, and everything in me wants him to take me, claim me, and never stop. He ends our kiss to stare at me, and I feel his cock right at my entrance. My hands move to his lower back pulling him closer, needing him inside of me, and the intensity in his eyes makes my pussy clench again with a feverous want. The need to be filled is driving me mad. "Carter, please." I beg.

"Fuck, Shel. I love hearing my name coming from your lips." He slowly slides the tip of his cock in and we both groan, feeling the instant pleasure from it. "Please tell me you're on some sort of birth control," he asks, stopping all movement.

"Yes," I breathe out. "I have an implant in my arm." I don't tell him Easton made me get it, but at the time I didn't want kids either.

I push all thoughts of Easton out of mind, knowing he doesn't belong here in this moment as Carter says, "Good because I can't have any barriers between us." As soon as the words leave his lips, he thrusts into me deeply making me call out incoherent words. My head rolls back, and my eyes close as he slowly pushes in and out of me. My hands move up to his arm, and to his shoulder as my legs tighten around him, keeping him right where I need him. I let the pleasure take over, as he stops to pull my chin down with his fingers. "Stay with me, Shel."

Slowly opening my eyes, I say with a sultry voice. "I'm here, Carter." My eyes stay on his as he takes me, claims me for his own, forever branding me. I can feel it in my heart, my mind, and my soul. I'll forever be his and nothing will come between us after this.

His thrusts are unrushed as he takes his time filling me with the bliss only he can bring me. I arch my hips meeting his thrusts, and his hands grab mine. His grip tightly holds onto mine as he pulls them over my head. I've never felt more connected to him than I do now. It's hard not to feel the love, the tenderness, and the absolute passion as he pushes deep inside me hitting my favorite spot over and over. I can feel my orgasm building, and it won't be long before I fall over the edge. Carter's pace quickens, but our gaze never wavers.

This isn't fucking. This isn't just another roll in the hay. This is special, meaningful, and it's us making love. Pouring everything we have into each other. I don't want it to end. I want this moment, the overwhelming surge of love and pleasure to last for a lifetime, but I know I can't hold my orgasm from taking over me any longer. My entire body is screaming for release. My toes curl as my body tenses, waiting for me just to let go and come completely and utterly undone.

Carter leans down and pushes his tongue deep in my mouth. I take all he gives relishing in the sweet bliss. He pulls back locking gazes with me again as he says with a groan, "Let me feel you, Shelby. Let go for me."

It's my undoing.

It's soul shattering, heart stopping, and absolutely breathtaking.

I cry out, letting the immense release rush through me. It's unlike anything I've ever felt before, and I never knew our love could be this powerful. Our hands tighten and when I feel Carter's release, it sends me in a carnal frenzy. A second orgasm takes me by surprise, and his pace slows, letting me ride out every wave of satisfaction that flows through me.

Carter's deep thrusts slowly stop and he rests his head on mine as our grip loosens, and I wrap my hands around his neck. He plants sweet and gentle kisses on my forehead, cheeks, and finally on my lips. I feel his heart racing in his chest just as fast as mine is. I take a deep breath trying to calm my panting, as he strokes my cheek and stares down at me with a loving gaze. I let my legs relax and rub my hands up and down his back, savoring the feel of his weight and warmth against me. He places a final peck on my lips and slowly pulls out of me, making us both groan. He lays next to me, still touching me, and I let out a deep and satisfied breath. I turn to him and smile as I caress his cheek. We eventually make our way to the bathroom to clean up, and he never once stops touching me.

Once we're clean, we get back in bed facing each other as our bodies intertwine. There isn't a part of us not touching, and it's exactly what I need to make this night even more enjoyable. Carter's hand roam down my arm, thigh, and slowly makes his way back up to brush my hair off my shoulder. I've craved intimacy like this for a long time. It's something I never once had with Easton, and my heart swells with contentment. Carter is the only man that can make me feel so loved, adored, and perfectly cared for. We talk about anything and everything. We laugh more than once, and I love how easy it is to be around him. Being able to be who I really am.

# Carter

Carter leaves for a few seconds to grab us some water, and I stare at his tattoo on his back as he leaves the room. When he returns, he hands me the glass of water first letting me drink my fill, before he does the same. He gets back into bed resuming how he was before he got up, and I ask, "Will you tell me what your tattoo means?" I have a feeling it means more than just a random piece of artwork.

He sighs, rubbing my arm, as he says, "It was my reminder." When I frown, he explains more. "It was a reflection of my pain for losing you, and what I did to myself. It was the only way I knew how to really show what my heart looked like after I pushed you away."

I gaze into his eyes, and wish I could take away the pain he's remembering. I caress his cheek telling him, "We'll heal each other, Carter. What we have is all we need, and one day those wounds won't hurt so much."

He grins, kisses me sweetly, and starts running his fingertips up and down my arm. His brown eyes never leave mine, and we just enjoy each other. He begins to trace his finger down the side of my cheek, then to my chin. I can't help but look away from his loving gaze as his finger moves down to the scar on my lip. I don't want our moment to end, and I know if he asks how I got it, it'll do just that. I won't lie to him. I won't avoid my past any longer because there's no point. I used to fear him not wanting me after what I went through, but he'll always want me. Even if I'm broken, he'll slowly repair the damage. He'll slowly put my shattered heart back together, and I know he'll never let me go again.

I suck in a deep breath when he asks me the question I knew he would. "Why did you leave South Carolina, Shelby?"

I swallow and look back up to him as I say, "It wasn't just one thing. It was a combination of regrets and betrayal."

"How did you get the scar?" He asks as he runs his forefinger over it once more.

I want to tell him everything. I want to purge myself of all the hell I went through, and get rid of all the pain I felt during that time in my life. But a part of me knows once I tell him, I can never erase it. He'll know everything there is to know, and I don't want him to blame himself like he did before. I most definitely don't want him to get angry and do something stupid. I sigh deeply and stare back at him, knowing he's waiting for me to open up to him completely. His caress on my cheek gives me the strength I need to begin. "I changed when I moved to South Carolina in so many ways. At first, it wasn't as noticeable. At least not to me, but I slowly began to see how vulnerable and lost I was without you." Carter continues to caress me with his gentle touch, letting me know that I can open up fully and trust him. "When I first met Easton, he was nice to me, and we quickly became friends. He was kind and was always showing me how caring he could be, but I never knew someone could hide who they truly were so well until I married him." I frown thinking about it now, and I wonder if I only agreed to marry him because of how lonely I was. How confused and hopeless I felt no matter what I did. I never felt the consuming love that flows through me now with Easton, and I realize I never loved him at all. How could I? I've always loved Carter and no amount of time apart will ever change that.

"Easton must have sensed how broken I was. It's the only thing I can think of as to why he latched onto me. Our first year of marriage wasn't so bad, but he slowly began to manipulate me into doing things I'd never even think about doing. Things like changing my hair color, what to wear, how to act, and what to think basically. He would twist his words in such a way that I thought I had to change, and had to be perfect for him. I felt insignificant when he would tell me how to talk properly to his friends, and I tried so hard to be flawless for him. But he changed me, molded me into the woman he wanted to show off to his rich friends and family. I can't tell you why I stayed after I realized what he was doing." I pause and I look away from him, ashamed I was that type of woman. I should've known better, or should've left when I first saw the signs all but slapping me in the face. I know why I stayed though. It's because I had nowhere else to go, nowhere that I belonged anymore, and Easton made damn sure to remind me of that on several occasions.

I stayed because I didn't have any other choice. I stayed because after a while, I thought I deserved everything Easton did, or said to me.

"When my mother moved down the road from us, things started getting worse than it was. She adored Easton, and she saw how he treated me. She egged him on when he would try to control me most of the time. She constantly belittled me, always agreeing with Easton. I couldn't do anything to please either one of them." I stare at Carter's chest listening to his heavy breaths as I continue on. I know he's not liking anything I'm telling him. His light touching has stopped, but his hand is still on my arm. I can't look up at him, and see the regret and guilt in his eyes like earlier. "I'd finally had enough about five years after we were married. I started to stand up for myself hoping Easton and my Mother would change, but it didn't work. If anything it made them crueler than before." My voice breaks and I clear my throat a few times before I can keep telling him all of it. "That's when Easton would leave for weeks, sometimes months on end, just to deprive me of touch. He would make sure I was alone, and made all the friends I thought I had stay away from me. His family name held so much power over the town we lived in, and it made me feel like an outcast. It showed me who I could count on, and who was just there for the social status. All I had during those times was my job, and it was the only thing that kept me going most days. Sometimes Mom would stay with me, but it wasn't to keep me company, and do what normal mothers do. I realized it became her job to continue with the mental abuse while Easton was gone. There's only so many times someone can say you're worthless and will never be loved by anyone, before you start to believe it. I started to believe everything they would tell me thinking I just had to stay and endure it. I slowly began to lose myself more than I'd ever had, and I didn't know what to do to change it from continuing to happen time and time again."

I feel Carter take my hand and I sigh, willing my tears away as he rubs the back of my hand with his thumb. He's still trying to comfort me, and I'm grateful for his touch. It's keeping me grounded and from not completely falling apart. "One day I came home early from work because I was sick. The flu was going around, and I knew Easton wasn't home since he was gone on a business trip. When I saw his Lexus parked in the driveway, I instantly knew something was wrong. I should've listened to my instincts and the alarm bells going off in my head, but I didn't. I ignored everything in me telling me not to go inside the house thinking I was overreacting, or was feeling so uneasy because I wasn't feeling good." I shut my eyes, knowing if I don't I'll lose control over my tears, and I don't know if I'll be able to finish. "I walked inside noticing the house was eerily quiet. I remember my heart racing for no apparent reason and when I walked into the kitchen, I saw two wine glasses sitting on the counter. An empty bottle of wine sat by the glasses, and I knew it wasn't from me. My first thought was that Mom came over with a friend. But that thought was quickly washed away when I began to walk upstairs. I heard them before I even got to the door. I remember my hand shaking as I reached for the doorknob, knowing what I was about to see. I wasn't stupid, but I never in my life realized how vindictive, and malicious Easton and Mom could be until that moment." Carter's hold on my hand tightens and I'm glad for it. He's holding me here, in the present, not drifting back to the absolute horrid day. "I pushed the door open, and my mouth fell open as I saw Easton fucking Mom. I was disgusted, and I had to cover my mouth to hold back the bile from spilling. All I could hear was her cries of pleasure and when she looked at me then smiled, I dashed back downstairs. I emptied my stomach in the sink, realizing this had to have been going on for a long time. It made sense to me as to why she moved there and quickly attached herself to Easton."

I open my eyes as Carter slowly raises my head with a finger under my chin. I gaze into his brown eyes trying to find the courage to let it all go. All the pain, suffering. The loneliness. Carter's eyes hold me captive, and when he brushes his fingers against my face as lone tear escapes. "What else happened, Shel?"

I don't want to tell him, but the feeling doesn't last long. I've kept so many feelings and regrets bottled up for so long. I didn't have anyone to unburden to when I left, and now that Carter is here, back in my life, I know I can tell him everything. He won't judge me. He won't make me feel weak for opening up, or for actually letting someone close to me. I can trust Carter. He uses his thumb to wipe away my tear when another one rolls down my cheek. "Easton came running after me. He tried to make excuses, to get me to listen, but I was done. I couldn't take it anymore. I'd reached my limit of being fucked with, and I told him so. He was shocked and for a second, he looked hurt. I didn't care though. I told him how much I hated him, how revolted I was that he'd been with my mother." I suck in a breath and clench my jaw as I replay the memory of what happened after I told Easton I was leaving. "I turned to leave and that's when he grabbed me. He'd done it before, pushed me a few times, but he'd never actually hit me. Not until that day at least. I tried to jerk my arm out of his grip, but he pulled down hard and when I yelled at him to let me go, he backhanded me. He hit me so hard, I fell and hit the counter before landing on the floor."

"That motherfucker." Carter's voice makes me stop and when he sits up, he pulls me with him. I sit in front of him, worried he's angry at me. "Don't even think for a second I'm mad at you, Shel." A rush of relief washes over me and I nod, letting him know I understand why he's angry. "I had a feeling that bastard hurt you, but hearing it and learning everything he put you through, I want to kill him." His jaw and fists clench, and I glance down at my hand in my lap knowing this isn't the end of it. Yes, the worst is over, but there's more to my past. "There's something else, isn't it there?"

I look up and nod. Carter's eyes are full of pain and I know it's for me. I wish I hadn't put that look there, but he wanted to know. I wanted to open up and when this is over, we can finally move on. We can forget the past. "I went to stay with a friend after everything, but when I got there, Easton had called her and told her that I hurt myself. He told her that I wanted attention, and that I was trying to cover up for being the one caught cheating." At the time, I was shocked and devastated. Now it seems comical. Easton turned the tables on me, and I knew it was his backup plan if anything ever happened between us. That's why he changed me so much. Rumors quickly spread of why I'd dyed my hair and acted so differently. "Needless to say, after my so-called friend turned her back on me, I knew what I had to do. I stayed in hotel rooms for a few months, but that didn't last very long. After I'd talked to a lawyer, and the divorce papers were drawn up, Easton started showing up every day to my room. He would threaten to take everything I had and leave me with nothing, if I went through with the divorce. The sad thing about it is, he went through with it. He got everything in the divorce, and I never felt so demoralized in my life. I give him credit though. He twisted everything to favor him and with his family's reputation, I was left with not a dime to my name." I shake my head, feeling so pathetic for letting myself go through everything I had. I was naive and stupid for allowing Easton's name to be on everything I owned. He took it all without remorse, and no concern what so ever of how I would survive. "Of course Mom was right by his side and afterwards, she told me I got what I deserved. I didn't know what to do and with limited funds, I tried to lean on a few so-called friends. One did let me stay for a couple of days before I realized she was keeping tabs on me for Easton. Throughout everything, he begged and pleaded for me to come back. He promised so many things," I let out a snort knowing everything Easton ever said was a lie. I knew better than to trust him and believe for a second that he would change. "Anyway, that's when I made up my mind to come home and try to start over."

Carter reaches for me and I willingly crawl into his lap. He pulls me close holding me tightly, as I place my head on his shoulder and wrap my hands around him. I relax in his embrace taking in all his love, knowing I'll never have to worry about him hurting me. I feel lighter, more at ease than I've been in years, and even though we're unclothed, it feels right this way. Nothing is holding us back, no barriers, and I don't mind for one second of opening up the wounds. Carter will heal me, strengthen me, and make me whole again. His hands slowly and lightly rub up and down my back as he says, "I can't imagine what you went through, or how you felt not having anyone there for you. I don't know why you had to face the terrible things you did, but I do know this." He pulls me back to look at me in the eyes. "I will do everything in my power to make you forget. Every second of every day, I'll replace those hurtful words with kind and loving ones. All the fucked up memories you have will be replaced with me loving you and caring for you like you deserve." My eyes fill with tears, but not of sadness. It's from feeling the surge of truth behind his words. His conviction, and the unconditional love he makes me feel. "I'm sorry I wasn't there to take you away from it all. I'm so fucking sorry I let you go, and let you stay away." His hands take my cheeks as he tells me, "If I could go back I would've never let you go. I would've shown you how much I loved you and how much you meant to me, and still mean to me. I can't change what happened, Shel. As much as I want that asshole to pay for what he did, and for what your mother did to you, I can't. All I can do is show you how you'll never ever feel anything but love from me. I don't care if it takes the rest of our lives. I'll never stop loving you, and proving to you that I'm exactly what you need."

He gently brings me to his luscious lips, and his kiss leaves me thinking of nothing but him. He's taking over, already making me forget what I went through. His tongue touches my lips, asking, wanting permission to invade my mouth. I don't hesitate letting him overload my very being. His kiss is tender, passionate, and takes my breath away. Desire fills me once more, but Carter pulls away before we both get lost in lust. I'm left panting, and as I gaze into his honey brown eyes as he says softly, "I wish I could find the words to tell you how much I love you." He grins and says, "There's just not enough words in this world to tell you, Shel. I know fate brought you back to me for a reason, and I truly believe it's because we both needed each other. You're my other half, the part of me that I can't live without. I regret that we spent so much time apart, missing a piece of us, and how we had to live not knowing if we would ever see each other again." His forefinger touches my lip, dragging it down. "But now that I have you back, there's nothing, not a damn thing that will ever take you away from me again. You're mine, Shelby."

"You promise?" I ask.

He smiles at me, before declaring, "I promise. Forever and always."

I reach up and stroke his cheek knowing how much his promise means to me. He leans into my touch, and I tell him, "I love you so much, Carter."

"I know you do. Now, let me show you again how much I love you." I giggle as he flips me on my back and he spends the rest of the night showing me everything he promised and so much more.

# CHAPTER 14

## Carter

It's been two weeks since Shelby opened up to me and finally began to move on. It's done wonders for us, and our relationship. I catch myself feeling guilty and responsible for what she endured, but I'm slowly getting better at accepting it was out of my control. One day, I'll be able to fully forgive myself for letting her go and feeling as though I'm the ultimate reason she was hurt so much. Which is why I've kept the promises I made her. I wasn't ever going to break them, but I feel the need to tell her multiple times a day what those promises were. I've showered her in nothing but my love, nothing but devotion, and I can tell she's enjoying every second of it. We lay in bed most days when we're off work, enjoying each other, and slowly making our relationship stronger than it's ever been. She's also been staying over most nights, and I'm more than ready for her to move in with me. I haven't asked her yet, knowing she isn't quite there. I'm trying to be patient, but I can't help but want her with me at all times. I have a lot to make up for, and I don't want to waste another second without her.

I chuckle as I place my coffee mug in the sink, hearing her singing very loudly in the shower. We're getting ready to head to my parents for Thanksgiving, and I have a pretty big announcement to make. I haven't told Shelby yet. Mostly because I hope she says yes to what I want to offer her. I've noticed every time she talks about her old job, she has a sad look in her eyes, and I know she misses what she loves doing. I also know she only took the waitress job at the Waffle House because there wasn't any job openings for her degree. I'm going to change that. She can work for the firm, and I already know Dad will be on board with it. I hope she accepts the job. If she says no, since she can be stubborn at times, I already have a plan B to convince her otherwise if she declines. It might include torturing her in sweet pleasure all night until she agrees, but she doesn't know I plan on doing that anyway.

My phone starts to ring, pulling me out of my thoughts, and I turn around to grab it when I see who's calling. "Hey, man. How's it going?"

"It's going good. How's everything there?"

Clark's voice is comforting to hear. It's been a few months since he's been able to call, and knowing he's safe while on deployment sends relief through me. I frown at his tone, and I can tell he's not handling this deployment as well as the others. I've always known when something is off with any of my brothers since we're so close. "Things are great here. Getting ready to head over to Mom and Dads. I wish you were here. It's not the same without the entire family."

"I know and trust me, I want to be there. I'm over the fucking desert."

Clark and I talk for a while, me mostly doing the talking as he listens. I tell him everything that's going on here, and let him know how Shelby and I are doing. He, of course, asks how everyone is, and I wonder why he didn't call Mom and Dad like he normally does. "Are you not going to call Mama? You know how pissed she's going to be if she finds out you called me first."

He chuckles and says, "I don't know about that. You're the oldest and the perfect child therefore, she'll forgive me. I'm going to call them soon. I just wanted to hear how things were going with you."

I ignore his comment about me being the perfect child, knowing he's trying to get a rise out of me. But I can't help the uneasy feeling that runs through me. He's not telling me something, and it's starting to worry me. "You sure you're alright, Clark?"

"Yeah." I hear him sigh deeply, and he says, "It's just … tough being here again."

"Maybe it's time to retire?"

"Yeah, maybe."

I can't even begin to imagine what it's like for him. Being in combat, and seeing the shit he does … it would scar anyone. I just hope he can hold it together for a few more months. "Almost done, man.

Then you'll be home, and we can make up for lost time."

"I'm looking forward to it." We talk for a few more minutes before he lets me go to call Mom and Dad. I clench my jaw as I place my phone back down on the counter, worry starting to overtake me. I know this isn't the first time he's been shipped off, but something's different this time.

"Carter? What's wrong?"

I snap my head up hearing Shelby's voice, and she walks over to me, then gently touches my arm. I didn't realize she was done in the shower, but I'm glad she's here. I can see the concern in her eyes, and I can't help but grin when I notice her hair is wrapped in a towel. "Clark just called, and I'm just worried about him. He sounded … off, and I wish this deployment would end so he could come home."

She runs her hand up and down my arm as she says, "I'm sure he's fine, and he's just missing being here for the holidays. Just think, in a few months he'll be back and hopefully he'll decide to stay around this time."

I grab her hand pulling her to me. Her other hand grips my arm as I wrap mine around her. "I want him to get out, but that's his choice. I just know he's not going to come back the same this time." I don't know it for sure, but it's a feeling I have. Something isn't right about this deployment.

"You do have every right to be concerned, and I have faith he'll know he has everyone's support when he gets back."

I grin, knowing she's right. "It's kind of hard to have a serious conversation with you when there's a towel on top of your head," I say jokingly.

She laughs and playfully smacks my arm. "You better watch it, or I'll tell William and Annie how awful you're being."

I shake my head at her idle threat. "Oh yeah? And what will they do about it?" I slowly pull the towel off her head, dropping it, and her eyes dilate with desire.

"Well," she starts as I lean in closer to her lips. I stop only inches away as she says with a sultry voice, "I forgot what I was saying."

"Oh, you did?"

I don't miss the sharp intake of her voice as I grasp her ass, pulling her into my now hard cock. "Carter, you always know what to do to make me forget."

I smirk and watch her as she licks her lips. "It's a skill. What can I say?"

I laugh as she shakes her head and pushes me away. "I'm on to you. We don't have time for that."

I huff, looking at the clock and seeing we only have thirty minutes before we have to leave. "I think we can get a quickie in."

"Ha, ha. Nice try."

"Fine." I sneak in a kiss, and when I pull back, she's smiling. "I do have something to tell you and ask you."

"Oh really?" I lean on the counter as she picks up the towel. She starts to run it through her hair and says, "I have something to tell you too."

"You first," I say, wondering what she has up her sleeve.

"Well, I was thinking." She continues to dry her hair with the towel and says, "Maybe Cason could teach me some self-defense moves?"

I nod in agreement, thinking it's a great idea. Every woman should know at least the basic moves of self-defense. "Yeah, I'm sure he'd be more than happy to teach you."

She holds the towel in her hands and looks away before saying, "I figured so. I've just been thinking about it a lot since we talked." I reach out and grab her hand as she glances back at me. "I don't want to be weak anymore, Carter."

"Shel, what you went through, it doesn't mean you're weak."

She sighs deeply, and I can tell she's still struggling to work through everything still, and I didn't expect her to be over it instantly. "I think if I learn how to defend myself I won't be so helpless if a situation like that were to ever arise again."

"I won't let that happen," I tell her and it's a promise.

"I know, but it'll give me piece of mind."

"Okay, we can talk to him about it when we see him soon." At this point, I'll do anything to make her not feel weak, and for her to know she can take care of herself. Granted she has me to do that for her, but knowing she's going in the right direction and willing to take the steps she needs to move on, makes me proud of her.

"What did you want to tell me?"

"I'm going to take over the firm." I watch as her eyes light up, and she smiles widely. "I'm going to tell Dad today."

"That's wonderful, Carter." She drops the towel on the floor then wraps her arms around my neck. I hold onto her waist, still getting used to her being so open and close to me again. "I'm so proud of you, and I know you'll do a great job."

"There's one other thing," I add.

She frowns and asks, "What is it?"

"I want you to come and work for me. I know you really don't like working as a waitress, and you can work from home if you're worried about spending too much time together."

"Carter, I ..."

I push her wet hair behind her ear before she can finish. "You don't have to say yes right this minute, but I would like you to help me run the firm. At least the business part of it. Just think about it, okay?"

"Alright, I'll think about it." She sighs as she glances down, I barely hear her as she says, "You're too good for me."

Placing a finger under her chin, I raise her head up to me. "Don't ever think that, Shel. We're perfect for each other, and I want to give you everything I can. If I can provide you with a job I know you love doing, then I'll make it happen. Don't second guess it."

"How is it you know just what to say to make things so much better?"

"It's easy when it's with you." I tilt my head down and place a sweet kiss on her lips. Her hands around my neck tightens, then move to my hair. I can't get enough of her hands on me, caressing me, and showing me how much I mean to her. I never thought we'd have this again. I never in a million years thought what we have now would be so intense, and heart stopping at times. I kiss her once more, and I have to make myself pull away. "We need to finish getting ready, or Mama is going to kill both of us if we're late."

She laughs, a sound I want to hear all the time, and slowly takes her hands off of me. As much as I want to ravish her, Mama will be pissed if we're late for our annual Thanksgiving lunch. I watch Shelby as she walks away, wondering how in the hell I got so lucky, and I send a silent thank you to fate for bringing her back to me.

Shelby and I walk inside my parents' home hand in hand, and my heart clenches seeing Shelby quickly let go as we walk to Annie and William then to Mom and Dad, hugging them. Pride and absolute joy fill me knowing she's here for the first time in ages to spend the holidays with me and my family.

I've always liked Thanksgiving more than the other holidays, but this one is probably the best one yet. It's all because she's here, she's with me, and I rub my chest trying to sort through the strong emotions overwhelming me. It's an amazing feeling, one that I know I won't be getting used to any time soon.

Caden slaps my shoulder, knocking me forward, as he says, "Happy Turkey day, old man."

I shove him back playfully, and shake my head. "You'll think old man when I kick your ass at Pictionary later." It's been a family tradition for us for years to play games after we eat and at times, we can get pretty competitive. Especially when Bethany would come over. It saddens me I've lost her as a friend, and how I haven't seen or heard from her in months. In a way, I guess it's a good thing because I honestly don't know how to repair the friendship we had.

"Thinking about Bethany?" He asks, and I'm glad he lowered his voice. The last thing I need is for Shelby to think I miss her. I do, but only as a friend. I've tried to talk to her about it, but it's hard when I see how jealous she still is about the whole situation. I can only hope one day everything will work itself out.

"It's just strange not having her here since she'd been coming almost every year since we became friends. All this change this past year is hard to get used to." Caden nods, and I look to the kitchen seeing Shelby laughing with Mom and Annie. I grin, and all thoughts of Bethany disappear. Only Shelby can do that to me. Cason is by Dad and William, sitting at the kitchen island, and I turn back to Caden to ask, "Caleb not here yet?"

"He's on his way. His plane got delayed, or something like that."

"Good. Mama would flip her shit if he didn't show."

Caden's face pales as he says, "Oh, fuck, we know better than that. I like my balls right where they are."

I laugh and shake my head. It's never a dull moment with him. I place a hand on his shoulder, and we make our way into the kitchen. He makes his way over by Cason, Dad, and William, as I walk to Mom. She's putting the final touches on a peanut butter cake, and I look over her shoulder and say, "That's mine, right?"

She laughs, and I see Annie shake her head. They all know how much I love Mom's peanut butter cake. "No. This is for everyone," Mom tells me, but I know she made an extra one for me to take home later since she does every year. When Mom turns to wipe her hands off, I swipe my finger in the frosting. I quickly put my finger in my mouth, but she catches me anyways. "Caden, I mean Caleb. Oh, whatever your name is, stop that right now!" We all laugh at her, knowing she always calls us by the wrong name when she gets flustered with us.

I hold my hands up as she shoos me out of the way, and take a seat on the stool by the island. I sit back and listen as everyone begins to talk amongst themselves. Caden, Dad, William, and Cason talk about sports, and the truck Caden and William are still rebuilding together. Mom, Annie, and Shelby pull out a sales paper for the after Thanksgiving sales. I grin, watching them make out a game plan for Wal-Mart, but it's necessary if they want to get everything they circled. Plus that place will be in utter chaos, and I won't be there if I can help it. Shelby looks up and smiles, catching me admiring her. She blushes, something I crave to see, and she tucks a piece of hair behind her ear. Beckoning her to me with a tilt of my head, she doesn't waste a second before she walks over to me. I turn her back to me and hold her waist as she stands in between my legs. I wrap my hands around her stomach, then place my head on her shoulder. I feel her sigh, and she leans back into me. I'm perfectly content with her staying right here for the rest of the day. We're oblivious to everyone else around us, caught up in each other's embrace. I kiss her softly on her neck as I tighten my hold on her. Feeling her shiver as my lips touch her earlobe, I know I need to stop before getting to a point of no return.

"Can you two please stop with all the lovey dovey crap? You're making me want to puke," Caden says and I chuckle against Shelby's neck. I pull back to stare at him wishing he'd leave us alone, but he's right. I don't need to be kissing her here anyway, knowing I can't devour her until we get back to my house.

I don't get a chance to respond. All of us turn to the door when we hear, "Sorry I'm late!" Caleb stumbles as he fumbles with his glasses, trying to get in the door, and I can't stop from laughing at him. He's so awkward for a twenty-three year old.

"Well look who it is. What's cracking, oops baby?"

"Caden, do not call your brother that," Mom scolds. Caleb ignores Caden's nickname, but it's actually very accurate. Mom told us the story once for Thanksgiving of how Caleb was literally their 'oops baby'. Mom and Dad had wanted to stop at four boys, but apparently Mom's birth control failed. Caleb walks over to Mom giving her a hug and a kiss on the cheek before she says, "Ignore Caden. He knows you're my favorite."

"What! I thought I was your favorite," Caden squeals like a girl. Cason, Shelby, and I can only laugh as Annie, William, and Mom shake their heads. Caden is such a drama queen. We all know Mom's teasing him, but it does make for high-quality entertainment. Caden huffs loudly, and Mom tells him to help her set the food on the table.

Shelby turns her head to me and says, "Your family is still just as crazy as they were before I left."

"They are, but you love it."

She smiles before saying, "I do and I have missed this. Thank you, Carter."

Frowning, I ask, "What for?"

"For bringing me here, and making me feel so welcome again. For just being you."

I take a hold of her waist pulling her in close, asking, "Have I told you how much I love you today?"

She blushes a bright pink, then says, "Yes, but you can tell me again."

"I plan on telling you for the rest of our lives, and thoroughly showing you later." Her eyes dilate with lust, and my hands wander down to grab her ass. I'm aware we're in a house full of my family, but I just can't help myself. "I love you so much, Shel. Sometimes it scares me of how much you mean to me, but I wouldn't change any of it. I love how you understand me. How you complete me, and especially how you make me feel like I'm the luckiest man alive."

Her hands wrap around my neck, and she says softly, "You know exactly what to say to make me fall in love with you even more than I already do. I love you, too." She leans in and sweetly kisses me. I savor it, letting her kiss fill me with an almost uncontrollable urge to take her back home, and show her all the sensations she brings me.

Our kiss doesn't last long as we hear Caleb's throat clearing. "Sorry, but Mama says the food is ready."

Shelby reluctantly backs away, and I get off the stool to follow her to the kitchen table. Before we sit down, she says, "Does anyone feel like the women are outnumbered here?"

I chuckle as Mom says, "I've felt that way for a long time."

"Just wait, Linda. It'll be equal numbers soon," Annie says to Mom. Caden's eyes widen as Cason sits by him with a brooding look. Caleb shakes his head as if he can't wrap his mind around it, and I kiss Shelby on the cheek then pull her chair out for her. Annie's right. One day all my brothers will find their 'one', and I can't wait to give them hell about it.

No one else comments on the subject. We're all too preoccupied with filling our plates with the food Mom and Annie cooked. The conversation begins to flow once everyone has their plates fixed, and I glance at Shelby as she laughs at something Caden says. These are the moments I cherish. The ones that I'll hold close to my heart, and always remember. Being with my family and the one woman that holds my heart, is exhilarating. I can't even begin to put into words how much I enjoy this time with everyone, and when Shelby turns and grins at me, my heart swells with more love that I could ever imagine it could. I take her hand in mine, and squeeze it. She does the same back, and I place a kiss on the back of hers. We stare at each other for a moment before turning back to our food, and I realize that this year, this Thanksgiving, I have so much to be thankful for.

After everyone is finished eating, we sit around the table for a bit longer before we start cleaning up. It's another tradition of ours that Mom and Annie cook while the rest of us clean up afterward for them. It's only fair since they spend so much time preparing a huge meal for us. Shelby and I start to wash off the dishes as Caden and Cason put away the leftovers. Caleb, William, and Dad clear off the table and make sure to put everything back where it belongs.

The task doesn't take nearly as long with all of us working together, and once Shelby and I are finished, I dry my hands off and gaze at her. She places her arm around me and whispers, "Don't be nervous. Your Dad is going to be so proud of you."

I smile down at her, and it's still amazing how she knows what's going through my mind. I plant a kiss on her forehead before I say, "Thank you, Shel." She beams at me, and she slowly pulls away so I can walk over to Dad.

He's sitting by William now in the living room, and they're watching the football game. When Dad notices me, he mutes the TV, waiting for me to start. "I know you've been waiting patiently for me to come to a decision on whether or not to take over the firm when you retire." He doesn't say anything, still waiting for me to finish. I swallow, feeling my nerves bubbling to the surface. I know I need to do this, but at the same time … I'm afraid I'm going to fuck it all up. I let out a huff as I say, "I'm going to take over when you decide a date to retire." I instantly feel my shoulders relax, and when Dad grins, I can tell I made the right choice.

"It's about damn time!" Caden yells from the kitchen, and I hear Mom scold him right after for his cussing. I just realized how everyone was listening in, but I can't be angry for their eavesdropping.

Dad gets up off the couch, and grips my shoulder as he says, "I'm proud of you, son. I knew you'd come around eventually, and I know you'll do a great job taking over for me. I wouldn't have asked you unless I knew you were ready for the responsibility." I nod, taking his praise to heart. It means a lot to me he has so much faith in me, and I'll do my best to keep making him proud.

"Can we start the game now?"

Dad shakes his head, and I turn around and say, "Caden, can you chill out for five seconds, or are you in that big of a hurry to lose?"

"Oh it's on! You're going down!"

I chuckle, making my way back into the kitchen as I ask, "Who's on your team then?" I quickly grab Shelby and pull her by me before he can pick her.

"Hey! That's cheating."

"Stop whining. You already knew she was going to be on my team."

"I'm right here," Shelby butts in.

I look down at her and say, "You don't want to be on his team. Caden can't draw shit to save his life."

"I heard that, Carter!"

"Sorry, Mama." I drop my head, as Caden, Cason, Caleb, and Shelby laugh.

"How about this," Cason starts. "Caden, Caleb, and I will be on one team and you," he points to me. "Shelby, Annie, and Mama will make the other team." I'm beginning to like those odds. William and Dad decide not to play, opting to watch the game instead.

Once we agree on the teams, Mama pulls out the drawing board, and hands each of us a pencil. We have a nice set up going on, and it's much easier having a bigger spot to draw on. Caleb gets the cards, and timer ready as Annie sets up the score sheet. We don't use the actual board game anymore, since it's much more fun to play by score. For each one each team guesses right, it's two points. Whoever gets to fifty points first is the winner and believe me, they will brag and rub in it for a whole year.

Like I said, we're competitive when it comes to Pictionary.

"Which team is going first," Shelby asks.

"Rock, paper, scissors," Caden says and Shelby nods, accepting his challenge. Everyone else sits back as they begin, and I have faith my girl will win. I watch her get her game face on, and I can't help but chuckle at how serious she is. Her eyebrows are furrowed and she stares right at Caden. She's focused and determined to win. They both close their fists, and place it on the palm of their other one. They hit their palms with their enclosed fist three times before, Caden chooses rock and Shelby does paper.

"I win," she says sweetly but I know it's her way of being sarcastic.

"Best two out of three," Caden tells her, but she shakes her head.

"Caden, she won fair and square. I don't want to hear any bickering like last year," Mom says to him, and I can't help but laugh as Caden's face turns into a scowl. He hates to lose and not get his way.

"Good job, babe," I tell Shelby and she turns to me, smiling brightly. She kisses me then picks a card laid out in front of Caleb. I watch her as she looks over the categories and when she finds one she likes, she gets up and walks to the drawing board.

"Let me know when y'all are ready," Caleb says. He has the sand timer in hand, ready to flip it for us.

Annie, Mom, and I move to the edge of our seats as we wait for Shelby to begin drawing. She stands on the side of the board so we can see what she draws, and she hovers over the board with her pencil and she says, "Ready," to Caleb.

She begins drawing and it takes us a few seconds to start guessing. "Box," Mom calls out.

Shelby shakes her head as I say, "Square." She shakes her head again as she continues to draw. All I can think of is squares because that's all she's drawing. I rack my brain of what it could possibly be as she starts to draw the pattern.

"Oh I know! It's hopscotch!" Annie says as she jumps out of her seat.

"I don't see it," Caden says, and I know it's his way of saying we cheated.

I see it more now that Annie put a name to it. The only thing missing is the numbers in each box. Shelby laughs and punches her hands in the air as she says, "Suck on that, Caden!"

"I swear. Y'all are going to be the death of me," Mom says to no one in particular.

I smile as Shelby makes her way back to me, and she wraps her arms around me and kisses me before sitting down. Caden rolls his eyes at us and starts to take a card before Cason stops him. "No way, you're going first."

"What? Why not?"

"Because you suck at drawing," Caleb tells Caden and Cason nods in agreement.

"My own teammates are against me!" Shelby and I burst out laughing because knowing Caden, he really means it. Mom and Annie shake their heads, and Cason ignores him completely as he picks a card. I reach across the table and take the timer from Caleb once Cason has his category, and I sit back as he makes his way to the board. I already know this is going to be good because not only is Caden horrible at drawing, he's the worst guesser. I turn and wink at Shelby, because she's about to see why Caden always tries to cheat.

Cason nods to me when he's ready and I flip the timer. He begins to draw, and to me it looks like a curvy line. "Squiggly line!" Caden yells and Shelby snorts beside me. Cason doesn't even acknowledge him as he adds more to his drawing.

Caden repeats his guess several times before Caleb tells him, "Just because you keep saying the same thing, doesn't mean it's going to magically change." Caden rolls his eyes as I turn back to the board. It's looking more like a snake now. "Water hose," Caleb guesses.

"Rope," Caden tries again. Cason still draws and Caden adds, "It is a noose? Damn, bro. We don't want you to hang yourself." Cason turns around, and I chuckle at the brooding look on his face. He's getting annoyed with Caden.

"Power cord," Caleb says, and Cason draws more, and rolls his hands as to say keep going and you're close.

"Uh, I've got nothing," Cason says in defeat. He huffs and sits back in his chair, and I call time.

Cason rolls his eyes, crosses his arms, and says, "It was an extension cord."

"How did you think we could guess that? It looks nothing like an extension cord."

"Caden." Cason stops, taking in a deep breath, before saying, "What's the point in our bond if you don't use it when we play games? We always lose because you suck."

"Alright, boys. Play nice or I'll stop the game now," Mom tells the both of them. Cason nods and sits back down as Caden mumbles under his breath.

I lean over to Shelby and say, "See what I mean?" She nods and laughs when Caden begins to pout.

We end up playing a few more rounds before Mom finally calls the game. Caden and Cason will not stop bickering back and forth, and I feel bad Caleb looks so defeated listening to them. I'm proud Shelby did so well. When I tell her, she smiles at me then kisses me sweetly. We help Mom and Annie put away the game, and then we join Dad and William in the living room. Shelby sits down by me, and I place an arm around her, pulling her close. Caden and Cason are still fighting, which isn't surprising, and Caleb sits by Mom and tells her how school is going. Annie takes a seat by William and I look around the room seeing how *normal and comforting this is. I run my hand through Shelby's hair, silently thanking her for being here with me.

If it hadn't been for her, I'm sure I wouldn't be so relaxed, content, and blissfully happy with the way things are going.

Caden and I spar in the ring in Cason's gym as Shelby gets her first lesson in self-defense. It's hard for me to concentrate on following Caden's jabs when all I can focus on is Shelby. She seems to be doing great with Cason's lesson, but I can't help but worry. I was proud of her when she asked Cason before we left my parents on Thanksgiving to train her, and I could tell she was excited to get started.

I turn back to Caden, and groan when I miss him, and he jabs with his right hand, catching me in my ribs. "What's up with you, Carter?"

I let out a breath and drop my hands. I put my boxing glove under my arm and pull, taking it off as I say, "I can't focus."

"I can see that. I whooped your ass today. Are you worried about Shel? You know Cason will teach her everything he knows."

I nod and say, "I know. I just don't want her to think she has to do this, or she feels like she needs to prove herself." I know how determined she can be at times, and I've told her more than once she didn't need to do this. But I also know if learning how to defend herself will ease her worries, and give her another reason to forget her past I'll have to find a way to stop worrying so much.

"Well they've been at it for over two hours. I think she's fine." Caden and I glance over at Shelby and Cason, and I smirk seeing her block Cason's attack. She already seems experienced, and I can't help to feel pride seeing her lock Cason's arm in a hold, making Cason bend at the waist.

Caden and I step out of the ring, and we make our way over to them. Cason sees us and says, "That's enough for today. You did great for a first day, Shelby."

"Thanks," she says as she wipes the sweat off her forehead.

I run my hand down her arm and say, "You did do great today. I couldn't take my eyes off you, and now Caden's never going to let me live down him kicking my ass today."

"Damn straight," Caden adds.

Shelby shakes her head, and I nod to Cason and Caden. They take my hint and grab their gym bags, and I turn back to Shelby when they leave. "Are you okay?" She has yet to meet my eyes, and I know something's going on.

"Yeah. I just want to make sure I'm getting everything down perfectly."

"Hey," I say softly as I pull her to me. I run my hands up and down her back as she relaxes in my arms. Her head rests on my chest and I say, "You can't expect to get everything down in one lesson. It's going to take time and patience."

She huffs out a breath as she says, "I know. I just feel like I'm not strong enough and even if I needed to defend myself, I wouldn't be able to take them down. I'm too weak."

I pull her back by her shoulders and firmly tell her, "You are far away from being weak." Gazing into her eyes, and seeing how her insecurities are starting to arise again, I quickly add, "If you want to add in weight lifting, Cason will make a regime for you. Don't get down about not knowing how to do everything at once. You know you can come here anytime during the week and practice with Cason."

"I know, and you're right," she says with a heavy sigh.

The uncertainty in her eyes lets me know the demons of her past are still plaguing her, but I knew it wouldn't be an easy or quick fix. She needs to have faith in herself, and I know she can overcome everything she's been through. I tell myself I have to start reminding her that she's not in this alone. I will be her rock, shoulder, and everything she needs to feel safe again and to be able to let the past go. I caress her cheek and say, "Don't let the past take over, Shel."

She nods and embraces me. I hold her tightly, knowing she's still dealing with her demons. "I know I'll get there and be more confident after I learn more, but it's just bringing up a lot of insecurities. Not to mention the things Easton would say."

"One day those memories won't affect you as much, but you're doing the best you can to overcome it. I hope you know I'm here for you, and here to listen anytime you want to talk about it."

"I know you are, and you have no idea how much that makes it easier to get past it. I honestly don't know what I would do without you, Carter." She glances up at me, and I can't help but lean down and take her mouth, and place my hand on her neck. I want her to know her past doesn't define her. It doesn't control her anymore, and I intend to show her how true that is.

She moans as I deepen our kiss and run my other hand down her back. I grip her ass as I push my hips into her letting her feel how much I want her. How much I need her. She pulls back breaking our kiss and says in a husky voice, "I'm all sweaty, and Cason will be pissed if we mess up his mats."

I smirk, saying, "I don't care. I want you, Shel. I have to have you right here, right now. Fuck Cason and his mats. What he doesn't know won't hurt him."

"You're so bad."

I nip at her lips and whisper, "You love it." I use my tongue and lick her neck making her head tilt back. Her hands grip my arms as I kiss, and softly bite her neck, as I move down. I can tell she loves it.

Her skin prickles in goosebumps, and I hear the intake of her breath. I want to hear her moan out my name, watch her as she let's go, and cries out in ecstasy. I want to taste every single inch of her body with my tongue.

I'm going to give her everything she desires, then do it all over again.

I stop only long enough to quickly pull her exercise top off, and find her succulent lips again. My kiss isn't as sweet as before. I take her mouth as though I need her taste to live. To breathe. She willingly gives me everything I'm taking without a care in the world. I know she trusts me to give her everything she wants, craves, and lusts for. Her back arches as I slide my hands slowly up her back caressing her while still devouring her mouth. Once I reach her sports bra, I pull away from her and quickly take it off, letting it drop on the floor. She's never been more beautiful than she is now. Her nipples perk at my gaze, and I give them my full attention. I want to reach out, grab her and take her right this second, but I will myself to slow down. To savor her. To relish in the sensations she brings me. My gaze meets hers, and she looks up at me with hooded eyes. Her lips are red from my assault, and I feel my cock twitch as I see how much she wants me in her eyes. Green sparks seem to flare back at me, and I remind myself that this is real. She's here with me, at this very moment, and nothing will tear us apart again. I also see it in the way her chest rises and falls as if she can't catch her breath. My eyes only leave hers long enough for me to take off my shirt and toss it aside. Her eyes travel down raking over my body, and an unquenched hunger flows through me. I'm being consumed by her gaze. Slowly being pulled into her seductive trance, and I groan loudly when she licks her lips. She has absolutely no idea what she's doing to me, and she's not even trying.

My breath hitches in my throat as she drops to her knees, and reaches for my gym shorts. She grins up at me, and I brush her hair back from her face. My body jerks as she pulls down my shorts, and my head falls back when she grips my cock with her hand. She slowly works me, making my stomach clench, and my entire body burn with need. I can't stop my hips from moving into her hand. I need more of her touch. More of what she can give me. I suck in a harsh breath through my teeth as I feel her hot mouth suck the tip of my cock. "Fuck, Shel." She moans on my sensitive cock, and I take a hold of her ponytail as she sucks my cock deeper into her mouth. I look down needing to see her take me, and my balls clench wanting to come. I fight the urge to spill in her hot and wet mouth not wanting it to end so soon. I let her suck, lick, and caress my balls for a few more moments, but I can't take any more of her delectable mouth.

I pull her away from me, and when she gazes up at me, I confess, "I can't handle your mouth anymore." I let go of her hair, kick off my shoes, and bend at my knees. She watches me as I crawl over her, and she's forced to lie back on the mats. I place a knee in between her legs and raise her hands above her head. I lean down slowly taking my tongue over her taunt nipple, and she hisses out a breath when I use my teeth, then suck the pain away. She arches her breasts to me, and I know she wants more.

I rub my knee over her hot pussy as I take her other nipple into my mouth. She grinds on me, moaning as I cup her other breast in my hand. "Carter, please," she begs, and I give her one last nip before I take her mouth again. I let her hands go and move away from her mouth. Trailing down her exposed torso with both hands, her nails start to dig into my back. The pain is dull, not even registering to my brain, and I know she's going to leave marks behind. The thought makes my cock twitch again, and I quickly move away. Her shoes quickly disappear and take her shorts and panties off as I move. I take in her naked body, enjoying every inch of her. She watches me as I look her over, appreciating the stunning woman laid out bare for me. Only for me. My mouth opens to suck in a breath as she uses her fingertips to touch her breasts, and I almost lose control when she spreads her legs wider for me. I swallow hard, seeing her ready and wet pussy. "Take me, Carter," she pleads, and I can't wait anymore.

I all but growl as I move over her and hover at her entrance. I suck in another breath as I steady myself. I can feel her warmth. Her very essence, and it's going to be a challenge not to spill into her as soon as I thrust in. Her legs wrap around my waist waiting for me to enter her. An animalistic need to fuck her into oblivion flows through me, but I clench my jaw stopping the urge from taking over. Instead, I move my hand down to my throbbing cock and guide myself painfully slow inside of her. Her head bows back, her eyes close, and her cries of pleasure let me know how much she craves me. Her pussy greedily takes me and grips me like a fucking vice, as I push into her more. I halt my movements, only for a few moments, letting her adjust to my size. I begin to move as her hips arch on me and pull out, only to thrust into her deeply. I do it again loving the loud cries she begins to make. I continue my slow almost agonizing pace, before moving my leg to the side. I take a hold of her thigh gripping it tightly, opening her more, and giving me a better angle to sink into her deeper than before. Our moans and heavy pants fill the room, and I gaze down at her. I watch as her eyes open then close, and her mouth opens making that perfect 'O' shape. I can feel our souls merging as we become one touching skin to skin as close as possible. I didn't think I'd ever feel the intense and almost overwhelming surge of love, desire, and absolute passion roll through me. It sends a tingling sensation down my spine and moves all throughout my body. I relish in the sensations she brings me. The feel of her pussy wrapped around my cock, the swell of her breasts teasing me to suck them, and the sound of her cries of pleasure, makes me want to love her with everything I have. Everything I am. It's our connection. The unconditional love that we have for one another. It's a rare feeling to have, and I never want our love to stop flowing through us.

My pace begins to quicken as her walls clamp down on me. I know she's close and when I reach down to rub her clit, my pace slows as she lets out a loud scream. I groan as I watch her as she comes undone, something that I'll never get tired of seeing, and let her ride out her orgasm. Her eyes slowly open, and she lets out a relaxed breath. Pride and satisfaction flow through me knowing I'm the one to put that satisfied look on her face. I thrust into her again and again, before I pull out for a moment to flip us. She lets out a surprised cry, and she lays on my chest kissing me sweetly. I shudder as I take her mouth. She dips her tongue in mine, and I reach down to grab her ass with each hand. She pulls away when I take her hands. Slowly pushing her up so she's sitting straight, and I love the view of her on top of me.

I take her waist and groan out, "Take me, Shel." She complies willingly slowly easing herself down on my raging hard cock. I'll never tire of feeling her tight walls suck me in deep. Never tire of seeing her body flush with desire for me as she takes me. She begins to rock back and forth, and I gaze up at her in amazement. Her eyes are full of lust, love, and her head falls back as I thrust into her. My hands roam up her body, and I caress her breasts as she takes her pleasure from me. She's beautiful, stunning, and breath taking as she brands me.

She sears my soul. Forever claiming my heart for her own and taking me for everything I am.

I watch as her head falls back savoring her cries of pleasure, as I run my hands down her body. The soft feel of her skin against mine makes me rise up, and pull her breasts to my chest. Her eyes meet mine as she grabs my neck moving me to her lips as we take each other. She rocks slowly on me, and I grab her waist, helping her reach the spot I know she loves. Gazing deep into her stunning blue eyes I declare, "I love you, Shel. I'll never stop loving you."

I know she can feel our connection. Her breath hitches before saying, "I know, Carter. I love you so much." I've always known she loved me, but every single time she says those precious words, it's like hearing them for the first time again.

I can feel myself ready to explode in her as her walls clench down on me again. I want this feeling to last, but I can't hold out any longer. I reach up and take her ponytail again pulling her mouth off mine as I demand, "Come with me, Shel. Let me feel you as I let go."

Her fingers dig into my neck as she speeds up her movements, and when her head falls back as she calls out my name, it's my undoing. My head drops to her neck as I release inside of her, and let out a loud grunt. She milks me taking everything I give her, and then some. I thrust into her a few more times feeling her walls clamping down on me still. I let her ride out her orgasm and when she's ready to come down, I lift my head and watch her as she smiles. She rests her head on my forehead as she tries to catch her breath. I close my eyes, not wanting to let this moment go. I'd die a happy man if I never had to leave her warmth.

I feel her move, and I open my eyes as she says, "That was …"

"Incredible," I finish for her.

Her hands run through my hair, caressing and thanking me for pleasing her. "Incredible, sensational, amazing, and exactly what I needed. How do you know what I need, Carter?"

I lift my hand to her face and rub my thumb on her cheek as I answer with, "It's because we're connected. You're my soulmate, Shelby. It's like your soul calls to mine when you need to be reminded of how beautiful you are. How strong you are, and what you mean to me." Her eyes shine back at me loving my sweet words, and I add, "And it's because I know you. There's nothing about you that you can keep from me. I've known you forever, and it's not hard to read you anymore."

"I'm glad you know me so well. It does make our relationship so much easier."

I chuckle as I say, "It does. I wouldn't change anything about it either." And I wouldn't. Shelby is one of a kind. She's special. Someone I'm more than happy to be with for the rest of my life. She's the one person I can truly say holds my heart and she'll protect it with everything she has.

Carter

I've always known our love was one of a kind, and I'd be fucking insane if I didn't savor every second with her. Every touch, caress, and kiss. All of it is burned into my mind. It's still surreal most days that she's mine again. I don't know what I did to deserve a second chance, but to hell with questioning it. I'll keep her close and enjoy all we have until the day I die.

Maybe even after that too.

# CHAPTER 15

## Shelby

The weeks seem to fly by and before I realize it, Christmas is only a few days away. Carter and I spend every minute we can together, showing each other multiple times a day how much we love each other. A part of me thinks he's trying to make up for our years apart, and the other is telling me he's filling me with new memories to replace the dark ones. Either way, I'm relishing in his affections. His unconditional love. He showers me with it, and I wouldn't change anything about how our relationship is growing stronger each day. Carter challenges me, helps me forget my past, and I tell him all the time how grateful I am to have him back in my life. He's even been coming with me to Cason's gym for my self-defense class. Carter cheers me on, giving me the confidence I need to be better. To excel at it, knowing it's giving me peace of mind. I still struggle with feeling weak and ashamed for what I let happen to me, but every time I take a step back, Carter is there helping me take two forward.

Things would be absolutely perfect if not for the times he brings up Bethany. I know I shouldn't be jealous, but it's hard not to be. I know he only cares for me, but a part of me hates he spent so much time with her while I was gone. Their friendship was true, and I know Carter wants to reach out to her. He's told me a few things about Bethany. How her family treats her and how she couldn't depend on anyone until they formed a friendship. It doesn't really change my feelings toward her, or the way she acted and treated me. Needless to say, it's still a touchy subject, and Carter doesn't bring it up much. Only time will tell if I can deal with her coming back around and them becoming friends again.

There's also a piece of me that feels like it's missing. It's like a hole, slowly growing, and even when I'm with Carter all the time, I know it's there. I should've figured it out sooner since it happens every year around Christmas, but it didn't fully surface until this morning. I'd gotten up early like every morning going about my daily routine, when I thought about my Dad. It hit me out of nowhere. This time every year, it was our month together. It was a rare time he wouldn't drink as much. He was more himself, more like a father should be. I cherished December because of it. It's as if my Dad being there for me caring for me and showering me with love I so desperately wanted was my Christmas gift. I missed him terribly, and guilt started to make it's way in. I haven't been to his grave since Caden took me months ago, and I tell myself I'll go soon. Even if it's just for a few minutes, I owe it to myself and my father's memory to pay my respects.

With my mind made up and my heart feeling a bit lighter than before, I walk down the stairs to find Annie in the kitchen making coffee. William has just finished eating, and I chuckle seeing him rub his pot belly. Annie and I sit at the kitchen table and have our morning coffee, and we catch up on what's been going on with everything. I've been trying not to work as much, and I'm still undecided on whether or not to take Carter up on his offer to work for him. Annie and William think it's a wonderful idea, but I'm worried about working with Carter too much. He can be stubborn at times. Partly because we challenge each other. I don't want our time spent together worrying about jobs or unnecessary things causing us to argue, but I also miss doing what I love.

I take a sip of my coffee as Annie begins to tell me again of all the reasons I should take his offer. "I don't understand why you want to think about it so much. It'll be a perfect job for you, and you can work at home. You work way too much as it is, and I hate I can't see you how as often I'd like."

I place my coffee down on the table feeling a twinge of guilt. She's right. Between working all the time then spending time with Carter, I hardly have rare moments with them like this. William nods then picks up his morning paper. I shake my head at him, because I know he'll be listening to everything we say. "I know, and I promise to make more time for us. You really think I should say yes? What if it's a disaster?"

Annie shrugs then says, "If so, then Carter can write you a letter of recommendation so you can find another job." She pauses for a second then adds, "Speaking of letters." I curiously watch her as she gets up, and walks over to the small table holding all the mail. I twist in my chair wondering what she's digging for in the pile of junk mail. William is eerily quiet, but I don't think much of it. William has always been a man of few words. It's his actions that you have to pay attention to. "Ah-ha! I found it," Annie proclaims and returns to the table. She glances at me and I tilt my head, trying to figure out what's going on. She holds a white envelope in her hand and sighs before saying, "I got this letter a few days ago. Remember that nice couple that moved into your old house?" When I nod, she continues. "Well they stopped by here, and they found this hidden in the attic. They also told me to let you know your mom didn't fully clear it out, and you're more than welcome to come over to go through it to get whatever you want."

I feel as if someone knocked the air out of me. How is this even possible? Is the letter from Dad? And why did my mother leave our possessions in the attic? I have so many questions, but no way to get my answers. I refuse to call Mom. I'm completely fine with never speaking to her again, but I'm still so confused about everything. "Who's the letter from?" I ask.

Annie lowers her head for a moment, then she looks up to me. "I'm not sure. It only says your name, and the couple knew you and your mother were the only people who lived there before them. If I had to guess … I would say it was from your father."

I sit back in my chair, reeling from this news. It's nothing I expected to hear today. I lean back up and ask, "Can I see it?" Annie hands the letter to me instantly, and I stand up. "I'm going to read it upstairs."

Annie reaches out to touch my arm as she says, "If you need anything, we're right here for you, okay?" I clench my jaw unable to speak. Instead, I nod and turn to William. He looks at me with such concern, and I only manage to give him a small smile before going upstairs to my room.

I close the door behind me gripping the white envelope tightly. I swallow hard, and my stomach feels as if it's in knots. I'm nervous to open it and scared of what it'll say. With shaky legs, I walk over to my bed and sit down. I breathe out a loud sigh letting myself look at the letter. It only has my name on the front, as Annie said, and I already know it is from Dad. I remember his manly handwriting so vividly. I swipe my finger over my printed name, and tears start to fill my eyes. It seems like a huge coincidence how I was just thinking about him earlier, and now I'm holding a letter from him. I almost decide not to open it, and almost want to toss it in the trash so I don't have to deal with the loss of him again. Instead, I close my eyes and think of

Carter. He's not even here but just thinking of what he'd say to me, gives me the strength I need to read Dad's letter. It's almost as if I can hear Carter's voice filling me and giving me the courage I so desperately seek.

*You can do this, Shel.*

*You are not weak. You're the strongest woman I've ever known.*

*I'm here for you and don't you ever think for one second I won't be here when you need me.*

I open my eyes, feeling stronger than I ever have. I know I can do this and whatever is written in this letter, I'll deal with it. Because not only have I grown so much since being back home, but I can always count on the people who love me and they will be here for me. I let the new found confidence I'd thought I would never get rush through me. It makes my heart beat faster and makes my entire body feel lighter just knowing I'm not alone anymore. It's powerful. It's remarkable and most of all, it drastically changes me. The way I've thought almost all my life has been wrong. I don't have a clue why it's happening now, but I don't question it. I also know, the fear of being hurt again, and the ones I care for letting me down, is something I'll have to battle every single day.

But not now. No, now I rip open the letter preparing myself for the worst. I take the white paper out of the envelope, and toss it on my bed. Staring at the paper for a moment, I slowly unfold it. It's most definitely from Dad. I look over his handwriting, realizing how much I've missed seeing it. A small thing that one might have forgotten, but not me. I remember every little detail about my Dad. I suck in a much needed breath, then begin to read his letter.

**My Dearest Shelby,**

**If you're reading this letter, it means I'm no longer a part of your life. Whether it be because you've learned the truth about me, or I've made another terrible mistake.**

I stop reading for a second, already having to blink the tears away. I also notice the date at the top. It's dated three days before he drove drunk, killing that family, and leaving their daughter without her parents and brother. I brush away a lone tear and continue to read.

**There's so much I've wanted to do with you my sweet girl. I don't know why I'm writing this letter to you. Maybe I wanted to try and explain myself and give you peace of mind. Maybe I wanted you to have something of me after I'm gone. Either way, I hope this letter one day finds you, and it'll help you understand why you had to endure what your mother put you through for so long.**

**But before I do that, I wanted you to know how deeply and truly sorry I am for being this way. There are days where I don't even know who or what I've become. Out of all the people I've hurt in my life, I never meant to hurt you so much, Shelby. I wanted to be the best father to you. I wanted to make you happy and watch you grow up to be the amazing woman I knew you could be. But I let my addiction run my life.**

**I let the pain of the way your mother treated me and you, control my actions when I should've done more. I should've been there to stop her from hurting you. I have never regretted anything so much. I missed a lot of time with you my sweet girl and for that, I hope you know I am so very sorry. I know you're too young to really grasp what is really happening, and I know one day you'll read this and know the truth.**

I stop reading trying to get my bearings. If anything, I'm more confused by his letter before reading it. I yearn to talk to him, and ask what all this means. But I'll never get that chance. On the other hand, just knowing how much he truly loved me, makes reading his letter a little more bearable.

**When I first met your mother, I fell madly in love with her. She seemed so perfect to me, and someone I thought I wanted to spend the rest of my life with. But your mother was cunning. She was conniving, and she would do, and say anything it took to get what she wanted. It took me for what it seems like a long time to realize why she wanted to be with me. I know you don't remember your grandparents before they passed, but they were very wealthy. When they died shortly after you were born, they left everything to me. Your mother began to change after your birth. There were times she'd say the most God awful things, and they're so bad I cannot even bear to write them now. I just want you to know, no matter how your mother felt about you or me for that matter, I loved you with everything in me. When the nurse placed you in my arms for the very first time, I remember crying with**

tears of joy. I'd never known what love felt like until I met you my sweet girl. You were my precious gift, and I hate how I've become over the years.

About a year after your birth, that's when I noticed how your mother truly was. She was pure evil and vicious at times. I know when your mother and I married, we were both so young, but I just knew she'd change once she saw you as I had. Sadly, there will never be a reason for your mother to change. She let me know why she married me on multiple occasions rubbing her affairs in my face, but I stayed anyway. That's when I started to drink. It slowly became my coping mechanism for when your mother would lash out at me. I was so scared my sweet girl that she'd take you away from me. She threatened more than once she would, and I'd never see you again. She knew how much I loved you, and how much it would kill me if I didn't have you.

It's no excuse for me drinking and becoming an alcoholic. There's no reason for it, other than I was weak. I knew deep down I could take you, and we could build a new life together, but God help me, I still loved your mother after all she did.

I flip to the next page, wondering what else about my mother I didn't know about. I knew exactly what Dad meant. I knew first hand that Mom could be downright cruel for no reason at all. I knew what it was like to be constantly teased as a child because she wouldn't bathe me, or sent me to school in dirty clothes. Mom never laid a hand on me. No, she used her harmful and damaging words. Words so awful that would make anyone step back and want to weep. I don't blame Dad for staying with her. In a way, I understand exactly what he's saying. I just didn't realize how bad it was for him. I realize even with my father's addiction, he still had enough love for me to shield me from the worst of it.

I still don't know what to think of my grandparents being wealthy. I didn't get a chance to know them, but it makes sense as to why Mom stayed like she did. She played my father using me against him in the most unspeakable of ways. I blink my eyes rapidly, making my tears stay away. I don't want to cry, but God I wish I could hold my father just once more. I wish there was a way I could tell him I forgive him, and how much I loved him. Even when he wasn't sober, he was my hero. It seems my father and I were more alike than anyone knew. From what we both went through, the mental abuse, and the pain. Maybe that's why I can understand what this letter means. Maybe that's why I'm not angry with him. With a heavy sigh, I read what else my father has to tell me.

**I hope you know I'm not writing all of this to upset you, or to bring up any unwanted feelings. I need you to know my side. The side I know your mother will never tell you, and I know for a fact she doesn't want you to know any of this. The day after you turned ten, I changed you to my sole beneficiary. If something happened to me, no matter what the cause may be, you would get everything I had and what my parents left me. It's a lot of money, Shelby. It's more than enough**

that would take care of you for a lifetime. I tried to keep it from your mother, but she found out anyway. She wasn't happy I would be leaving you with everything, and she hated me for it. I just couldn't have her treating you the way she did and reap the benefits from me. I left your mother with enough money for her to live very comfortably until you turned eighteen. After that, the money would stop, and she'd have to figure out what she wanted to do.

I also thought one and a half million was too much money to handle for a girl your age.

What the fuck? I reread that last line again and then once more, making sure I read it correctly. I also read over the entire paragraph just to be certain. What money is he talking about? I never knew my father left me anything, let alone knew I was a fucking millionaire. Yes, I knew we had money, but we didn't flaunt it around like everyone else did.

I split the money into three parts. When you turn eighteen, you'll receive two hundred thousand. I want to make sure you have more than enough to pay for your college dues, and be able to support yourself at the same time. I know you'll be smart my sweet girl. I know you'll never be like your mother. Which is why if and when you get married, the first year you'll get another part of the money. If you're still married after five years, the rest will be put into your account. If you need to speak with my lawyer, his name is Henry Willington. He'll answer any and all your questions by the time you get this letter.

**Shelby, I'm so sorry if I'm not there to see you grow up. I'm sorry if I won't be there to see how many achievements you get, or to see you go through your first heartbreak. I'm sorry if I'm not there to tell you how beautiful you are for your prom. If I miss being there to walk my sweet girl down the aisle, and tell you how lucky your groom is to have you in his life. I know I'll be missing so much of your life if anything happens to me. I hate I can't go back in time, and change all the things I could've made better. I regret so very much of not being the father you deserved. I do want you to believe me when I say, I do love you my sweet girl.**

**No matter how much you don't want to think so, I swear with everything I am that I do. I loved you from the moment you were made, and I'll never stop loving you, Shelby. Please take care my sweet girl, and know you'll always be Daddy's little girl.**

**With all my love,**

**Dad.**

I let his letter fall to the floor as my tears unleash. I place my hands over my eyes and hold in the bittersweet scream I want to yell out loud. My body shakes uncontrollably, and I try so hard not to let Annie and William know how much Dad's letter hurt to read. Not because of the way my Mother treated both of us, but because I finally realize he did love me. He just never got the chance to tell and show me. I hate he was drinking and driving the night that cost him his life. I hate I feel cheated out of more time with him. I also wonder if he knew he couldn't handle life anymore, and just gave up. Did he feel if he left, I would be better off without him? I'll never get the answers I want or need. He's gone and there's not a single fucking thing I can do about it. His letter shows me how much he cared about me, but it still cuts me so deep knowing he didn't tell me these things, or had enough sense not to drink and drive.

I wipe my tears away and pick his letter off the floor. Now I feel as if I've let go some of the hurt I need to figure out what Dad meant about this money. It's not that I want it, I don't need it, but something happened to it. That much money doesn't suddenly disappear, and I have a feeling Mom had something to do with it.

There's only one person who can help me, and he's the only one I want to help me at this moment. Carter's always been the one to make me see the bigger picture, and I know this time won't be any different.

I walk into Harlow: Attorneys At Law and the secretary, Mary, immediately lets Carter know I'm here. I'm grateful she knows me and does her best to let me to see him. I don't have to wait long, before he comes out of his office, and I sigh, instantly relaxing when he smiles at me. I move towards him, and he takes me in his arms.

He slowly pulls me back after a few moments and asks, "What's wrong, Shelby?"

"Can we go in your office and talk?" He nods and leads me inside his office. I watch him tell Mary to hold his meetings and calls, then he slowly shuts the door. I can feel my Dad's letter burning in my pocket, and I don't want to burden him right off the bat.

"Tell me what's going on. Did something happen?" I can't help but smile up at him. He always knows when something is going on with me. He always has, and I don't think that trait will ever stop.

"No, nothing really happened," I stop, and pull out the folded letter from my jean pocket. "Annie gave me this earlier." I hold it out to him, and he slowly takes it from me. He stares at it, then glances back at me. "She said the couple that moved into my old house found it along with some of my things in the attic."

"Is this from your Dad?" I nod, and he huffs out a breath. He knows exactly what I went through when Dad died. "You want me to read it?"

"Please. There's something in there I need you to check out for me. Plus you always know how to put things in perspective for me."

I can see the pride and how much he appreciates that I came to him with this. It's not hard to miss the love shining back at me in his eyes. He caresses my cheek with his hand, and I can't stop myself from leaning into his gentle touch. "Thank you, Shel."

I frown as I ask, "For what?"

"For trusting me. For coming to me when you needed a shoulder to lean on."

"Is that what I did?" I say, jokingly.

He chuckles, then leans down to give me a peck on my lips. "Do you want to sit down while I read over it?"

"No. You sit. I'm too antsy." He kisses me sweetly again, and he takes a seat at the chair in front of his desk.

He begins to read Dad's letter, and I can't stop the nervousness from flowing through my veins. I start to pace around the room and bite down on my thumb nail. I glance over at Carter, and wonder what he thinks about Dad's letter. Will he think less of him? Will he feel sorry for him? I shake my head and turn away, knowing these types of thoughts aren't going to help the situation. I pull my necklace out from my shirt and twirl it with my fingers as I wait for him to finish reading.

To distract myself, I look around Carter's office seeing his Harvard diplomas hanging on the dark colored walls. It's a small office, and I wonder if he feels cramped in here when he works all day. He has two tall bookshelves on the left side of the wall with a water cooler in between them. On the other side is a tan couch with fake plants on the each side. He has a huge bay window directly behind his desk, and I smile thinking of him turning around in his chair to look outside during downtime.

I also think about working for him. I know he wants me to, and the money would be a lot better than waitressing. I would love nothing more than to get back to what I love most. Working with numbers. Numbers are easy, simple, uncomplicated, and they rarely surprise you. I've always had a knack for math, and it made the most sense for me to major in accounting. Although I've never worked in a law firm before, I'm sure it wouldn't take me long to catch on how Carter handles the business side of it. Maybe I should say yes, and if it doesn't work out, then I would at least have a sparkling recommendation from him. But I know Carter, and he'd never let me leave if I agreed to work here. I need to make a decision soon, but I'm still unsure about it.

"I don't know where to begin, Shelby," Carter says, and I instantly stop my pacing. I take the chair next to his as he folds the letter back up and hands it to me. "How are you handling all this?"

I clutch the paper in my hands, thinking of how to put into words. "It's strange really."

"How so?"

"I … I feel free. As if this letter has set all my doubts about how Dad felt about me go. It doesn't seem like I should be feeling this way, but I am."

"If that's how you see it, then it's not wrong. No one can tell you how to process his letter, and I'm glad you're taking it better than I thought. I don't mean that in a bad way. I just mean you've come so far from where you were when I first saw you. I told you how strong you were, and I think you're finally believing in it for yourself."

I reach over and grab his hand. I squeeze it, my way of thanking him, because he's right. I'm not the same lost and hopeless woman I was months ago. I feel like I'm finally finding my own way. My way to Carter, to freedom, and to being happy. "I did cry about it," I tell him and let out a small laugh.

"It would surprise me if you didn't, Shel. He told some heavy truth in his letter. You know, you really never do cease to amaze me." I feel my face flush at his compliment, and he reaches over to tuck my hair behind my ear. "You know I love seeing you blush for me."

"Carter," I shyly say and playfully slap his hand away.

He laughs, then his face turns serious. "So, I'm with a millionaire now. Should we go out and buy us a mansion?"

I snort loudly, which causes both of us to burst out in laughter. My laughter dies down before his and I say, "That's the one thing I didn't understand." He frowns, and I add, "I never got any money. At least, not that I can remember. My tuition was paid for by scholarships. I had a full ride for the full four years."

Carter rubs his chin, seeming deep in thought. "You didn't sign anything while you were married?" I shake my head because I honestly can't recall signing away one and a half million dollars. "Okay, I need you to think back. When you left, did your mother have you sign anything and not read it?"

I suck in a breath and close my eyes as I try to recall that day. I remember nothing but being hurt and utterly broken. I dig deeper, knowing the truth has to be somewhere in my memories. When I came home the next day, Mom was in the living room on the phone, and once she saw me, she smiled. I thought it was creepy, but then again, I knew she loved to watch me suffer. I remember her asking me tons of questions, drilling me really, about what had happened. I broke down and told her, thinking just once, one fucking time, she'd be a mother I needed. Instead, she told me it would be best for me to leave and start over in South Carolina. She said she knew Carter would end up hurting me, and he'd never take me back. Her words worked. She made my choice to leave that much easier, and I went directly to my room to pack. I recall her coming into my room asking me to sign some paper. I cannot remember what it was, but she was adamant about me signing it. In my emotional state, I jerked the paper out of her hand and signed my name. I tossed it back to her and went back to packing.

I snap my eyes open and look at Carter. "I did sign something. It was right after you and I broke up and I was a fucking wreck. She kept badgering me about signing the paper, and oh God, I didn't read it."

Carter gets out of his chair and sits on his knees in front of me. He takes my hand, careful not to take the one still holding Dad's letter, and says, "It's okay, Shel. We're going to figure this out, I promise. I know Henry, and I can call him right now to figure out what happened."

"It's not about the money to me." I pause for a minute as I compose my thoughts. I don't care about the money at all. "I'd rather have exactly what I have now, than be the richest person in town. I just want to know what happened to it. If I knew, maybe I could get it back and donate it to a charity or, I don't know do something good with it?"

"I know where your heart is, Shel. I know you just want to figure out what happened, and why your mother tricked you. I'm positive she had you sign over the benefits to her, but we can try and prove she did without your knowledge. It'll be hard since it was so long ago, but I'll call Henry and we'll go from there okay?"

I place my hand on his cheek as I softly say, "Thank you, Carter. I really have no idea what I would do if I didn't have you in my life. You're the best thing that's ever happened to me." He smiles at me, and I lean down to thank him properly. It never fails. Every time I kiss him, he takes my breath away. Makes my heart beat faster, and makes my stomach flutter as if I'm about to fly away.

His thumb rubs my face as he takes my lips, but he doesn't let the kiss go too far. He slowly pulls away, groaning, as he says, "I really don't want to scar Mary."

I laugh, saying, "No. I wouldn't be able to look at her the same." As much as I would love for him to take me on his desk, I'm not willing to risk the embarrassment afterward. Plus Carter's office isn't sound proof.

Carter gives me one more peck on my lips, then stands. He holds out a hand, and I place mine in his as pulls me out of the chair. "I'll walk you out." I nod, and let him lead me out of his office. Once we get outside, he says, "We'll figure out what happened to your Dad's money. I promise I'll get to the bottom of it."

"I know you will, Carter." And he will. Carter knows how much it means to me to find out why Mom stole from me, and no matter what, I can always depend on Carter to help me along the way.

Carter and I have spent every second together for the holidays and of course, we had more than a few laughs at the Harlow Christmas dinner. Carter spent way too much money on me as far as presents go, but I showed him many times just how much I loved them. Now it's January, and it's a new start for us. I feel it, and I don't even try to question it. Even though Carter hasn't made a lot of progress with figuring out what's going on with Dad's money, I know he tries almost every day to put the puzzle together. At this point, I've decided not to worry about it anymore. I still wish I knew what happened to the money, but at the same time, I don't need it. I have everything I could ever want, and if I never find out what happened, then I'll be okay with it. Carter also helped me go through the items in the attic of my old home, and now I have more pictures of Dad.

There wasn't much to go through. It was mostly old toys of mine that I donated to the Salvation Army, some ratted old clothes, and tons albums of Dad's family. I kept what I could, mainly the photos, and now I feel as though I can move forward with my life. I've come a long ways from my old self, and I know this is just another step in the right direction.

I can't remember the last time I was so blissfully happy, but I don't over think it. I'm going with it and holding onto my happiness tightly. Which is why when I pull up at Annie and William's after my shift at the Waffle House, my heart sinks. I park William's truck by the silver Lexus letting it idle for a few moments, wondering if my eyes are playing tricks on me. They have to be because there's no way Mother is sitting on the porch swing. When she waves at me, I know I'm not dreaming. I pinch my arm just to be one hundred percent sure. I take in a much needed breath, and turn off the truck getting out shortly after.

I slam the truck door shut, and notice Annie's car isn't in the driveway. I'm guessing Annie and William are gone, which is why Mom is sitting outside. I know Annie doesn't care for my mother, but she'd never leave her sitting outside. Annie is just too nice to be rude to anyone, no matter how much she doesn't like them. I slowly make my way to the porch already dreading her visit. It can't mean anything good, and I thank God Carter will be here soon. He's off today, but he's with Caden and Cason, helping them move new furniture into their apartment. I'm really not sure why. Carter mentioned something about Caden and fire, and I knew it wasn't anything serious since Caden wasn't in the hospital.

I walk up the steps to the porch, but I don't make a move to go inside the house. Annie might be a nicer person than I am, but I refuse to let my horrid mother inside their home. "What are you doing here?"

"Can't a mother come visit her only child?"

I'm not stupid to think she really wants to actually visit me other than for a reason. I mean nothing to her, and she's done nothing but show me that my entire life. "Just tell me why you're here." I'm not playing into her childish games. You'd think for a woman in her early fifties, she'd be a bit more mature, but no. She makes sixteen year olds look like the damn Dalai Lama.

She rolls her eyes and fluffs her hair over her shoulder saying, "Honestly, Shelby. I don't know why I even bother with you." I clench my jaw, trying to reign in my anger. I don't want to end up in jail for punching her, but it's getting hard not to give into it. "I know you've had your boy toy looking into your father's account."

I frown, wondering how she knew about that. "Does privacy mean nothing to you? What gives you the right to check on anything I do, and do not call Carter that."

"I know everything that goes on in this shit town. Haven't you figured it out already? Henry's an old friend, one that still falls to his knees when I say so."

Oh, God, I'm going to be sick. I grimace, trying not vomit all over the porch. "I'd rather not have that mental picture thank you. And what does it matter if I'm checking into Dad's accounts? It was my money. I should know what happened to one and a half million dollars, don't you think?"

"Always such a child," she sneers as she moves off the swing. "You know, you're nothing but disappointment after disappointment. You could've had anything you wanted, but no. You couldn't handle anything that was given to you."

"What the hell are you talking about?" I'm seriously considering her having some sort of mental illness at this point. She keeps talking in code, and I have no clue what she's getting at.

"Do you really want the truth?"

"I already know the truth. I found Dad's letter."

"And you really think that's all of it?" Please tell me there's not more to it. I can't handle any more revelations. When I don't say anything, she takes it as her cue to fill me in. "You think it was a coincidence you met Easton? You think everything you've been through is by sheer chance?"

I step back, her words cutting me open. Slashing every wound I thought had healed. No, she wants me to bleed. I shake my head saying, "No, you wouldn't be that cruel."

She laughs as I back into the front door. I don't know who this woman is standing in front of me. She's not my Mother. I have no fucking idea who she is. "This is comical really. But yes it's true. Once

Carter finally figured out you were nothing but trash, I made you sign over all the money your father gave you, and you didn't even know!" She lets out a laugh, one that sounds like she's happy with herself, and she finds this situation hilarious. I don't see anything funny about any of this, and I have a feeling it's only going to get worse.

"Easton and I knew each other long before you ran off to college, and you know how much his family is worth." Tears swell in my eyes hearing her tell me all of it. Every single thing my mother has ever done has been for herself. "Of course, Easton couldn't marry me because his parents wouldn't approve of my age, but you were quite the bargaining chip. You see, Easton was my toy. My shiny new pet that I loved to play with, but sadly some toys must be put away. Then there was the fact that I had some pretty hefty dirt on him. He was willing to do anything and everything I asked. That included giving me anything and everything I wanted." Her face turns cold, hard, and the viciousness in her eyes make my breath catch in my throat. "Then you fucked everything up. Easton was more than happy to marry you, and let me keep the money, but no. He had to go and fall in love with you. I knew if he started to care for you, he wouldn't let me get that money your father tried so hard to keep from me. I had no choice, but to intervene and make him realize what you really are."

It's all making sense now. Why in the beginning Easton was so nice and caring to me, then as soon as she came, he changed into a man I didn't recognize. "That's why you came. That's why you both broke me down to my weakest point. All for fucking money, that I didn't even know about, or even wanted. Why would you do that! I'm your daughter, your only child. How can you be so damn cruel?" I hate how weak and sad my voice sounds, but this hurts. It cuts me straight to my damaged soul, making those wounds bigger than before.

She steps closer to me as she says harshly, "I didn't even want you! I begged your father to let me abort you, but no. He had to have his precious baby. You fucked up my life, and I was just taking what I was owed. You don't think I didn't see how much your father loved you? He adored you, and he forgot all about me. I was left alone with no one because of you!"

"Let me guess. You thought the best way to punish Dad and me was to manipulate my entire life, solely for your benefit? All because of the money?"

She points a finger in my face as she declares, "Of course for the money! I didn't give a damn about you, or your father. He was a nice distraction, and of course I loved how he used to give me everything I wanted. My life was perfect until I got pregnant with you. But then you ran away like a child, and Easton stopped giving me what I wanted. I want what's mine, Shelby. Don't you dare say you didn't love all the lavish gifts Easton gave you. All those beautiful parties, all the pampering, and how much he doted on you."

Her hand falls as I shake my head. "I never cared about the money! If anything, I felt like someone else, someone shallow, and selfish. That's not me, Mother. I would've traded every bit of that if I knew I could have what I do now back then."

"You really are pathetic, aren't you?" She rolls her eyes at me again, and I'm about to tell her to leave when she says, "No matter. It's time to grow up, and take responsibility."

"Excuse me?"

"Come on, Shelby. It's time to go back home, and makeup with Easton."

My eyes widen, shocked, she would even think of this. "You have got to be fucking joking. Why would I ever go back to him?"

"Because I told you to. Because you're his wife, and he wants you back." My heart begins to pound, feeling the fear taking over. Just thinking about going back to him makes me sick to my stomach. I won't do it. I can't do it. "Don't fight me on this. Go pack your things. We're leaving."

"No, I won't go back to him. Did you forget about me divorcing him? I'm no longer his wife. I know all you want is another paycheck, but I refuse to leave with you."

She laughs, a disturbing sound, as she says, "You don't have a choice! Easton may have given up on you, but I will not let you run away and take everything away from me again." I don't really know what comes over me after she says this. Something in me snaps, and I release a deep laugh. I don't hold it back. I laugh loudly, as if what she wants is the most hilarious thing I've ever heard. I bend at my waist, holding my sides, as my laugh rolls through me. It's freeing actually. The fear, the pain I felt, and the sick feeling in the pit of my stomach vanishes with my laugh. "What's so funny?"

I slowly rise, wiping my eyes, as I tell her, "You, Mother. You really think I'd ever go back to Easton?" I shake my head smiling as I say, "If you think that for one second, you need fucking help. I will never ever go back to him, or to South Carolina. I don't give a damn what you want. I'm finally happy here. Finally living my life the way I want to, and I will be damned if you will come here and mess this up for me." She starts to cut me off but I hold up my hand as I narrow my eyes at her. She quickly shuts her mouth, and I can tell I'm still shocking her of how I'm acting. I'm done letting this woman control me. "I'm done, Mother. Never in my life have you given a single thought about me. Not once have you cared about my wellbeing, or if the choices you make will affect me. You're selfish, ruthless, and you manipulate everyone around you. I've done enough for you, and I cannot believe you would even think I would endure all I did again! All my life I knew you hated me. I knew you never cared how I was teased as a child, made fun of because I wasn't like everyone else, and that's all your fault!" I step closer to her as I say through clenched teeth, "If you dare to try and mess up what I have right now, I swear I will make you regret it. I'm done with you or anything to

342

do with you. You're just another sad, lonely, gold-digging whore, and I never want to see you again." All the anger from my entire life fuels me, giving me the courage to stand up to her for once. Her words may hurt and they may make me doubt myself, but I won't let her know that. She's not going to control me, or influence me anymore. I can't guarantee Easton won't come back, but I have a feeling he won't. He got everything, and I'm sure by now, he's found someone else to degrade. She just wants me to go back to make me suffer for her own sick ways.

She finally finds her bearings, and she does exactly what I knew she would. "That was a very touching speech, but you forgot one thing."

"I'm sure you're going to tell me whether or not I want to know," I say, preparing myself for her harsh words that I know are coming.

"Yes, I will tell you because you need to hear them. You've seemed to have forgotten your place." She smirks, a disgusting look shining in her eyes, as she says, "No matter what you do or wherever you are, everyone around you will see what you really are. You're just a sad pathetic little girl. You're nothing, but a worthless piece of trash." She shakes her head, as if she can't believe she's even looking at me. "You'll never amount to anything, and I've never been so disappointed in you." I suck in a breath, slowly letting it out. This is nothing I haven't heard before. In fact, she and Easton used to say the same things to me on a daily basis. The only difference now, I won't believe it. I refuse to let these words affect me, and change who I am just so she'll accept me. I'm sick and tired of trying to gain her affections, and for her to finally start being how a mother should. I don't need her in my life anymore. I don't really know why I spent so much time and effort trying to make her proud of me, but I know now that I never needed it. She's shown me so many times she doesn't give two shits about me, or about my happiness.

I really think the biggest shocker to her is when I don't respond. I show zero emotions, even if I'm ready to run away from her. It's taking everything in me to stay and listen to her. I don't lower my eyes like I use to. Thankfully, my eyes don't swell with tears. I don't plead for her to stop with her hateful words, and think about me like I use to. I don't do anything to show her I care about what she says, and when I see Carter's truck pull up, a grin forms on my face.

I don't even look back at her as I run off the porch.

I run to Carter realizing, I'll always find my way to him. I don't need my mother's approval or love because I have all that, and so much more with him. Why I didn't do this years ago baffles me, but it feels amazing knowing he's here for me. My eyes focus on him as he steps out of his truck, and when he sees me, he smiles opening his arms as I reach him. He stumbles back as I wrap my arms around his waist letting his manly scent embrace me as his arms do the same. I hold him tightly resting my head on his chest. He rubs up and down my back caressing me, loving me, and showing how much he can comfort me. After a few moments, he pulls me back and takes my face in his hands. He glances up at the porch, then back to me as he asks, "Are you okay?"

"I am now," I say truthfully.

"I would've been here sooner if Caden and Cason hadn't been arguing so much." I grin, knowing how the twins are.

Carter's hands slowly move from my face, and I see Caden and Cason walk up to us. I stand by Carter's side, our arms still around each other, and his continuous comfort helps me keep Mom's words from creeping in. "Is that your soul-sucking Mother?" Caden asks, and I can't help but let out a chuckle.

I dart my eyes to Cason, noticing he's stiff as a board, before answering Caden. "Yes, that's her."

I glance up at Carter, seeing he wants to ask why she's here, and what she wants. I can see it in his eyes, but Caden interrupts him from asking. "Want me to arrest her for you?"

"It's fine, but thank you, Caden."

He starts to walk back to the truck, but stops as he says, "I mean I can go get my handcuffs." He shrugs. "Some chicks dig the cuffs."

"Dude, you're disgusting," Cason tells him as Carter and I laugh. Watching Cason clench his jaw as he looks towards the porch, I wonder why he's acting so strange, but my attention is elsewhere. Our laughter fades as we watch Mom walking towards us. I'm assuming that's why Carter stops, or it could be because my grip on his waist tightens. He doesn't say a word as my fingernails dig into his skin, but I need him to keep me grounded.

"Well, haven't you boys grown up," she says as she stops in front of us. I can't help but watch as she looks over Caden first, then Cason. Her eyes start to shine in approval as she gazes over Cason, and I wonder for a second if she wants to use him as her new boy toy. The thought sickens me, and I don't miss the way Cason slowly begins to back away from her. "Yes, I see both of you have grown up very much," she says, but her eyes never leave Cason. Caden looks over at his twin, and I know they're using their twin bond. When Cason lets out a disgusted sound, and Caden makes gagging ones, it's hard not to laugh. Caden is bending at his waist, acting like he's about to puke. Mom shrugs then says, "If you boys change your mind, you know where I am."

"I highly doubt that will ever happen," Cason tells her with such malice in his voice, and shortly after, Caden agrees.

"I think you need to leave, Tabitha." Carter's voice is hard, sharp, and I can feel him tense under my grip when mother turns to him.

"Please. I'll leave when I'm good and ready." They stare at each other for a few moments before she smiles a sinister smile, then turns to me. "It's time to go, Shelby."

Carter

"She's not going anywhere," Carter snaps. I'm grateful he's standing up for me, and putting Mom in her place.

"I won't tell you again," she tells me, completely ignoring Carter. "It's time for you to come home."

"Shelby's already home, and she's never leaving again." I smile up at Carter and he looks down at me, caressing my face. He doesn't even look at her as he says, "She's right where she belongs." My face flushes, but it's the look in his eyes that hold me captive. So full of love, and I know he means what he says. Even though I'll never leave him, this was his way of reminding me that I belong with him.

"Alright, soul-sucker. It's time for you to scat." Carter smiles and shakes his head, as I let out a chuckle hearing Caden talking to her that way.

"This isn't over, Shelby!" She says something afterward, but I tune her out. I'm not worried about what else she has to say. I have Carter taking over, and that's all I need right now.

He gazes back at me, rubbing his thumb on my cheek, as he asks, "Are you sure you're okay?"

"Yes. I'm perfect now that you were here to back me up."

"Good. I'm sorry you had to go through her bullshit without me."

I pull him closer to me, saying, "You're here now, and that's all that matters." He shows me my favorite grin, then slowly leans down to kiss me sweetly. It's just simple kiss, but it holds so much power. It takes my breath away, making my heart soar with an overwhelming sensation of love. It's beautiful. It's perfect. It's everything I've ever wanted.

He pulls away with a groan as we hear Caden clearing his throat before saying, "If y'all are done sucking face, then can we get a move on? We got a party to plan, remember?" Smiling, I step away from Carter, and look around seeing Mom's car is gone. It's nice to know I don't care about her anymore. I didn't even hear her leave.

"Alright, Caden. Get in the truck and we'll go." Caden lets out a whoop and gets inside the truck. Cason snakes his head, then follows behind him. I start to walk over to Cason to ask him what's gotten into him, but Carter turns back to me asking, "My house soon? You can help plan Clark's welcome home party."

I glance over to Cason, seeing him getting inside the truck. For now, I decide to let it go, since Cason isn't the type to open up. Turning back to Carter, I nod as I say, "I wouldn't miss it for the world."

After talking to Annie and William, and filling them in on my crazy Mother situation, I arrive at Carter's house. I quickly make my way to the door and open it to utter chaos.

"I told you not to mess with it!"

"Stop yelling at me!"

"If you would fucking listen to me, this wouldn't happen."

# Carter

"Oh my God, why don't you just cry about it?"

I step inside, checking to make sure the coast is clear. Caden and Cason are standing in the middle of the living room arguing as usual. Carter has his back to me in the kitchen. It's sad really that Carter can tune them out so easily. It looks like he's making something, and I dash to him careful not to get in the middle of whatever's going on with the twins.

I set my purse down on the kitchen island quietly, and wrap my hands around Carter placing my head on his back. "There you are," he says. I let him go so he can turn around, and he instantly kisses me. I don't even think about stopping my hands from wrapping around his neck, and standing on my tip toes to reach him better. He kisses me deeply and passionately. When I moan in his mouth he pulls away, resting his head on mine and says breathlessly, "If we don't stop, I'm going to take you right here, right now."

I bite my lip, wishing he could, but it would be super awkward with his brothers being here. "Later then?" I ask.

"It's a promise, Shel."

"Good." I slowly unwrap my hands from around his neck and lean against the counter. "What are they arguing about anyway?" Yes, they're still going at it, and I really don't know how they can stand to live together.

"I really don't know this time. Something about Caden messing up Cason's phone." Carter shrugs and adds, "There's really no telling, but I'm glad you're here. Now, we can really start planning this thing for Clark."

I nod, turning around to grab the salty snacks Carter has laid out. I pop a few in my mouth then ask, "When is he coming back?" I know it's getting time for him to return home, and I'm glad it's soon. I know Carter has been worrying so much about him since Clark's phone call at Thanksgiving. I also know it's been hard on Carter that Clark hasn't been calling him as much. I'm not sure if it's because he's not able, or if he just doesn't want to talk to Carter. Either way, when Clark gets home things will be easier.

"He said sometime in March. Mama said she'd let me know for sure on the date when he tells her, but you know how Mama is with her parties."

"Yes, we all know how Linda can be. Plus I know she's excited Clark's returning, so I assume it'll be epic." Even as kids, Linda would throw the biggest birthday parties for us. I loved it because it always made me feel special, and part of the family. "What do you have done?"

"Well," he turns around and cuts off the stove. He takes the pan, holding some delicious smelling chicken, then moves it to the side before finishing what he was saying. "I haven't gotten much done."

"I can't imagine why ever not," I tease. I know it's because he's not getting any help from the twins.

"They've been at it for over an hour." He shakes his head, adding, "Maybe now that you're here we can actually get some planning done."

I start to comment, but Caden walks into the kitchen, placing his hand on my shoulder as he says, "Is the food ready yet? I've starving."

"You know," I say, poking him in the ribs. "You really should be more grateful Carter cooked for you."

"You wound me woman with your hurtful words. Old man knows I love it when he cooks for me."

"Hey, I didn't cook just for you," Carter says back.

"Caden! What did you do to my phone!" We all turn back to the living room to a frustrated Cason shaking his head and cussing.

"I don't know what you're talking about," Caden shouts. Carter and I can only shake our heads. "I really didn't touch his phone."

"I'm sure you had absolutely nothing to do with it," I say to him sarcastically.

"Again, you wound me!" I laugh and lightly hit his arm. He fakes being hurt of course. He's such a drama queen.

A few moments later, Carter announces supper is ready, and we make our way to the kitchen table. I take a seat by Carter as Cason narrows his eyes at Caden before sitting by him. My mouth starts to water as the aroma of the chicken hits me, and I quickly make my plate before everyone takes all the food. It's happened before, and I know to grab it as fast as I can. We eat in silence for a while, enjoying our food. Caden lets out a few moans as he bites into his chicken sandwich, but we don't even give him a second thought. He's always been this way, but it's good to know he'll never change. He definitely keeps everyone entertained.

The silence doesn't last very long as Caden asks me, "What did your soul-sucking Mother want?"

I knew eventually someone would bring it up, but it doesn't bother me like it would before. I glance at Carter when he takes my hand, squeezes it, then says, "I wish you wouldn't ask her things like that. What if she doesn't want to talk about it?"

"It's fine, Carter." He's always looking out for me, but I really don't mind talking about with everyone here. "She told me she wanted me to go back to South Carolina," I stop when I see the look on Caden's face. His eyes widen, and he seems so shocked he even stopped chewing his food. "Don't worry," I quickly add. "I'm not going anywhere."

"Good because I'd come after you if you did," Carter says sweetly while squeezing my hand again.

"I'm glad you told her no, but man your mom is a piece of work for sure. I swear it felt like she was trying so suck my soul out just by looking at me."

"You're so full of shit, Caden. Admit it. You wanted to go with her," Cason says, and I cover my mouth to laugh. I can tell Cason is being playful, but he still seems tense like earlier today.

"Dude, that's not funny. Seriously not into cougars."

Their banter goes back and forth for a few moments, and eventually I get to tell them all what happened. From her randomly showing up, to the part about Dad's money, and her being the reason for me being put in such a horrible situation. I can tell Carter doesn't like hearing it, but he does his best to hide it. Caden of course, makes jokes at every chance he gets, but it's nice. Even if it hurt finally finding out the truth today, at least I know I have the Harlow brothers to help me through it. Caden will always find a way to make me laugh, Cason will sit and listen, and then there's Carter. The one I know will love me no matter how broken my past made me.

I glance around the table, watching as Caden laughs, and Cason actually lets a rare smile form, even if it doesn't reach his eyes. Once I get to Carter, he's staring right at me. I smile, feeling my face flush, and he reaches over to pull my chair closer to him. He puts an arm around me, and I lean my head on his shoulder. I let out a content sigh when I feel his fingers running through my hair, and my heart skips a beat when he whispers, "I love you, Shel."

I lean up to gaze into his beautiful brown eyes as I say, "I love you, too." Caden and Cason fade into the background as Carter gives me a peck on my lips.

It's in these small simple moments that I will cherish forever. It's the ones that are going to slowly make all the bad ones disappear, and I know I'll never take any of this for granted again. I'll hold onto it, storing it forever into my soul. And it's all because of Carter's unwillingness to give up on me, and his strength to fight when I thought I'd given up.

I owe him so much, and I plan on never letting him go again. Because our love is one of a kind, and I'll be forever grateful for our second chance at finding one another again.

# EPILOGUE

## Carter

## Two months later

I open the armoire searching for the two small boxes I want to give to Shelby. I'm certain now's the perfect time to ask her two very important questions, and I don't think she'll say no to either. We've come such a long way since last year, and I want to make sure we both continue to grow. To make our relationship stronger than ever. I rummage through some of my socks and for a small moment, my stomach drops when I don't find the boxes right away. I exhale slowly as I pull them out, nervous I'm wrong. If she says no, I tell myself I'll respect her decision, but I'm confident she'll say yes.

She has to say yes.

I quietly shut the drawer back, careful not to make too much noise. I left her asleep on the couch, and I want to ask her before we leave to head to my parents for Clark's welcome home party. I debated whether or not to ask her in front of everyone, but in

355

the end, I chose to wait until we were alone. It'll be more intimate, and I know Shelby would rather enjoy this little moment between just the two of us. My heart begins to pound as I walk away from the armoire, and out of the room. I can still hear the TV in the living room, and I hope she's still asleep. I hope my plan goes perfectly, and I don't fuck this up. I reach the kitchen, and I can see her sleeping form on the couch. I grin seeing her finally able to sleep soundly, and I can't remember the last time she had a nightmare. I would like to think her bad dreams stopped because she finally had some closure with her Dad, and with her Mom. It still makes my jaw clench every time I think of Tabitha, but I'm trying to erase that woman from my memory.

I'm trying to do as Shelby has.

She's extraordinary, and she never ceases to amaze me. I really thought with all the revelations she found out within this past year would make it harder for her to move forward, but she's doing better than ever. Besides not being plagued with nightmares almost every night, she sleeps soundly. She doesn't get lost in her head anymore, and every time I ask if she wants to talk about it, she tells me she's perfect with that beautiful smile I love. I feel terrible with what I found out about the money her dad left her. All of it is gone. Not a penny left, and I'm still working on figuring out how Tabitha managed to spend one and a half million dollars. Shelby tells me constantly to leave it alone and forget about it, but I just want to know out of curiosity. I know Shelby has never cared about money or wanted expensive things, but I want to take care of her. Which is another reason for two boxes.

Once I reach her, I bend down sitting on my knees, and set the boxes beside me as I gently brush her hair out of her face. She stirs only to move toward my hand, and my stomach dips feeling nervous about asking her what I want. I smile when she calls out my name, and wonder what she's dreaming about. I lightly touch her shoulder trying to coax her awake. Her blue eyes open a few moments later, and she smiles at me widely. "Hey," she says with a raspy voice. "How long was I out for?"

"Not long," I swallow hard, trying not to lose my nerve.

She must sense something's off, because she places a hand on my face. "Are you alright? You look a little pale."

"Yeah, I'm fine." I touch the boxes by my legs, wondering how to ask her what I want. She eyes me curiously as I look away. I pick up the one of the small boxes, thinking it's now or never. "I have something for you," I start. I hold up the first box and her eyes widen as she sees it.

"Carter, you didn't need to get me anything."

"I know, but it's not what you think." She slides up on the couch as she takes the box. She grins at me and I nod, encouraging her to open it.

I watch her as she begins to open the small box, and I hold my breath until she sees what's inside.

Brie Paisley

Her eyes dart to mine, and I smile as she asks, "Why is there a key in here?"

I place a hand on her calf as I explain. "That key is to the firm. I know you've been going back and forth with your decision about working with me, but I want you to know I need you there. I need you to be a part of my team, and this key, it's just for you to come and go as you wish. You can set your own hours, work at the firm or at home." She opens her mouth to say something, but I hold up a finger to stop her. I grab the other box and hand it to her. She sighs, knowing she has no choice but to open it.

Her eyebrows furrow as she opens the second box and holds up another key. I can tell she's confused to why I'm giving her a bunch of keys today. "Why do I have another key?"

Before I answer, I stand and grab her legs. I place them in my lap as I sit and gaze at her and say, "That key is to my house." My heart drums rapidly in my chest as she sucks in a breath. "I want you here with me every single day. I want to wake up to seeing your gorgeous smile. I want to be the first you see, talk to, and share your morning coffee with. I want to listen to you sing in the shower every morning, and to sit on the couch to watch scary movies at night with. Shelby, I can't live without you. You're the only one I want to share my life with, and I would be honored if you would move in with me."

Her eyes fill with unshed tears and for a second, I think I fucked up. She takes the keys, holding them tightly in her hand as she says, "Yes."

"Yes?" I ask, just to confirm what I heard. She laughs and a lone tear slides down her cheek as she nods. I use the pad of my thumb to wipe it away, then ask, "Why are you crying?"

"Because." Another tear rolls down her face and she shakes her head. "Because I'm happy, Carter. You've made today amazing, and I never expected this."

I move her legs on each side of me as I lean over her. Hovering over her lips as her hands go to my back, I use my hand to cup her cheek. "Just so it's clear, you're saying yes to both?"

She gazes at me, making my heart clench, as she breathes out, "Yes to both. I can't wait to move in with you, and spend every day with you. I can't wait to get back to doing what I love, and I know you wouldn't be doing any of this, unless you were ready."

"I'm more than ready, Shel." And I am. I'm ready for it all and more. I glance over at the clock on the wall as I say, "We still have a few hours before we have to be at my parents."

"Really?" She makes a sexy moaning sound then asks, "Whatever shall we do to pass the time?"

I grin as I touch her lips and whisper, "I have a few ideas." She giggles as I take my finger off her lips, and take her mouth with mine. I barely hear the keys falling to the floor. I'm entranced, consumed, and only focused on her. I slowly dip my tongue in her mouth loving how she tastes.

Her legs wrap around me, and I groan as her hips arch into mine. I pull back, looking deep into her eyes. Our breaths come out in pants, and I hope she's ready for me to show her just how happy she's made me today. Because I don't plan on stopping until she begs me to.

Shelby sits in my lap, laughing loudly as Caden and Cason roll around on the ground horse playing. They've been at it for a while now, I'm just waiting for Mama to finally break them up. I grin, then take a drink of my beer, watching Cason wrap his legs around Caden. Caden grunts as the slaps Cason's arms while trying to get free. I run my hand up and down Shelby's back enjoying spending the day with my family.

Cason seems to be back to his normal self after Shelby explained to me how he acted when Tabitha showed up. I tried talking to him about it, but he told me more than once he was fine. I let it go knowing if something was wrong, Caden would know and he'd tell me.

Dad should be back soon from picking up Clark from the airport, and my parents backyard is full of family and friends awaiting Clark's arrival. It's been a long awaited day, and I for one, am glad to get my brother back. Shelby and I ended up being the ones to plan the party with Mama's help of course. Cason and Caden wouldn't stop bickering long enough to help, but overall I think we pulled it off. We decided to have it outside, since it's a perfect day out, and it wouldn't be as crowded inside. We had a local caterer come and set up three tables of buffet style food. They're lined up on the back porch, and I'm quite pleased with how the welcome home banner turned out. There's so many people waiting for Clark, and I know he'll be happy to have so much support.

"Caden and Cason! Stop that right now!" I turn hearing Mama's stern voice, and when the twins don't instantly stop she yells, "I'm going to get my whoopin' spoon!" I cringe away, as Shelby lets out another laugh, and the twins finally stop messing around. They get off the ground and brush their clothes off, pushing each other in the process.

They make their way to the food, and I laugh hearing Mama shoo them away from it. Shelby leans back against me sighing, and I wrap my free arm around her. "Have you ever been so happy that you think it's not real?"

I place my beer down as she turns, and I think about her question for a moment before answering. I know what she means. It's still surreal knowing she's mine, and soon, she'll be moving in with me. "Yeah, I've done that a lot since you came back into my life. The thing is." I tuck a strand of her hair behind her ear as I say, "It's these small moments with you that make me love that feeling. It may sound strange, but this exciting feeling you give me, I want to feel it every single day. Nothing is going to take our happiness away this time."

"You promise?"

I grin, knowing how much she needs to hear my vow. "I promise, Shel. With all my heart, and with everything that I am." She gazes into my eyes for a moment, then she slowly leans down to kiss me sweetly. I run my fingers through her hair savoring her kiss, her taste, and her very being.

"Caden was right about you two," I pull away, turning to see Caleb moving a chair by us.

Shelby blushes bright red and gets up. I watch her make her way to Mom, and my heart swells seeing her getting along with Mama so well just like she used to. "One day little brother, you'll understand."

I see him shake his head out of the corner of my eye, as he says, "I highly doubt that. I'm too awkward around chicks."

I turn to him, saying, "When you meet the right one, it'll come naturally."

"I can't believe you're giving me love advice," he says with a chuckle.

"Well," I bend down and grab my beer, then take a drink before telling him, "When you know, you just know. I knew I wanted to be with Shelby when I was six, and knew I loved her when I was eleven." It was a strange feeling looking back. I didn't really know what it meant, but as I got older, I knew exactly what I was feeling.

"I'll take your word for it." Caleb turns to me and says, "I am glad you got your girl back. It's good to see you so happy again."

"Thanks, man. And she does make me happy. She's all I've ever needed." I'm not surprised at Caleb's approving gaze. All my brothers know how much she means to me, and how much I regretted leaving her. I turn my gaze back to our family and friends, seeing them talking, laughing, and having a good time. Pride and contentment flow through me, and I've never been so thankful for such an amazing family and friends.

I set my beer back down as I notice Caden walking over to Caleb and me. I wonder if Dad is back with Clark, knowing Dad's been gone for a while now. He left early this morning, headed to Jackson Airport, to meet Clark. "Dad just called. They'll be here in five." I nod, grateful the time is finally here to reunite with Clark. It's been a long time coming, and I can only hope my worries about him will be eased once I see him.

Caleb, Caden, and I make our way to the back porch impatiently waiting for them to arrive. I see Shelby sneak a piece of chicken, and she shrugs her shoulders when she notices me watching her. I shake my head, beckoning her to come stand beside me. She complies instantly and wraps her arm around my waist. Annie and William stand close by us, and I watch Mama stick some tissues in her bracelet. I already know Mama is going to shed some tears. I know how much she misses Clark, and how much she worries about him. I hate that it's so hard on her, and I can only hope Clark finally decides to retire. He's been in going on ten years, and it's time he stays home for good.

Everyone begins to crowd around the back porch eager to greet Clark. I shift my weight from side to side anxious for him to get here. Shelby's embrace tightens, and I still. I look down at her, and she smiles widely at me saying, "It's going to be fine, Carter." I nod, grateful she knows how much I'm worried. I think when I see him things will be better, and I'll know for sure he's alright.

Moments later, I see Dad walking through the house through the glass window. I see Clark walking beside him wearing his Army uniform and when they come outside, everyone cheers when they see Clark. We clap, we cheer, and for a brief moment, Clark smiles. It doesn't reach his eyes, but I don't think much of it as Mama hugs his tightly. They stay embraced for a while it seems, and I notice Mama's shoulders are shaking. Dad steps over to them, and he rubs Mama's back as he leans down to tell her something. I see Shelby wiping a tear off her cheek, and I pull her closer to my side. Caden, Cason, Caleb, and I patiently wait our turn to greet our brother as they stand beside me. Mama finally lets Clark go, and he makes his way toward us.

He stops at Shelby first, and she wraps her hands around his neck. I watch them thankful Shelby is still accepted by everyone, and how much she belongs here. Clark slowly pulls away moving to me. I suck in a breath, not believing he's finally home. He's safe, and I couldn't be happier he seems fine. I embrace him as he does the same, and I lightly slap his back. He slowly moves away doing the same to the rest of us. I watch him, and I can feel our brotherly bond strengthening. We've always been close with one another, and it's hard when one of us isn't here. I know Caleb still has until May until he's finished with school, but at least he comes home when he can. Soon, all of us will be back home living our lives just like we want.

A few hours later, Caden, Cason, Caleb, Clark and I sit outside talking, and catching Clark up on what he's missed. It's nice to be able to spend time with Clark, and he's actually able to relax since everyone has left for the night. Each of us has a beer in hand, and we laugh more than once at Caden's jokes. Shelby's inside with Mama helping her finish cleaning up. I have noticed Clark won't talk about his time overseas. I would say it was normal, but after his other deployments, he had some great things to say about his friends with him. We catch on quickly doing our best to keep his mind off anything that might upset him. I have a nagging feeling that this time is going to be harder on him. I just hope he knows he can lean on any of us, and we'll do everything we can to show him we support him.

My gaze finds Shelby inside, leaning on the counter talking with Mama. I can't help the grin from forming, and I honestly don't know how this could get any better. I have everything I could ever want. "There he goes again." I frown as I turn to Caden. "She sure does have you whipped, old man."

"But out already, Caden." Cason scolds.

"I'm just saying. He does it all the time now."

"You sound jealous to me," Clark says. Caden scuffs, and I actually think he is jealous.

"Whatever. Y'all don't know anything."

"Why are you so defensive then, Caden?" I ask, truly curious. The last time it was brought up about him getting serious with a woman, he said he didn't want a relationship.

Caleb laughs, as Cason rolls his eyes and Caden says, "I'm not! Y'all always gang up on me, and it's not right."

"Are you pouting?" Cason asks, and I can only shake my head seeing Caden really is pouting.

"Alright, we get it. You're jealous and don't want us to know. Dually noted," Clark chimes in.

Caden shakes his head, mumbling as I try to change the subject. "Can y'all help me move Shelby in the house next weekend?" I know Shelby doesn't have a lot of stuff, but Mama told me she wanted to take Shelby shopping to add more of her style in my home. I agreed thinking it was a great idea. I want Shelby to know my home will be our home soon.

Everyone agrees to help, and Caden adds, "I still can't believe she said yes. I thought for sure it would take a bit more convincing."

I nod, saying, "I know. I thought I'd have to ask more than once, but she has changed a lot."

"I just hope she doesn't pull a runaway bride when y'all get married." I laugh as Cason smacks

Caden on the arm. "Dude! What the hell was that for?"

"Think before you speak dipshit," Cason tells him.

They begin to argue of course, because it's not a family get together without the twins fighting. Caleb tries to help break them apart, but I think it's making it worse. I chuckle as I listen to what they're saying, then Clark leans over towards me, tapping my knee with his beer. "I am glad you're happy again. It's good to come home and see you two back together."

"Thanks, Clark. She means the world to me, and I honestly don't know what I would've done if she hadn't come back into my life." Clark nods, and I find Shelby again. I watch her head fall back as she laughs, and she slowly turns to me, showing me that stunning smile.

I barely hear Clark as he says, "Go get your girl," as I get up and make my way to her. She notices and meets me halfway.

Her arms take my waist as I use both hands to cup her face. I don't care if anyone's watching, because all I can see is her. I gaze into her eyes, loving the sparks of green shining through. I trace my thumb back and forth on her cheek, as I say, "I love you more than words can describe, Shel."

She sighs, a smile spreading across her face as she says, "I love hearing you say that." I know she does. Every time I do, her eyes light up, and that smile I crave to see forms. It's something I want to see every single day for the rest of my life. I lean down and slowly take her lips. I kiss her sweetly, tenderly, and pour every single bit of love I have for into our kiss.

I pull away when I hear Caden yell, "Get a room already!" I chuckle, but I don't let go of Shelby.

As I hold her gaze, I realize that one day, maybe soon I'm going to ask her to marry me. One day, she'll officially be mine. My heart beats faster thinking of giving her my last name, and one day seeing her carrying our baby. It's something I've always wanted with her. I know it'll happen for us. I have faith she'll prove Caden wrong, and she won't be a runaway bride.

Either way, if she runs I'll always chase her. Wherever she goes, I'll follow.

I pull her to me, running my hands down her arms then to her back, as she leans her head on my chest. I know she can hear and feel how fast my heart is beating. It's all because of her. Everything she makes me feel is because of how she loves and cares for me. I hope she knows how much these small simple moments mean to me. If not, I can't wait to spend the rest of my life showing her. Loving her. Being everything just for her.

Forever and always.

# The End

# Carter

Brie Paisley

# More from Brie Paisley

## Standalones

Temptation
Addiction

## Worshipped Series

Worshipped-book one
Betrayed-book two
Redeemed-book three

## The Harlow Brother Series

Caden-book two
Caleb-book three
Carter & Shelby: Ever After-coming soon

## The Transcendent Series

The Foreseer
The Predestined-coming soon

# ACKNOWLEDGEMENTS

Okay, I'm going to get a little sappy for a moment. I have so many amazing people to thank, but I don't want to forget anyone. Instead, I'm making this thank you for all of you. Firstly, I would not be here, doing what I love, if it were not for you, the reader. Thank you for taking a chance on me, a still fairly new author. Thank you for taking a chance on Carter, as this book is by far my favorite. I honestly don't have enough words to express how grateful I am for you wanting to read my books, this one in particular. I hope you love it as much as I did while writing it, and thank you again from the bottom of my heart for reading.

Secondly, to the wonderful ladies in my fan group. Thank you for sticking by me when things weren't going so well. Thank you for keeping me sane, and for all the laughs. Thank you for the naughty posts, as they were highly appreciated. You guys are absolutely amazing, and the love and support each, and every one of you show me, is awesome. Ladies, you keep me going and for that, I cannot thank you enough.

Thirdly, to my wonderful street team. We may be small, but size doesn't matter. You babes rock it and pimp your hearts out. I cannot thank you enough for all the support, and pimping you do. I really do appreciate all the help in getting Carter out there, and making sure to enter in contests. You babes are the best.

To my beta team, thank you for reading and giving me the wonderful feedback. Y'all know how nervous I was about Carter, and hearing how much you loved it, gave me the courage and reassurance it would be great. Thank you for your honesty and wanting to help make Carter the best. To my review team, you ladies rock it. I'm so glad to have such an amazing group willing to read and review for me. It really means the world to me.

I can't forget about my lovely ladies from Saints and Sinners Books. Thank you so much for going above and beyond to make Carter's cover reveal and release day such a success. From all the hard work y'all did, down to tagging me in each post, I can't thank you enough. You ladies are the best. To the amazing team with Give Me Books, thank you so much for helping me promote and get Carter to new readers. You have a wonderful team, and I cannot wait to work with you again.

Thank you to my amazingly talented cover designer. I'm really sorry it took us so long to come up with the perfect cover, BUT, it came out truly beautiful and stunning. As always, you rocked it. You have some serious skills, and I cannot wait to see what you come up with next.

A big thank you to Christopher Correia for capturing the perfect photo for the cover. You're so talented, and I cannot express how thankful I am for everything you did to make sure I had the right picture. You're amazing to work with, so kind and sweet, and I can't wait to work with you again. To the models, BT Urruela and Jessie Reis, both of you are such an inspiration. I couldn't have picked anyone else to fit the characters so perfectly. A huge thank you for both of you for inspiring Carter and Shelby. It was a pleasure working with both of you, and I can't wait to plan more books with you.

To my brilliant and ever patient editor, thank you for helping me polish and make Carter the best it can be. As always, your suggestions were great. You've helped me with so much, and of course, helped me learn what to do and what not to do. It's always a pleasure working with you.

I know I said I wouldn't name anyone, but it's needed with this thank you. Nikki, thank you so very much for supporting me and helping me so much when I needed it. You always cheer me on, giving me the courage to step out of my comfort zone, and I really have no way of thanking you enough. You've been there for me from the very beginning, and I'm so glad I have you on my team. Thank you again for everything you do, no matter how small it may seem.

Last but not least, thank you to my husband. Thank you for your support and telling me more than once how proud of me you are. The support and love you give me every single step of the way means more to me than you know. Thank you for understanding when I disappear for days, and the housework slips. You've always understood me, and I love you for that. Thank you, babe, for being everything I need.

# PLAYLIST

Springsteen by Eric Church
Hotline Bing by Drake
Far From Home by Five Finger Death Punch
How Deep Is Your Love by Calvin Harris &
Disciples
Gotta Be Somebody by Nickelback
Just A Kiss by Lady Antebellum
Lovesong by Adele
Tears Don't Fall by Bullet for My Valentine
Moving On by Asking Alexandria
Let Her Cry by Hootie & The Blowfish
In Chains by Shaman's Harvest
Wash It All Away by Fiver Finger Death Punch
I Found a Boy by Adele
I'll Be Waiting by Adele
Habits (Stay High) by Tove Lo
I Want Out by Young Guns
Feel It In Your Heart by Cold
There for You by Flyleaf
I Apologize by Five Finger Death Punch
Words As Weapons by Seether
I Won't Give In by Asking Alexandria
Missing by Flyleaf
Angel by The Weeknd

Brie Paisley

Stay by Flyleaf
Stay With Me by You Me At Six
Don't You Remember by Adele
Walk Away by Five Finger Death Punch

# About
# Brie Paisley

Brie Paisley was born and raised in a small town in Mississippi, and now, she currently lives in different locations, due to her husband being military. She wanted to write at a young age and was always filling journals with her thoughts and short stories. Brie started with an idea for her debut novel a few years ago, and with the encouragement of her husband and sister-in-law, she was able to write and publish her first book. When she isn't writing, you can find her reading a good book, watching a good movie, or spending time with her wonderful husband and beautiful daughter.

Facebook: @authorbriepaisley
Instagram: @authorbrie_paisley
Twitter: @author_brie